FIREWING

BY DALE AYCOCK

Published by: Inkling Press
P.O. Box 2598, Menlo Park, CA 94026
www.inklingpress.com

Cover illustration: Darian Lee

ePub ISBN 978-1-943682-17-1
Print ISBN 978-1-943682-18-8

Preface

Kama Mountain
New Earth

Earth's mothers gather around their sacred fires as do those of Lissone, high on the slope of Mt. Kama and the ancient ritual begins:

We started out midst fire and ice, a thousand of us strong, untried
and too young to bear the burden but we bore it. Moving into the
caverns and caves prepared for us by an earlier race—
we hid and waited.
When the smoke from the world fires did clear
still we hid and waited.
When the ice descended, and the long night came
still we hid and waited.
When the clouds vanished and the stars shone bright,
when the great Inland Sea appeared,
then did we emerge into the light.
And when we emerged
We were ten thousand strong.

Earth's Mind supplies the pictures, and the voices around the sacred fire grow soft.
Oh how the world had changed.

Shallow seas there were where once a land had been
scorched with fire. Vast oceans hid
the desecration of centuries.
Mountains there were where no mountains had been.
And we had changed.
We had grown powerful in our caves and caverns.
We had used that which we were given and
We had increased in kind. Our children shall inherit the Earth.

PART 1

PLAYER

Chapter 1

Arcolan Domes, Mars
(In the 47th year of the Return)

Ellis Hagan dreamed he killed his father.

In the theater rehearsing the final scene of the play, Julia at Candlemas, due to open in a scant three hours, the dream still reverberated in his mind, more potent than troupe leader Josh Ormandi's voice reverberating against the false timbers of the theater roof.

"What's wrong with you, Ellis? The word is debilitate. Debilitate. Why can't you say it right?"

Why couldn't he? He might have told Josh about the dream, but Josh would only call it nerves and accuse him of drinking lotus tea.

Josh pounded the table in front of him. "Damn it, man, pay attention! The way you're going, Ben could do a better job."

Ben, Hagan's understudy for the Jolando part, might at that. Hagan pulled his long cloak tighter, wishing warmth where there was none. Playing Jolando would've been easier if he hadn't been awake half the night, afraid to sleep for fear the dream would return.

However, the play was important. And yes, he could do it. Wasn't he Jolando? Didn't he know the soldier-priest better than he knew himself? Yet—

Why dream of Earth now? Six years he'd been gone, yet the dream made it seem like only yesterday he'd slunk to Mars, his tail between his legs. In spite of his resolve to forget them, details of the dream kept coming back. A view of the Kama Valley from high above. A scorching sun. He'd had the body of an enormous Eagle, talons extended, giant wings folded flat as he plummeted toward the ground, diving for the kill. He'd felt anger, fear, and a strange determination. And there was his father on the ground, and blood. Blood everywhere. He'd killed—his father!

"Ellis, are you listening to me?"

Hagan focused on the leader. Josh was right. He had to put the dream aside. "Sorry, Josh. I'll be all right." He smiled. "Must be stage fright."

"Or you've been drinking lotus tea!" With that expected shot Josh spun on his heel and strode across the stage. Four young apprentices who had been eavesdropping behind a scrim scattered like borobirds spooked from a bush.

Still cold, Hagan settled more deeply into Jolando's velvety cloak. He'd make it. If nothing else, he'd take a spoon of Dani's mind-soothing powders, and once within the play he'd forget the dream.

Considering the dampening effect of Dani's potion, the fiery play went better than Hagan expected. Josh, who'd authored the parts based on a two hundred and fifty year old manuscript, played Marcos, the King, with brilliant sincerity. Dani, his real-life daughter, played Julia, daughter of Marcos, giving pathos to a part that could've been merely pathetic, and Hagan's own rendition of the usurper Jolando had the necessary combination of priestly fanaticism and soldierly cynicism the part called for. The audience of manager-technicians and middle-rank soldiers had roared their approval, then gasped at the reality of Jolando's death.

Now, dream safely stowed in the recesses of his mind, Hagan stood in the wings waiting for the final curtain.

He felt good. More whole than when he was merely Ellis Hagan, player.

To survive the inevitable celebration following one of their opening nights, he need only pretend he was still the soldier-priest.

Easy.

A sharp grunt from behind the curtains in the rear ruined his sense of well-being. Hagan, already moving toward the sound, heard Ben's soft panicked call.

Ben's tone twisted in Hagan's belly like a knife. Reaching the dim back hall, he found Ben and another apprentice holding an Arcolan Military Policeman between them. Ben's hand was tight over the man's mouth and nose.

Hagan's heart sank. Manhandling an AMP was a punishable act.

"Let him go!" Hagan whispered. Quickly the apprentices did, and the soldier slid to the floor, gasping, his eyes still closed.

"I couldn't help it," Ben whispered. "I couldn't—he came bursting in the back door during the black-out—"

Hagan knelt and touched the pulse at the soldier's neck. It was strong and fast. Not injured at all. Relieved, Hagan started to rise, but at that moment the soldier grabbed out, long fingers clutching Hagan's wrist. The movement caught them all by surprise, and the soldier came to his feet, lithe as a gymnast, Hagan manacled by his hard grip. His other hand hovered over a lens-capped s'darm at his thigh. The soldier peered at Hagan through the shadows. "You're Hagan, aren't you? You're the one I want to talk to."

The knife in Hagan's belly twisted deeper. "Why?"

"Can't talk in here. Come outside."

The soldier's grip didn't loosen. If necessary Hagan knew he could take the soldier under a grip like that. He could, but it wasn't worth chancing a month's punishment in the Caverns. "All right. Outside."

The soldier released him and moved past the apprentices to the exit.

Emerging into the alley behind the theater, Hagan closed the door, shutting off the first round of applause for Marco's final impassioned speech. In the light of the ball lamp above the door the soldier appeared of medium height. Older than Hagan had first thought, perhaps only a year or two short of his own thirty-six earth years. The soldier was blond, and Hagan guessed him to be from Araxes, under the Southern Domes. Nordic, he would have been called before the Leaving.

With effort Hagan drew himself together. "What do you want? What did I do? Forget my work permit? Walk on some stinking General's shadow?"

"You treat the Service lightly, Captain Hagan. Especially for one who at one time made it his life."

Captain Hagan? The rank that tripped so lightly off the soldier's tongue zinged along Hagan's nerves, undoing all the good wrought by Dani's powder. How had the soldier known who he was? "Who are you?"

"Name's Kali. Liaison to the Expansion Council."

Hagan stared at the hand Kali extended until the soldier drew back. (The eagle stirred in his mind.) "So?"

"You're the son of the Colonial—"

"Wrong man." His military record wasn't known here. Few even know he was from Earth.

"No I haven't. The records say you're Captain Ellis Hagan, the son of the Colonial, Elias Hagan, the Commander of Kama. It's that man I've come for."

Come for? In spite of his efforts to control his reaction Hagan felt the fine sweat bead on his brow. How had they found him? Why had they. . .(The eagle spread it's wings, coasting on an updraft.)

"Well? You are, aren't you?"

Shunting a dozen questions aside Hagan took a quiet, controlling breath and made himself relax. He was not Hagan, son of the Commander of Kama. He was Jolando, the soldier-priest, facing his accusers once again. His smile was deliberately arrogant. "Am I what? Certainly not a Colonial. Obviously there's been a mix-up in your records."

"No, Captain. You might cleanse the colonialisms from your speech, but you can't remove your resemblance to the Commander."

Resemblance? Not bloody likely. But the denial he wanted to say wouldn't come.

After a moment of waiting, the soldier lost patience. "This is ridiculous. Of course you're Hagan's son. I wouldn't be here if I wasn't sure. Your—" He hesitated. Looked almost apologetic. "Your father's dead, Hagan, and we thought you should know before the news hits the nightscreens."

Elias dead? Hagan still clutched at the Jolando pose, but inside he started to shake. Dead? As he had died in the dream?

The door beside him slammed opened. Sound rushed out. Ben tugged at his arm. "El, hurry. The audience is wild and Josh will kill you if you don't get in here."

Shrugging him off, Hagan stared at the soldier. "Dead? How?"

"We're not sure. We'll know more tomorrow. Come down to Xanthe with me tonight. You can be there when the reports come in. You'll have everything we know, as soon as we know it. It'll be more than the propaganda you'll get from the nightscreen."

Jolando's mask was Hagan's only defense. Hiding behind it, containing a pain he had hardly expected, he gave the only answer he could. "I'm sorry to hear the Commander is dead, Captain. I'm sure he's been one of civilization's mythic heroes, but this means nothing to me personally. As I said before, you have the wrong man."

"You—you fool!" Kali growled. When Hagan didn't respond, the officer threw up his hands, turned on his well-polished heel and marched down the alley in the direction of the sub train terminal. His steps echoed against the empty alley walls.

Hagan watched Kali's departure with only one thought pounding in his head. If Elias Hagan was really dead, had an eagle killed him?

Later that night there was nothing on the nightscreen about the Commander's death. Leaving the party early, Hagan and Dani had returned to his apartment, and he'd turned on the screen, hoping there would be news, hoping there wouldn't. When there had been nothing said about the Commander, he and Dani had gone to bed.

But now, unwilling to sleep for fear he'd dream the dream again, Hagan thought of his fruitless watch for colony news. Was the Commander really dead? If so why hadn't the nightscreen mentioned it?

Resolutely he turned on his side and curled around Dani. He laid his cheek against her smooth warm shoulder, smelling the faint flower scent of the lotion she used before she went to bed. Deep in dream-sleep, she didn't move when he touched her.

A world of minute sound filled the sleep-dimmed room. The low-pitched hum of the bed machinery keeping their bodies feather light, the slightly higher hum of doorlocks and window locks, the faint hiss of fresh, temperate air replacing stale, body-worn breath. Breathing, hers soft, his loud in his own ears. Beating hearts, his strong, hers only felt, quiet and regular. As it would be whether he was there or not.

Impatiently he turned on his back again. He should have begged a jar of lotus tea from that spurious Pax Domini priest who lived on the second floor. Too bad the stuff made him sick. Another hour of this and he'd try anything that would let him follow Dani into that dreamland.

A dream land, not a nightmare land. How had the Commander really died? How had Kali and the Expansion Council found him so soon?

And if Kali had found him so easily, how long before the High Council of Mars found him? Not long, when the last Original Share hung in the balance. Damn the Share. Let them have it!

The ache in his throat grew more painful. There'd been no colony news at all tonight, which in itself was ominous. Usually there was something, if only statistics about the latest Hojoi shipment.

Drawing further away from Dani, Hagan stretched to ease his tension. Thinking of Hojoi, the raw food crop originally bred from the tobacco plant, brought images of the Kama Valley, turned to the plow and planted in stark, endless rows under the hot sun. Brought images too of the cool shade along the Kama River. Images of the glen where he'd killed—

No, he'd not remember. He couldn't and stay sane.

If Kali could be trusted, there was only one fact. The Commander was dead.

And all the conflicts he and the Commander might have resolved, given time, were dead with him.

Hagan rolled out of the bedfield and padded across the cool cerafoam floor to the water dispenser. He was more wide awake now than when he'd gone to bed, and his mouth was as dry as the Kama Valley in late summer.

"El—" Dani rolled over and felt for him without opening her eyes. "What's the matter?"

"Nothing. Go back to sleep." He punched in for an issue of water.

"Are you worried about that soldier?" Her voice held a floating quality, as if she were still half in her dream.

"No." The water was cool, but not cold, and suddenly Hagan was swamped by the images of water, running water, the Kama

Falls, the long, winding river, the almost endless ocean that stretched off the shore of the colony, forbidden swimming in Norcanna Bay when he was young. Another blond girl, long hair flowing down her back like smooth spring water. And another, dark eyed, dark haired, watching him with such compassion when he was in such pain. For a moment the images came so fast he swayed, dizzy with them.

"El, what did he want to see you about?" Dani was watching him. Even with his back turned, he could feel her gaze. It prickled his skin.

"I already told you, it was about my papers. They were in order. That's the end of it."

"I don't believe you. Josh didn't believe you either."

"I don't care what Josh believes."

"You should. If he cuts you out, no other troupe will take you on."

True. The tenth quarter under the Arcolan Domes of Mars was a closed community, and Josh carried a lot of weight. But Josh's concern was for the players, and if they weren't threatened, Josh wouldn't care what Hagan did, as long as he could play the parts Josh assigned.

But this Kali of the Expansion Council—he could ruin everything. And what could it matter to Kali whether he acknowledged his father or not? Was it the Share? They could have the damned thing if they'd leave him alone.

Hagan rubbed his cold arms. Kali's information—so damned accurate. He'd been a fool to think he was safe. If those people at Xanthe could find him so easily, others could too.

Drawing more water, Hagan studied Dani over the edge of the small cup. In the shadows her bare form of soft valleys and peaked hills lay completely relaxed in the bedfield, inviting exploration—offering comfort.

Hell, it wasn't comfort he needed.

Moving to the window he leaned against the sill and looked out on the dark, empty street, the red-shadowed dome low overhead. No, what he needed was to banish the dream of the screaming, diving eagle. But more than that, he—he needed to know what had happened to the Commander. Should he go to Xanthe like Kali said, and find out?

7

"El, come back to bed." Danielle's voice was again dream touched.

Hagan sighed and stretched. If he slept, he'd dream, and if he dreamed, it'd be of Earth.

Of himself as an eagle.

He crushed the empty cup and tossed it into the recycle well. A trip to Xanthe might be necessary though even the thought of it gave him chills. No, he couldn't. No matter what Kali had promised, he couldn't.

Yet, perhaps he should.

If only to lay the eagle to rest.

There was no time for tears.

As she strapped herself into the recliner flight seat in the third passenger-bay of the Diana-Earth shuttle, Meeriam of Lisson fought a sense of doom. Poor Doctor Portus, already suffering for the loss of Commander Hagan, had been summoned back to Earth by General Graeber. The soldiers had come while she'd been talking to him in the workers' dining hall.

Now a sense of darkness grew with each breath she took. When Graeber told him of the Commander's death, could Portus hide the fact he already knew? Or where he'd learned the information? Yet Uncle had said it was imperative Portus know what had happened, imperative he take the truth back to Mars. Who would have guessed General Graeber would act so quickly?

She shut her eyes and tried to calm herself. Immediately impressions impinged themselves on her mind's eye. The guards at the gate, peering into faces, studying identification papers, were jittery and distracted. Fear lived in their eyes. Three soldiers in the bank of seats above her were talking in whispers about the Commander's disappearance. They'd also heard the rumors.

Officially, Commander Hagan was only missing, but no one expected he was still alive. Many would suspect the man who had killed him, though most would be too afraid to say so out loud.

In spite of her resolve, Meeriam felt tears well again. Not here, she thought, not now. It was too dangerous to give in to grief now. Instead she made herself think of other things. Of home in the mountains. Of the People going about their daily lives in harmony and joy. Pain filled her. They, too, would miss the Commander. He had been their advocate in the Norcanna Council. She ranged further, sweeping through the Diana colony on Earth's moon, where most people were still not aware of the tragedy that had taken place on Earth. And then her thoughts moved on toward Mars and anger intertwined with her grief. The Commander's son was on Mars. How would he feel when he heard the news? Would he care his father had been murdered by a madman? She remembered the fury that had been in the younger Hagan's face the last time she had seen him. She had also seen the pain. So like the Commander's own. Portus had thought he'd come home when he heard the news, but Portus was wrong. He would not come. Let him stay safe in his comfortable life on Mars. No one needed him on Earth.

She pressed her fist to her lips. She wouldn't cry. But the ache grew in her throat.

Sitting in his office off the mezzanine in Xanthe's Administrative wing, under the Domes of Trithonius, Kali had just finished telling his superior, Major Simon Harris, the results of his abortive trip to the Arcolan Domes. Still simmering, he threw himself back into his chair. "Maybe it was the costume, Si. Or the beard. Made him look like someone right out of the dark ages."

"Perhaps going to the play first colored your perception."

Kali barely heard Si's note of conciliation. "When he kept denying he was the Commander's son, I wanted to deck him."

"He's going under an assumed name?"

"Hell, no. Out there plain as day."

"I'm surprised no one else has picked up the connection."

"They'll make it soon enough. Hagan's a fairly common surname up in Arcola, one of the old military families, but even with the beard the bastard was wearing you can see the resemblance to the Commander." Kali stared at his half-empty cup of cold coffee. "Doesn't he have any idea what will happen when the news reaches the Grand Council? The moment someone remembers the Commander had a son, the vultures will be after him."

"Including us."

"Well, damn it—" Kali laughed. Of course, including them. He'd just gotten there first, that was all.

"I feel sorry for him," Si murmured.

"I don't. Imagine the bastard, denying his paternity when any fool could see the lie." Kali drained the rest of his cold coffee and tossed the cup at the recycler. It was Portus who'd suggested six months ago, when they first realized the Commander needed help to keep General Graeber in line, that the younger Hagan might be approached about returning to Earth. The Commander himself, though, had nixed the idea. Knew better than the good doctor how his son would reply. Maybe too much cheery was addling the doctor's brain. Or was he, too, dead?

A knot of anxiety grew in Kali's gut. "Did anything come from Portus while I was gone?"

"Nothing."

"Where the bloody hell is he? We should have heard by now."

Si's shrug said he agreed. All the helpless anxiety Kali had tried to bottle up spilled out. "Graeber's getting away with murder while we just sit here and twiddle our thumbs. Damn it, Si, tell me. What can we do?"

"We wait," Si said. "We wait."

Chapter 2

Norcanna Colony, New Earth

What could he do?

Portus, waiting outside Graeber's massive door beneath the newer wing of General Headquarters, barely contained his trembling. When Meeriam had told him about Elias, two days ago, around his horrified numbness, he'd felt totally inadequate to the situation.

He wasn't Elias. He couldn't take up the cause where Elias had left it. He was no eagle, like Elias had been. No, he was, in fact, a small brown wren. Silent, perhaps persistent, but not very brave.

His small breathing mask firmly in place, Portus hid his unsteady hands within his coat, took hold of his wavering dignity. Mustn't let the General see. . .

Before he was ready the door opened and he was exposed.

General Gordon Graeber didn't look up. The general, born in the year of the Return forty-seven years before, to a minor matriarch of the House of Pavonis and thus, as fate decreed for sons of minor matriarchs, thrust into the military life at an early age, sat behind his desk engrossed in whatever the reader was telling him. He was short, with shoulders like a wrestler, and hands as big as a Freefarmer's. Deep-set eyes rimmed by puffy lids, a pallor to the skin caused by too much time spent here in his hole. A red flush across broad cheekbones might possibly be temper—Graeber was not noted for his even temper—jerky movements denoted a lack of control. Perhaps he was ill.

When he finally looked up he smiled, a slight movement of heavy lips that bared yellowed teeth yet did nothing for the coldness in his eyes.

"Ah, Doctor Portus, do come in. And do remove your mask. The air is pure here." Reluctantly Portus did as he was bid. The general nodded benignly. "I hope I've not unfairly burdened you by requesting your return?" As Portus had only been gone less than a week and wasn't due back here for several months, it seemed an honest question, but before Portus could form an answer, Graeber was going on. "Have you brought your bag of medical tricks?"

"I—I would be as naked as a soldier without his s'darm if I had no bag full of tricks, General." It was hard not to speak of Elias, and worse, to have the General act as if nothing was wrong. "H-how can I help you?"

Graeber smiled gently. "You can give me your medical opinion, doctor."

"For yourself?" Portus remembered his impression when he'd first entered the room. "Are you ill?"

"Hardly, doctor." Graeber frowned at the telereader which was still running words across its screen. "The Firewing have killed the Commander of Kama, Elias Hagan. I want you to—"

So damned blunt—so damned final! Portus swayed, then steadied himself against Graeber's desk. "Elias?"

Graeber's expression didn't change. "I'm sorry, Doctor. I forgot you and the Commander were friends."

Portus groped behind him for a chair, and sat heavily. "Of—of long standing, I'm afraid—I really must—" He pulled out his handkerchief and mopped his face. And then Graeber's words sank in. "The Firewing? Are you sure?" He could not hide his incredulousness. It couldn't be. It wasn't possible. Meeriam would have said.

"Absolutely sure, Doctor, but that's where we seek your expertise. Examine the body and tell us how he died. It seems obvious, but we must be certain when we send our report back to Mars."

"N-no. It would never do to be uncertain—" An ache tightened Portus's throat. Examine Elias's body? Did he have to do this? Couldn't someone else just as well? "Where—where is he?"

Within an hour of the time Portus had finished his examination, Graeber produced the report for his corroborating signature. Reluctantly Portus signed. "We should reserve final judgment until we've tested those metal fragments," he said, but in his heart he was sure. Sure that the metal had come from a Firewing weapon. Only an old-style scatter-gun such as an occasional Firewing carried would make that large and bloody a wound. But it made no sense. Why would the Firewing shoot the one man who had championed their cause in the halls of power? He wouldn't believe it. He simply couldn't.

"Naturally, Doctor I agree," said Graeber. "But I am bound by my commission to forward a report to the Expansion Council on Mars as quickly as possible. It's time they were made aware of the seriousness of this matter. At this moment we verge on a state of war with the savages. If they can turn on Commander Hagan, is anyone safe?"

Portus's mouth went dry. Did he have to answer? Badly did he need to warm himself upon a glass of cheery.

But Graeber seemed in no hurry to release him. "About that metal, Doctor. There's no question in your mind, is there? It's undoubtedly of Firewing origin, isn't it?"

Portus tried to swallow. "I'm no forensic expert, General. If you want an analysis of the metal I suggest you have it sent to Xanthe." Frantically Portus searched for a way of removing himself. He was becoming clammy with cold sweat and the effort to appear calm was almost more than he could bear.

"Yes," the General leaned back in his chair, "it's a damned shame that when we have questions like this we must go to Mars for answers. How long, Doctor, will they keep us undersupplied with men and equipment? I'm sure you realize," Graeber went on, as usual not waiting for an answer, "we are understaffed at all levels? And equipment—"

"Sir," Portus tried to stem the rising tide of Graeber's complaints. "I agree wholeheartedly. I've mentioned it more than once in my own reports. I'm sure if we had qualified people applying for immigration—"

"Exactly. I ask for soldiers and they send the Matriarch Kassine more farmers. I ask for doctors and she receives fertilizer experts. I ask for carriers and road equipment, and all I'm sent are promises. Perhaps if I substituted sand for the next few shipments of Hojoi they might give the matter more attention."

"No doubt." Portus knew exactly what the General meant. Elias also had wanted the Colony to be self-sufficient. Given the right complement of technicians and support groups, it would have been possible within a reasonable length of time. It would have been even more so if Elias's plan to adopt Firewing methods of living off the land had been accepted. But in some quarters on Mars such thoughts had been considered quite mad. Do without Hojoi? Eat raw, unprocessed food? Most citizens of the Domes found the idea more repugnant than incest or open sores. In truth, Portus didn't like the idea himself. It couldn't be good for the digestion, letting all those strange microbes in. He also doubted he could ever comfortably dispense with his face mask. Once more Portus mopped the sweat off his brow. "We can only keep trying."

"Yes." Graeber surged forward again, his sausage-like fingers drumming on the wing of the chair. Portus shifted restlessly. Why didn't the General dismiss him?

"Doctor, I remember now, you and Hagan were very good friends. Did he ever confide in you what arrangements he made for his widow?"

"Velia?" As he always did when Velia Hagan was brought to mind, Portus suffered a pang of irritation. If the woman had even a smidgen of decency, how different so many lives might have been. How Elias could have—and to think it had even been Portus's own well-meant suggestion—

"Yes, the Commander's widow."

"I—I don't know. Why? Is there some problem?" Of course there'd be a problem. Though he had avoided her for years, without a doubt, with Velia there was always a problem. She'd not let Elias rest in peace. Not if she could help it.

"She seems to have become irrational, if you know what I mean."

Portus didn't. Velia had always been a little irrational. For Velia it was as natural as breathing. "I don't, General," he said. "Velia Hagan is a woman of strong opinions."

"This is more than strong opinion." Graeber frowned. "When I sent Captain Galt out to tell her we'd found the Commander, she demanded an attorney be sent to her at once so she might send her claim to Mars with all possible speed."

"Her claim?"

"To the estate, and to the Original Share. My aide said she seemed to feel if she didn't do this immediately she would forfeit the holdings."

In spite of himself Portus laughed. Nice to know she hadn't changed. The knowledge restored his faith in the immutability of human nature. "She knows very well no matter how fast she submits her claim the share will still go to Ellis. He's the heir, not she."

"Ellis?" Graeber's voice grew cold. "Ellis? An heir?" Had he been standing, Portus would have tried to back away from the lethal expression growing in the General's eyes. With alarm he watched the General's massive hands come together, grip a thin metal light wand, watched the metal bend under tremendous pressure.

Portus felt light-headed. Wasn't it the ancient Greeks who killed the bearer of bad tidings? No, surely, now, he was misreading the expression in the General's eyes. However, in any case, dismissed or not, he had to leave. Abruptly he stood and edged toward the door, speaking as he went. "Yes. The son. On Mars."

Graeber barely noticed when the old doctor scrambled through the door and out of sight. An heir, God damn it! With a shower of sparks, the light pencil in his hands snapped.

Vana Darrow, a tall, angular woman who made up in loyalty what she lacked in beauty, opened Darrow Tower's outside door to Portus before he could ring the bell.

She led him to the lift, and off again at his floor, talking all the time. "Ah, Doctor, heard the carrier, and couldn't guess who'd be upon my walk. Certainly didn't expect to see you again so soon. You heard the news about the Commander, didn't you? Missing most a week now. Everyone hoping for the best but not expecting it. That's how we always are, isn't it so?" Vana Darrow also talked a lot, which was sometimes a comfort and at other times not.

Wearily Portus nodded. Vana Darrow's younger son, who'd shown up to retrieve Portus's bags as soon as he heard his mother's voice at the door, placed the bags inside the bedroom arch, and Portus gave the boy an obligatory credit. Vana Darrow retrieved the coin without a word, shooed the boy out the hall and placed the coin on the sideboard. "We'll not take it from friends, Doctor. Not in these hard times."

"You should take it while I have it, Vana Darrow. If I'm forced to stay too long you'll have to kick me out for non-payment of tariff."

"Never you, Doctor. Are you then thinking of a longer stay?"

Obviously the general hadn't broadcast yet that Elias had been found. How could he explain without saying too much? "I'm grounded by this alert."

"That's the General's doing, no doubt. Military never can let decent folk go on with their living without they interfere. But it wasn't different under the Domes when I lived there with Darrow."

Vana Darrow had lived in the Southern Domes, and had been among the first big surge of settlers to Earth at least twenty years before. Her husband had died twelve years later, and since then she'd made a living for herself and two boys with this transient's tower. A good living, by the looks of it. Portus's inner voice laughed. Could do worse, old man, if you have to stay on Earth.

Grimly he chided himself. He couldn't stay. He wouldn't even think of it. So much to do, and so little time. Elias dead. God, he needed that drink. Why didn't the woman leave? Wasn't there a bottle of cheery in the cupboard? He licked dry lips, and the hands he'd managed to keep steady in the general's presence trembled as if he had the palsy.

Vana Darrow straightened a chair and flicked a speck of nonexistent dust off the windowsill. "Everyone a-saying the Firewing might have killed the Commander, you know. That is, some do. Now myself, I'm not so sure. Howsomever, you mark my words, there'll be misery either way. The Freefarmers are a-clamoring for protection and Matriarch Kassine herself talks about arming them."

Arms for Freefarmers? Portus shuddered. Protection from whom? The Firewing? Graeber's army? God help them all.

Finally, after assuring Portus she would set supper for him at her own table, Vana Darrow withdrew, and Portus hurried to the cupboard and poured himself a small glass of ninety-proof cheery, downed it, then poured another and carried it back to the recliner in front of the curved window. The heat of the alcohol created an artificial glow in his stomach.

Going limp in the chair, Portus gulped down more of the cheery, and though it finally warmed his cold body and stilled his shaking hands, it did nothing for his mind. The moment he started to relax the ache in his heart deepened. Elias. God, it would be lonesome without him. Better not to remember the cadaver in that sterile room—it wasn't Elias, anyway. Not any more. If the Firewing were to be believed, Elias was—still, somewhere—Elias. And perhaps, after all these years, he was at peace.

Portus closed his teary eyes, remembering—remembering—the story Elias had told one cold and rainy day over a shared cup of cheery.

—that Elias, informed of the impending birth of his child had traveled since the previous daybreak to Lissone, a canyon valley high on the slope of Kama, the sacred mountain, hoping to get there before the event. He'd come alone, under a new moon and during a summer night, unencumbered by civilization's weapons. Indeed, here he had no need for weapons. And once out of his own camp, he'd donned the soft, tough mountain boots and neutral clothing worn by the Firewing. He'd found them easier wearing in the low brush country, and an absolute necessity on the higher reaches of the mountain.

He knew the way. He'd been to Lissone many times.

A stadt, which was less than two kils, outside the Firewing camp he was met by young Patlos, 'Driana's brother. "We thought you would be here soon. You came quickly."

"I came like a Firewing," Elias said. "Will it please her?"

"I don't know. Women are a mystery to me, 'Lias, my sister no less than others. But there's some concern among the women. She's been in labor two days now. It is a boy babe, and he is large."

Though he was concerned about 'Driana, his wife by Firewing custom, Elias was also filled with pride. A boy! He would father a boy! He didn't question that the Firewing knew the sex of the baby before it was born. The Firewing had a power beyond his understanding, but he accepted that fact and didn't feel inferior. Envious, perhaps, but not inferior.

Now, in the middle of the night, walking beside Patlos, he felt a joy that all was right with the world. The feeling lasted until they reached the camp.

Even in this late hour of the night the large encampment was awake. The elders had waited for him, and greeted him with gentle hands. Some children stared at him with wide eyes, perhaps wondering that this stranger looked no different than their elders.

He was no different, he insisted. But he didn't have the Power.

'Driana's tent was open to the warm night air. She was waiting for him, eyes as large as mountain pools, as dark, as deep. He knelt full of wonder, full of fear, by the cushions where she lay, and took her in his arms. Her skin was dry and feverish.

She spoke into his mind. Her words were tinged with pain. *I knew you would come. I was waiting.*

"I would've been here sooner, but I couldn't get away."

I know. I know. Her words were a barely heard whisper. A spasm convulsed her small body and she gasped. He held her tightly until it receded. After a quiet while she seemed to draw strength from him. She smiled, and reaching up, touched his air-shaved face with a hand as gentle as silk. Again she spoke and the words were only in his mind. *What name shall we give our son?*

"Our boy?" He smiled at the thought. "You choose. Give him a Firewing name."

No. He should bear your name.

Elias laughed outright. "My name? God forbid there be two of us in the world." He thought of the line of Hagans stretching back into antiquity. His own father had carried the ancient biblical name of Elijah. His grandfather had been a Timothy, his great-grandfather, departing from the biblical tradition had been an Ellis. "Ellis?"

Ellis. I like that name. Now she smiled. *Yes, Ellis. It sounds strong, yet gentle. He will be like that. Oh, 'Lias, how happy*—her thought broke off. Beneath his hands Elias felt another spasm engulf her, felt the baby shift as if impatient with this birthing process. Gently he settled 'Driana against his shoulder, waiting for the pain to ease, soothing her with his hands, with his voice, nodding quietly but firmly to the women who came periodically to check on them. He was here, she was his, he would take care of her.

Toward morning, with the mountain breeze turning cool, 'Driana passed into unconsciousness, and the baby finally entered into the world. Elias, watching the women work over his wife's still form took the babe when they offered it to him. A love almost as great as his love for Adriana of Lissone filled him for the squalling bundle.

Though the babe was big and loud, 'Driana never saw him. Before the sun broke over Kama's high shoulder, she died.

Elias, as befitted a man of his rank and upbringing, contained his tears. Quelled the outward evidence of his anguish, controlled the darkness that tried to engulf him in black flame. For the following two days he resided in the tent where 'Driana had given birth and died, watching the women who came with loving hands to care for the baby. He held aloof. He'd not blame the blameless for her death. The baby was but a product of their love, and as such was precious beyond belief, but he found himself wondering: Why was one life traded for another? Was it fair? Was it right?

Why?

When it came time to leave, the Firewing pointed out he was not equipped to raise a son with power. Elias left the baby with them knowing they were right, and also knowing if he appeared with the newborn infant there would be more questions than he could answer.

Not too reluctantly he returned to his post at Kama Garrison, but the knowledge that his son lived on the slopes of Kama Mountain ate like a cancer at his heart and the questions turned his days sour. The next time Portus came Elias got drunk on cheery, and then he cried, and Portus cried with him.

And still the tears welled.

Thinking he heard someone call his name, Portus stirred, but his eyes were too heavy to open, his muscles had no strength, and his mind seemed to observe from the depths of a deep, dark hole. Slowly his tongue formed an answer, but then he forgot the question.

"Poor man," someone said. "Let him rest."

Yes, he agreed. Let him rest. Let him finally rest in peace.

Chapter 3

Trithonius, Mars,

Under the shadow of Nix Olympica within what is known on the oldest maps of Mars as the Northwest Quadrant, lay the Domes of Arcola, a city under eight cluster domes of unbreakable glass. A city of artificial atmosphere, low-profile buildings and even-measured streets, where each growing thing was carefully monitored so it received only its share of life-giving water. Where cleanliness became fetish, and the night domes were always tinged with red.

South in the same Quadrant, down the immense slope of Nix Olympica and out across the vast, empty lava plains of Araxes, lay the Southern Domes, more properly called the Domes of Araxes. Here, in another cluster dome city that was the twin of Arcola, spread the industrial center of the population of Mars. Here was where the machinery was made that turned Mars sand into cerafoam, the ubiquitous construction material that everywhere formed roads, buildings, signposts and sidewalks. Here also at one time was the artisan's center, which had almost claimed its independence in the upheavals of 2990. In those hard times one fourth the habitable space of Araxes had been destroyed, and only now were the domes being rebuilt.

Memories were long in Araxes.

And so were they long within the Domes of Trithonius Lacus, or, as commonly known, 'Thonius, the smallest of the three domed cities of Mars. Here, at 'Thonius, one thousand and ninety stadts east of Araxes and built within deep basalt canyon walls, were the domes housing the University of Xanthe, named after an ancient scar on the face of Mars. Here, at 'Thonius, was the repository of history, the Archives of a dark and fearful past, and harbinger of an uncertain future.

Here at Xanthe the skills were taught that enabled mankind to survive on the harsh surface of the planet Mars. Here the sons and daughters of power were instilled with a sense of history and purpose. Here was found the seat of the Expansion Movement which was sending colonists back to Mother Earth. And here, under the Domes of 'Thonius Lacus, within the black walls of the University, were found the most subversive elements of Arcolan society, the scholars of Mars.

Four days after Kali's visit to the theater the news about the Commander of Kama had been shown everywhere. On the nightscreen tapes Dani had replayed over breakfast, and on the cab-screen every half hour all the way from Arcola to 'Thonius. Stepping from the travel-tube exit onto the platform at 'Thonius, Hagan felt as if everyone should know him now. Not the player Ellis Hagan, but Ellis Hagan, son of the dead Commander of Kama. Killed by an eagle? The thought fluttered like a disturbed spirit in the subcaverns of his mind.

It was the flagrant rhetoric against the Firewing that finally made him step into the travel-tube for the trip to Xanthe. Truth, Kali had promised him. What was the truth? Repressing a shudder, Hagan shook out his heavy Jolando cloak and drew it over his shoulders, then took the moving stairway to the surface.

Waiting for Kali in the soldier's office off the mezzanine of the Administration building some minutes later, Hagan studied the sparsely furnished room. Four chairs, a bare desk with a small built-in telereader. A glass-topped sideboard with a terra-scene at one end. On the other side a narrow gray glassed window, with only a view of low roofs, and part of a pathway visible. The view stopped abruptly at a sheer obsidian cliff which by its very sheerness carried the eye upward to the dome abutment.

Claustrophobic.

Swallowing away an incipient panic, Hagan turned back to the terra-scene, letting his gaze rest on the miniature green tree, the pond made of tiny gray pebbles, and the fine green grass that made a perfect miniature meadow.

Earth? He stared at it, almost losing himself in the effect.

"So you decided to come after all."

Startled, Hagan turned. Kali had entered and stood just inside the door, arms crossed, watching him with cold eyes.

Hagan shrugged. "It was an irresistible invitation."

"I didn't think you'd come. Not the way you were denying

any relationship."

Within the folds of his cloak Hagan tensed. It was obvious Kali didn't like him any more than he liked Kali. "How could I resist? Haven't you seen the nightscreen?"

"Of course I have."

"Is it true? Did the Firewing kill him?"

"What do you think?"

Hagan stared at Kali, resenting the young soldier's seemingly unshakable calm. "I think it's a goddamned lie."

"I'm glad we agree on something. Here, have a chair."

Kali's change from arrogant young officer to something more approachable caught Hagan off guard. He took the chair Kali indicated.

Kali sat down behind the desk and popped the telereader into work position. Studied Hagan with dark curiosity. "All right, so why did you come?"

"You promised me the truth."

Kali waved a hand at the reader. "You don't think the nightscreens are truthful?"

Hagan considered his words carefully, wondering if they somehow would be used against him. "No. It—it sounds too senseless. They were his friends. There isn't one of them who would have killed him."

"Tell that to Graeber." Kali keyed a code into another small machine and turned the screen so Hagan could see the words running across the reader's broad eye. "The whole medical report is here. It came through from Norcanna an hour ago. Signed by Dr. Portus himself."

Portus? An image of the kindly old doctor flashed into Hagan's mind. He forced himself to read the words Portus had written. Stopped at the end of the first paragraph. "The Commander was shot?" Like another man was shot—he blinked away the memory and forced himself to make sense of the medical jargon describing the Commander's injury.

"Yes. By an old-style scatter shot. A fact pointed out in Graeber's addendum to Portus's portion of the report. He wants everyone to believe the Firewing are armed to the teeth."

"Why?"

"So the High Council here on Mars will send him more

23

soldiers and weapons is my guess."

"But who'd believe it?" Hagan didn't.

"No one with any sense. The Firewing have nothing to gain by such an act."

"Who, then?"

"We know there's only one man who profits by your father's death."

Remembering the Original Share he would inherit Hagan's jaw tightened. "Other than myself?"

Kali waved his comment away. "Your father was one of the sane voices in the Colony. After Graeber's promotion a year ago, every push he made against the Firewing was countered by the Commander. Every repressive order was argued. No one but the Commander could have gotten away with bucking Graeber for as long as he did." Bright pain appeared in Kali's pale eyes but was quickly shuttered. "We should have seen this coming, and didn't."

"Even if you'd seen it, what could you have done?"

"Not much," Kali admitted. "Warned the Commander, for whatever good it would do. Even if he'd known, he wouldn't have backed down."

Raw pain darted through Hagan. No, the Commander wouldn't have backed down.

Kali, still watching the screen, went on. "He might have taken the problem to the High Council, perhaps, but Graeber is well-placed as far as family goes. His mother was a minor matriarch of Pavonis, and he has high backing. He's one of the few people to go to the colony who've not been screened through here. But he had a clean record. He'd been Commander of the Caverns for two years before requesting the transfer. Both his transfer and his promotion came directly through the High Council. I wish to God we'd made at least a token objection. I'd feel better now."

"Then you believe he had the Commander murdered."

"That's what we believe, but we can't prove it. Not from here."

"A clash of personalities, even an opposition of views, is no reason to do away with someone."

Kali's pale blue eyes harden to gray stone. "Madmen are not

reasonable. Graeber's colony can't expand until the Firewing are removed. He's already pushed them as far into the mountains as they are willing to go. The Firewing are fighting back, but not with weapons."

"What do they do?"

"They destroy newly laid roads, they damage military equipment, they destroy crops. In return, if Graeber catches them, he kills them. Hardly tit for tat, is it? Your father was just barely keeping Graeber in line, holding down the damage. Holding expansion to a minimum."

Hagan frowned. Why did Graeber need expansion? The colony hardly teemed with people. Thousands of additional colonists could go to Earth before the colony needed more room. There had to be something more. Something Kali wasn't saying. He waited.

Kali tilted his chair back and rubbed his red-rimmed eyes. "From the moment we knew Earth had an indigenous population, we tried to protect it, and at the same time we've tried to protect ourselves. We need Earth. I wish the Firewing needed us as badly."

The chill of premonition touched Hagan. "How badly do we need Earth?"

Kali hesitated. "The Colony already supplies over half of our food crop."

"They could open other domes here." Or expand Pavonis. Earth couldn't be that crucial.

Kali pushed the reader aside and leaned forward. "Have you heard of the Ancient City? The one the Firewing call Phinx?"

Hagan bit back a smile. Was that what this was all about? The Firewing's mythical city? "Of course. The Firewing mean Phoenix. The City of the Leaving." It should also have been the City of the Return, Hagan remembered. But when the first colonists formed their corporation and bought their shares in the grand adventure forty-seven years ago, a detailed map of that whole quadrant had been made. There had been no City of Phoenix on it. No cities anywhere. He knew, because he remembered when he was young studying his father's copy of the old map. It had hung in the Commander's study, behind his desk.

"But what if it was there and simply hidden?" Kali insisted.

"Even so, it's been over a thousand years. What would be left? Buildings crumbled to dust? Metal artifacts rusted beyond recognition?" The idea was ridiculous.

"What about hardware? Rockets that could leave earth's atmosphere? Weapons that could be made operative?"

"After a thousand years?" Not likely. Hagan wanted to laugh, but a chill suspicion made him almost breathless. He said it aloud anyway. "Not likely."

"Not even if the Firewing had been taking care of them all these years?"

"That's—that's impossible." Wasn't it?

"Your father didn't think so."

A sense of desperation filled Hagan. He tried to fight it with logic. "So what? That doesn't make it true. And even if some remains are still there, Graeber would be insane to try to use them. There were rockets. Fission rockets. Radioactive."

"Yes, and if they still exist, they must now, at all cost, be destroyed."

Momentarily speechless, Hagan stared at Kali. The thought of ancient horrors tugged at him, but he caught himself. By God, none of this was his problem! It wasn't.

He'd gotten what he'd come for, hadn't he? The accounting? There was nothing he could do about the rest.

Feeling as if one more second in this small office would make him vomit, he rose to his feet. "I have to leave. We do another show tonight."

Dismay crossed Kali's face. "But—don't you want to—are you sure you don't want to go back to Earth and get to the bottom of this—?"

"Me? Are you cavern fodder?" What good could he do if he went? Surely Kali didn't think he could take the Commander's place? That was the most ludicrous thought of all.

Kali's voice sharpened. "What will happen here when the council remembers you've inherited the last Original Share?"

The Share? Hagan's heart sank. Other Original shares had either been broken up by inheritances or been redeemed by the Expansion council. The Commander, however, had been proud of his Share. Had sworn he would never see it sold or surrendered.

But for he himself, it meant only notoriety. He didn't want the Share. Let the Council have it. Or let Xanthe have it. He didn't care.

Kali leaned forward, desperately earnest. "Hagan, damn it, you have to help us. There's no one else who can go to Earth with the power you would have. The Share even gives you a seat on the Norcanna Council, if you want it. And if Phoenix really is sitting out there beyond the mountains somewhere you'd be in the ideal position to find it."

Hagan hid a shiver. If his father hadn't found it in forty years of looking, what made Kali believe it was there to be found? Besides—he couldn't go back. The haunting image of a Firewing lying in a pool of blood rose from his memory, and with it a pain greater than any the Commander had ever inflicted. No, he couldn't go back.

"You have to do this, Hagan," Kali said. "You're the only one who can stop that mad man."

"How, for God's sake. By killing him?"

"If necessary, yes!"

"No, by God, I won't—" Hagan gave Kali one last anguished look, then propelled himself through the door.

Kali, shaken by the blatant pain he'd seen in Hagan's eyes, sank back into his chair. He'd played it all wrong. Yet—yet what could he have said differently? He barely heard Si enter from the next office.

"Well?" Si asked. "How did it go?"

"Couldn't you hear it through the walls?" Not wanting Si to see how shaken he was, Kali swung his chair and faced the window. "I couldn't get through to him, Si. Nothing I said made an impression."

"Doesn't he see how much we need him?"

"No. He's blind as a cavern rat." Kali frowned. No, the player had seen it clearly enough. Something else was eating at him. Why couldn't Hagan return to Earth? Had Hagan really thought Kali was asking him to kill the General? Well, Kali thought, in the heat of the moment, isn't that what he'd said? But he hadn't meant it. No, removing Graeber from power would be enough.

"Frankly," Si went on, "I'm surprised you brought him this far. You can't force him any further."

"But he could stop Graeber." Kali fell back on the argument he'd used to Hagan. "He'd be in the ideal position."

"Ideal for us, not for him."

Kali groaned. Si was right. And there was something else. "Because of the share, they'll be on him like a flock of vultures, won't they? How long will it take? A day? A week? Let's hope to God he changes his mind before it's too late."

As far as Hagan could see, he had few options. Though he'd spent the three hour high-speed train ride from 'Thonius thinking about it, nothing presented itself but to hide until the furor passed. He'd drop out of sight, at least for a while. There were jobs to be had in the Southern Domes. In the Agridome of Pavonis. It was not his job to go to Earth and kill his father's killer. It was not his job to find and destroy the ancient city, assuming it was even there, and even if it was, assuming the Firewing would permit such an act.

Kali was crazy. He couldn't go back.

Emerging from the tunnel into the artificial warmth of the Arcolan late afternoon, he felt a protesting tension in his shoulders. He was a good actor. He liked the stage. He liked losing himself in a part. He felt more alive there than he ever did away from it. Yet, he couldn't stay. He'd tell Josh, tonight, after the play. Thinking the decision would ease his tension, Hagan turned onto the narrow Street of Players, and felt the hair prickled on his neck.

The street was empty. Empty when the crowd should have been gathering. He slowed his step, every sense alert. Or was he just being—

In a fractured second he saw the fist barreling at him. Then pain exploded in his midriff. A strangled cry rushed out of him, and he doubled over, gasping for breath, reaching out to break his fall. A boot in his ribs sent him sprawling. Pain engulfed him. The twilight grew darker.

Abruptly, from somewhere more distant, a sharp voice halted his grunting tormentor.

In the pause, he wretched, then heard a soft, sobbing cry.

28

"No, no. Leave him alone."

Dani? He shook his head, trying to clear it. Was she here? Had she been hurt? He whispered her name, then coughed and tasted blood. He wanted to push himself up but sensed someone close by.

Blinking to clear his vision, he saw a pair of black AMP boots planted firmly in front of him. Soldiers.

Come for him?

"On your feet, Player." The point of the black boot nudged Hagan's already painful ribs.

And then a soft, feminine hand was on his cheek. "Do as he says, Ben." Dani sounded sad, defeated.

Ben? "I'm not—" What the hell? She knew who he was.

Dani's hand, buried in his cloak, poked him sharply. "You are too getting up. Josh is inside and he's furious with you."

Josh? Holding his head, Hagan fought his confusion. They were still in front of the theater—now he knew why the street was empty. Three soldiers had emerged from the wide theater doors and were standing to one side, watching Dani, who wore a diaphanous robe of iridescent blue and green, Julia's costume for the first act. Her face, devoid of makeup, looked older, her long blond hair was partially dressed for the role and a dark bruise stained her graceful white neck.

A rage grew in him. "Dani—"

Under the robe she held him tightly, but her smile trembled with vulnerability. "It's all right. They thought we knew where Hagan was."

Abruptly another soldier drew close, pushed Dani away. "That's enough, woman. You—" he pointed at Hagan, "your papers!"

His papers? Fear fine-tuned Hagan's speeding thoughts. Dani wanted them to think he was Ben—the papers would prove them liars! He let his shoulders slump. "I—I don't have them."

"They're inside, Ben. You left them in our dressing room."

Hagan lifted his hands helplessly, conscious of the pouch of papers under his cloak. All they had to do was search him.

The soldier watched without emotion. "What's your name, Player?"

He was in too far to back out now. "Ben Palmer.

Apprentice—" Though God knew how long he could get away with the charade. "My papers—I left them inside."

"No papers on you? That's a credit offense, Player. You know that, don't you?"

"Yes sir." Hagan put a heavy whine in his voice, and begged silent pardon from Ben for assassination of character. "I was just needing to be out a moment."

Dani turned on him. Where the moment before she'd been protective, now she was furious. "You went to see her again, didn't you. You said you wouldn't, Ben, you said—"

"Didn't either—" It was a scene straight out of one of their plays. He hoped the soldier hadn't seen it.

"Enough!" Though the soldier grinned, he cut them off. His voice dropped. "I won't cite you this time. If you're telling the truth."

If he was? Hagan nodded eagerly, trying to keep his disbelief from his eyes. At that moment, from the shadows down the street, another figure appeared, a nondescript man in a civilian uniform, gray and undistinguished by either colored collar insignia, family emblem or rank stripes on his cuff.

The soldier in charge saw the civilian too, and walked away from Hagan and Danielle. The soldier and the civilian conferred quietly.

Dani pressed closer to Hagan. Though she still appeared angry, he could feel her heart racing. "Where were you? Did you go to Xanthe? Who is that man? What do they want with you? What are they talking about?" she whispered.

"God knows," he said, answering only the last question. "Where's Ben?"

"Gone. Josh sent him away. Why didn't you tell me who you are?"

"It wasn't important."

"Not—" Dani's whisper was almost a squeak.

He put a finger to her lips. "Sh."

Before Dani could protest, the soldier returned. He jabbed a finger in the direction of the door. "Get in there. Stay off the streets. And tell your leader the minute that bastard Hagan shows up he's to let us know." Into Hagan's hand he thrust a small call-disk, the kind that could be dropped into any call-box. It had no identifying marks nor did it have an origination symbol. He shivered.

Ducking his head subserviently he pulled Dani up the steps and through the door. Heart hammering, he slammed it shut, leaned against it, heard the clipped footsteps of the soldiers moving off.

Gathering with the others backstage a few moments later, Hagan heard what had happened before his arrival.

"They were waiting when I got here this afternoon." Josh pressed a folded ice-cloth to his cheek. His muted voice held an angry bite. "I had no choice but to let them in." Hagan glanced at the other players and guessed what they were thinking. They could protest this treatment, but what good would it do? He had to agree. What grievance was heard, what wrong addressed, if you weren't of the military cast or connected to one of the great Matriarchal houses? He'd learned that quickly, once he'd removed his uniform.

Dani picked up the story. They'd all seen the screens about the Commander. How the hunt was on for the heir to the Original Share, and how Josh said it was Hagan himself. When she spoke of the Original Share, awe touched her voice. The others were watching him now as if he might sprout horns, or break into Pax Domini speech. Luckily, she continued, no one seemed to know who they were actually looking for. The picture flashing on all the screens looked nothing like he was now, thanks to the Jolando beard and player's clothes. A good thing he and Ben looked so much alike.

Good thing Ben had deliberately increased the resemblance while he understudied the Jolando part.

Hagan looked at them all, wanting to say he was sorry for what they'd suffered because of him. He wanted to say it, but didn't know how.

"Ben will hide until morning," Josh said. Added what Hagan already knew. "By morning you must be gone."

Shortly after midnight Hagan stood in the silent street behind the theater, the Jolando cloak pulled tight around him. Josh had shut off the light, and with everyone asleep, he had let himself out the door and stepped into the grey night. Yes, he would be gone, but gone where? Only one place came to mind. He had to make his way back to Xanthe.

Chapter 4

New Earth

At their sacred meeting place high on the slopes of Grandfather Mountain, Anahata sat with the Elders of the Clan of Lissone, her head bent toward the central fire, Mind calling—calling to all those who were far away to come to their sacred fires. Calling over distances too great to be visualized. Calling with heart as well as Mind, as she had so many times in the past. Hoping especially to break through the barrier a special one had placed around his heart.

Mother—a hand touched her on the shoulder just as a soft voice touched her thoughts. *Mother, Meeriam has come.*

Meeriam? Slowly Anahata extricated herself from Mind. For a moment the effort left her weak. Now drawn to a consciousness of the Sacred Place, she frowned. The child had made good time, traveling from Norcanna. Ana had not expected her so soon.

Mother? Are you all right?

Yes, she sighed, *yes I am*. Nodding to the others seated around the fire, she quietly withdrew.

Still, pausing at the edge of the circle, she hesitated to leave this sacred place. There was an ugly dark power building on their precious Earth. One they must try to contain, channel so the least harm might be done. Strangely enough, in all of their years since the Leaving no such dark power had been seen, though some said it was inevitable, being inherent in the human heart. This she did not believe. Yet that power was here now. They had already felt its burning touch.

But Meeriam had come, and was also important to her heart.

With grace and a skill earned over many years, Ana picked her way down past the ancient growth of red-barked trees, past the large spring of Lissone and the creek flowing from it. Past the rock outcrop where some ancient artist had left the imprint of his soul in the imprint of his hand. Beneath the dense canopy of trees that hid the well-traveled path into the small canyon of Lissone.

The Camp was quiet this afternoon. Those who were not

at the Spring Calling high up on the slope of the mountain had other tasks, and the soft sounds of their activity filtered through the still air; a distant hammering that could be either one of the people building a new shelter, or a tree-beater seeking grubs; a soft rustling that could be either an errant breeze or a quiet loom where a woman might be making cloth for her family from flax or cotton puffballs spun to thread. Much was done here as it had been done for millennia, done for the pleasure of the doing as well as for the usefulness of the finished product. And done in such a way that it never intruded on the natural life around them. That, she sometimes thought, had been their greatest accomplishment since the Leaving. Within fifteen minutes of her arrival, Meeriam heard her grandmother's soft step on the path outside the tent. Unable to hold her tears in, she ran into Grandmother's comforting arms.

When the first rush of tears finally abated, Meeriam said *I tried to reach you. I tried so hard, but I couldn't. I was afraid you had shut me out.*

Only briefly, dear heart, and only to protect the children, the old woman said. *I'm glad you came.*

Meeriam followed her great-great-grand-mother to the cushions, then watched her touch a pot of water sitting on a small ritual table. By Grandmother's intent the water heated, and in the time it took the tea to brew, Meeriam's flow of tears stopped.

She smiled her thanks for the tea her Grandmother offered. *I loved him very much,*

I know you did, the old woman answered. *I loved him too. He was a most worthy man.*

I loved him more, I think, than he loved me.

Grandmother agreed with a gentle smile. *He was, after all, much older than you.*

And I was foolish, wasn't I? Meeriam drew a last deep shuddering breath. *Is that always the way it is?*

No, child, not always.

He would not let me share his thoughts. He said his thoughts would disturb me. But sometimes I think he did love me.

Perhaps you reminded him of someone else. Someone he used to know many years ago, before you were born.

Grandmother's words were spoken with loving tenderness and an undeniable certainty.

Simple words, yet as Meeriam considered them, she gradually understood so much. Of course. She had loved a man. He had loved a memory. The thought brought pain, and a flash of jealousy that was acknowledged, flowed on and away. As she sat still listening to her thoughts, Grandmother's words of comfort came softly into her mind. In return her thoughts flowed outward, and her sorrow and her love. Her loneliness. Her need for reassurance and comfort and peace. All of these she received, and renewed herself.

A calmness settled over her. *You knew all along what was really in his heart.*

Yes, child. I knew.

You could have told me.

Would it have done you any good to know?

But it hurt so.

Yes, but the hurt will pass.

Meeriam wanted to deny that it would, but she bowed to Grandmother's wisdom. She watched a wisp of steam rise from the spout of the ancient pot that sat on the low table between them, and shared her troubled thoughts.

I—I don't know what to do now. Should I stay with you? Should I go back? Uncle Gerald says he still needs me.

Would you be happy here?

I don't know. I've tried to think it out, but I can't. I was hoping you could tell me.

Grandmother took her hand, opened it out flat, palm up, peering at it like a fortune teller at a fair. Her face took on a studied expression, a deep frown formed on her parchment-skinned brow.

Meeriam submitted, watching, until quiet laughter bubbled from the well-spring of her mind. She turned her hand and gripped Grandmother's delicate bones with her own gentle fingers. I understand. You cannot foresee any more than I can.

Smiling, Ana rested in her own thoughts for a brief time, then looked down at the firm young hand clasping hers. *There is always a place here for you. There are men to chose from, if you are ready for marriage.*

I don't think so, Grandmother. Not yet.

Grandmother nodded. Turned her attention back to the tea. Meeriam knew why she had mentioned the possibility of marriage and was sure Grandmother had known what the answer would be.

The message was, knowing what she didn't want, Meeriam would be able to see more clearly what she wanted, what she needed.

Chapter 5

Norcannan Colony, Earth

Heart ponding, Portus emerged from a strange dream of Elias. One in which they were standing on a bridge over a bottomless abyss, discussing a fine point of history while someone rhythmically chopped away at the bridge supports.

Even as full memory returned, the anxiety caused by the dream was slow to fade.

Earth. Four long months had passed since Ellis died, but he was still on Earth.

Portus buried himself in the pillows. His head ached, and his mouth was dry. God, could he face another day?

He was in his fourth month of imprisonment on Earth. He could think of it in no other way. Four times he'd gone up the hill to the General's headquarters and demanded Graeber allow him to return to Mars, and each time the General was a little less polite, a little more arrogant. No one could leave until Commander Hagan's killer was found.

Though it might have been easier to enlist Meeriam's help, Portus had resisted the impulse to seek her out for fear her connections with Elias would become known.

Yet, without Elias, without Meeriam to talk to, and with nothing useful to do, he led an empty, useless existence, broken only now and then by the presence of Vana Darrow or one of her sons. It was that sense of uselessness that was baring down on him.

This morning, like every other morning since Elias's death, Portus felt no inclination to get out of bed. He was drifting closer to the dream again when a sharp tap came at his door. He tried to ignore it but the tapper was insistent. Grumbling wordless words, he pulled himself out of the tumbled covers and grabbed an old robe to cover his short nightshirt. The sharp tap came again before he could slip the small breathing mask over his mouth and nose. "All right, all right. I'm coming. Who's in such a hurry—" He released the door lock just as the tapping renewed itself. The door opened and he looked down on the frightened face of a young man—Portus corrected himself, a mere boy who did not even come to his shoulder. But not one of Vana Darrow's. "Yes, what is it, boy?"

"Are-are you Doctor Portus?"

"Of course I am, or you would not be knocking on my door, would you?" His voice was hoarse behind the breathing mask.

The boy's eyes widened with a look of additional fright. "N-no. V-vana D-Darrow said I should c-come and w-wake you-she's watching—" Trembling, the boy swallowed hard and looked as if he would cry. "P-please, sir, c-can you come?"

Impatience surged through Portus. "Where is Vana Darrow? Has she fallen ill? Is she hurt?"

The boy brought his trembling under control. "No sir. Downstairs, sir. Please. If you just could come down."

Giving in, Portus growled "Wait a minute. Let me put on some clothes." Making his way back across the room he stumbled over a pair of slippers, and an empty tray on which he'd had his supper the night before. Ignoring the mess he rummaged for clean clothes in his closet. A few minutes later, decently clothed for the first time in days, Portus returned to the gathering room. The boy was still just outside the door, not having moved a centimeter while he waited.

Portus frowned. "Tell me, then, what manner of event is taking place downstairs that you must rouse me from my bed?"

"It's my s-sister, Susan."

A convention, thought Portus. They're having a damned convention down stairs. "And what is wrong?" It had to be something, surely, though what he couldn't imagine.

"S-Susan—" the boy swallowed, seemed to struggle to hold back tears.

Feeling a rush of anxiety, Portus quickly belted his long shirt at his waist and shrugged into his grey jacket. Drawing his small medical kit from the sideboard, he went on. "What's the matter with sister Susan?"

Without answering, the boy darted down the open hallway to the circular lift. Portus pulled his door shut and followed.

The boy's urgency filled him. He cursed the slowness of the open platform that took him to the bottom floor.

The heart of Vana Darrow's home was her kitchen. A large room, it followed the curve of the circular outer wall, and was divided by a bank of synthesizers, a separate recycler, a large kitchen table that could seat fifteen if she so chose, and held along an inner wall a series of sinks and cupboards. It also contained Vana Darrow looking concerned, and two very frightened young people, one of whom was a young woman of maybe eighteen years who was very large with child.

"What's wrong? Is she in labor?" Portus asked of Vana Darrow, but in truth, the girl looked as if she shouldn't even be on her feet.

"Yes, Doctor. Thank you for coming down. As you can see, she needs—"

"Yes, of course she does." He focused on the girl. "How far apart are the pains? Why aren't you in the hospital?" At his second question the girl looked to the young man, and for the first time Portus realized that the young man he supposed to be the father, wore the black and red uniform of the Venati Military Police. A soldier. One of Graeber's so-called peace-keeping forces. The thought shot a bolt of fear through him.

The next moment the girl paled, folded over and was caught in her young husband's strong arms, and Portus forgot his fear.

Vana Darrow wiped her hands on her apron. "Can you help her, Doctor?"

"A bed, Vana Darrow," Portus said, "she needs a bed."

"She'll have my own."

As Vana Darrow bustled around, preparing her bed, the couple's story poured out. The young woman, she didn't appear much older than her younger brother, was only in her eighth month, if she and her husband could be believed.

"We think," added the young soldier, who said his name was Richard.

"You think? Don't you know? Hasn't she been seeing the doctor regularly?"

Portus's horrified tone caused the young soldier's eyes to darken. "No."

"Why not?"

"She saw a lady."

"A what?"

Vana Darrow interrupted. "A midwife, Dr Portus."

Another facet of colonial life. "Why not the hospital with a regular doctor?"

Susan, on the bed, shook her head vigorously. Portus, with his hand on her wrist, felt her heart rate increase alarmingly. Vana Darrow, on the other side of the bed, took her other hand and made soothing sounds.

"There, there, child. Don't fuss. It's all right. You did right in coming here. We'll take care of you now, don't fuss."

Sitting by the bed, Portus found the words and tone almost as soothing as Susan seemed to. Only his hand shook slightly as he continued his physical examination of Susan and his verbal examination of her husband. "Well, all the same, she should have seen a doctor."

The young soldier shook his head. "That hospital out there's no place for a girl like Susan I know what goes on out there now. I was on guard duty for a month during the winter. I know."

Guards on a hospital? Why would they put guards on a hospital. Uneasily Portus glanced at the soldier's tight, worried face. It was a hospital he'd helped set up himself. He'd written the requisitions for men and equipment. He glanced up at Susan's face. She watched him with trepidation, but he had the feeling her fear was more for what her husband might reveal than for herself. Then another contraction came and a spasm of pain crossed her face. Portus wanted to hear more about the hospital but this was neither the time nor the place to question them. Not with a short-termed baby on the way.

Three hours later Portus held the squalling new-born infant girl, wonder in his heart at how life continued to renew itself even in the midst of adversity. Passing the infant to its proud, exhausted mother, who immediately put the baby to breast, he felt his own almost unbearable exhaustion and his whole body trembled. He was too old for this.

"Come out and have a bite to eat, Doctor." Vana Darrow had bustled around with her inexhaustible energy, changing bedding, cleaning up the infant, helping the new mother. Her efforts had been practical and efficient. Now she took his arm and led him back into the kitchen and sat him at the kitchen table. "Here," she said, reaching for the mask on his face, "let me have that—" Not waiting for permission, she removed it. Portus was too tired to protest. Within moments a cup of coffee and a bowl of fruit and gruel were on the table before him. The sight of the food turned him bilious. His hand trembled for a glass of cheery but under Vana Darrow's stern eye, he tried to eat. To take his mind from the food, he turned his thoughts to what Richard, the young soldier, had said about Norcanna's hospital and when, a few minutes later Richard came into the kitchen saying his Susan had gone to sleep with the babe at her side, Portus invited him to sit and share the food.

The young soldier seemed more than happy to do so.

Portus wondered how to ask the questions which would elicit answers the young soldier wouldn't want to give. What was going on out at the hospital that made normal, ordinary people afraid?

Portus studied the young man, waiting until Richard's first hunger had ben appeased. "Have you been in the Colony long?"

"Not long. We emigrated last year."

"You, Susan and the young brother?" Who was also, at Vana Darrow's insistence, eating gruel and fruit.

"Yes."

It wasn't unusual for family groups to emigrate together. "To soldier?'

Vana Darrow, bustling around in the back ground, paused, as if she too were interested in the answer.

"No sir, of course not. I'm an Irrigation Tech, but that's not a priority field here. When we arrived, I was given a choice of VMP or Construction."

"Soldiering is a high priority, I take it." Portus couldn't help his dry tone. Having been given no choice in the matter of his staying, he had a good idea what kind of choice Richard had been give. Not much at all. "And Susan?'

"She teaches." The young soldier frowned down at his food and corrected himself. "She taught. When she became pregnant they told her she could no longer teach. They—they said out at the hospital that she should abort the baby. When she wouldn't they sent her out to one of the homesteads.

A chill slid down Portus's spine. "They?"

"The General's Location Committee."

There was no provision for such a committee in the Colonial Charter. Not that Portus had ever heard of, anyway, nor that Elias had ever told him of. He filed it away as information that Merrick and Kali would be interested in. "And you?"

"I was assigned to a Road crew down the coast."

In effect, the Location Committee had tried to break up the family group, Portus realized. In this case the attempt had failed, but how often in the past had it succeeded? Portus almost hated to ask the next question. "And what now? Does your Commanding Officer know where you are?"

A hard smile touched the young soldier's face, giving him additional years, making him someone to reckon with in spite of his age. "No. When Susan and the babe can travel, we'll all go—" He paled and broke off. Cast a guilt-ladened look at Vana Darrow. Finished lamely. "We'll find a place."

Vana Darrow broke in. "Pioneer Cove will be a good place for you. They're needing settlers down there. And the General's arm isn't quite that long. Not yet." She picked up the food that had grown cold in front of Portus and clucked her tongue. "If you weren't needed here so bad, I'd say that would a good place for you, too, Doctor."

Needed here? Hardly, Portus thought. He stared at the fresh hot coffee Vana Darrow placed in front of him, and his stomach turned over again. Maybe once he'd been needed. When Elias was alive. How could things have changed to drastically in only a just a few months? Or were the changes happening all along and he just hadn't noticed? Lost in thought he barely heard Vana Darrow's suggestion that she bring his supper up early and later, stepping onto the circular lift to return to his room, he couldn't remember whether he'd said yes or no.

How, he wondered, could he get word off the planet and into Merrick's hands? How long, he wondered, before he could contact Meeriam? Once in his room he dropped all pretense of optimism. Sadness engulfed him. The Cheery helped, but only a little.If there was still a God somewhere, please, he prayed, let Him see that Ellis Hagan did not come back to this.

Knowing the time was not yet right, Meeriam marked the days until she could visit Portus by keeping herself busy at the job she had been trained to do within the Matriarch's organization. With work still piling up from the change of seasons she was staying late at her desk of carved darkwood when she felt a friendly gaze. Meeriam looked up from the old style journals in which she was recording farm statistics from her uncle's notes. Gerald Nilander smiled at her from the doorway. "You've been working hard since you came back from the mountains. How does it go?"

"It goes well, Uncle. I'm almost caught up. I'm glad you left these for me to do." Working left her less time to worry. She frowned, remembering another worry that had bothered her since noon. "Is Vana Kassine all right, Uncle?" Usually at least once a day at midday meal Meeriam saw the Matriarch, whose responsibility was to oversee all the farms and farmers of Kama Valley. Today the Matriarch had been absent from her usual place at the table. Meeriam knew Kassine had an indomitable will, but physically grew weaker with each passing month. The old woman worked too hard, and worried too much about her Freefarmers. Kassine, like others in the Colony these days, seldom received her quota of workers, equipment or supplies. Slowly and out of sheer necessity, her Freefarmers were learning to depend on Mother Earth for other things than Hojoi, Vana Kassine had been heard to say. She hoped it would be otherwise. Though she would breathe unfiltered air and had for years, she held the same view as most Arcolans about the safety of eating anything but processed food. And hope dies hard, thought Meeriam. Hadn't the Matriarch also hoped that her daughter would take up the battle to make Earth a home for the returnees when she herself could no longer continue?

Everyone except the Matriarch knew her daughter's ascension to power wouldn't happen. Meeriam suspected that Kassine, too, had finally accepted the fact. The arguments that used to come daily from the private floors of Kassine's residence tower had almost ceased since the Commander's death. Kassine, too, had been saddened greatly by losing a good friend.

Tears pooled in Meeriam's eyes, and to take her mind from their loss she lowered her gaze to the books she had been filling with neat, foreign numbers. Record keeping of the kind employed by the Matriarch didn't come naturally to the unfettered mind of one of the People. Putting her to the task of learning how, Uncle Gerald had still sympathized with her. Now she did it without thinking of the mechanics. It was, in fact, fairly boring and she only did it because the job was a good excuse to be here in Norcanna, helping where she could.

After a short time her tears dried. Gerald, who had entered the small office overlooking the inner courtyard and taken a chair by the window in a rare moment of relaxation, still watched her with empathy. Of course he would have known the minute her thoughts turned elsewhere.

"Uncle, when do you think it will be safe to visit Portus?"

"A while longer, I'm afraid, child. The General suspects he was acting as courier for Elias. Not only has he forbidden Portus to leave the colony, he's set a guard at Vana Darrow's tower to keep an eye on the good doctor."

"Just one?" Meeriam smiled. They could handle one guard easily.

Even one is more than I want you to tangle with, child. The words spoken into her mind were a quiet warning. Gerald seldom spoke into her mind, being always aware that a slip like that in the presence of other members of the household might give them away. He'd had many years of this deception, and she knew the caution was second nature to him.

Meeriam started to protest. *I would be safe enough—*

The look in Gerald's eyes stopped her. "Vana Darrow is looking out for him."

"She plays a dangerous game too. Does he know?"

"I hope not."

"What can we do, then?"

"Wait." Gerald smiled though, obviously knowing his answer was not the one she wanted.

"Wait?" She jumped to her feet. "Wait? The General is not waiting before he destroys the farms, he's not waiting to move into the mountains. You yourself told me he's sent crews out to Kama."

"He is, though, child. He's waiting for Ellis Hagan to come home."

Meeriam's heart did a strange little flip. She remembered Ellis Hagan, though no doubt the younger Hagan was unaware of her existence. He had been somewhat older than she. He and Luan Kassine, the Matriarch's daughter had, for a short while, been everything to each other. It was shortly after Meeriam had come to stay with Gerald, and unobtrusively started learning how best she could help him in his work. She remembered Ellis Hagan on his visits to this house as a dark, serious young man who wore his uniform with pride, a young man with a natural arrogance and confidence who had been so in love with Luan Kassine he could see no one else. He had failed to see Vana Kassine's disregard of him as a mate for her daughter until it was too late. Meeriam vividly remembered the expression on his face the last time she had seen him. Hurt. Furious. He had left this house not even knowing she'd been an unwilling witness to his pain. Within days he had been sent from Norcanna to the mountains, to his father's post at Kama. And two years later he had gone to Mars. Would he really come back? If he did he would find many changes.

Strange how she'd followed him in her thoughts. Stranger still that the thought of his return could make her shiver with something akin to fear.

He wouldn't come. General Gordon Graeber, who for six months had waited for Ellis Hagan to return to claim his Share was beginning to doubt that he ever would. It seemed that on Mars, the player had dropped out of sight, no one knew where.

As if that weren't bad enough, for the first time he'd run into opposition from the High Counsel on Mars, the Council of Five as they called themselves. There were those on the council who said his conclusions about the Firewing killing the Commander must be wrong. Demands had been made for further proof. Hard evidence was requested. And now the good Doctor Portus was drinking himself into a stupor. Twice recently he'd been unavailable when the General sent for him, that information according to the dragon who ran the tower where Portus resided. If he could only get the doctor to add more to the conclusions he'd made about the death of the Commander, those idiots on Mars might be put off long enough that they would no longer be dangerous to his plans. Considering all of this, Portus now took his place beside Ellis Hagan as the dual focus of Graeber's rage.

Nothing could go wrong. He refused to think anything might. He was adaptable. Flexible. If necessary he would change his scheme, add to it, twist it, braid it with another. How he arrived at the ancient City wasn't important. When he arrived, and what he would do once he was in charge of the deadly hardware encased in steel, those were the important factors in his plan.

Ellis Hagan was only important insofar as he could help Graeber attain the Ancient City.

All of this was still in Graeber's mind an hour later as he pursed his lips and looked over the tips of his fingers at the three townsmen standing before his desk. He hid his fury well. He had noted them all, these three nondescript men, shopkeepers, he thought with disdain. Only with effort did he check the curl of his lip.

"Sir," said one, Barnes by name, "we must insist you give this matter some consideration now. We've presented this request to the Norcanna Council and have their backing."

They hadn't done that originally, Graeber knew, and it infuriated him that they'd thought to do it now. "So what is it this time?"

"Sir—" obviously the men had discussed the best way of broaching this subject. "Sir—we know the townspeople's medical problems tax your military facilities. We seek permission to establish our own clinic in Norcanna itself. It would certainly relieve your medical facilities—" The man's voice faltered.

Graeber understood what they were doing, and his contempt exceeded his caution. "When you need medical facilities, I will let you know."

"But sir, the Council—"

A small warning sparked in Graeber's mind. He didn't control the council yet. Not completely. Else why wouldn't they have let him know about this matter before these men appeared at his door? Perhaps, for the moment, it was wiser to appear to give in. "Yes, of course, the Council. Will they fund it?" Where on Earth or Mars would they obtain the funding? He kept a tight grip on Colony finances. He knew where every credit went.

"We'll fund it privately, General."

"I can spare neither the men nor the equipment for such a place."

"We understand that, Sir."

"There are no doctors to man your clinic."

"We thought of asking Dr Portus. It's said he'll be staying for a while. If nothing else, at least he could help us put it together. Train personnel. That sort of. . ." The shopkeeper's voice trailed off.

Ah, the good doctor. Graeber's eyes narrowed. Yes, there would be advantages accruing to him, now that he thought of it. Keeping Portus too busy to spy on him, for one. It would also be a sop to the townspeople. He knew many were becoming uneasy about the use of the hospital for retraining. Yes, he could see benefits. But he must not seem to give in too easily.

He frowned at them for a long minute. Started to shake his head. They moved uneasily under his expression. Finally he said, "Very well, you have my permission. My blessing, so to speak." He forced a smile that made at least one of the men before him squirm. "I want to see the final plans before you begin."

The men silently consulted each other. Then came to a silent consensus, and Barnes, the elected spokesman, accepted the condition. "As soon as they are finalized, General."

After the townsmen had departed Graeber hunched forward. The fools. How dare they think to manipulate him! He'd noted their names on a light-board, and now he looked at the list. Ludwell, Barnes, Parrish. He knew them. Men who had been here too long. Shop-keepers! They thought they wielded some power. But he'd show them who held the power here. He'd show them.

He smiled as, with his thick light pen, he ran heavy lines through each name. It amused him to see the names vanish before is eyes.

And then he added another name to the vanished list. Ellis Hagan. And then drew another thick line through it so that it too vanished.

It hadn't happened yet. Not yet, but it would. When the player turned up, if he was of no use, he would die.

It was at noon the next day when the explosion was heard across Norcanna. At first some thought it was an earthquake, rattling windows and dishes, and they waited fearfully for the continuation, but the black smoke, rising in a dark column from the base of the hill between the town and the bay soon told the true story.

Portus, shaken from a stupor by the shock, was drawn to his windows and could see where the smoke began. At the process plant. Next door to Matriarch Vana Kassine's resident tower. His first thought was for Meeriam, but no, she must have returned to the mountains. He'd not seen or heard of her since their parting on Diana Colony some months ago.

None the less, something bad had happened. Black, black smoke billowed into the brilliant blue spring sky. Drawn by the same morbid curiosity that made him watch the General's nightscreens for word of Ellis Hagan's whereabouts, Portus donned his clothes, pulled on his cloak and face mask, and picked up his small medical pack. Perhaps someone would need his help.

The afternoon was crisp. After the early heat wave the weather had returned to normal. The smell of rain rose from the earth even though the deep sky contained no clouds. Rain had fallen during the night, perhaps, or maybe even during the last couple of days. Portus's memory of the days since the baby was born in Vana Darrow's bedroom were hazy at best. God, it was so stupid, drinking himself blind. He knew better, but sometimes the pain—He shivered, pulled the light cloak tighter. A walk in the air would help clear his head.

Portus hurried down the hill path beneath the broad ribbon of streetbelt above him. Dimly he noted there was more activity about than he'd seen the last time he'd ventured out. Units of VMP patrolled on foot, their s'darms glinting brightly in the afternoon sun. A few farmers in brown tunics and cloaks hurried by. Vehicles hummed on the streetbelts overhead. The path he was on led down into Old Norcanna, the nucleus of the town that spread around the curve of the bay. Once on the flat, the path widened and turned into a regular stone-paved walk. The original settlers had tried to make it as precise and neat as the metered blocks of Arcola under the domes, but they hadn't counted on the abundant water and the rank, wild growth of vegetation, the native bushes and trees which grew faster than crews of men could cut them down. Coming from a planet where each spark of life had to be carefully nurtured, they had been surprised by Earth's verdancy. Not only the abundance of water and the vegetation, but the deep blue sky. Portus tried not to look at the sky, and the black smoke from the explosion hanging low in the air. The closer he came the more he could smell the acrid stink of raw Hojoi even through his mask.

Past the center of Old Norcanna he turned left and continued on down the hill toward the bay, until the noise of men and machinery made him slow his pace.The high fence that surrounded the processing plant finally drew him to a halt. He joined a crowd of farmers and townspeople where a wide gate stood open. He might have entered to offer his service but just as he arrived a small military carrier, a HOGG, hushed to a quick stop where the streetbelt grounded outside the gate.

Portus eyed the emerging officer with uneasy surprise. It was Galt, Graeber's staff Captain. He was followed by four soldiers.

The people around Portus also seemed to recognize the officer. Quickly they melted away until Portus stood alone, watching.

Hand resting ominously on his s'darm, Galt led his men into the milling workers who filled the foreyard of the plant. The crowd parted like waters parting for Moses.

"What the hell happened here?" The stink of raw Hojoi reached even to Portus who was still back by the gate. "You, over there. What happened here?"

When they became aware there were soldiers in their midst the workers stilled. The hiss of giant water hoses became the only sound breaking the quiet. Galt grabbed the nearest worker and shook him."Tell me what happened here."

The worker stood dumb, his face pale with fright. Galt pushed him away and seemed to seek another victim. His voice fought the angry hiss of water and won. "Who's in charge here?"A man stepped from the crowd. Portus recognized him immediately. Nilander, Kassine's Superintendent. He was a darkish blond and appeared to be of early middle years, tall and on the thin side. He wore the usual uniform of the farmer, brown trousers, a beige long-sleeved shirt and a dark brown vest. Only his calm assurance separated him from the other workers. "I'm in charge here."

Galt also recognized him. "You're Nilander, aren't you?"

"Yes. And you are—?" There was no insolence in Nilander's question, but it seemed the tone of authority in his voice brought an angry flush to Galt's high cheekbones. Obviously, Portus thought, everyone was supposed to know who he was.

"Captain Galt, General's Staff," he snapped. "What the hell happened here?"

"Nothing that concerns you, Captain." Nilander's eyes grew hard. "We have the situation in hand."

"The General wants a report immediately. Was any matrix lost?"

Portus noticed Galt didn't ask if there were any injuries.

Nilander's mouth tightened. "You'll have to ask Vana Kassine, Captain. I'm not authorized to give out reports to the Military."

Galt gripped his s'darm. "We'll see about that." Galt's quick, predatory smile seemed to welcome Nilander's answer.

Before the promise in Galt's smile could be acted upon, a small private auto-carriage slid to a halt off the streetbelt and came to rest inside the gate in front of the larger vehicle. The crest on the opening door was easily recognizable, as was the woman who emerged, Vana Glena Kassine.

Portus appreciated the woman's regal bearing, knew it was the product of years of training, and supreme effort. Though she was more than a head shorter than any man in the foreyard, her bearing made her tower above them all. Her hair, piled high on her head, was a delicate pink, her eyes a pale green. Her age indeterminately old.

At that moment the hoses manned by the workers were shut off. In the sudden silence her words cut with rapier sharpness. "The military is trespassing on Matriarchal grounds. Remove yourself and your men at once, Captain Galt!" Turning her back on the soldier as if he were no more dangerous than a recalcitrant schoolboy, she eyed her manager. "Good afternoon, Gerald. What happened?"

"Number Two valve, Ma'am. It blew."

Vana Kassine's mouth drew tight. "Didn't we just replace—"

"Four times we've replaced that valve, Ma'am. Four." Nilander rubbed the back of his neck, a puzzled look on his face. "This time it should have held. I don't know—" Kassine's frown and quick glance at Galt stopped him.

"Was anyone hurt?" she asked.

"Two workers, Ma'am."

"Ask Dr. Portus to come in and treat them." She indicated Portus standing beside the open gate.

It was true, Portus thought, though elderly she missed nothing. Galt turned, saw him and his mouth momentarily gaped, then snapped shut. Portus, drawn into reluctant participation in the scene, stepped forward.

Galt opened his mouth to protest but before it seemed he could form the words, Nilander strode to Portus. "Good afternoon, Doctor. I'm sorry I didn't see you standing there. Could we impose on your good graces? Will you look at our injured?"

Clutching his cloak to still his shaking hands, Portus nodded. He tried to ignore Galt as he walked at Nilander's side past the Military men.

Galt's face darkened. "The general will hear of this," he ground out.

"I'm sure he will" Portus breathed, knowing whatever damage accrued to the situation was already done.

Nilander's hand on Portus's elbow tightened almost imperceptibly, giving Portus an unexpected feeling of support. "This way, Doctor."

As Portus moved with Nilander past Galt and the soldiers, he heard a hiss of simmering rage from Galt, then a barked order. Moments later the HOGG started up. Hurrying with Nilander toward a small shed, Portus drew a shuddering breath. Another crisis averted, or was it perhaps merely postponed?

Chapter 6

Norcanna Colony

After dark the fog crept in off the ocean, rolling wave on wave over the rough shoreline. The trees, dry from the day-long breeze, drank the moisture like thirsting men. Sentinel pines stood out on the headlands, lonely watchers of an empty coast. Watching, always watching for the ships that never came.

And the waves broke high on the lonely rocks.

When the fog moved in after dark, it swallowed sound, muffled the lonely borobird, silenced the distant coyote. It dampened pine needles underfoot, swallowed the moon and chased the children and the dogs inside to cluster around the family ballstoves. Stole the street-lamps' light.

At night, in the fog, the land came alive with soft sound and vibrant smells of pine and rich dark earth. In the fog Earth refreshed itself. Life slept and renewed.

And, as always, the waves broke high on the lonely rocks.

Hagan hadn't thought of the fog when he thought of coming home, and even the increased artificial gravity did not prepare him for the extra pull of Earth. Heat, or wind, yes, or if they arrived at night, the brilliant canopy of stars overhead. But not this suffocating, soul-penetrating fog. Ignoring the tired babble of voices around him, he'd grabbed his shuttle bag from the baggage line and pushed through the crowd of incomers and those who were meeting them, toward the entrance of the pink-domed terminal. Only moments ago his papers had passed inspection, he received his limited-stay visitor's pass, and had been assigned a transient's room at Darrow Towers. He had moved quickly, aware that any moment Graeber's men might swoop down on him like a vulture on a kill.

Then he'd stepped out into the fog and paused. It had been less expected than the greater gravity.

The ball lamps around the wide terminal entrance glowed

against a blank gray wall. To his right, curbing stretched out like a silver ribbon and disappeared before revealing the bow. The air smelled of salt, and ocean, and rampant growth. He took a deep, soul-satisfying breath. Then, hesitating only a brief moment more, he searched the dark. If there was a public call box where he could call up a little automatic carrier, he couldn't see it from where he stood.

Hagan pulled the Jolando cloak tighter around his Xanthe tunic, and stepped into the fog, remembering with a grimace the argument that had ensued over whether he should come back in military garb, the Xanthe cloth or ordinary tenth-quarter civilian clothes. He'd refused the protection of the military clothes and the rank which once had been his, and Kali had, in turn, pointed out the dangers of coming back as a mere civilian. They all agreed the University uniform was the least dangerous.

Stepping from the curb, he let the fog swallow him. After all their planning, after all of Si's warnings and Kali's dark forebodings, this arrival seemed anticlimactic. No delegation to meet him and demand he hand over the Share, nobody lying in wait to do him bodily harm—at the thought Hagan momentarily tensed and paused, but no, he sensed no danger for himself out here.

Of course, Kali had warned, even though they weren't expecting him Graeber would know the minute he stepped off the Diana shuttle. They always surveyed the incomers. And Hagan thought he'd sensed the surveillance of the cameras even though he'd not bothered to spot where they were hidden. Still there would be an element of surprise. Enough perhaps to throw Graeber off stride and let Hagan make the contacts he had to make and perhaps accomplish what he'd come to do., before the General caught up with him.Though he'd insisted he would have nothing to do with Graeber's death, he had agreed to try to reach the Ancient City. Of course the Firewing, too, would know he'd arrived. They always were aware of what went on in Norcanna, though he wasn't sure how. They sometimes knew what was in a man's mind before he did himself. Wasn't that what the Commander had always said? Wasn't that what Patlos had indicated, before—

Quickly Hagan drew back from the thought. Frowned.

Now his various nightmares were vying with each other for mindspace. If Graeber didn't make him a Cavern-case, he'd likely make himself one.

Somewhere in the near distance a dog barked, and the bark echoed with that particular hollowness that made the sound seem to have no source.

Hagan smiled again, with more enjoyment. Home. In spite of the bitter memories tied to Earth, he'd missed it. For tonight he wouldn't think of what he'd agreed to do. He'd walk this path up to the transient tower and enjoy while he could the dark, damp, fragrant earth under foot, the muffled sounds of the night, the pull of a different, much heavier gravity. The paths had not changed in six years, and his sense of direction was unimpaired. As a child he'd roamed these pathways by day and by night, in the fog and under the stars. He and a group of other Colony brats. Velia hadn't been able to contain him, no matter what harsh punishments she'd tried. Until she'd insisted upon the Military Academy, when he was ten. Then life had been different. He had grown up.

The smooth texture of the paved path underfoot changed to crunching gravel, abruptly bringing his mind back to the present. The sound of his boots upon the gravel was loud in his ears, and he stepped off the path into the softer surrounding terrain and paused, alert with every nerve in his body to the soft muffled sounds of the night.

Hearing nothing out of line, he went on.

Though it was after midnight, General Graeber's office complex beneath the Gathering Hall was still brightly lit. Graeber, ensconced in his wide chair behind a desk screen, leaned forward intently. "Run it again. Let's have another look at him." Still shocked at the suddenness of Hagan's arrival, Graeber fumed. Why had no one told him Hagan was on his way? What did he pay spies for? Why hadn't someone on Diana spotted him during the transfer from the Mendoza?

Captain Gal punched the panel inlaid on the desk and once again the screen filled with the images of men, women and children dismounting the shuttle ramp. Most looked tired and rumpled from the long trip. Almost all of them were dressed in the freefarmers green and brown tunic, though several Xanthe uniforms were also seen. "There. There he is." The player was dressed in a gray Xanthe tunic and tight trousers which were tucked into low topped boots. The whole was covered by a long black cloak of strange design, clasped at the high-collared neck by gold fastenings.

When he faced the hidden camera fully Graeber hid a gasp. Here was what the Commander of Kama must have looked like thirty years ago. A face of certain arrogance. A touch of disdain. A touch of fastidiousness in the way he held himself aloof from the pressing crowd.

"Doesn't look like a threat," Graeber growled softly.

"Bears a resemblance to the Commander," said Galt.

Graeber nodded. Galt was good at stating the obvious.

Galt went on. "Why is he wearing the Xanthe uniform?"

"That's where he went to ground. Must have been staying there."

Graeber frowned. When the player had finally emerged from hiding, he'd been safe in the arms of the university. Safe from Graeber's reach. The nightscreens had finally tired of his story, and he'd once more faded from view. Only Graeber had remained interested. Scheming how best to use the Commander's son. But he himself had no friends at Xanthe, nor had he ever wanted any. Those sons of prolific mothers made him sick with their hypocrisy. Suspicion narrowed his eyes. What was old Merrick up to? "Why is he here now?"

Though the question was rhetorical, Galt answer. "The report says —"

Graeber slammed his fist on the desk. "I know what the damned report says. Why is he really here?" It was not something he expected Galt to know but he turned his fury on his captain as if Galt himself was responsible for Hagan's arrival. Hagan had the effrontery to show up here without notice!

Blanching, Galt stepped back, prudently taking himself out of Graeber's reach. "Original Share? Money's a pretty good reason—"

Graeber grunted derisively. In Galt's mind wealth was power, and power was what he most wanted. Graeber himself could think of several other reasons the Player might return.

Did this Hagan hope to take up where his father left off? Did he mean to exercise his right to a seat on the Council? Fight with his step-mother over the Commander's estate? What did he want? Drumming his fingers on the polished desk top, Graeber stared at the face on his screen. An idea struggled for birth but when he tried to grasp it, the idea was gone. In the months since he'd learned that young Hagan had turned up, he'd composed one plan after another, from outright mayhem to more subtle methods of persuasion, all the time knowing that until Hagan returned to Earth most of his planning would be useless. So much depended on the man himself. And for months he'd been out of reach. Was it the widow threatening to sue that had brought young Hagan back? Graeber glared at the screen. He suddenly shook with fury. Why had no one told him Hagan was on the way?

Even so, this Hagan would stand in his way no more than the other had. He would see to that. Of course the Player had spent so much time in the forefront of public consciousness his too-speedy death would be too coincidental. It would bring an official scrutiny for which Graeber was not prepared.

How long did the player mean to stay?

Graeber regarded his aide with narrowed eyes. Galt's hunter instincts were well-developed. "What do you think of him, Galt?"

Galt's usually greedy eyes became expressionless. "You'd best be rid of him. He's dangerous."

"Dangerous? Surely he doesn't look dangerous. A player? You aren't afraid of a player, are you Galt?"

Galt flushed. "No." Hot angry eyes watched the image of the player crossing the terminal floor to the dispersion desk. "No, I'm not afraid of him!"

Graeber frowned, catching more than ordinary interest emanating from Galt's stance.

Graeber pounced on it. "Do you know Hagan, Galt?"

The angry flush receded from Galt's face, leaving him pale. "Yes, sir."

Icy fury burned in Graeber. Why hadn't Galt said so before? He stared coldly at his aide. "How well?"

Galt seemed unaware of the General's anger. "Well enough.

Moss and I both served under him at Kama seven or so years ago."

"Under him?"

"We were in his unit. Moss was there longer than I was."

Graeber's mouth tightened. It was like carving stone to carve answers out of Galt's granite mind. "Then you know quite a bit about this Hagan that's not in the official reports?" The documents he'd surreptitiously pulled from the files had been uninformative.

"Some." Galt's glance shifted uneasily.

Graeber frowned. There was something here—an anger—or was it fear? That would be interesting, wouldn't it? Fear in this sniveling braggart? Graeber smoothed his frown away. "Tell me about him, Galt. Did you like him?"

"No more than I liked the Commander."

"Why? Did he push his weight around? Take advantage of the fact he was the Commander's son?"

"Yes." Abruptly Galt's eyes shuttered, and his lips tightened.

Knowing Galt's proclivities, Graeber's mind made the leap. "A woman?" Ah, of course. There would have to be a woman. Galt was in and out of enough beds to make it a subject of gossip in the ranks. Hagan, too, looked like he might be the type. At least he had the looks for it. Merely because when he found a wound he could not help but salt it, Graeber prodded. "Who was she, Galt?"

Galt hesitated. When he finally answered his tone was deliberately bland. "Luan Kassine."

Kassine? The name sank into Graeber's mind with delicious irony. Luan Kassine? The Matriarch's wild bitch of a daughter? He wanted to laugh. The girl was cavern-fodder. She spent her days at the Baths, and her nights immersed in Lotus tea. She slept with anyone who would scratch her itch. He knew her. Oh, yes, he knew her. She reminded him of his mother. The bitch. "And which of you won her?"

"He did, much good it did him." A wolfish grin flicked across Galt's face. "I owe him for that."

Graeber almost didn't hear Galt's answer. Another image had risen in his mind. Kassine. More than an mere irritant, the old woman, head of the Freefarming community, had become

58

another roadblock on his path.

Kassine—Hagan—Galt—

The idea took on sharp edges in his mind. Kassine, Hagan, and Galt. For the first time since he'd learned the Commander of Kama's son had arrived on Earth, he felt an easing of anxiety. Ah, yes. Kassine, Hagan and Galt. It was becoming clear.

Abruptly he leaned forward and slammed off the screen. "It's time we took a face-to-face look at him. Pick him up."

Hagan had shifted his shuttle bag onto his other shoulder for the last steep ascent into the old section of Norcanna when he became aware of a presence behind him. He paused, listening, but the fog was like cerafoam fluff, stopping his ears. The sounds of his own exertion quieted, his breathing slowed. The hair prickled on his neck, but strangely he didn't feel a sense of danger. Only of presence.

Straight ahead the path he was on led to steps which were lit by a low-riding ball lamp. He'd not yet entered into the light of the lamp, but he'd be silhouetted against the glow to anyone following. But nothing he could do about it now. Straightening his shoulders he proceeded toward the light.

When he reached them, the stone steps were wet with fog, and the crevasses covered by deep green moss. Moss also grew up the bank on his right. Somewhere water ran, the sound merrily incongruous with his harsh breath. His legs, fighting the denser gravity of Earth, ached with the effort to step gently, quietly.

A branch breaking up the hill to his right startled him, and he glanced up in time to see a dark shape slipping into the denser trees.

He was being stalked, and again there was nothing he could do about it but pretend it wasn't happening. Friend, or enemy, he wondered, or perhaps neither. Perhaps merely someone who wanted to know why he was walking the paths this time of night.

In spite of the chill in the air Hagan felt the clammy dampness of sweat between his shoulder blades. Still moving slowly, he reached the bottom of the steps where the path broadened and joined another. Overhead he recognized the understructure of a streetbelt. Another ball lamp lit the stairs upward to the belt. Carefully he skirted that pool of light and kept to the broadened pathway. It would, he knew, lead him to the transient towers which sat in a group together at the edge of the old town. Overhead a carrier passed, its air generator hum drowning out all other sound. Then quickly it disappeared leaving only a memory of sound.

The presence stayed with him until he reached the gate of Darrow Tower ten minutes later, then it too was gone. Neither fading nor growing, it simply vanished.

Were you curious, friend, Hagan wondered, or were you unseen protection? If so, who sent you?

The door of Darrow Tower swung open at his pulling of the bell, and an angular, harsh-faced woman looked out. "Yes? What is it? Don't you know how late it is?"

"Yes ma'am. I'm just off the Diana Shuttle, and I understand you're holding a room for me."

"I do have a single waiting. They filled me up with young couples mostly, this time. They're long gone to bed. What's your name? Where's your visitor's pass?"

Hagan handed over his papers and the woman gave them a cursory glance before she handed them back. The formalities being served, she opened the door wider. "Come in, come in. You're letting the night in. Don't worry about this fog. It'll be gone by morning. Always is this time of year. The single is on the top floor. I hope you don't mind walking up. The lift is out of order, but only temporary, mind you. The single has a small kitchen."

Hagan found he didn't have to use words. Replacing his papers, he merely had to nod at the proper times. Quietly he followed the woman to the narrow stairs. Although he'd never before had occasion to stay in a transient tower, he'd had friends who did and had visited them enough to be aware of the main features. Six floors, three or four apartments per floor. A central circular open lift. Inside each apartment the decor could be as elaborate or bleak as the owner allowed. Somehow, from seeing Vana Darrow again after all these years, he knew the rooms would be clean, neat but hardly luxurious. He was grateful she didn't seem to recognize him.

"Just sign the slip," she was saying. "How long are you here for? First time in years I've had a full house. Course, no one's being allowed to leave, not even to Diana, I understand. There's something going on, but plain folk are better off staying out of it, if you ask me." She eyed his gray University uniform and the long black cloak. "You from Xanthe?"

Hagan nodded again, wondering how she could manage to talk full speed and still have breath for climbing up six flights of stairs. He was relieved when they reached the top and she opened a door right off the stairwell.

Vana Darrow's eyes slid away from him. "Soldiers came a little earlier, looking for someone. I wouldn't let them in. I know my rights. I showed them my slips. That's all they needed to see. Here you go. The ball stove's already lit. Bed's not what you're used to, I imagine, but it's clean and fresh. Take my word for it, there's none better in Norcanna."

"Thank you, Vana Darrow. I'm sure there's none better, and it'll be most welcome. Much better than what I've slept on these last months, you can be sure." He smiled, and the woman almost did a double take. But to forestall any more questions, he gently bowed her to the door.

After she was gone Hagan dropped onto the edge of the flotation mattress and tried not to think about what the soldiers might have wanted. Graeber was moving quickly. Well, at Xanthe they had expected him to.

Which meant that Hagan, too, would have to move quickly. Tired as he was, Hagan pulled off his boots, and removed the small packet of maps from the space built into the broad cuff. Maps of the high desert beyond Kama. On the long trip from Mars he'd studied them until he'd have been able to draw them from memory.

Not sorry to see the last of them disappear, he tore them into small scraps and carried them to the kitchen recycler. When they had disappeared into the recycler's small, yawning mouth, he returned to the bed.

Now he'd sleep. And no doubt dream.

At three a.m., Graeber gripped the arms of his conforming chair with his enormous hands. "Where is he now?"

Galt stood tight-lipped before him, having come back only moments before empty-handed. Hagan had disappeared. "We'll know as soon as the trip-cards come in." All trip cards used by the small carriers were automatically fed into HQ intelligence banks. More than once Graeber had found the information useful. That was how he'd found out about the elder Hagan's visits to Vana Glena Kassine. Visits that had precipitated the Commander's death.

"Oh, yes," he ground out. "We will certainly know where he's been, but where the hell is he now?" Graeber glared at his staff captain. Of all the inept, stupid, careless— "You checked the transient tower?"

"Yes sir. When he wasn't at the terminal I immediately went to the tower. He wasn't in their register."

"Did someone meet him?"

"Not that I could discover."

"Keep looking, Galt. If it takes you all night, I want that man found!"

"Yes sir." Galt spun on his heels and exited the general's office as if devils were chasing him. Barely noticing that Galt had gone, Graeber sank back into his chair and summoned Moss from the antechamber.

With malevolent eyes, Graeber studied the man who entered and stood before him. Not quite at ease, but neither was he subservient. Moss, Graeber knew, had many qualities Galt lacked, but he also lacked one vastly important quality Galt possessed. Although the perfect soldier, always doing what he was told, Moss had no thirst for power. Graeber didn't understand a man who had no ambition, and what he didn't understand, he mistrusted. He often wondered what Moss was thinking. With Galt he always knew.

Cold, thought Graeber now. The man was cold. Abruptly he gestured at the captured image on the telereader. "Galt tells me you and he served under this Hagan out at Kama?"

Moss paused as though shifting through memories like files in a seldom used databank. Then he nodded. "Yes, sir, we did."

"What kind of a soldier was he?"

Without hesitation Moss answered. "A good one. Very good."

"Galt didn't like him."

Briefly amusement flashed in Moss's eyes. "No."

What would it take, Graeber wondered, to surprise Moss out of his icy calm. "Did you know Hagan has already disappeared? Galt lost him between the terminal and the Transient Tower."

Moss nodded shortly. "I heard."

"Can you do any better?"

"It's possible."

"Then get on it. We can't have Commander Hagan's son wandering around on his own. Something might happen to him. We couldn't have that, could we?" Graeber's smile should have sent shivers through a soul more staunch than Moss's. Moss merely nodded.

After Moss's departure, Graeber stared thoughtfully at the empty doorway. So young Hagan had been a good soldier? By Moss's standard that must be high praise indeed. So how did a good soldier become summarily dismissed from a service for which he was bred and born? For which he'd been schooled and groomed?

There had to be some falling out between father and son, or why would the Commander have acted as he did? The questions were those he'd been asking himself since he'd dug into the records and found only the bare bones of a military life. They still had no answers that he could discover.

And this thing with Kassine's daughter.

Graeber frowned. The elder Kassine, the Matriarch, had become uncomfortably vocal in the Norcannan Council. Every month she voiced her Freefarmer's complaints, and every month the Council listened. Only if he could convince her that the Firewing were a danger to her freefarmers, only then would she support him, and only then would he have the support of the whole council.

Ah, to hook young Hagan—to silence Kassine—those were his immediate goals.

Spinning in his chair, Graeber focused on the model of the Earth and Mars, in perihellic conjunction. He must never lose sight of the ultimate goal. Never. Too much was at stake.

Earth must rise again to its former magnificence. Civilization must once more flourish. And he would be it's guide, it's savior.

By whatever means necessary.

It was meant to be.

And—the idea was growing—young Hagan would be the key.

Meeriam stirred in her sleep, then came quickly and fully awake. Sitting up she reached for the heavy quilt that had fallen to the foot of the bed and wrapped it around her, sensing outward to find what had disturbed her dreams. Her room behind the kitchen of the large residence was dark, silent. The halls of the house were empty of life. The hour, way past midnight. Everyone overhead deep in sleep. Almost everyone.

Gerald's voice spoke into her mind. *It's all right, child. Go back to sleep. I'm sorry I woke you.*

Is something wrong? She sensed a disturbance in Gerald, but could get no clear picture of what it was. She hadn't talked to him all day. He'd been out to the farms, but she'd thought he'd returned much earlier.

Nothing's wrong, child. I merely had to go out again.

Meeriam heard his hesitation and waited.

He finally said, *You'll hear tomorrow, anyway. Ellis Hagan arrived tonight on the Diana shuttle.*

The Commander's son? Ellis? Her heart tightened with a familiar pain, followed by an unfamiliar anger. Why did he have to come back? What. . .what would he be like now?

She was egged on by a strange curiosity. *Where is he?*

At one of the transient towers.

Which one?

No, child, I'll not tell you. You must have nothing to do with him. It's too dangerous. Gerald's thought was gently admonitory. *Go back to sleep. We'll talk in the morning.*

She wasn't a child, to be told when to sleep and when to wake, although Gerald seemed to think that because he was old enough to be her grandfather he had the right.

Suddenly she felt his laughter. *Surely, father, perhaps, not grandfather.*

She sank back on her pillows, smiling. *I apologize. You're not that old.*

And so do I. You're not that young. How is the Council's clinic coming along? Did you find a building yet?

Gerald had lent her services to the town's citizens who were working to build the town its clinic. As an effort to distract her from thoughts of Ellis Hagan, the question was effective.

Yes, Portus and I found it. Since Portus had helped them the day of the Plant explosion, she'd seen him regularly. *The building needs much work. It's as dirty as a bear's den, but Portus said when it was cleaned out and decently lighted it would be fine. It's right above Old Norcanna on a side-path. Centrally located.*

Good. When will the request go to the Council?

As soon as possible. They're still afraid the General will stop them.

Gerald laughed and Meeriam flinched at the harsh feeling she got from him. So unlike Gerald, who was gentleness personified. *Graeber has more on his mind than keeping the townspeople in line. He's already scheming. . .* Abruptly Gerald shifted paths. *I'm tired, child. I'll say good rest and see you in the morning at breakfast.*

Good rest, then. We are Earth.

We are Earth, he replied.

Moments later Meeriam relaxed against her pillows. Gerald was tired, and she'd kept him talking longer than she should, but her thoughts, too restless to still, went back to Ellis Hagan, and as she drifted to sleep she was still trying to conjure up a picture of what he was like.

Chapter 7

Norcanna Colony

Hagan half-woke to a strange, beautiful cacophony of sound outside his window unlike anything he'd heard in six years on Mars. He lay enjoying it. Birds. A million birds. He smiled and cataloged other sounds coming through a half open window. The traffic on the streetbelt nearby. A cat meowing.A dog barking furiously, then suddenly and strangely silent.

The hair rose on his neck.

Shaking off the dregs of sleep, Hagan pulled himself from the bed, and stepped to the large curved window. Six floors below the path and courtyard area were busy.

Where the streetbelt grounded at a turnaround, a military carrier rested on its air pad. Three soldiers stood beside it, half hidden by the trees and bushes. Another soldier was making his way up Vana Darrow's path, his footsteps plainly heard on the gravel walk.

Coming for him? Why did he think so?

Hagan's stomach knotted. He'd find out soon enough.

He started dressing and was almost ready when a knock came on his door. He answered it to find Vana Darrow's younger son, looking subdued.

"Van Hagan, there's a soldier looking for you. Are you here?"

Wish that he could say he wasn't! Hagan smiled down at the boy. "I'm here. Tell your Mama thank you."

The boy looked at him with puzzled eyes. "For what?"

For warning him?"She'll know." Hagan snapped his boots around his ankles, grabbed his cloak and went out, pulling his door tight. It would open again only to Vana Darrow's master key or his own key plate. That should have made him feel secure, but it didn't.

The lift was evidently working this morning. The boy

stepped on the flat platform then looked back over his shoulder, waiting. Hagan stepped on, then let the boy touch the control. Slowly and smoothly the circular platform descended.

Murmured voices from the bottom floor came to him softly, growing louder as the lift carried them down.

"Is he in now?" A male voice, authoritative and a trifle impatient.

"Yes sir, I think so." Hearing the lift Vana Darrow glanced back over her shoulder, and looked relieved to see Hagan.

Beyond her, a soldier clad in the VMP's black uniform with narrow red strip down the leg, stood in the doorway, bareheaded in the early morning sun. The soldier had not yet seen him.

"Would you send for him, please?" There was something familiar about the soldier's insistent voice.

"He might still be sleeping—"

The platform came to a stop even with the entrance level and Hagan stepped off. Instantly he recognized the soldier who faced him. Moss. Images of Kama came flooding in, and abruptly he shut them off. Moss had Captain's bars on his collar now. Which meant he'd climbed the organizational ladder in Graeber's Colony Police. Did that make him friend, or foe?

In that same instant he recognized the cool appraisal in Moss's eyes, and made his decision. Trust no one. Not even Vana Darrow, who seemed, at the moment, to have his best interests at heart.

Vana Darrow clutched at her sky-blue skirts. "Sorry, Van Hagan. Had I known you were awake, certainly now, I'd have let you know you had a visitor here—"

"Thank you, ma'am." Hagan whipped the Jolando cloak around his shoulders and met Moss's cool appraisal with his own. "Captain," he acknowledged, "what can I do for you?" If Moss could pretend they'd never been friends, then so could he.

A shadow of emotion came and went in Moss's eyes. He nodded briefly. "The General wants to see you this morning, Player Hagan."

"Right now?" Hagan fell easily into the Norcannan way of speech. "Before breakfast?" His stomach was empty. He'd had nothing to eat since a quick meal on Diana the day before. But perhaps it was best to get the meeting with Graeber out of the way. Face him and then get on with it. He was suddenly thankful he'd disposed of Merrick's maps.

Turning to the tall, angular woman Hagan surprised a look of concern in her eyes. "I'll be back tonight in time for supper, Vana Darrow, if you'll but tell me the hour."

"Of course, Van Hagan. We eat at six. We'll be expecting you." And raising a hue and cry if he didn't appear when he should. The promise was implicit in her nod. Somehow it made him feel better to know that she was concerned.

Murmuring a thank you, Hagan turned back to Moss. "I'm ready, Captain."

Ready or not, Hagan thought some minutes later, it was all happening. Escorted to the big HOGG, the name, he remember was more due to it's looks than any acronym, he sat in silence across from Moss. A driver controlled the vehicle, and the three escorting soldiers were sitting in the rear. He'd caught their curious stares before he stepped into the cab. Young, he thought, and green. Not soldiers at all, but what they were he didn't know. Farmers? Fishermen? Junior technicians?

Displaying a nonchalance he didn't feel, he stared out the window. Norcanna had changed too, while he'd been gone. The area the City covered seemed greater, but fewer people were in evidence. Hardly anyone rode the streetbelts, but on the paths below he saw a few people. Was it his imagination or did they flinch when they heard the carrier overhead?

The streetbelt wound it's way up the steep hills toward the huge building that sat at the top. Norcanna's great Gathering Hall, with strange throwback architecture of a much earlier age. The first settlers had chosen here to pattern their new Meeting Hall on much earlier Earth styles rather than the precise and measured architecture of Mars. Except, that was, for the huge dome that covered the Gathering Hall proper, and the dome over the terminal where the Diana shuttle's passengers disembarked to Earth. These touches of home they kept. Hagan had often wondered why they had bothered with these domes. They weren't translucent like the domes of Mars. The interiors of both were painted a dusty pink, as though the returnees needed to be reminded of what they'd left behind. The dome of the Gathering Hall was covered on the outside with a gold leaf that now gleamed brightly in the sun. Wisps of fog which still drifted through the trees lower down the hill toward the bay already had disappeared from the top of the hill.

Then, as they crested the ridge, the city and the bay disappeared from view, hidden behind the vast complex that was built around and under the Gathering Hall. General Headquarters of the Venati Military Police. Why the name Venati, he'd asked Portus when he was a child, and the doctor had explained that the Venati Matriarchs had been one of the important families who gave First Settlers and money to the Exploration. The name itself had been dropped within twenty years of the first return, was retained only in the name of the Venati Military Police. There had been none to complain. Like with so many of the Matriarchal lines, the return had drained the Venati resources and the Venati family had died out shortly after, her few sons dead, her one or two remaining daughters absorbed into other lines.

As their carriage skirted the edge of the complex and made its way to the long carriage pad at the back of the huge Hall, buildings appeared that Hagan had never seen before. They stretched out in long wings, one following the top of the hill, the other forming an L-shape and edging the green common area toward the Academy. Barracks, he guessed. A carrier shed had also been added, and housed two private carriers and three military HOGGS, with room for six or seven more. But over it all, like a giant bird spreading protective wings, towered the Gathering Hall where he'd graduated on Lottery day fourteen years before.

He shivered at the memory.

When the carrier settled on its deflated cushion Moss stepped down and indicated Hagan should follow. Wishing he didn't have to, Hagan did. He paused, breathing deeply of the air that held the scent of 'clyptus trees, and the damp winter earth that was already turning dry from spring heat.

Then, drawn by a force he couldn't name, Hagan turned, searching. Here, from the highest point surrounding the great Norcanna Bay, he sought out the most distant line of mountains punctuating the horizon. The sweep from this spot was immense. And there, there where he knew it would be, thrusting its snow-covered peak to the stark blue heavens, stood Kama Mountain. Grandfather Mountain, the Firewing called it. The sacred mountain. Somewhere on its slope, hidden and safe from the intrusion of civilization were the Firewing. At two hundred and fifty stadts, more or less, the mountain was still stark and clear on the horizon. No other peak in the range approached it in sheer size. Or beauty.

Abruptly the enormity of what he'd agreed to do hit him. Cross those mountains, reach the high desert on the other side. Find the ancient city and destroy its deadly firepower before Graeber got there. Sure. Only, on Mars he'd forgotten how big Earth really was. Suddenly the task seemed too formidable to achieve.

"Hagan?"

The sound of his name on Moss's tongue jolted him. He spun back to face Moss. "Pardon?"

Moss indicated the bright cerafoam path that led to General Headquarters, and General Gordon Graeber. "I said, are you coming?"

Oh yes, he was coming, thought Hagan. Too soon, he was coming.

Moments later Hagan entered the underground chambers of the General's Command Center.

Graeber, behind a huge flat desk inlaid with the controls of a telereader as well as a light board and pencil, looked like nothing so much as a gigantic toad crouching in the middle of his pond. His bulk almost hid the chair he sat on.

Glancing up, he allowed himself one small grunt of surprise then recovered quickly.

Was it because, Hagan wondered, he looked so much like the Commander? Smoothly Hagan moved into the breach. "General Graeber? I'm Ellis Hagan. Were you looking for me?"

Graeber leaned back in his oversized wrap-around chair and studied Hagan through small, heavy-browed eyes. "Ah, the elusive son."

The man before Hagan exuded an odor of danger. Kali had been right. A fat, poisonous toad. An evil soul. With effort Hagan kept his voice even. "Elusive, General? Hardly. In fact, I thought I was right where I was supposed to be." Right where you wanted me to be, his thought continued.

"Perhaps I assumed Commander Hagan's son would have the courtesy to present himself when he arrived."

Hagan felt the sudden need to tread lightly. "You were first on my list today, General. Of course, I thought the courtesy was in not bothering you last night. It was quite late when I arrived." An inner devil prompted him to add, "Perhaps I misjudged your eagerness to get a look at the flesh and blood heir to the Original Share." As soon as the words were out, Hagan realized his mistake. Graeber's eyes grew smaller in the folds of his face, his furious gaze holding Hagan's like a mesmerizing snake. A contest of wills. The silence stretched between them, grew brittle. Hagan's skin began to crawl with an unnamed fear.

Don't push too far too fast—from somewhere the warning nudged Hagan's mind and he recognized its validity. Changing his stance slightly, he allowed his gaze to drop before the General's own, and heard the grunt of satisfaction that issued from the General's throat.

With the proper tone of defeat, Hagan said, "What did you want, General?"

As he contemplated the closing door fifteen minutes later, General Gordon Graeber was immensely pleased with life. He smiled. After just these few minutes with the Player he felt he knew all there was to know about the bastard. Arrogant, reckless and weak. No wonder there'd been bad feeling between the father and son. Spitefully Graeber's smile broadened as he contemplated the pain having such a son must have caused the oh-so-upright Commander of Kama. But it happened even in the oldest of families. Slowly the strains were degenerating, the strong loyalties dissolving. Corrupting. Corruptible.

Slowly Graeber's smile faded but he shrugged aside a frisson of uneasiness. If anyone expected help from that sorry son of a prolific mother, they would be sadly disappointed. He'd be able to help no one.

Not even himself.

As always when confronted by a problem, Graeber turned and rested his gaze on the model built into the niche behind his chair. No matter what the obstacles, there was only one goal to keep in mind. Time was growing short. He had only eight months left. Only eight to reach the ships abandoned by fleeing humanity and then he too would start his journey back to Mars. He slid his hand down to the psychoprobe and stroked it, and in his mind he was already seeing the fear on the faces of the members of the Grand Council of Mars as they listened to his ultimatum. It would happen. He would make it happen. But now there was much to do. Much. And, as he'd informed Hagan, it would start with a grand reception in three days time. One in which the Commander's son could be reintroduced to the colonists. Raising his voice he called his Chief of Staff.

Hagan, with a chill that had nothing to do with temperature, left General Graeber's dark office and stood on the common green, soaking up the warm spring sun. Slowly he let out his breath. The battle was joined. And he'd let the General win the first round. Or had he? Could it have gone any other way? Shivering, Hagan pulled his Jolando cloak close.

Go to a damned party? A reception, the general had called it, to be held in his honor in three days. For the son of the Commander of Kama. It would be held at the General's town residence. God, of all the things he didn't want to do. But the General had given him no choice, in that or anything else. He'd be given a military escort, and for escort read guard, he thought sourly. And further, because of the Firewing threat he would confine his activities to Norcanna itself. The only item Hagan had been able to insist on was that he'd not use the General's personal carriage for his transportation around the Colony. He'd cited mobility, but the true reason was that it would have tied him too closely to the General, and he was afraid the General had sensed that.

Striding down the hill path toward the center of the town, Hagan thought of the other things he had to do. Find Portus. See Velia. Present his claim to the Council as if he were worried about whether or not it would be received. That was the plan he, Kali, Si and Merrick had devised while he was still on Mars.

And of course he must see Kassine. She was the key. Though he'd rather not have to deal with her, he had to have help if he was going to get through the mountains to the ancient City of Phoenix, and she was the logical choice. Her freefarmers ranged to the mountain's edge. She could provide the transportation he needed. She had to help him. Kassine had to be his first order of business. If she refused, then he was truly on his own.

Stilling his sense of urgency a few minutes later, Hagan watched the young attendant in charge of the public carrier-shed count the credits Hagan shoved at him. The young man, his hair shaggy and unkempt, and his face the color of Firewing leather from years of direct Earth sun, had recognized Hagan immediately as the son of Commander Hagan, and let his curiosity get the better of him.

"You come back alone?"

Hagan admitted he had.

"You staying long?"

"It could be."

"Not in the military anymore? Can't say I blame you for that. Those of us that have a choice wouldn't choose that kind of life. Not any more. 'Course, some don't get the choice."

It was a statement Hagan wanted to explore, but with an abrupt about-face the young man grabbed the credits, and thrust a pile of trip-cards and a small yellow control box at Hagan. "Take the cards, Player. You got it for a week." Turning quickly on his heels, the young man slipped into his little guardhouse and shut the door. Searching for what had spooked the attendant, Hagan saw the soldiers standing on the far side of the streetbelt, those the young man must have seen that sent him scurrying for shelter.

Hagan had no doubt the soldiers had been sent to keep an eye on him. They were so obvious that he almost laughed. But it wasn't amusing that Graeber wanted to keep tabs on him. Either the General was naturally cautious, or he already suspected something. Either way, the soldiers' presence left him as cold as when he'd stepped out of the General's door.

Slipping into the cab of the small carriage a few moments later, Hagan flipped through the trip cards, chose one, and dropped it into the control box. First he would try to see Kassine, then he would find Portus and pass on the messages from

Merrick.

"That's what I've been telling you, Doctor." Vana Darrow stood outside Portus's door, unconsciously wringing the blue apron that covered her bluer skirts, her lean face full of worry. "He has rooms right here. Came in last night. I was going to let you know then because I remembered that you and the Commander were such good friends, but it was late. And then this morning that soldier came and he left—"

Portus raised shaking hands to rub his whiskery face. Trying to rub the foamy feeling out of his mind. Ellis here? Would he bring word from Xanthe? He couldn't let Ellis see him like this. He needed a bath, a shave. The old robe he'd thrown on for warmth covered the clothes he'd slept in. "Where is he now?"

"He hasn't come back yet. I don't know what I could have done. That soldier was one of the General's men. I couldn't—"

Portus's mouth went dry. His fear of Graeber had increased daily. Only when he was working with Meeriam on the new hospital did he seem at all in control any more. Only then. And how much longer could she continue to help without drawing Graeber's attention to herself? Now Ellis was here? Why? Why had he come back? Didn't he know how dangerous it would be for him? Without a blink of his evil eyes Graeber could squeeze the life out of them all.

Just the way he'd snuffed out Elias's life. Portus had no doubt about that now. He'd heard too much, seen too much these last months since Elias's death. It was common knowledge that Elias had opposed his General on all fronts. Yet even if it was whispered by some that the General had taken his revenge, no one was brave enough to say so out loud. Yet Portus knew, and the knowing made him afraid.

Vana Darrow peered more closely at him. "Doctor, are you feeling all right? You don't look well. Why don't you come down to the kitchen and let me make you something to eat. I do believe you skipped your supper again last night. You shouldn't do that, you know. It really isn't good for you to skip meals."

Because complying was easier than refusing, Portus followed Vana Darrow first onto the lift and then on down the narrow steps to the first floor and into the kitchen. Minutes later, sitting at the long kitchen table Portus sipped at the clear black brew that had little to do with synthesized coffee. Watching her make it he'd wanted to protest that he'd not put such poisonous stuff into his stomach, but after the first sip his protest had died. The coffee seemed to have an amazing effect on his mental processes.

And now that he could think more properly, one thing was clear. Ellis must not be brought under suspicion by contact with him. With that determination, Portus explained to Vana Darrow what they must do.

Reluctantly she agreed.

Portus was nowhere to be found.

For three days now, though he'd searched all the haunts he thought the doctor might inhabit, Hagan met with no success. He ran into a dead end everywhere he turned. And there was no one to talk to, to question outright expect perhaps Vana Darrow, and even she was surprisingly noncommittal. It didn't help that everywhere he went he was dogged by Graeber's soldiers.

By today, though, the day the General had designated for his reception, Hagan had devised a plan that might let him elude his pursuers without triggering their suspicion that they'd been out-maneuvered. He hoped the General would think it was either coincidence or incompetence on the part of his men. Removing the trip card from the little yellow control box, he manually wound his way through town, doubling back on himself, randomly choosing the lower streets and paths, and finally, having eluded his escort, sped out onto the long Avenue of Estates.

Here the raised streetbelts and lower pathways gave way to ground level cerafoam roads gleaming whitely in the noon-day sun. He passed no traffic, and spied none following him.

It was a small victory, but one he needed. God, he felt so stymied. So damned helpless. Each move he'd made so far had ended in failure and frustration. Kassine was in residence at her home down by the Hojoi plant, but she had denied him an audience. Almost everyone he spoke to of Portus recognized the good doctor's name, but no one knew where he was, or when they'd last seen him, so he was on his way once more to see Velia. It hadn't been the first item on his list, but one Kali had said would be natural. Knowing how she'd received him the first day he'd arrived, he'd hoped to put it off indefinitely. But here he was. This time, he hoped, she wouldn't slam the door in his face.

The deserted Avenue of Estates was a long, tree-shaded road situated at the very edge of the city of Norcanna. The Commander of Kama had possessed one of the most imposing. Most of the dwellers of the homes set back from the road in park-like settings worked at their various functions as if what they did mattered, and once, before Graeber had taken charge of the Colony, they really had. As he passed the distinctive gates belonging to people he'd known from childhood, Hagan ticked them off. This ornate artifact was the gate of Harmon Landen, who governed the Department that controlled the common utilities. He was a small dictator who had always been afraid of military usurpation of his duties. How was he dealing with Graeber now?

Not very well, Hagan guessed.

And there, on the opposite side, was Phelin Crocker's gate, he who had started out as a shopkeeper, being a third or fourth son of a minor matriarchal house, and had used his organizational abilities to wield the other shopkeepers into a united group who usually swayed the Norcanna Council to any point they wished. His father had often said, given time the shopkeepers would rule the colony, maybe someday, even the world itself. The Commander had not meant it as a compliment.

Envisioning Graeber crouched behind his wide curved desk, taking over every little detail of Colony life, Hagan wondered if that was still true. Somehow he doubted it. Phelin Crocker would be no match for Graeber's vast ambition. Few people would.

Except, perhaps, Kassine, the Matriarch of the Freefarmers. It was her responsibility to produce the Hojoi that fed the replicators on Mars. It was also her life work, and she had expected it to be her daughter Luan's too.

Luan had objected, but it had done no good.

Kassine's estate was next.

Slowing the carriage, Hagan frowned. The gate at the Avenue entrance to the Estate hung open. What had once been immaculate green fields clipped and groomed like an Arcolan park were now brown and dry under the hot spring sun. Grass had gone to seed along both sides of the private carriage lane that led from the Avenue to the house. The house, weeds growing up along the walls, boards over some of the windows, appeared to have been abandoned.

A high blank wall that started at the front corner of the house and surrounded a huge back area, a design for house and garden that had been set by the first returnees and copied by everyone since, was covered with dead brown vines. The neglect seemed recent but thorough.

Did no one live here any more?

On impulse Hagan turned his carriage into the lane. Immediately a sense of isolation washed over him. No one was here, not even a caretakeing freefarmer. How strange. Surely Kassine hadn't died. Of course not. Hadn't he just been told she was in residence in Norcanna? No, that wasn't it. She simply must not be using this place anymore. But what about Luan? Luan had always loved this house. She'd called it her castle, and the walled garden her private kingdom. Their private place. He twisted with an imitation smile at the thought. He hadn't seen Luan yet. He hadn't asked about her and no one had mentioned her. It was even possible that she'd finally made it to Mars. That had been her dream. To live on Mars. With him. Or so she'd always said. But the dream had died. For both of them. No, he didn't want to see Kassine. But he had to. Sooner or later, she would talk to him.

Stopping the carriage in front of the wide stone entrance, Hagan dismounted, leaving the carriage door swinging open behind him. Somehow the small sound in the silence was comforting.

As he walked up the steps to the door, his footsteps were loud against soft whispers of grass nodding in a faint fragrant breeze. He quieted his own steps so that the sound he made became another whisper, and stopped in front of the door.

The elegant sweep of the inner entry was barred by a heavy lattice-work gate that was locked with an old-fashioned key-lock. For a brief fanciful moment he imagined that if he touched the lock it would open for him, but then he laughed at the thought as being an adolescent fantasy. He'd spent a lot of his youth pretending he was a Firewing and could levitate over obstacles and could open locks merely by wishing it so. Luan had called him a silly dreamer.

Making as little noise as possible he went down the other side of the stone stairs and emerged on a dry path that led to a closed gate in the garden wall. With a hand already out to nudge the gate to see if it would open, he paused, every nerve suddenly alert. Was there another footstep not his own? Or had it been a small animal—no, not something—someone!

Someone, who stood on the other side of the wall waiting—for what? To see what he'd do?

The possibilities whispered through his mind. A groundskeeper? One of Kassine's freefarmers? Hesitating a moment longer, he heard a soft shuffle, and then with a quick shove, he pushed the gate wide.

A heavy-muscled figure shadowed away into the dark-leaved trees and overgrown bush, and before he could stop to consider the sanity of the action, Hagan sprinted after him.

This garden, like every other great estate garden, had comprised of three-eights of a square stadt, the large residence always sitting on another eighth. As Hagan ran into the dense shade of the trees he saw where the garden had not dried up completely. Where the stream still ran, moss and green grass lived along its bank. Now, though, he had no time to be grateful for that sign of life. The man running ahead of him angled for the distant back wall, his footsteps so soft they were only at the edge of sound. Hagan already felt himself out of breath. Too much sitting, he derided himself, too little exercise, but the pattern of this garden was ingrained in his memory. If he cut through to the smaller pathway he could reach the wall first. Slipping between two overgrown thorn-bushes, feeling the thorns grab at his clothes and sting his arms as he protected his face, Hagan drove ever deeper into the dark recesses of the miniature jungle. Huge unkept broad-leafs had crowded the life from smaller more delicate plants and the dead sat like grotesque skeletons next to the living.

Coming to the path that ran parallel to the wall he stopped. No longer able to hear the soft sound of the other intruder's passage over the pounding of his own heart, and the gasp of his own breath. Cursing himself for all kinds of fool Hagan froze into the shelter of a topiary animal whose outlines were now blurred into non-recognition. Had the man he was chasing gone over the wall already? His view of the area was restricted, but his senses seemed doubly alert.

A prickly sensation crawled up his back. He felt the other's presence somewhere close by. As his heartbeat returned to normal and his breathing grew slow and quiet, he had the strange sensation of being searched for, found and lost again, as though someone were using a bright beam in a dark night, sweeping in wide arcs.

A Firewing.

Old, dark fear touch him, the old panic. Ruthlessly he repressed the memories that tried to surface and kept his mind totally on the present. He'd not fight a Firewing. And left alone, he was sure the Firewing wouldn't seek a fight with him. Easing himself from his shelter, Hagan moved back in the direction from which he'd come. By God, he thought, go in peace.

Picking his way carefully past fallen branches and dead bushes, Hagan couldn't help wonder who the intruder was. A member of which clan? What was he doing so far from home? Didn't he realize how dangerous it would be for him if he were caught this close to Norcanna? Graeber would like nothing better than to have a real live body he could show off.

Hagan had almost reached his starting point at the open gate when his feeling of ease abruptly vanished.

There was no sound to warn him, nothing he could see, but the sure knowledge of danger was suddenly on him.

Reacting with a speed that afterward seemed unreal, Hagan dove sideways and down and the tangled roots of an old barrel tree gouged into his shoulder and ribs. Twisting, he brought his feet up in time to catch the man's upraised arm. A branch of deadly thorn-bush winged harmlessly away. Hagan got a flashing look at a pain filled grimace as he rolled and hit the broad torso midsection. The Firewing went down, the breath knocked out of him. Breathing heavily Hagan came to his feet and stood over the Firewing's still form.

Young, Hagan though. And angry.

But even as he watched, the Firewing recovered, drawing

strength to himself. He lay still. Only his dark eyes were watchful.

Hagan stepped backward and gave the young Firewing room to rise if he so wanted. "I am unarmed." He wondered if the young man would understand him. Portus had told him once the Firewing language was an old mixture of pre-holocaust French and American, though how such a mixture had come about, or how a millennium later it seemed to have created the liquid mixture of sounds they now spoke Portus had never been able to say, other than Language evolved.

Hagan tried again. "I mean you no harm."

"Then why were you chasing me?"

Though softly inflected, the man's Norcannese was perfect. Hagan barely contained his surprise. "I merely wondered who was trespassing in the Kassine Garden. Who are you?"

Ignoring Hagan's question, the Firewing's gaze flicked over his now dirty clothes and a sneer grew on his face. "You're not a soldier." His tone was almost accusatory.

"I never said I was. And you're not a farmer." Although the young man was dressed as one.

Cautiously the young Firewing pushed himself to a sitting position, his hands clutching for support on the ground beneath him. His gaze remained glued to Hagan's face, and Hagan felt the mesmerizing pull of the Firewing's dark eyes. The old fear resurfaced as though newly born. Concentrating on the younger man's strong, arrogant features, Hagan steeled himself against his own memories. Shunting an image aside of another strong, yet gentle face, whose eyes had also been dark and mesmerizing. He shut his eyes against a flash of pain.

Hagan's small lapse of inattention gave the Firewing the moment he needed.

A fine cloud of dirt flew up into Hagan's face and at the same moment the Firewing launched himself forward.

Hagan, with only an instant of warning, threw himself to one side, and was caught by the point of the Firewing's shoulder on his hip, throwing him off balance.

Head first he spun toward the ground, hit the roots of the barrel tree and exploded into painful darkness.

Breathing quickly, Condor crouched by the inert form of the stranger and felt a moment of dizzy triumph, followed by a swift shaft of regret. It hadn't been his prowess so much as a lucky accident that had taken the stranger down. But he shrugged away the feeling. Was the stranger dead? Dead or not, what did he care? He bent lower. A trickle of blood from a head wound pooled on the ground at the base of the roots and he stared at it, fascinated and yet repulsed. For all his talk, he'd never before drawn blood from the strangers. Yet it was what he'd meant to do, wasn't it? Wage war on the strangers the way they waged war on the People?

Quickly, before he could change his mind, he withdrew from his boot the beautifully crafted knife he'd found at Phinx. The forbidden knife. Merely having it had made him feel more powerful, in a strange, dark way. Now he felt that power more strongly. Holding the point steady, he knelt over the inert form at the base of the tree. This was a stranger. An intruder. He had no right to be here on Mother Earth.

But the closer he came to bringing the knife into contact with the stranger, the greater he felt the life force of the man sprawled unconscious on the ground.

A life force strong and pulsing—and— A thought struck him so forcefully he blinked in chagrin. I am one with my enemy.

An anguish of a kind he'd never known before filled Condor and the sharp point hovered over the pulsing life line at the stranger's unprotected neck.

He couldn't do it. Confused, he rose to his full height and stared down at the stranger.

Someday he might face this man, they might fight, and one of them might die. However it'd not be like this, with one helpless before the other.

Moments later the man stirred and Condor nodded with satisfaction.

His thought was a promise.

We will meet again.

Hurting in areas he hadn't known he possessed, Hagan shook his head, trying to clear his thoughts, tasting dirt and grit against his teeth. His hand came away from his head sticky with blood. As his vision cleared he realized the Firewing had gone.

Using the protruding roots of the barrel tree, he pulled himself upright and used the tail of his tunic to wipe blood off his head. Why hadn't he known the Firewing could do something like that? Sure as hell he couldn't see Velia in this condition. Not that he had really wanted to. He grinned without amusement. Assessing the damage done, bruised ribs and hip, grit in his eyes, a cut on his head still oozing blood, he shuddered.

How could he go to the General's reception looking like this? If he hadn't hoped to make contact with Kassine, or someone else who could help him cross the mountains, damned if he'd go! Making a final effort Hagan pulled himself to his feet, and stood until the dizziness left him. He grunted derisively.

Damned if he would go!

Doubly damned if he didn't.

Chapter 8

Kama Valley

Meeriam heard about the coming reception for Ellis Hagan while on her way to the Thomas Homestead with Gerald to investigate the site of another fire, the third in as many weeks. Over the muted roar of the landhopper her comment was acidic.

Gerald chided her.

"But it seems so senseless," she protested. "Elias wouldn't have—"

"Elias has been gone eight months, child. The General moves on, and so do we."

Meeriam frowned her unhappiness. She still missed Elias so. It occurred to her that perhaps she was only jealous because she wouldn't be one of the people invited to the reception. In spite of Gerald's warning to stay away from Ellis Hagan she wanted to see him, to meet him. Surely the Commander's son would be someone who could step in and—and what? What did she expect of him? Her memories of him were so specific and yet so limited.

And then, as the landhopper approached the largest homestead in the Kama valley, all thoughts of the Commander's son vanished from her mind. A black pall of smoke rose up to greet them, turning the morning sun red and blackening whatever it touched. As they traveled through it and came out on the other side the homestead proper came into view, with its loading pad, drying and packing sheds, equipment barn and large, sprawling house surrounded by green grass, fences and bright spots of color where Belle Thomas had planted flowers. As the landhopper sank to its berth, the orderliness of the homestead was belied by the small crowd gathered around the far side of the large pad, their faces drawn, their clothes ash-covered. Outside the perimeter of the pad, and away from the farmers stood a unit of VMP. A large military HOGG was parked at the end of a roadway, and another soldier leaned against its door with negligent ease.

Hardly waiting for the landhopper's engines to shut down, Gerald was out the door and down the ramp. Freefarmer Liam Thomas stepped forward to greet him.

Meeriam, at Gerald's side, said into his mind, *The soldiers, Gerald. They haven't been fighting fire.*

Grimly Gerald noted what Meeriam had already seen. Clean uniforms and shiny boots. He nodded.

Liam Thomas was an older man, his face weathered by sun and wind, and now blackened by ash and soot. His eyes held anger, his body a bone-deep fatigue.

"Greetings, Van Nilander. You're a little late for the party."

"But needed nevertheless," Gerald replied softly.

"God, yes." The Freefarmer wiped sweat from his sooty face on his yet-blacker sleeve. "I don't know which is the worse menace. The fire, or—" His glance went to the soldiers, confirming what his words didn't say. "We lost twenty ton of green Hojoi, Van Nilander." He lowered his voice. "And that's bad enough, without that idiot over there—" his gaze rested momentarily on the leader of the small unit beyond the pad, a tall rail-thin soldier who looked as if he'd just stepped from the domes of Mars, uniform pristinely clean and mouth obstinately and scornfully set. Liam Thomas heaved a tired sigh. "Can you believe it? He wants to arrest someone. Thinks the fire was deliberately set."

"Was it?" Gerald's tone invited confidence.

"I—I don't know."

Meeriam frowned. The freefarmer was lying. Gerald knew it too, even before her thought was clear.

"Freefarmer Thomas," Gerald's words grew quieter. "I'm not trying to assign blame. I only want to know the truth of what happened." Meeriam read his fleeting thought that he'd said this more than once lately.

"You might not be assigning blame, Van Nilander, but the Matriarch will."

"But I deal with Vana Kassine, not you. Tell me."

A long sigh drew the staunchness from the Freefarmer's stance. "The fire was set. The soldiers tell me a group of

Firewing was sighted at the head of the valley last night, but we didn't see any here on the homestead. When they're in the area they usually stop. My wife—" Abruptly Liam Thomas stopped, seeming to become aware to whom he was speaking. The homesteaders weren't supposed to trade with the Firewing, but they did.

Meeriam, Gerald's thought shot out, *go up to the house and talk to Vana Thomas.*

Without drawing notice to herself, Meeriam left the group by the hopper pad and made her way between well-kept sheds and past patches of colorful flowers that the Freefarmers seemed to delight in. She'd often wondered why they didn't turn their expertise to food, but Elias had explained the aversion most domes people had to putting anything real in their stomachs. She still thought it odd. Having eaten the synthesized food herself, she wondered how they could tolerate a life-time of it.

By the time she climbed the wide steps to the deep-covered porch of the house, the Freefarmer's wife had seen her coming and was waiting in the doorway.

Belle Thomas, short and slim, was a third-generation farmer herself, and at least twenty years younger than her husband. She was known throughout the Valley for her industry and common sense, as well as for her sweet personality. She and Meeriam had become friends from their moment of introduction several years before.

Now Belle stood, her hands outstretched. "Meeriam, love. It's so nice to see you. I was hoping you'd come with Van Nilander today."

"When I heard the news I couldn't stay away, Belle. What's been happening?" She noticed automatically that Belle's hands were damp, and trembling slightly, and that Belle exuded a nervousness that wasn't in character. Quietly Belle drew Meeriam to the chairs sitting in deep shade against the gray walls of the house.

"You mean besides being overrun with soldiers, fighting fires and listening to angry talk from Liam's men?" The woman's smile was not quiet convincing. "Am I pregnant again?"

Meeriam laughed, helpless not to in the face of the woman's exasperated expression. "Are you?"

"Yes, but don't tell Liam. It's all he needs at the moment."

Meeriam sobered. "Are things worse then, Belle?"

The smile that had started in the woman's eyes disappeared. "Liam wouldn't let the children stay here. He sent them down to Pioneer Cove to stay with his brother and sister." Meeriam remembered the younger Thomas children, but before she could comment, Belle was going on. "The soldiers have set up a permanent camp down by the river between us and the Jordan Homestead. They fouled the pump on the Number 4 well two days ago. Liam was furious. Then last night this fire—"

"Van Thomas said the soldiers are trying to blame it on the Firewing."

"They're trying, but I don't believe it."

"Who else, then?"

"I wouldn't put it past Graeber —" Abruptly Belle stopped speaking, her hand over her mouth. Meeriam waited but the Freefarmer's wife took a deep breath, then shook her head. "Liam says my mouth will get me into trouble someday."

Meeriam pretended not to understand. "Why should that be?"

"Garth Peters—you know him? Has the homestead down beyond Stadt Ten? One of his sons disappeared not long ago. Just after—" the woman's voice lowered, "Just after he got into a brawl with a soldier, and beat him, I should add." Meeriam felt the woman's frustration mixed with a very real fear. Belle's fingers plucked with restless energy at her green tunic. "It wasn't this way when the Commander was alive. We never had this kind of trouble. All we worried about then was the weather or a mechanical failure. We got along well with the Firewing. Now they avoid us, and I can't say I blame them."She laid a hand on her stomach. "Now I don't know what will become of us all. Liam bought sidearms for the field workers—" Belle's face paled. "Oh, lord, I did it again. Please—don't mention that to anyone. Liam didn't want anyone to know."

"I won't tell." She wouldn't have to tell Gerald something that important. He'd already know. "But why did he do it?"

Belle's tone became defensive. "Liam said it wasn't fair that the men shouldn't be able to defend themselves. And he's right. You know he is."

And so violence would beg more violence.

Meeriam had been raised by the mothers of Lissone, after her own parent's death in a rock slide when she was ten, to believe that only in compassion and love could a person hope to find happiness. When she'd gone to Norcanna to live with Gerald at Grandmother's behest at the age of eighteen, she had learned that the domes people, although they gave lip service to those same ideals, often resorted to coercion if not outright cruelty to get what they wanted. Even Elias easily could resort to violence when he thought it necessary. It'd been a part of him she'd not understood. At least not until he himself had been a victim of that violence, and then in her despair and anger, she too felt that need in herself. It had taken the healing presence of Grandmother, and the merging with Mind to wash her clean of anger and hate, but the experience had left her with a comprehension she had not had before. Now she could understand what Belle was saying, even if she did not agree.

She sighed and started to arise. "I must get back to Uncle Gerald, Belle. He'll want to return to Norcanna before too long." To escort Vana Kassine to that unholy barbaric display—

Disappointment flashed across Belle's face. "Oh, please, not yet, surely. We haven't had a good talk for weeks. We heard the Commander's son came back the other day. Have you seen him yet? What is he like?"

Not amazed at how fast the news had traveled, Meeriam laughed. "You probably know more than I do, Belle. He just came in three nights ago on the Diana Shuttle. I haven't laid eyes on him yet."

"Well, they say he's the image of the Commander, and the Commander was such a fine, handsome man."

Oh, yes, he was. Meeriam thought the unexpected shaft of pain might cleave her in two. It must have shown on her face.

Immediately the other woman reached out and touched her arm. "Oh, Meeriam, forgive me. I know you and the Commander were close."

Close? Meeriam blinked back tears. Something in Belle's voice intimated an even greater closeness than she and Elias had actually had. "It's all right, Belle. I—I do miss him."

"Of course you do. That's how it is when you've loved

someone. If I should lose Liam—"

Meeriam sighed, knowing that for Belle that would be even worse. Belle and Liam Thomas had produced life between them while Elias had never even taken her to his bed. And she understood now that he never would have.

Seeking comfort, she stared out beyond the confines of the homestead to the mountain posed with majestic beauty above the distant rim of the valley floor. She was soothed by the knowledge that on the mountain's flanks most of those she loved dearly were still safe.

When she'd drawn to herself a measure of calm she turned back to Belle and smiled and if it was a smile filled with sorrow, it was also a smile of reassurance. Liam Thomas would be safe. She knew it with the knowing given her by her heritage, though she didn't say so. "You won't lose him, Belle. Don't worry."

Belle smiled ruefully. "I know. It's only sometimes that I get so worried. I don't know what it is, Meeriam, but when you come to see me, I always feel so much better. You give me faith that everything will turn out all right."

"Good. You just keep believing it."

"I will. Please, let me get you something cold to drink. Can you imagine what summer will be like if it's this hot now?" Before Meeriam could protest, Belle had jumped to her feet and disappeared into the house.

While she waited for Belle's return, she let her gaze wander over the nearer buildings, the drying sheds. She had just spotted a soldier, standing in the deep shadows of the nearest shed when Belle returned, bearing two glasses. The juice, Meeriam noted silently, was fresh and not synthesized. Good for Belle. Her thoughts then went back to the soldier.

"Bell, why are there soldiers on the homestead?"

Belle's mouth twisted wryly. "Supposedly for protection, though that's a horrendous joke, don't you think?"

Belle's eyes flicked nervously toward the drying shed where the soldier leaned so nonchalantly and her face paled. "They scare me sometimes," she admitted. But Meeriam hadn't needed proof. Belle's fear was a palpable blanket surrounding her. Her hands tightened around her glass and she trembled with it.

Those soldiers shouldn't be allowed to terrorize Belle and

her family. No wonder Liam sent the three children away.
Perhaps he should have sent Belle too, but knowing Belle,
perhaps he tried and she refused to go. That would be like her.
Meeriam's mouth tightened with resolve. The least she could
do for Belle was to rid her of the soldier who stood so openly
watching her.

With no compunction this time for invading another's mind
Meeriam briefly touched the soldier's thoughts. His blatant
sexual imagery brought a flush to her cheeks.

Suddenly angry, she sent her anger out like an arrow, and
saw the soldier straighten and put a hand to his head. Shifting
her concentration to his stomach she let her anger work there too.

Looking decidedly uncomfortable, the soldier's hand went
from his head to the area just below his belt. His thoughts were
no longer sexual. Pushing himself away from the Hojoi racks, the
soldier turned and disappeared around the corner of the shed.

"Look at that," Belle said. "Perhaps the heat got to him.
Most of these soldiers can't stand the heat. They're newly
arrived from Mars, you know."

Meeriam knew. Though where they came from on Mars
she couldn't begin to imagine. Now that the soldier was gone,
Belle's color had returned, and the tension went out of her. The
conversation turned to the children, and the minutes passed
pleasantly. The soldier didn't return.

Later, when Gerald was ready to leave, and Belle had
accompanied Meeriam back to the landhopper's pad, Belle
whispered an aside in her ear. "You get a good look at the
Commander's son and tell me what you think. From what
I remember of him—" Her grin was a quick, irrepressible
invitation to laugh.

Liam Thomas chose that moment to cast a glance at his wife
that made her involuntarily clasp her hand over her mouth again
and roll her eyes. A blush crept up under her sun-browned
cheeks. Meeriam didn't need to hear the words, "Oh dear, I did
it again," to know what Belle didn't say.

"Never mind," she whispered back, laughing. "I'll let you
know what I think."

After a subdued leave-taking, Gerald pulled the door
closed, set the controls and settled back into one of the

landhopper's four passenger recliners. "How did you find the Freefarmer's wife?"

Meeriam, strapping herself into another seat next to Gerald, let the recliner adjust to her weight before she spoke. "Tense. She said Freefarmer Thomas sent the children to Pioneer Cove. She's frightened by the soldiers but she tries to make light of it." Meeriam repeated everything Belle had told her and Gerald listened, his long face growing harder by the moment. When she was through he leaned back and closed his eyes with a tired sigh.

"Thomas, too. I can't blame him. I'll have Vana Kassine lodge a protest in Council about the soldiers on the homestead. I'll also warn Thomas to keep one of his men near the house."

"Then you do think the soldiers are a bigger problem than the fire."

"I think without the one we'd not have the other. By the way, have you been in touch with Condor within the last few weeks?"

Her cousin from the Valley of Water? Meeriam frowned. "Not since before I went to Lissone." Condor always sought a meeting with her when he was near. More than once he'd threatened to take her back to the mountains with him. He'd even spoken for her at the Sacred Fire, but she'd turned him down. As she'd explained to Grandmother at the time, as a lover Condor might be wildly exciting, but as a husband and father he would be horrible, and besides, she was looking for neither lover, husband nor father for her as yet un-conceived children. No, Condor had no place but kinship in her life. "Why? Has he been around?"

"He was on the homestead last night. Van Thomas said he'd seen Firewing," Gerald smiled slightly at the use of the name the Arcolans had put on the People. "And when I walked over the ground I sensed it was Condor who'd been there."

"But surely he didn't set the fire."

"No, of course not, but he might have seen something useful. Can you reach him?" Meeriam knew though he was occasionally at one with Mind, Gerald himself had no contact with the various tribesmen who came over the mountains and into the valleys, feeling that his position as Vana Kassine's right hand must not be jeopardized by suspicions not easily allayed. Grandmother, sensing his growing isolation and need had sent him Meeriam, an act which had earned his gratitude. Meeriam, whose questions renewed his interest, and, he said, whose intelligence sometimes astounded him. As well as whose help at times went beyond what he expected of her.

"I'll certainly try. Do you sense him still in the valley?"

"No. Not nearby. Do what you can. I'll be escorting Vana Kassine to the reception tonight, but we'll not be late. I'll talk to you when we get back."

Meeriam knew the elderly Matriarch had not been feeling well. For several days now Gerald had been trying to convince the Matriarch she should see Dr. Portus. So far the indomitable old woman had refused. That she should be required to attend a social function at the General's whim was more than Meeriam could understand. Why didn't she refuse? Had she, like Liam Thomas and his wife, become afraid?

Feeling a wave of dread she resolved that she would, come evening, cast out her thoughts and search for Condor. If he was anywhere within the Kama Valley or coastal areas, she would find him.

Chapter 9

Norcanna Bay

Putting off her preparations for the General's reception, Vana Glena Kassine stared into her mirror. Every one of her innumerable years exposed themselves in the wrinkles on her brow. How many years, how many wrinkles, she wouldn't even consider. She had learned not to. On those rare moments when she did so she became physically ill with the immense number she counted.

Considering age also made her irritable, because it made her remember and remembering was a painful and useless exercise.

Unless, like tonight, it was less painful than what she looked forward to.

How dare that man order her to come to a reception for the Commander's son. If it didn't suit her own purpose, she damned well wouldn't go. Of course, what better place to discover what new alliances were being formed, which rats had deserted the ship and which were still hanging on.

She breathed a tired sigh. Perhaps Luan would—no. She wouldn't let herself do that. Even if Luan were there, it would more than likely be to flaunt a new parasite. Her mind closed painfully around that thought and she leaned her head on her arms. In spite of her best efforts the memories rose.

She herself had been approaching mid-age when her lover had impregnated her. She was already a Woman of Responsibility, and she had thought of the one experience that so far had been denied her, that would make her complete. With her usual determination, she chose the experience even over the protests of her family and friends. Why, she asked, when ordinary women still could choose to bear children, why shouldn't she? Almost every woman she knew had borne at least one child.

But early in a difficult pregnancy she determined that what was right for other women was not necessarily right for her. Yet in spite of the difficulties, because she considered herself above the common herd, she chose not to abort. So, stoically, she bore her pregnancy being sick often and violently. For this she gave up her beloved job—for this she turned away her lover—ah, now she knew a secret shared by millions of women down through time.

It wasn't worth it.

When the baby arrived Kassine hired a nurse, and as soon as possible, picked up her life where it had left off some months before. Strangely she felt no different after the experience than she'd felt before. Accepting that knowledge, she put the experience behind her, and over time moved up the rungs of responsibility, changed lovers once, then twice. The baby, a fretful infant, grew into petulant childhood, and slipped into atrocious adolescence almost without notice. The ladder of success for a woman of Kassine's organizational ability and knowledge was easy to climb. Her abilities took her finally to the New Earth Colony of Norcanna.

Eight years ago, when the nominal head of the Processing Complex resigned because of age and infirmity, a position that had actually been handled by Kassine during the previous Matriarch's long and lingering illness, she, Vana Glena Kassine, was prepared to step in. That was also the year her daughter, age twenty-two and beautiful with a brittle charm that reminded her of herself at the same age, chose to violate tradition and become involved with a soldier—worse, a son of soldiers! Furiously Kassine had set about to destroy the relationship. "If you want to take a lover," she had said, "that is your prerogative. But to actually talk of marriage—" she left the unspeakable unsaid. Marriage was for commoners and soldiers, not Matriarchs. Using her position and influence, she saw that the young cock was transferred out, to the furthest possible post.

Her beautiful, willful daughter, stymied in her impulsive love, grew more brittlely charming, discovered the joys of lotus tea and the best way to claim attention from her mother.

Too late Vana Glena Kassine had discovered that the experiences she'd sought twenty-two years before had become the anchor around which her spirit would sink. Desperately she issued orders which were ignored, ordered punishments which were endured or derided, and finally, with tears too deep to surface, realized that the neglectful sin of the mother was punishable in kind. Aware that she'd lost the war, Vana Glena Kassine had withdrawn from the battle and again buried herself in her work, surfacing only when she was needed to put back together the broken pieces of her daughter's existence. Perhaps, if she was lucky tonight, Luan would miss the reception. But, remembering who the party was for, that self-same young cock she'd managed to banish eight years before, she knew better. So she would go, and see what could be salvaged from the matter. Maybe there'd be something of the Commander in him after all.

An hour later, gathering her reserves of strength, Kassine paused at the glittering entrance to the General's Gathering room, a combination of living space and audience chamber that had become common in the great houses of Mars. At least a hundred small floating ball lamps cast a warm glow from their positioned paths just below the high ceiling and sparkling streamers that caught the light and broke it up into rainbow colors helped weave a festive air. Music, faintly martial in tempo, came from an alcove opposite the entrance, and the voice level had already risen in direct proportion to the amount of hard-chap, Cheery and other heady brew consumed.

Graeber, she thought with disgust. Ostentatious upstart. Didn't he know how out of place such a show as this was? Disdainfully she raised her chin, and pulled her breath in, girding herself for what lay ahead.

Placing her hand lightly on Gerald's hard-muscled arm, she nodded her readiness to enter.

Gerald, ever concerned for Kassine's health, had urged her one last time to miss this glittering display. What good would come of it, he'd asked, but she had grown morbidly curious about the Commander's son, especially since she'd had him turned away twice in the last two days. What could he have wanted?

Close by the silvery entrance curtains a young man in a barely acceptable servant's uniform was accepting wrap-arounds and cloaks. If Kassine found the sight of so much bare skin offensive, she indicated so only in the slightly contemptuous smile she bestowed on the boy from behind her mask of manners.

Although outside the spring night had enfolded them with liquid warmth, the atmosphere inside the Gathering Room was cool and Kassine shivered with the loss of the wrap Gerald had handed to the attendant. One of the greater evils of getting old, she thought with an angry sigh. Gerald glanced down, and drew her slightly closer, sharing some of his warmth without its being too obvious. His staunch presence was protective, and she appreciated his gesture in the deep recesses of her mind even though she denied a need for it.

The room was filling rapidly with people from all levels of colony life.

Steering her clear of the entrance, Gerald leaned closer. "Do you wish to meet the Commander's son first, Vana Kassine, or—"

Kassine didn't let him finish. She usually didn't. "He may be the man of the hour, Gerald, but I hardly think it fitting that I rush right over and present myself to him!"

"Yes, Vana Kassine. I was merely thinking it might speed up matters and we could go home again." The touch of dry humor in Gerald's voice saved him from sounding presumptuous.

Kassine allowed a real smile for the first time since receiving the summons from General Graeber. "My dear boy–" because she had twenty years on him and a world more authority, she often lapsed into that informality, "we must observe protocol. We will join the other Council Members. . ." her voice trailed off as her searching gaze found the other four members of the Norcannan council. They were gathered at Graeber's side like sucker fish on a whale. "Or maybe we won't." Quickly she turned, searching for the drink dispenser she knew would be somewhere close by. A drink of anything would be welcome right now.

As if he read her mind, Gerald guided her in the direction of a dispenser being tended by a handsome young man who smiled at them with exceeding familiarity. Then, recognizing Kassine, the smile faded as he nodded with reluctant and probably feigned respect, and asked what he could serve.

Drink then in hand, Kassine turned again to the crowded room. "Is the doctor here, Gerald? Can you see him?" She had seen the doctor earlier in the week and had been shocked at the sight. Poor man. Could not the healer heal himself?

From the advantage of height, Gerald encompassed the large Gathering Room. "Portus?" Women in more formal wear than one usually saw in the Colony, men dressed in the finest materials obtainable, none of it Earth made—Gerald discovered the good doctor half-hidden in another small alcove, his hands rigid around a glass, staring down, miserable and not bothering to hide it.

Masking his pity for the doctor Gerald glanced down at Kassine, seeing only the pink hair pulled harshly back from the prominent bones of her finely chiseled face. Not that he needed to see her face to know what was in her mind. "He's here. Do you wish to speak with him?"

"Not yet. Who else?"

"Everyone." Gerald's voice was again humorously dry. He knew who she was looking for, though she wouldn't admit it. He had nothing but compassion for her crushing love/hate feelings for her daughter. It'd been a week since the younger Kassine had been home and though the house was more peaceful without her, the elder Kassine suffered for her absence. "Vana Luan is in conversation with—" Gerald's hesitation was so slight as to be unnoticeable, he hoped, "Captain Galt."

"She would be in his pants were not so many people around." Kassine whispered bitterly.

Gerald pretended he hadn't heard. "The transient Householders are here. Vana Darrow, Van and Vana Stedtman and Van Nelder."

"They dare not be absent if Graeber summoned them." Kassine sipped sparingly of her drink. "He has taken over the issuing of permits." Gerald knew she'd been outvoted at the last council meeting on the issue and still resented the fact.

Gerald nodded, but before he could continue his litany of those present a man, perhaps fifty, in an old-fashioned robe that swept to his ankles, approached. The flicker of his eyes barely acknowledged Gerald.

"Ah, Vana Kassine. You have come after all. We had heard that you were ill, perhaps."

Kassine's pink head nodded in polite acknowledgement.

"Not at all ill, as you can see, Van Corman. One stays busy at one's desk and immediately the rumors start to fly. Is your family well?" Corman had returned his whole family to Mars for a visit shortly after Graeber's arrival. Now he heard from them only by the tapes they sent by outliner. His wife was refusing to return. In private he blamed the whole matter on Graeber, but to the General's face he was obsequiousness personified.

Gerald also knew Kassine had no use for such duplicity and had been heard to say that his wife was no loss to the Colony and that it was obviously a bad breeding to begin with. What else could you expect when mere free-holders were allowed to marry into the Minor Matriarchal houses? Her smile was serene.

Corman's frown, never far from his face, deepened. "The family is fine. Fine. My daughter has met a soldier and is seeking permission to marry."

"No doubt Vana Corman is objecting?"

"No. No, not at all. Would like to see the girl settled you know. I would too. My wife says there's talk of opening up a new City Dome, you know. Might as well get on the list. Might take forever. . ." His voice trailed off as if his train of thought had withered and died.

"Why," said Kassine, "would she choose to live and breath under a dome when she could come back here?"

Corman reddened, no doubt suspecting the sarcasm even though it was well hidden. "Not everyone can tolerate Earth, you know, Vana Kassine. Some are too delicate."

Kassine barely contained her lady-like snort.

Seeming to sense he was getting the worse in this duel of words, Corman quickly changed the subject. "Have you met the Commander's son? Now there's a fine specimen. The Domes certainly put a polish on him, I should say."

"Really?" Kassine's disbelief was obvious. "He looks no more polished than the other of the General's lackeys to me." As she'd obviously not yet come close enough to Hagan to pass judgment, Van Corman's smile held a sudden trace of maliciousness. "Whores and lackeys, they're all the same."

Gerald felt Kassine's wash of rage and quickly intervened. "Vana Kassine, Vana Gatsford beckons you." Vana Gatsford, a tall, gaunt blonde somewhat less than Kassine's age had inherited part of the mining interests on Diana but made her home in the Valley of Estates here in Norcanna. As such she was one of a small number in Earth's colony who could be considered Kassine's social equal. She had indeed beckoned but wasn't sure why, knowing only that she had felt the irresistible urge when she had seen Gerald looking her way.

Without waiting for Kassine's decision, Gerald guided the old woman away from Corman and into the crowd.

With eyes narrowed against the glare of the many lamps floating just above head height Hagan watched Gerald Nilander steer Kassine through the press of people. Hagan's day which had started poorly, and grown worse in Kassine's abandoned garden now looked to end in disaster. When he'd gone to see Kassine he had at least expected to be granted a moment of her time. Add that frustration to the fact that his head hurt, and his muscles ached because of his confrontation with the Firewing. His ribs contained two purplish splotches and his head sported a knot he'd reduced with icy spring water before climbing back into his rented carriage and making his way back to his temporary home at Darrow Tower. He repressed a tired groan.

He'd never liked a crowd of people. An audience come to see him perform was one thing. There was, after all, a certain distance between the actor and the audience. But here? With disgust he realized that Graeber had put him on display like a prized dog. What did he hope to gain by it? As Kali had warned they might, people who remembered him eyed his player's costume askance, perhaps whispering how little of his father he had in him, and wondering if the General had him in his pocket. And those who didn't know him assumed as much. The General who circulated among his guests with his retinue of hangers-on, minus Kassine of course, kept a close and benevolent eye on him, fostering the impression.

Letting his glance slide by the General's gaze, Hagan continued the game of identifying people he had once known.

He'd already spotted Luan Kassine, looking outwardly much as she had eight years before, except now she glittered with the newest Arcolan fashions, a flowing metal-thread dress that molded to her too-thin frame, her pastel hair pulled high into

a diamond-studded hairpiece. The moment she had entered
the room she had turned her back on the crowd and devoted
her attention to Galt. Even from this distance she looked brittle
and hard, and invitation was in her stance. Danielle, for all of
her stage artifice, had been more real. Lost for a moment in
the memory of Danielle, he was hardly aware that someone
approached and spoke, but he must have answered satisfactorily
because with a hearty laugh the speaker moved away again.
Hagan's head throbbed and he had no doubt his eyes were
slightly glazed. He took another sip of cheery, and hoped the
man pushing his way through the crowd with determined feet
and elbows wasn't coming to talk to him.

He was turning away when, through a break in the crowd an
old, familiar figure appeared. Portus? Could it be? Huddled in
a small alcove, staring into a glass of cheery. Sweat stood on the
old man's face, and without knowing its source a surge of pity
swept Hagan. The old Doctor liked his Cheery, Kali had said.
Perhaps too much. And then Portus looked up and met his eyes,
and his gaze was filled with an angry hopelessness that pierced
Hagan's core.

Hagan started forward but was stopped by a clutching hand.
"Van Hagan, surely you remember me?"

The speaker was a heavy-set man of middle years, and
Hagan looked at him with blank impatience. "No, I'm sorry
to say I don't." He stared at the hand on his arm, each finger
containing a family signet that had he been so inclined he could
have read like a family tree. He wasn't so inclined.

Under his impatient gaze the hand sprang from his arm
but the words continued. "Freemerchant Henry Charles.
Used to keep you and your father in uniforms. And this is my
daughter Anna," he dragged a young girl forward. She came
reluctantly. "Seventeen and a beauty, if I do say so myself. Good
worker too." The girl blushed beneath her painted mask and
looked miserable. "If she could just stay here a moment while
I get us drinks. Her mother couldn't come tonight." The man
disappeared into the crowd leaving the girl at Hagan's side. He
sighed. "How old are you, Anna?"

"Fifteen, Van Hagan." Her voice was a mere whisper.

"What's your father thinking of, thrusting you at me?"

"Probably no less than every other father is thinking of." Obviously alarmed by her own boldness the girl blushed again.

In spite of his headache, Hagan had to smile. "And what is that?"

"That you'd make a fine match." Emboldened by his smile her words slipped out in a rush. "My papa says you're a most eligible match. In spite of the way you're dressed."

"I don't doubt, if he's thinking of the Share. But fifteen is a mite too young for my taste."

"Oh, I know that," she dimpled beneath the mask of paint, "but Papa has four girls and can't help hoping."

Hagan laughed, and then wished he hadn't when the silent drum in his head beat louder. "Find yourself a handsome young Firewing."

Though he'd been speaking softly, the young girl's eyes grew wide with alarm and she looked around as though wondering who might have heard. "Please, Van Hagan, don't say things like that, when the Firewing killed your own father."

That was the prevailing fiction. More than once as people had offered their condolences the Firewing had been named as culprits. Repeat a lie often enough and it becomes truth? "The Firewing didn't—" he started.

At that moment Van Charles reappeared and the real girl slipped behind her mask of glitter again. Though he wanted to tell Freemerchant Charles just what he thought about the parading of adolescent girls before possibly hungry bachelors he held his tongue. Young Anna was embarrassed enough as it was. He gave her a slight smile as her father drew her away. Then his smile faded. Now that his attention had been drawn to it, it did seem like he'd been introduced to a preponderance of young women since he'd arrived an hour ago.

Disgusted, he turned, hoping again to search out Portus. At least, if he could connect with Portus, some good would come of this blasted party.

So intent was he on his need to find Portus, that he almost stumbled over Vana Glena Kassine and Gerald as they approached. But her soft, sibilant voice cut into him.

"So this is the Commander's pup, all grown up. Primping and preening in fine Arcolan clothes and eating the bastard's food and—"

"Vana Kassine." Gerald's warning tones were accompanied by the obvious tightening of his fingers on the old woman's arm.

Startled Hagan stared down at the small woman, slowly taking in the stylishly pink hair, the subdued but intricate mask that hid her everyday wrinkles. Kassine herself?

He stifled his surprise and bowed slightly. "It's also a pleasure to see you again, Vana Kassine. I'd almost forgotten how welcome you make a person feel."

Kassine's eyes glittered through her subtle mask. "None of your sarcastic remarks, young man. What are you doing, wearing those ridiculous clothes?"

Hagan had dressed as a player, rejecting the more formal Arcolan wear his good sense told him to don. Anything tight around his chest where the bruises were deepening would have made him gag. The flowing white shirt, loosely belted, and tight only at cuffs and collar, worn over the deep magenta tights, set him apart more surely than his size, his carriage, or his speech, but he was beyond caring. Not even Kassine's question could divert his increasing headache. "I'm sorry my clothes don't please you, Vana Kassine." He turned to Gerald. "Hello, Nilander. I see your job ever increases in its complexity."

"Have you now," Kassine went on as though he'd not even acknowledged Gerald, "been approached by every marriageable daughter in the Colony?"

Even though he'd hoped for her cooperation, Hagan's hold on his temper slipped. "All but your own, Vana Kassine."

Instantly he regretted his words. The old woman turned white under her mask. It was as if he'd hit her.

Gerald Nilander stepped forward, steadying Kassine while his words took no note of the exchange. "Are you planning a long stay in the colony, Van Hagan?"

"Long enough," Hagan replied, his attention still focused on Kassine. Slowly the old woman recovered her color. Hagan glanced around for a chair, but there were none in sight, and impatiently he turned back to her, his voice gentled. "I'd offer you a chair, Vana Kassine, but there seem to be none in sight." She was, after all, merely an old woman, not the dragon of his youth. Even though she still breathed fire. The thought brought him a reluctant inner smile. Perhaps it wouldn't be so hard to obtain her help after all.

For a brief moment something close to approval seemed to flicker in Nilander's eyes, but then it was gone again, and Hagan decided he must have misread an errant thought.

Then, as though the subject of her daughter had not arisen, Kassine said, "It's a shame you had to wait for the Commander's death to return to the Colony, young man. He could have used your help."

Hagan's wry smile came in spite of himself.He almost had to admire her. She never let up. "Doing what?"

"Why, quelling the vicious Firewing, of course. Haven't you heard how besieged we are by the savages?"

"On every side," Hagan agreed softly. "But may I say, Vana Kassine, that it's always been hard to tell the civilized from the savage here in the Colony?"

"You may," she replied dryly, "but don't say it too loudly. The savages may take offense."

Gerald Nilander's jaw set with disapproval, but Kassine continued to ignore him. Hagan did the same, concentrating his energy on trying to keep up with her thoughts, both spoken and unspoken. Because obviously she was saying more than she seemed to be.

"And how grow your Free Farms, Vana Kassine? Do they also suffer from the savages?"

"Everyone suffers. I don't know why they don't do something about that odious toad." Once more Gerald's fingers tightened on the old woman's shoulder, this time in a way she couldn't ignore. "It's growing late, Vana Kassine. I'm sure the General wouldn't appreciate our monopolizing Player Hagan's time."

"Poppycock." Kassine's old eyes hardened with anger. "Do I concern myself with what—"

"No," Gerald interrupted grimly, "but you should. Hagan, it's been good to see you. We'll meet again, I'm sure."

Hagan could see that Nilander was truly irritated with the old woman, and perhaps Kassine could see it too. She nodded abruptly. "Very well, then, we'll move on." She looked up through her expertly done makeup into Hagan's purposely bland face. Her voice quieted. "Come see me tomorrow, young man."

Not giving Hagan time to speak a yea or nay, the old woman moved on.Watching her, Hagan chilled with a strange, dark premonition that he'd not see her tomorrow. That there was a good chance he'd never seen her again.

Hagan was still watching her, trying to understand the feeling when a hand touched his arm and a soft voice purred in his ear. "Welcome home, Ellis."

He started, and jerked around and looked down with a feeling of deja vu into Luan Kassine's inviting blue eyes.

With knowing eyes and cynical silent laughter, Graeber had watched the parade of girls presented to young Hagan. Because of his newly inherited wealth, had they been on Mars the same thing would've been happening, but on a much grander scale. Every minor house would be scheming to draw him into its fold, and a few of the major ones as well.

If Graeber was puzzled by Hagan's lack of response to the girls, his puzzlement lasted only a moment. He was more interested in the feeling he was getting, the comments made. The young pup looked enough like his father that people stared. But he was soft. Pliable. Yes, he could be made to look like a leader. He was a player wasn't he?The people were practically ready to crown him a king. Hadn't he, Graeber thought, with an almost obvious smile, always fancied himself a king-maker? The power behind the throne, so to speak.

From the corner of his eye Graeber saw Luan Kassine still talking to Galt, and his sense of complacency fled. If ever a woman looked like an in-heat bitch that one did! As he watched a moment longer, Graeber's shoulders tensed imperceptibly. Not Galt, you stupid little fool. That's not why we pulled you from the Baths this afternoon—and Galt—he was looking down at the younger Kassine as though he might take her right there, regardless of who watched.

"Moss," Graeber's guttural voice was harsh, "get Galt out of here."

Moss nodded without expression and moved away from the General's side. Moments later he was speaking to the couple. Galt's face paled, and he flashed a wary look at the

General before he turned abruptly on his polished heel and walked away. Moss said a further word to the younger Kassine, seeming to ignore the thin hand she used to explore his arm, and the predatory smile she turned up at him. Moments later he returned to the General's side.

Graeber felt himself stir at the young woman's obvious need. She was young, but not inexperienced. Even so, there were things he could teach her. Then he shook his head at his own errant fantasy. Her need was only tea-induced. Soon she would sleep the sleep of the drugged, and when she awoke tomorrow morning the evening would be only a vague memory in her befuddled mind. He liked the women he took to his bed to be aware of what he was doing to them. He liked the fear he saw their eyes before he pounded into them.

Abruptly Graeber realized he'd lost sight of Hagan and searched quickly, frowning as he now saw the elder Kassine was with him. For the moment everyone else was giving them wide berth. Graeber felt frustrated that he couldn't know what they were saying to each other. He moved toward them. Kassine must not use her vile tongue to poison young Hagan's mind.

As though they were figures choreographed in a strange dance, Graeber moved toward Hagan, as did Luan Kassine. At the same moment Gerald Nilander deliberately moved the old woman away. The look on his face was grim, and Graeber thought for a fleeting moment he'd like to have a Firewing's power to read minds, if indeed they could do so. What had been said to make Kassine's superintendent express any anger at all? Most unusual. Graeber watched as Nilander quickly moved the elder Kassine toward the door, and his mouth tightened with displeasure. It was a snub. A deliberate snub. Without conscious volition his hand tightened around the probe that rode unseen at his waist. She would pay. That old woman would pay. And then, as he glanced back at Hagan and saw the young cat finally approach him, his previous thought sank beneath another. One more satisfying. If the girl dared let Hagan go before she had him in bed this night, she would answer for it.

But even as he watched, the expression on Hagan's face, which had been aloof with the proffered adolescent girls, mask-like with the old woman, softened as he looked down at the

Matriarch's daughter. Inwardly Graeber laughed, all of his doubts eased by this new act beginning. And the plan that had been nebulous in his mind for three days now grew and took on solid shape. Young Hagan, whether he knew it or not, would be the prime player in his play. The bastard would be his instrument, his whip.

His weapon to destroy the Matriarch and bring the colony to heel.

His steppingstone to ultimate power!

Chapter 10

Norcanna Bay

Sharp, stabbing fire jolted through Hagan's chest, bringing him to sluggish consciousness. Turning in an unfamiliar bed, he felt a warm body, and froze. What the pain had started, the feel of the woman finished. His eyes flew open, then shut quickly again against an aching flood of sunshine. Memories of yesterday came back, cold memories of the fight with the Firewing in Kassine's abandoned garden, hot memories of Luan Kassine that left him icy with momentary fear.

He stifled a groan. What the hell had he done? He didn't have to open his eyes again to see her. He remembered too well the silky feel of her hot skin, the metallic dress that fell away under his searching hands. Luan. He'd left the General's residence last night with Luan. She'd taken him to her own apartments near the Baths. Talk, she'd said. It'd been so long since she'd had anyone she could really talk to, the way they'd once talked, sharing secrets, dreams. He'd ignored the brittleness of her laugh, the feverish glitter in her eyes, seeing only the body sending hot signals to his, and feeling his own response. He'd remembered how many dreams they'd dreamed together, how many hopes they'd shared. He'd wanted to believe she was just the same, so he'd believed it. He had seen only what he'd wanted to see. And God, he'd wanted her. Wanted her so badly that her strange intensity didn't matter. Only afterwards, as he was drifting toward lethargic sleep did he start to think it strange that she didn't question the bruises on his body. It was as if she hadn't seen them. She didn't even ask why he'd come back, or proffer any other question about his stay. Her wild need assuaged, she'd fallen asleep and still she slept, though the morning light pouring in the open window covered them both.

Drunk on lotus tea, he now guessed, or something worse. And here he was, the stupidest goddamned man on Earth.

Disgusted with himself, he rolled off the bed and straightened, stiff to the core of his being from his fight with the Firewing. He had to think. He had to consider. How much damage had he done? His glance at Luan told him she would probably sleep her drugged sleep until after noon. He wanted to be angry with her, he wanted to hate her, but he couldn't blame her for what he'd done. He could blame no one but himself. If he'd been set up, he'd fallen into it headfirst with no murmur of protest. Had he been? Or was she merely acting true to her own nature? Remembering how close she'd clung last night to Galt, who had reached the unenviable position as Graeber's top aide, he'd guess his first choice was the right one.

But why?

To cut him off from Kassine? Possibly. Had he been thinking last night he wouldn't have been so ready to fall into Luan's bed.

Thinking. God, how could he have been so mindless?

Coming face to face with himself in a mirror, he smiled bitterly at his reflection. As usual, he had only himself to blame.

How long before Kassine found out he'd fallen into bed with her daughter? He had no doubt she'd get the news sometime this morning. Earlier than late. Graeber would see to it. Was it possible he could get to her first? He grabbed up his clothes and padded toward the bath in the large open alcove off the bedroom proper. It was worth a try.

But, running down the circular stairs from Luan's apartment fifteen minutes later, clean on the outside even though he did not feel so inside, he knew what little luck he possessed had deserted him.

General Graeber's private carriage sat on the roadway, its door wide open. And Graeber sat inside, waiting.

He had to give it to the young pup, Graeber thought, watching Hagan hesitate only slightly when he realized who waited for him. There was something of his father in him. But not enough to matter.

As Hagan approached, Graeber smiled. If there was a subtle difference in the player this morning, he chose not to notice it. He'd show off well in uniform, wouldn't he? And the sooner the better. That player's garb with that ungodly color was offensive.

"Good morning, Ellis. I thought I might find you here."

The player smiled tightly. "Good morning. Have you been waiting long?"

Was he being mocked? Graeber narrowed his eyes, seeking weakness or impudence and finding both. His temper rose before he could check it. "Was bedding her worth it? I've always wondered."

The player's blue eyes grew darker, and for a moment Graeber felt their touch as an almost physical blow. He shook the feeling away with a sharp laugh. "Anyway, Galt seems to think so. Get in, get in. I'll give you a ride back to your resident tower."

"I'll walk."

"I think not." Graeber had not grown to power without learning the trick of impinging his will on subordinates. He pinned Hagan with an icy stare, allowing his angry contempt to spew forth without words. It was a look that had quelled hardened criminals in the Caverns of Mars, as well as High Council Members. It was the same look which at the age of fifteen he had used to quell his mother and her last lover who was not his father. Hagan faltered under it, and Graeber did not bother to hide a surge of satisfaction. No, this Hagan was not the man his father had been. "Get in," he repeated. This time it was an order. And it was obeyed.

Hiding his thoughts behind an impassive player's mask, Hagan sank back into the soft cushion of the private carriage and Graeber coded a trip into the control then turned to him again. If he'd not known it before, the General's lethal smile told him the answer at least to one question. He'd been set up. But then, not since the moment he'd seen the General's carriage had he doubted that.

If, in some small aching part of his mind he wondered how Luan could have done it to him, in another small part he knew it was only what his stupidity deserved. He put both thoughts aside for later consideration.

Now he would concentrate on not letting his fear of Graeber goad him into further rashness. Hiding a shiver, Hagan tried to treat the situation rationally. Heaven knew, he'd been afraid before, and probably would be again, but never with such good cause. Graeber's barely concealed fury, a fury that seemed as much a part of the man as his obese body or his heavy brows, emanated in waves that beat at him like storm waves against rocks along the ocean's shore. It created a lump of fear that left his heart beating rapidly and his hands icy cold. If Graeber so chose, Hagan knew, the General could have him killed out of hand. Another death, maybe, to blame on the Firewing. Or perhaps he was supposed to fall apart, sign over the Share and play tame pet for Graeber's conquest of Earth. Or better yet, perhaps he was supposed to fight with Galt for the privilege of Luan's bed.

Not likely. A saving dose of anger drew rein on the insidious creeping fear. He could deal with whatever Graeber did. He had to. And whatever Graeber did, whatever he tried, whatever happened, he would use it, and let it take him closer to where he needed to go. He'd use Graeber just as Graeber sought to use him.

"I think," Graeber, leaning back into the soft cushions of the carriage, spoke harshly, "it is time to consider your future here on New Earth."

Kali stared at the screen, numbness creeping into his mind. The Colony news, lately sparse, ran the one line announcement of Hagan's rejoining the VMP, resuming his rank, as a member of the General's staff.

"God damn it, he's supposed to be on his way to Phoenix. Why the hell isn't he?"

Si turned the screen so that he could also see the latest Colony news. Read with a gathering frown.

"He's in trouble."

"He's in trouble? What the hell are we?" Kali slammed out of his chair and stalked to the window. Gripping the window's edge, he resisted the urge to put a fist through the grey-glass. Outside the gathering dusk cast a reddish glow across the measured streets of the Xanthe community. People hurried between low buildings, others converged on the entrance to the sub-train. None of them was aware of the drama being played out on far-off Earth. God, if he could only be there! "I expected more of Ellis Hagan. I thought he'd at least try to make it to

Phoenix. But he's there four days and he's right in Graeber's lap. There's no way Graeber will let go now. No way."

"He's there, and we're not. Maybe he figures this is the best way." Si's usual voice of reason sounded somewhat uncertain.

Kali spun and faced Si. "That's right, damn it. He's there and we're not."

"And?"

"And I'm going."

Si paused only a moment, then smiled. "How?"

"The Mendoza is already on her way back from Diana, isn't she?"

Si considered, then with a shrug, discarded the Mendoza. "It'll take her too long a turn-around time. A couple of months, anyway. That new ship, what are they calling her? Nix Olympica? She's due for commissioning in a week. There'll be all kinds of ceremonies."

Kali flashed Si a determined grin. "Then I have one week to convince Madam President Demar that she should send me to Earth."

For a moment it looked as if Si might argue. "What about Merrick."

"I'll leave the boss to your inimitable charm. I'm going to Arcola. The High Council sits again in two days. I'll have an audience with Madam President before then."

"Very well. Be careful, though. It would surprise me if Graeber doesn't have his spies everywhere, even on Demar's staff. God, I'd like to know what he used to coerce Hagan's cooperation."

Kali's mouth twisted in a mirthless smile. "A woman, no doubt."

Meeriam heard the gossip in the kitchen just before mid-day meal. Vana Kassine was sick again, and no wonder, went the tittering stories. Her waiting up all night for the young one to come home, and she, tramp, or child, or poor lamb or ungrateful brat, depending on who was whispering the tale, had taken the Commander's son to bed, and him back only three days, flaunting him right before the poor old woman's nose, so to speak. Meeriam thought with an angry gasp that

113

surely it wouldn't be true, but the stories were too many, and too certain, to be false. Her great anger with Elias's son seemed disproportionate to her knowledge of him. Her memories, slight though they were, did not correspond to the vituperation heaped on him. The same kitchen whispers admitted he wasn't the caliber of man Elias had been. And somehow Meeriam found her anger was for him, as well as at him.

Sitting down to mid-day table with Vana Kassine and Gerald, Meeriam tried to gauge the old woman's feelings, but Vana Glena Kassine had seen too many disappointments, and knew well how to hide her emotions behind the business of the day. If her lips were tighter, and eyes more bleak, there was no one to notice but Meeriam and Gerald.

Only once did she mention Hagan, and then she did not refer to the Commander's son by name.

"He will not be allowed in this house."

"Even though you invited him, Vana Kassine?" answered Gerald gently.

"Even so."

With a slight nod of acceptance, Gerald acceded to her wishes, and the discussion went back to the devastation wrecked by the fire at Thomas's farm two nights before.

Under cover of the discussion between Vana Kassine and Gerald, Meeriam's thoughts gravitated to the conversation she'd had with her cousin Condor last night. He'd come here to the house, something he'd never done before, and she'd been shocked by the bruises on his body. He'd fallen, he'd said. He'd wanted her healing hands. She'd berated him for taking such chances, coming into Norcanna like this. Did he not know how dangerous it was? He'd laughed and said there was no danger to him. If the soldiers knew what was good for them, they'd stay out of his way. His boasting made her angry and she'd told him in no uncertain terms what she thought of it.

Later that night, when she'd told Gerald about Condor coming, he'd only frowned.

While he was there, Condor had also admitted knowing nothing about the fire out in the valley. He had, he said, spent the night in a garden on an abandoned estate. His scorn for those who would build walls around gardens was great. As it was also for those, he said, who felt they had to live with the intruders in their houses.

Having had all of his superiority she could stand in a shorter time than usual, Meeriam had told him to leave. Because her strength of mind was greater than his, he'd left, scowling darkly and muttering that someday he would take her home. Like a child deprived of a favorite toy, Meeriam thought as he went off in a huff.

But there was no great harm in him. Of this she was sure. He wouldn't take out his frustrations on hapless Freefarmers. Nor would he entrap anyone the way Vana Kassine's daughter had done. Meeriam stopped pushing food around on her plate. Now where had that thought come from? Perhaps it was just wishful thinking on her part. Or was it because she simply wouldn't believe the Commander's son to be someone so cruel or thoughtless of others that he took what he wanted, when he wanted it.

Even as the thought came, she wondered how she could be so certain of that. She didn't know him. Not at all. Except that he was Elias's son.

Sensing Gerald's gaze on her she looked up. She would have to save her thoughts for later. "I'm sorry, Gerald. I wasn't paying attention."

After that her thoughts of Ellis Hagan receded beneath a discussion of the Freefarmer family's needs and only much later did she let herself dwell again on the Commander's son.

BOOK TWO SOLDIER

Chapter 11

Norcanna Bay

As carefully as if it had been the finest c'foam silk Hagan smoothed the material of the black tunic top across his shoulders, pulled it snugly across his ribs, ribs that had finally healed from his fight with the Firewing in Kassine's garden, then tucked the formfitting blouse into his belt.

Three weeks since his return to Earth to find the ancient city and stop Graeber in the process, and all he'd managed to do was to alienate Kassine, the one person who might have helped. In that same three weeks he'd had his claim postponed by the Norcanna Council twice and found himself again a member of the service he hated.

In that same length of time he'd made no further attempts to see his step-mother Velia, nor had his few covert attempts to find Portus accomplished anything. Portus could only be hiding from him. Not that he blamed the old man. God knew, he probably wasn't the safest person to be around. Not with Graeber watching every move he made.

Sometimes he wondered if Graeber didn't guess why he'd come back. Yet, would he still be alive if the General knew?

Standing in front of the long mirror he studied the image he made. The image of the Commander, Vana Darrow had said. Was he? Strange how his memory of Elias had faded over the years, until all he remembered was the anger. The pain in his father's eyes. The final contempt.

He raised a hand as if he could block out the accusing eyes staring back at him, as if it were the Commander truly there, not his own reflection.

Sunshine from the skylight overhead glinted off the shiny leather strap across one shoulder and at his waist, and his mouth twisted wryly.

Like it or not, here he was. A captain on Graeber's staff.

What a farce. A sense of urgency ran through him like liquid fire. With each step he took he was further from his goal, and could feel Graeber's web drawing tighter around him.

The rank, the new apartment, the visibility at Graeber's side, all strands of the web, pulling tighter and tighter until soon it would choke the life out of him.

Visibility. That was what this particular day was all about.

A military show for the colony, Graeber called it. A Celebration of Death, was the phrase that kept running through Hagan's mind. Men reputed to have killed Firewing were supposed to receive commendations this day. Had they really done so? Somehow Hagan doubted it. But Graeber said they had.

A sound behind him shot adrenaline into his system and then a moment later Luan Kassine's honey-gold head appeared in the mirror at his shoulder.

"It's time to go." Since he'd moved into this apartment in General Headquarters she'd made herself at home. He should have been used to her frequent appearance, but he wasn't. He'd not taken her to bed since that first night. He was, he thought with a grim smile, cured of that particular disease. Better late than never.

Her voice carried a sharp impatience. "Are you ready?"

Ready for what, he wondered, but not aloud. Since that first night Luan had stayed as close as a shadow, not her own idea, he'd soon realized. She would rather have been at the Baths, or perhaps at a party at one of the estate houses. Instead, he guessed, she reported his every move to the General. She had a small circle of friends, mostly men, who had looked at him askance but, being afraid of the General, had said nothing. Some of them, like Galt, worked at Graeber's headquarters. Others were newcomers from the Domes of Mars. Luan, he'd discovered, hadn't been too particular in her choice of friends. Anyone would do as long as they could scratch her tea induced itch.

Now, as their gazes collided in the mirror, she pouted with irritation. "We should have left fifteen minutes ago. We'll be late."

"No we won't. But if you're worried, go on without me."

"No. We should have gone to the party last night. You know the General wanted you to go."

Her voice held an irritating petulance that grated on his ears. "Go sit around with a bunch of soldiers drunk on hard-chap, telling us how brave they are? Spare me, Luan."

"You didn't used to be so nasty."

"And once you didn't use to drink lotus tea."

Angry spots appeared on her translucent cheeks and her eyes narrowed.

Ignoring her he reached for the brushy comb and used it on his newly cropped hair.

Luan didn't seem ready to let the argument go. "We made the General mad by not being there."

"Too bad."

He almost missed the slight, malicious grin that played across her even features. "Galt thinks you're jealous."

"Of what?"

"Of him, of course." Luan preened lightly in the mirror, watching him from the corner of her eye. "Are you?"

Giving up all pretense, Hagan stared at her in the mirror. Him jealous of Galt? God forbid. Was she vain enough to think so? But it was as good an excuse as any. Shrugging off the hand she placed on his arm, he reached for the leather s'darm case that still felt so unfamiliar to his palm, slapped it around his waist and slammed the buckles together with a loud snap.

Let Galt think what he would. It was none of Hagan's business. He hadn't liked Galt six years ago and he liked the General's chief of staff now even less.

Hagan looked again into the mirror. Now he was identical to the rest of Graeber's minions. His mindless robots. His hard-faced, soulless soldiers.

Except that now he looked exactly like the Commander.

As though impatient of his private thoughts, Luan jerked at his arm. "Well, are you?'

Hagan quelled the impulse to push her away. Was he losing his mind? He seemed to have forgotten what the question was. "Am I what?"

"Are you jealous?"

This time the question struck him as ludicrous, and he

almost laughed, but laughter wasn't called for. Luan seemed to be deadly serious. How should he play it?What would be most convincing?He turned, facing her. Touching her smooth cheek, he smiled down at her. "Do you want me to be?" And for the moment his answer seemed to satisfy her.

As they reached the wide green common ground between the Gathering Hall and the Academy, whose cerafoam walls had taken on the patina of age beneath the forces of the seasons as they never would have under the domes of Mars, Luan's question still galled him. Was he jealous? Only the most insecure of women would ask. Or the vainest. When had she reached that apex of vanity? Or had it been there all those years ago and he'd been too enamored to see?

Allowing her to walk ahead, he wished that he could lose himself in this crowd gathering today in the late spring air. At high noon, under a bright sun and incredibly blue sky the scene was more beautiful than the most artful terra-scene treasured by the richest matriarchal house of Mars. In the near distance lay the blue curve of ocean and bay at the foot of the spreading City of Norcanna. White residence towers punctuated green trees and from this vantage point even the flat processing tanks in Vana Kassine's shoreside complex added perfect counterpoint and balance to the picture.

It looked more peaceful than it was.

Drawing his gaze from the distant view Hagan surveyed the nearby scene. The reviewing stand had been thrown up on the flat, circular drive that skirted the green and separated it from the wide Gathering Hall steps. Every Norcanna-based unit would be represented by a marching squad. Banners streamed in a warm breeze flowing from inland and smelling of the promise of heat.

From his position he couldn't see beyond the buildings to the distant mountains. Just as well. He remembered the overwhelming urge he'd experienced to go there. The mountain calling him, his father would have said. Kama Mountain, where, if Graeber had his way, men would die before the end of summer.

Today he was glad he couldn't see the mountain. If he did his face might give away his pain.

The general, almost ready to mount the staging platform, turned, saw him and beckoned.

Stealing himself, Hagan obeyed the summons.

Meeriam wondered why she'd come. She'd sensed Condor earlier, his deep hot anger had touched her, but from a distance. No, it wasn't because of Condor she was here. Maybe curiosity, more than anything. And unease.

She was finally going to see the Commander's son.

Slowly, as she watched, the crowd filled the stands and the area on either side. There was some noise, some laughter, but it was subdued, as if the people were attending a religious service rather than a celebration.

Even without touching a mind she felt the tension. It was a tension that had built steadily over the preceding weeks, helped along by vague announcements from the council, more visible troops on the street belts and on the pathways. There were short, sharp clashes between soldiers and townspeople, townspeople and freefarmers, freefarmers and soldiers. And of course between soldiers and Firewing. The Matriarch Kassine, looking older than ever, was having problems controlling her farmers. Just yesterday Gerald had reported another incident down at the plant, soldiers bullying their way in with the excuse they were looking for illegal s'arms. They found none, of course.

Shivering in spite of the warm breeze, Meeriam glanced around. She didn't feel safe. Should she have come alone? Perhaps she should've at least told Gerald she was coming.

"Meeriam? Is it really you, child?"

Startled to hear a voice she recognized, Meeriam turned. Portus? Where was he? It almost sounded like someone else.

The crowd had grown thicker. She couldn't see over taller heads. "Doctor?" She sent the thought out, found him at the far edge of the viewing stand, leaning against a lower support. Quickly she made her way through the press of bodies.

When she finally reached him, he engulfed her in a hug and for a moment she felt only joy at seeing him again. "Portus, it's been too long a—" Almost three weeks, in fact. In that length of time she'd made another trip to Lissone, and two to the farms with Gerald. She'd not yet seen Ellis Hagan, though everyone still talked about him. Now they said he'd even put on the General's uniform and taken his place at the General's side.

Perhaps that was why she was here. She had merely wanted to see it for herself.

Swaying unsteadily on his feet, Portus nodded. He seemed overcome by emotion. Suddenly repulsed by the alcoholic smell of him, Meeriam pulled away. "What—" Then she understood, and sympathy fought with revulsion. "Oh, Portus, what have you done?"

But the good doctor didn't seem to notice anything wrong. "Love—ly day—going to be hot—haven't seen you—long time—" He pulled a sad white handkerchief from inside his heavy coat and wiped perspiration from his face. His hand trembled.

"You—you don't look as though you feel well, Portus." She didn't know how to acknowledge all she saw. "Are you here alone?"

"Came up—came up to see—" An expression of helpless confusion swept his wrinkled face, as if he suddenly wondered where he was—why he was—

Doctor, she said speaking only to his mind, *let me take you home.*

"Home. Good idea. Chance to talk—haven't seen you—worried—"

Conscious of the crowd around, Meeriam felt another wave of uneasiness, stronger than before. She didn't want either of them to attract attention.

A silence falling on the crowd gave her pause. Concentrating on Portus, she had not been aware of what had drawn the attention of the people around her, but quietly the crowd parted, letting a couple make their way through. She caught her breath. The shock of recognition caused her heart to pound. Ellis Hagan. It could be no other. Once or twice she'd almost caught glimpses of him, arriving at a place to learn that he'd just left. But always, always just missing him. Yet, here he was.

With Luan Kassine possessively clutching his arm.

Knowing that Grandmother would chide her for being judgmental, still Meeriam couldn't control the contempt that swept her as she eyed the Matriarch's daughter. How could she flaunt Hagan before the whole colony? Didn't she have any idea what it did to her mother? And Hagan—how could he allow it? Yet, as they passed she was caught by another emotion in

Hagan's eyes. A fleeting, bone deep bitterness that was gone the moment he realized she was staring at him with such intensity.

Blushing, she turned away, but still felt shaken by a strange resonance that seemed to have passed between them.

"Elias?" Portus wiped his face again, his voice a rough, shaken whisper, and his eyes watery. "Was that Elias?"

"No, not Elias."Meeriam put her arm around Portus's shoulder. She was frightened. This was no place for either of them. "Let's go home, Doctor."

Lurching from his support beneath the stand, the good doctor agreed.

Obeying the General's silent command to join him, Hagan felt the civilian crowd grow quiet as he and Luan passed through. It was the first time since the general's reception he'd been on such public display and he was surprised at how deeply he resented it. Luan, who'd been with a group of young officers, hadn't missed the General's gesture, and had come hurrying to his side. No doubt proud to be seen with him. He felt like he was shriveling up inside. This wasn't a play. It was a bawdy-house joke. And the joke was on him. Maybe in the dream the eagle killed himself.

Unlike an audience before which he could play someone not himself, this crowd gave him no comfort. Two thousand people, maybe more, had come to the ceremonies this day. Had come to stare at the participants the way an angry audience at a badly performed play might stare at the responsible players. Could Graeber be so insensitive he didn't feel the hostility radiating from these people?

And then to come so suddenly upon Portus. Looking sick, and old, and confused. His first impulse had been to stop, but he knew he couldn't. There'd been no sign of recognition in the doctor's watery eyes. And the last thing he wanted to do was draw Graeber's attention to the old man.

As the crowd closed in behind them Hagan thought of the dark-haired girl who'd been with Portus. He'd felt her contempt like a knife, and it made him angry. Who was she? What right did she have to judge him?

Climbing the stand, he glanced back, searching until he

found them again. The girl seemed to be urging some action on Portus, though what good it would do he didn't know when Portus seemed too blind drunk to hear. Kali had been right. The good doctor was drowning in his cheery.

"Ah," the General's unctuous voice radiating anger brought him abruptly back to the matter at hand. "Captain Hagan, so glad you could grace our little celebration with your presence."

Graeber, standing on the next step up, pointedly waited for Hagan to approach. Hagan hesitated, and the words that he'd been thinking all morning once more rushed to the surface of his mind.

"A celebration in honor of death. It boggles the imagination, General."

He heard Luan's sharp intake of breath, felt her withdraw from him as though afraid of guilt by association. He almost was amused. Nothing else had pried her away.

Graeber's thick white brows beetled over his deep set eyes. His skin took on a mottled hue, and he fingered the tool at his thigh as though he wished he could use it. The psychoprobe. Hagan's brief amusement fled. He met the General's fanatic eyes and what he might have added was silenced by the General's convulsive shake of the head. "Not death, captain. Victory. We celebrate a victory."

Over people who refused to fight back? Sickened, Hagan was the first to look away. Out, over the heads of the crowd, to the edge of the common.

Almost in passing he noticed the girl and Portus making unsteady progress in the direction of the path that led down into the town.

Though he couldn't meet the general's eyes, he felt Graeber's unspoken insistence that he play his part, that he treat this whole wake as a party.

Then Graeber spoke again, softly, for his ears alone. "You sometimes exhibit your father's more intolerable qualities, young Hagan. Walk carefully, lest you follow his path."

Stunned to silence, Hagan watched the General turn away. The softly spoken words were the closest thing to an outright threat Graeber had yet delivered. And the General's eyes— Hagan hid a shiver. The man was mad. He had to be. Glancing at Luan to see what she might have made of the General's words, he discovered the Matriarch's daughter was already making her way to the seats left vacant for them at the General's side.

Then, from somewhere off to the left beyond the Gathering Hall, came the sound of marching music, and a shouted command. From the crowd rose a feeble cheer that gathered strength and swept over the common green and the crowded stands like a giant wave. A marching unit came into view, colors flying in the breeze, whipping over the color-guard's sleek black-helmeted heads.

Sick to the point of nausea, Hagan knew he couldn't join in this celebration. If Graeber wanted to show off a tame Ellis Hagan, he'd have to find another way. While everyone's attention was riveted to the marching units, Hagan slipped back down the aisle and pushed his way through the standees at the foot of the steps.

Cynically he realized these people didn't care why a celebration was being held. All they wanted now was to lose themselves in the pageantry as humans had lost themselves down through the ages. They wanted to forget their woes. Any excuse would do. Even death.

Blindly Hagan walked away from the noise and the crowd. How could these people not see what was happening? How could they not realize how Graeber pushed them, molded their thoughts, how he used them for his own purposes and schemes?

Hagan could almost hear Kali's dry voice urging him to see for himself. Well, now he had, and the sight made him ill.

Minutes later, without watching where his steps had taken him, Hagan found himself on the same path as that chosen by Portus and the girl, and he hesitated. Portus wouldn't want to see him. Not after going to such great lengths to stay out of his way these last few weeks.

With a sigh, Hagan had almost decided to turn back to the so called celebration when a sudden cry pierced his mind.

Then was gone again.

His skin prickled. Had he heard it? Imagined it? No, of course not. He'd actually heard it. From ahead of him, on the path. Had the girl cried out? Had Portus fallen?

Moving quickly to the edge of the green, Hagan caught sight

of them only a short way down the path, the girl struggling to keep Portus upright, Portus leaning so far over he looked as though he would push her into the ground.

Quickly reaching them, Hagan shifted the weight of Portus off the girl's shoulders. "Here, let me help."

Though she paled at the sight of him, the girl seemed to recover quickly. "You? What can you do?" A world of scorn laced her husky voice.

As though in answer to her question, Portus's knees gave way, and Hagan took the older man's full weight into his arms, lifting Portus before he reached the dirt of the path. As her attention darted back to the doctor, dismay touched eyes. "Is he—is he all right?"

"Drunker than a pig eating lotus weed." And twice as heavy, added Hagan to himself, grunting with effort.

The girl's dismay turned to anger. "You don't have to make a joke about it, Captain Hagan."

Not surprised by her recognition, Hagan grunted again. "Believe me, it's no joke." He felt a spasm pass through Portus's body. "Quick, now. Let's find a place to lay him down. He's getting sick." Indeed, Portus had begun to retch, deep dry heaves that shook his whole frame. Moving off the path into thick trees, Hagan found a bare grassy hollow and knelt, letting Portus slip gently to the ground. Groaning, the old man turned on his side and curled in upon himself, spasmodically convulsed, then lay still. Though he wouldn't tell the girl so, Hagan was worried. Portus looked awful. His breathing was shallow and gasping, his skin hot and dry and flushed.Carefully Hagan removed Portus's heavy cloak and made a pillow for the old man's head.

"I think we should take him home," said the girl.

"Where does he stay?"

"He has rooms at Darrow Tower."

Had he been that close? Hagan felt a pain that was almost physical. Why hadn't Vana Darrow told him when he asked? But even so, today no one would be there, and obviously Portus needed someone to take care of him. "No one's there.Will you stay with him?"

The girl worried her lip. "No, I can't.And the clinic's not

ready."

Decision entered her eyes. "I'll take him home with me. No one will mind."

Though she said so, for a moment she appeared doubtful.

Sitting back on his heels, Hagan watched the various emotions running across her face. Worry seemed to be predominate, but there was also something else. Something he couldn't identify. Twenty-five earth years, he'd guess, with a smooth, sun-drenched complexion that went well with her dark hair and darker eyes. Her skin, he knew, would feel like the finest Mars-made satin.

Irritated at the direction his thoughts had taken, Hagan pushed the idea away. But still he studied her. Not tall, like a native Arcolan might be, yet she was built in perfect proportion of waist to breast, of hip to leg. Even dressed in the long green tunic of a Freefarmer and kneeling by Portus in the high and concealing spring grass, there was an inherent grace about her that kept him staring long after it was polite to do so.

Again that feeling of subtle recognition pushed its way into his mind. The feeling grew that he should know her. Then she turned to him and the feeling fled.

"Don't just sit there. Do something!"

"What do you suggest?" His tone seemed to catch its asperity from hers. He was reminded forcefully of the earlier contempt in her eyes. "Or are you one of those people always willing to complain that nothing's done, but never willing to be doing it yourself?"

Her mouth tightened. Obviously she hadn't expected his attack. Before she could vent a sharp retort Portus groaned loudly, and tried to sit up.

Forgetting each other, Hagan and the girl were one in gently restraining the old man.

"Meeriam?" Portus peered up into the girl's face, confusion clouding his eyes.

"Yes, Portus." She caught his hand and held it tightly.

"Y'shouldn't be here. Dangerous. Elias knows better—"

Tears filled the girl's eyes. "It's all right, Portus. We're safe."

"Not safe. Not safe anywhere." Portus's voice roared into the quiet and battled briefly with the echoes of distant marching music and distant cheering crowd. "Damn Elias. Not safe. I've told him—" Abruptly Portus turned and stared directly into Hagan's startled eyes. "Damn you, 'Lias, you'll get her killed. I told you."

"It's all right, Portus." Hagan gripped the old man's thin shoulder in gentle reassurance. "I'm taking care of it."

Portus's face grew slack, and his eyelids drooped. "Send her back to Lissone, 'Lias, you promised you would. Do it before— too late." His voice slid to softness and he slumped against the girl.

Send her back to Lissone? Shock rippled through Hagan, but he schooled his face into deliberate miscomprehension. "Poor old man is delirious. The sooner we get him to bed the better."

"Yes." Meeriam choked on the word, but Hagan gave her no more than a cursory glance, though it was a glance that told him much. She had paled, and seemed to be waiting for him to make the obvious connections.

His thoughts churned, splintered. She was a Firewing, and that thought brought its own fear. She also was the girl his father had been involved with—oh, yes, more than one person had mentioned her, including Luan. Even Velia, with her vituperative tongue, though they all thought she was a Freefarmer. At first he'd disregarded the gossip as being totally without foundation. Whatever he was, the Commander of Kama hadn't been foolish enough to have a young camp follower hanging around.

But if she really was a Firewing—that thought spawned a realm of possibilities, but before he could examine them, Portus groaned again, clutching at his stomach, heaving again.

"Please," Meeriam's voice was softly pleading. "We must get him home."

All other matters aside, Hagan agreed that Portus should be put to bed. He'd knelt to scoop the old man back into his arms when the girl abruptly stood and placed a restraining hand on his shoulder. "No, wait. Someone's coming down the path. Soldiers."

Again Hagan had to agree. He, too had just heard them. "Yes. Here, keep Portus quiet, will you. I'll go head them off."

"Wait." Before she could utter the protest Hagan was on his feet and moving toward the path. "Please," she called after him softly, "be careful. They're looking for you. The General's orders."

Her words made his skin prickled with unnamed fear. Her knowledge scared him. And what would the General's orders be, Hagan wondered bitterly. Would she read their minds and let him know? Would she read his thoughts and know how much he feared her kind?

The voices of the approaching soldiers made him thrust those thoughts aside. He had other worries more pressing than the Firewing girl. He sensed that Portus was a bigger danger to her right now that the Commander had ever been.

Not questioning why he should want to protect her, he moved silently down the path. Here in the thick trees below the curve of the hill, shafts of sunlight penetrated to the hip-high brush and cast areas of brilliant light next to splashes of dark shade. Standing very still against an ancient tree, Hagan watched the soldiers at a distance grouped around Captain Moss.

There were four soldiers beside the Captain.

Even as Hagan watched, Moss pointed down the trail toward the town and the four men trotted around the first curve, then disappeared from view. Then, deliberately, Moss turned his head, searching. Hagan remained frozen, knowing he would be almost impossible to see, but wondering why Moss seemed so sure he was somewhere near. Had Portus already given them away? If so, why hadn't Moss sent the men in their direction?

Patiently he waited, hardly daring to breathe. Willing distance and shadows to hide him. Finally Moss, as if accepting that his instincts had for once played him false, gave up his search, started down the path that the other men had taken.

When Moss disappeared around the same curve that had swallowed his men earlier, Hagan broke his stance and hurried back to the girl and Portus. But the question puzzled him. If Moss was so certain he was still hidden on the hill, why hadn't he sent his men to search here?

Moss, he decided, also would bear thinking about.

Though she gently quieted the old man, Meeriam's mental eye followed Hagan back down into the trees. Her reactions to him had astonished her. She'd thought to stay angry, but she wasn't. She'd thought, from the few curt words Elias had spoken about him, that she would mistrust him, but she didn't. She'd thought, moreover, that he looked cruel and unfeeling in his black uniform with its blood red stripe down the leg, but somehow he wasn't. Not any more so than Elias had been. In truth, Ellis Hagan wasn't anything she believed him to be.

So much like Elias, and yet—and yet—on the verge of a strange discovery, Meeriam drew back. Elias had been a fine, strong man. A friend who had shared some of his deepest thoughts with her. His son had been shown to be—was—shallow. He wasn't worthy of the respect Elias had drawn from all who knew him. Elias's son didn't dream the dreams Elias had dreamed.

As it had in the past when memories of Elias came, the pain of loss swept over her, but now it was a gentler pain. A tiny voice of hope seemed to insist on rising. Perhaps Elias hadn't died in vain. Perhaps this son—

Rocking Portus against her, quieting him as if he were one of the children of Lissone, Meeriam couldn't voice her hope. Against all odds, it was enough to know it was there.

Why had he really come back?

When Hagan reappeared in the clearing, Meeriam searched his face, trying to pick up his thoughts without penetrating his mind. Why she hesitated to do that when it came so naturally to her she wasn't sure. Somehow she knew he'd resent her probing, that maybe it would even frighten him. She didn't want to frighten him. But though she studied his expression, his face was hard and unyielding of his intentions, until, looking down at Portus, his expression softened into concern.

"Did the soldiers go back?" Meeriam asked.

"They went on down the path toward town." Hagan knelt beside her. "Can we move him now?"

"I think we must."

"All right." Hagan slipped his arms under Portus. The necessary contact with his hands made her catch her breath and then Portus's weight was gone from her arms and Hagan stood smoothly, as if he were lifting a child rather than the dead weight of an unconscious man. He smiled reassuringly. "Lead the way."

The trip down the hill, through thick forest and sun-dappled glades, deep shadow and patches of golden afternoon sun seemed to take forever. They spoke little, Meeriam concentrating on avoiding soldiers and citizens alike, Hagan seeming to concentrate all his effort on giving Portus a safe and easy ride. Twice he called a halt, allowing himself a small respite, and each time Meeriam agreed, though her impatience would have made them move on.

The third time was when she would have had him turn in at the back gates of the Processing plant.

Hagan stopped and allowed Portus to slip down into the tall grass. "Is this where you live?" His tone was definitely disapproving.

"Yes."

"With the plant workers?"

"No. At the house."

Suspicion flared in Hagan's eyes. Portus's words had not fallen on stone ears. She damped down a sudden pain.

Stupid Arcolans with their more stupid prejudices. Why should she care? Why indeed? She was proud of the abilities she possessed. And Elias had been proud of her too. Firewing, the Arcolans might call them, but they were more than that silly name implied. They were Earth's Children. She had more right here than this—this —

"Does Kassine know what she harbors under her roof?" Hagan's voice was harsh with a mixture of anger, and a touch of the fear she hadn't wanted him to feel.

An unaccountable pain brought tears to her eyes. No, please don't be frightened of me, she wanted to say. But she had no chance.

Hagan's voice was cold. "I'm sure you can get someone to help you from here." Before she could reply, he turned on his heel and disappeared the way they had come.

Chapter 12

Norcanna Bay

Hagan stalked up the path through the forested hill toward the common green. The soft cadence of martial music drifted like the scent of smoke through the trees. The sound of it sent a shiver down his back.

God, didn't she realize what a chance she took living in the Colony right under Graeber's nose? As he reached the stone steps and started climbing his anger at her foolishness vied with his anger at the Commander of Kama, who should have known better than to have involved her in Colony affairs.

Had the Commander been in love with her? No, damn it. As he had before, Hagan rejected the idea. Not that it wasn't possible. Hell, anything was possible. But Elias had been so single-minded about the safety of the Firewing. The standing order had been to avoid them at all cost. The Commander had never let his troops enter a Firewing camp, nor had he ever thrown a cerafoam road near a sacred ground. He'd kept all Freefarmers to the valley side of the Kama River. It'd been Hagan's own disobedience of the rules that had brought about tragedy. The death of Patlos.

Deliberately his mind slid away from that memory and its ensuing pain. He considered instead Graeber, who now had road crews busy throwing ribbon roads for the HOGGS across the river, spanning the gullies, climbing ever deeper into the high country where the Firewing could no longer hide.

There was no doubt in his mind now that Graeber was pushing toward the Ancient City. Probing the various passes for an old roadway that had once been there. Hagan himself expected soon he'd be given a unit and sent to the mountains. Graeber had hinted as much not two days before, and he was looking forward to it. Surely the further he went before he had to strike out on his own, the better off he'd be.

He frowned. Maybe today's small mutiny would change Graeber's mind. Or make Graeber more determined. Again Hagan shivered.

Catching a dark movement in the shadows above him, Hagan felt the hair raise on his neck. He thought of the young Firewing in Kassine's garden, then rejected the idea at some inner level of knowing before he even realized it.

A soldier. It was a soldier up there waiting for him. The sure knowledge didn't make him feel any better. He'd rather meet the Firewing again than some of the soldiers Graeber had brought from Mars. Kali would be sick when he realized how easily Graeber was slipping them through. Cavern soldiers, most of them. Experts at retraining. Continuing upward Hagan tried to pierce the lengthening shadows. Only one? Yes, one. He sensed no others. The martial music, louder now, almost drowned out the quiet afternoon birdcalls, stilled the wind sounds and made loud accompaniment to his quick-beating heart. There. There he was.

Spotting Hagan, the soldier, who'd been leaning against a lichen-covered retaining wall straightened.

Moss. Hagan was relieved it wasn't Galt.

Hagan's relief lasted only a second before being replaced by wariness, and he paused in his climb. There was no surprise on the lanky Captain's face. Obviously Moss had been waiting for him.

Nor was there menace in the soldier's stance. What did he want? Hagan climbed a few more steps, then stopped, waited for the soldier to speak first.

Moss walked down the steep steps toward Hagan, a small, unexpected half smile moving across his face. "You always could outwit me."

Warily Hagan acknowledged the captain. Should he trust the incipient friendliness in the other's smile? "You've always had a streak of impatience hidden beneath that placid exterior."

"Unfortunately not tempered with age." The smile faded from Moss's eyes. "I wondered if you'd come back this way."

"Were you looking for me?" Not for Earth itself would Hagan admit he'd seen the soldier earlier. Though they'd once been friends, this Moss was still a stranger, one who jumped to the General's commands as quickly as Galt did.

"Yes. As you well know."

Hagan let that comment pass. "Did the General send you?" In spite of his resolve bitterness slipped into his voice.

"Yes. But I've already sent word back that I was unsuccessful in the hunt. I said I'd keep looking."

"Very commendable," Hagan said dryly.

"I do my job." Moss's smile disappeared altogether. "You had me worried, you know."

"Why? Where is there to go?" Hiding his uneasiness behind a borrowed Jolando intensity, Hagan shrugged. "I had to come back eventually."

"Come back to Earth, you mean?" asked Moss, seeming to read a different meaning into Hagan's words.

With a strange jolt of recognition, Hagan realized that Moss was sounding more like the friend he'd had at Kama Garrison than a member of Graeber's staff. But could he accept this turnabout at face value?

Moss seemed to understand his hesitation. "You're wise to be careful what you say, El. Things are never what they seem any more, and there are few now in the Colony one can trust."

"Even you?"

"Maybe." The lanky soldier eyed him sadly. "When word came on our nightscreen that you'd disappeared after the Commander died, I was afraid you'd been eliminated like so many of our other dissidents. Bets were being laid in the messroom that you wouldn't turn up alive."

"Which way did you bet?"

Moss turned a rare, quick smile on him again. One that seemed to draw them back to an earlier, more carefree time. "Both ways."

Hagan laughed. This was the Moss he remembered, the friend he'd thought he'd lost. "Hedged your bets, did you?"

"Of course. Wouldn't you? Anyway, I just wanted you to know that it was damned good to see you turn up."

Moss's words left Hagan with an even deeper chill. "But I wasn't soon enough, was I?"

"Had you been here, you couldn't have prevented the Commander's death. He was on a collision course with Graeber

135

from the moment Graeber arrived, and he knew it. In the end it seemed he didn't even care."

Hagan studied the open grief that shone from Moss's eyes. "He always thought highly of you. Couldn't you have helped him? Or at least, talked to him?"

"You know better than that. When the Commander got an idea into his head, nothing dislodged it."

Hagan knew that, better than anyone. Hadn't the Commander proved it himself, that last time—the pain of memory weighted his shoulders. He'd never understood his father's fury that last time they'd met. Anger he'd expected. He was angry with himself. Sick at what he'd done in a moment of blind panic. But his father's unreasoning rage—his wild words—

Moss was regarding him curiously, and Hagan stifled the memories. It served no purpose to remember it all now. "The Commander thought all Firewing were his brothers. What Graeber was doing must have been hard on him."

"Made him well-nigh wild. Worse than he was after you left." Moss held Hagan's gaze and his sincerity couldn't be mistaken. "The Commander took it hard when you left."

Though he'd struggled to repress them, the memories flooded back again, and Hagan couldn't escape the pain. "It wasn't my choice. He cashiered me without ceremony. He banished me from the Colony. He told me if I ever came back he would kill me."

Moss's dark eyes reflected Hagan's pain. "By God, Ellis, for what?"

Briefly Hagan thought of the girl, Meeriam. What would she think of him if she knew—his anguish became a physical thing, making his whole body ache. "For killing a Firewing."

Had he actually admitted to Moss he'd killed a Firewing? In the early evening after the civilians had all gone home, and the soldiers had moved to the the barracks mess to continue their celebration, Hagan had returned to his new barracks apartment to change his clothes, and await the summons he was sure the General would issue. Luan was nowhere to be seen and if his small rebellion today had driven her away he would think it a good day's work.

The fact that he'd said out loud to Moss what he'd never said before to another living soul except his father made him doubt his sanity. What would Moss do with the knowledge? Face to face with Moss, the old trust that had once been between than had returned, but after they'd parted, Moss to go back and report Hagan had been found, Hagan wondered if he hadn't made a gigantic mistake. Moss, after all, had made himself into someone Graeber also trusted.

Life had been easier under the Domes.

Shrugging into a fresh shirt, Hagan visualized for a moment that special time just before the curtain rose, the intensity, the flutter of dread. Meeting Danielle's eyes and exchanging unspoken excitement just before Ben whispered "time."

Now he felt only the dread, not the excitement. Then, inexplicably, an image of the Firewing girl, Meeriam, took Danielle's place. The way she'd looked down at Portus as she cushioned him within the circle of her arms. A loneliness, an almost desperate longing, rose in him. There would be a place to find comfort, to find forgetfulness.

But then, as he enlarged on that image, another arose. Himself baring her breast for his lips and tongue.

Before he had time to banish the thought, and its effect on him, a sharp rap came on the door. A voice called out. "Captain Hagan? You in there, sir?"

At the first word the fantasy splintered. Was this Graeber's summons? "Yes?"

The voice was young, and uncertain of its reception. "Sir, Lieutenant Loomis here. The General sent me. He wants you in his office, sir. On the double."

Hagan drew a deep, steadying breath. It was indeed what he'd expected.. "All right. I'll be there in a moment." Quickly he tucked in the tail on his shirt and shrugged into his jacket.

Out in the long hall that led to the barracks common room, the young soldier drew himself to attention. Surprised to see him still waiting, Hagan cocked an ironic eyebrow. "Still here?"

The young soldier's cheeks flushed. "I've been appointed your aide, sir."

In spite of his worry Hagan laughed. "Aide? An aide to

137

an aide? Or to aid me to the general's office?" Wryly Hagan
wondered where he'd picked up this habit of babbling.

'"N-no, sir. Just Aide." Lieutenant Loomis didn't elaborate.

With the young lieutenant walking quickly at Hagan's side,
Hagan strode off down the hall. What the hell did he need with
an aide? With as little as he had been given to do an aide would
be superfluous. "Has the General told you what you were to
aide me in doing?"

"The General mentioned maps, sir. You're also to have your
own private carriage, and I'm to drive you—and, and if you go
out, I'm to go along—"

Abruptly Hagan halted. "Oh, I see," he was no longer
amused, "you're my keeper." In other words, the General would
have no more of this disappearing on the pathways.

Lt. Loomis, whose smooth cheeks made him seem very
young, flushed more deeply than before. "He didn't actually say
that, sir."

No, of course he wouldn't. But would the lieutenant go
running back to Graeber if Hagan met the girl in town? Would
he report conversations like the one Hagan had with Moss this
afternoon? Taking another deep breath to still an incipient panic,
Hagan eyed Loomis. "I need you like I need a third boot."

The youngster drew himself up in youthful dignity. "I'm
sorry you feel that way, sir."

"So am I." Abruptly Hagan started off again, ashamed that
he'd taken out his irritation with the General on a hapless young
man who looked no more dangerous than someone's pet bird.
Another young soldier who, Hagan reminded himself, was also
only following orders.

"I suppose you come highly recommended?"

Relief on his face, the young man lengthened his own stride
to match Hagan's. "Captain Moss suggested it, sir."

An hour later as Hagan shrugged deeper into his jacket
against the chill of the map room, he had time to consider
Loomis's last statement. Graeber, coldly informing him that
his absence had been noted, had in the next breath ordered his
presence down below. Graeber himself had led the way down
the steps carved into the bedrock under the Gathering Hall,
through massive doors that might better guard a king's tomb,

and into a long, well-lit room of low ceilings, flat file-tables, and blank white walls.

Loomis accompanied them, but stayed unobtrusively on the edge of the room, and beyond the edge of the conversation. Hagan liked the way the younger man carried himself around the General. Respectful without being subservient. After one raking glance, the General ignored him. Hagan almost smiled. Being ignored by the General was no mean feat. Moss had chosen well.

"Our maps of Earth are pitiful," Graeber growled, still enlarging on a theme he'd begun almost the moment Hagan had appeared. "Those fools on the High Council think they can point their telescopes in our direction and find out all they need to know. And those idiots at Xanthe are even worse. God knows they think they can punch in the coordinates of this and that and come up with a complete picture." The General's heavy brows lowered, giving his face that flat, toadish appearance. "It's impossible of course. No one knows what Earth is really like."

Pulling a tray from a bank of similar trays that lined one cabinet, Graeber went on. "One of our prime functions should be to map Earth as it is now, but where are the cartographers? Why hasn't Mars sent me cartographers? Why didn't they make maps during those first few trips, before they actually landed on the planet? Or did they?"

Hagan hid a jolt of surprise. What was Graeber getting at?

Fishing through the templates Graeber's fingers seemed too massive to be capable of the delicate maneuvering needed to grasp one small square, but when he dropped a template into a waiting slot, Hagan forgot the incongruity of size. One white wall became a screen, and the lights altered subtly, leaving the map appearing in full relief and the rest of the room in shadows.

Hagan's soldier-trained eye immediately appreciated the detail in the map on the wall, even as he felt an instant dismay that so much of the adjacent Firewing territory had already been penetrated. The Commander wouldn't have allowed it, came his first angry thought.

"As you see," Graeber went on, "we've made some progress in the last few months."

Since the Commander had died?

"But, as you can also see, the mountains to the South-east remain a barrier. Xanthe has informed us that all that remains beyond is high barren desert. That we must expand North and West. Bah! North to the ice? West to the Great Ocean? Do they think I am a complete fool?"

Against his better judgment Hagan felt impelled to comment. "Surely the ocean would temper the climate and the continent in that direction perhaps give us other valleys like the Kama?"

"For what? Do they want us to be a nation of farmers?"

They don't want us to be a nation at all, Hagan thought, but a moment later when Graeber spun on him, was glad he hadn't said it out loud.

"Those idiots on the Council think they will keep us a small subservient subculture on the face of this immense planet. But this world is too vast, too vast I say, to be contained and it's our natural element." Graeber's eyes took on a mad gleam. "Think of it, Ellis, think of the world once more teeming with life, think of us once more reaching for the stars!"

With what technology? That hidden at Phoenix?

Hagan studied the map more closely. Nowhere was there indicated the possibility of the Ancient City beyond the mountains. He thought of the map Merrick had given him that he'd committed to memory and then destroyed. As though his memory were a template, he fitted it over the map on the wall. There. Right there was where Merrick thought the Ancient City lay.

Maybe Merrick was also insane. He became conscious that Graeber was waiting for his comment. "It's a fantastic vision," he said slowly.

"And it is our destiny." Graeber's cold eyes pinned Hagan, willing him to seek the same vision. "Ours, Ellis." His voice softened persuasively. "With your help we can make it happen in our lifetime."

"Make what happen?" Hagan didn't have to pretend astonishment. Graeber was admitting an ambition that could only get him in trouble. He must be either very sure of himself, or very sure than Hagan would go nowhere to spread the tale. Either way, Hagan felt the chill of fear.

Graeber snorted. "The High Council thinks it can keep us

contained here in Norcanna Bay. They think the Firewing will block my crossing the mountains. But nothing will stop me." Graeber's voice dropped to a whisper. "Nothing."

"And what of the Freefarmers, General? What part will they play?"

"Farmers!" The General spat out the word as though it burnt his tongue. "We don't need more farmers. We need the technicians, the engineers. We need our own factories, our own industry. We need machines and air ships. Those are what we need to conquer this Earth." With his final words Graeber slammed his hand down on the flat-topped counter, and from the corner of his eye Hagan saw Loomis wince.

Kali had called Graeber crazy. He was, and it took all of Hagan's acting skill to pretend that he didn't see it. "There's nowhere on Earth we can get what we need, General."

A flash of cunning appeared in Graeber's eyes. "Yes there is. The Ancient City. Phoenix. It's out there on the high desert waiting for us. Filled with more technology than we can use."

Goosebumps raised on Hagan's skin. "That's a tale told by the Firewing, General."

"No, more than that, Ellis. Much more than that." The General drew himself to his full height and still came no higher than Hagan's shoulder. Throwing an arm out, he indicated the whole of the map room. "This is now your domain. You will correlate all information as it comes in, and produce the maps we will need to cross the mountains."

Hagan knew it would be in character to protest the assignment, what he said was only the truth. "I know nothing of maps, sir."

"Then you'll learn. We have one technician. One. He runs that drawing machine over there. A month's work is backed up, waiting to be entered. We need that information as soon as possible. You have one week, Ellis. One week in which to learn and produce." Graeber's smile struck a chill. "I expect results."

For five days, cut off from Colony events while she sat by Portus's bed, Meeriam wondered what had happened to Ellis Hagan. Surely if he'd not made it back to the barracks on the hill the news would have been all over Norcanna by now. And surely, if the General had leveled some punishment against him for leaving the ceremonies, that too would have made the rounds.

She finally dredged up a measure of courage and asked Gerald, and was reassured by his answer. Gerald had contacts within the General's staff that even she did not know about, and his contacts told him that Ellis Hagan was safe.

Truly, with Portus so sick, she should not worry about the Commander's son. Portus, in his delirium, made little sense, but she came to realize that Graeber was the shadow Portus feared, the hunter that stalked his dreams and she was saddened. If Graeber had deliberately set out to drive poor Portus mad, he could have done no better job. With all her healing arts she could do no more than quiet and soothe the old man, and wait for his own spirit to heal him.

On the fifth day Portus slipped into a more natural sleep. When Gerald came to relieve her while she went to eat, she could not help but smile. "He's better." Though she spoke softly, the relief she felt made her voice light.

"Good."

Meeriam's smile faded, and abruptly she felt the weight of the past five days pressing her down. "It is the alcohol, isn't it?"

Gerald agreed.

"Will he—can he—" Meeriam wasn't sure exactly what she was asking, but Gerald seemed to know.

"Don't expect too much, child. He may be fine, but also he may not. Alcohol's an insidious master, and Portus is a troubled man."

Thinking of some of the incoherent ramblings she'd heard over the past days, Meeriam understood what Gerald meant. Poor Portus. Poor man. So much fear in him. So much fear everywhere, if the truth be known.

In sympathy with her thoughts as always, Gerald gave her a small hug. "Go eat your dinner, child. I'll stay with Portus awhile."

Meeriam let herself be comforted. "I won't be long."

"Take your time. Vana Kassine has already retired." Gerald's eyes grew cold. "She had an early meal with Vana Luan."

Immediately Meeriam understood what Gerald wasn't saying. Any meeting with her demanding daughter exhausted the Matriarch, and any meal, no matter how palatable, became ashes on her tongue when eaten in Luan's presence. Meeriam had tried very hard, early in their acquaintance, not to pass judgment on the older girl, but it was hard not to do so. Especially now, when she was linked by everyone with Ellis Hagan.

Or am I merely jealous? That thought was also unpalatable.

Before she had time to even consider it a soft knock sounded at the door and a young house-girl entered. "Van Nilander, there's a soldier at the gate—"

Alarmed, Meeriam turned to Gerald, but he was already pushing his inner sight out to encompass the perimeters of Kassine's property. He frowned. It wasn't who he'd expected. "Young Hagan?"

The girl nodded. "Yes. Captain Hagan."

Meeriam's startled gaze sought Gerald, but if Gerald was surprised, he at least gave no indication to the young girl at the door. "Who is he asking for, child?"

"Dr. Portus, sir, and like you said to do, I said he wasn't here. Now the Captain is asking for you. I said I would see if you were in."

Glancing at the old man who was sleeping naturally for the first time in days, Gerald frowned. Would young Hagan be a hindrance or a help? And then he studied Meeriam's pale face and sensed the feminine turmoil just below her schooled features. Easily he read in her both the strong attraction she had for Hagan and the fear of that same emotion. He read her, in fact, better than she read herself, and though he wished he could protect her from the pain the attraction might bring, he knew he had no right. "Very well, let him in. But see that he comes straight down here. I'll not have him disturbing Vana Kassine."

"Yes, sir."

Meeriam argued in her mind. *Gerald, is it wise to let him in?*

He's worried about Portus, Gerald replied. *Let him see that we're taking care of the good doctor.*

But—

143

Allow it child. I have my reasons.

Not sure that she actually wanted to see Ellis Hagan again, Gerald sensed that Meeriam would've argued further, but at that moment Portus groaned softly and his eyes flickered open. Panic flashed into the old doctor's mind, and both Meeriam and Gerald read it in the changed atmosphere of the room. As Gerald paused at the door, Meeriam hurried to the old man's side and caught his trembling hand in her strong firm grip. "Hush, Portus, it's all right. You're safe with us."

"Meeriam?" Relief filled Portus's watery eyes.

"Yes."

"Thank God—" With vaguely unfocused eyes, Portus swept the unfamiliar room. "Where—"

"Vana Kassine's. I—we brought you home."

Portus accepted her statement without question, his hands trembling in hers, his eyes closing on a new source of pain. "I—I thought I saw Elias."

"No. Not the Commander, Portus. His son."

If anything the old man grew more pale. "Ellis?" he whispered. "Here?"

"Yes. He's been here some weeks now. Don't you remember??

"No—yes—"

With a frown, Gerald shut the door on the old man's anguished voice and paused in the silent hall, considering. He had compassion for the old doctor, thrust as he was into a situation totally beyond his control. Feeling so separate, so alone with his fear. Loneliness was an emotion rarely experienced by the People, who had only to reach out with mind to touch Mind. But not unheard of, as he himself could attest.

Especially, he smiled wryly, when nothing seemed to go as it should. Taking a deep breath, he fortified himself for the coming confrontation, because he knew with certainty another was coming.

Gerald reached the bottom of the stairs just as the click of hard boots filled the late afternoon silence. Caught in the last rays of the sun slanting through the tall thin windows of the stairwell Hagan came halfway down, then stopped, his gaze colliding with Gerald's. Hagan more slowly descended the last few steps.

"Welcome to the House of Kassine," Gerald said, his voice echoing softly in the vastness of the lower hall.

Chapter 13

Norcanna Bay

Pulling rein on his impatience Hagan studied Gerald Nilander, trying to read in unreadable eyes what his reception might be. "Am I welcome?" His quiet words echoed. All week, cooped up in the basement-level map room he'd worried about Portus, and about the Firewing girl who was protecting him. Even so, had it only been the worry driving him, he wouldn't have come. No, there was something more now. Something damaging that demanded answers only Portus could give. Confrontation with his step-mother Velia was at hand, and he had to have the information locked in Portus's mind so that he would know how to counter her wild charges. God, if even half of what she said was true—

"If you truly come in peace, you are welcome."

"I do. I've come to see Portus. I know the girl at the gate said he wasn't here, but—" Hagan couldn't explain the feeling of knowing that he had. He had no explanation of it himself. He simply 'knew' that Portus was still at Kassine's. Just as he 'knew' there had to be some truth to Velia's charges.

"Purely a safety measure, Captain." Nilander gestured back down the hall. "He's with my niece at the moment. He's only just now awakened from a long sleep. He's still very ill."

"I hoped he'd be better now. He was in a bad way when we brought him down the hill last week."

Not by a twitch of a muscle nor the darkening of the eye did Nilander show Hagan's words surprised him, but Hagan had the impression it was true. "We're all happy that he seems lucid," Gerald finally admitted.

"May I see him, then?"

Kassine's superintendent hesitated. Hagan read indecision in his eyes. Then Nilander smiled. "Could I stop you, even if I wanted to? Come this way."

Had Portus been Kassine, Hagan knew he'd never have been

allowed to enter into her presence. Nilander's protectiveness toward the Matriarch was legendary, as was his knowledge of everything that went on in the Colony. In earlier, less wise years, Hagan had resented Nilander's intrusion into business he considered his and his alone. Now he accepted that Nilander was a man whose years of authority under Kassine had given him a wisdom and knowledge any intelligent being would acquire under the same set of circumstances.

Until he stepped into the shadow-washed room and saw the girl who knelt at Portus's side.

What the hell—

The Firewing girl, Meeriam? Unbidden, both fear and fantasies returned full-force. Then Nilander banished the fantasies and increased his fear, saying from the doorway, "You've met my niece already, I take it? Meeriam—"

Looking up from where she knelt by Portus's side, Meeriam frowned a warning that came and went so quickly Hagan wondered if he'd really seen it. He caught his breath.

Firewing.

Quelling an atavistic shudder, Hagan forced himself away from another shattering discovery. The thought was too preposterous. Gerald Nilander was only who he seemed to be. A Freefarmer grown powerful in Kassine's organization. Soon, Hagan derided himself, he'd be like Graeber seeing Firewing behind every rock and bush. Surely the girl had even Nilander fooled.

Hagan thought it, but he didn't believe it.

Drawing a calming breath Hagan slid his gaze beyond the girl to the old man resting against the soft white pillows.

Portus. He had to concentrate on Portus. Leave the rest for later. Portus was here, and Hagan had questions to ask.

The old doctor was still deathly pale, but his skin had lost the greenish cast it'd had that day they'd brought him here. Dark circles sagged under his closed eyes, and the skin of his hands looked almost translucent in the light of a low hanging lamp.

Meeriam rose swiftly to her feet. "He's drifting in and out of sleep, but I'm sure he'll wake if you speak to him."

Not trusting himself to speak, Hagan merely nodded that he understood. Meeriam herself looked almost as tired as Portus, he thought. Her eyes were wary, and —and sad. Filled with the knowledge of his fear of her.

Then, as if Nilander had spoken, she glanced at him where he stood by the door and stepped away from the bed, allowing Hagan room to approach. "He'll be hungry soon. I'll get some broth from the kitchen."

Frozen to the spot, Hagan was torn between wanting to follow and apologize for his fear, and the certain knowledge that when she found out why he'd come back to Earth she, like all the Firewing, would think even less of him than she already did.

He wasn't even conscious of Nilander until the older man touched him lightly on the arm, urging him forward to Portus's side.

"Speak to him, Captain. I think he'll be glad to see you."

Hagan flinched from Gerald's touch, then drew another deep breath, steadying his mind as well as his nerves. Concentrate on Portus, he reminded himself again. That was what he had to do.

As he approached the bed, Portus, without opening his eyes, put a hand to his face, rubbing as if he could rub away an ache behind his eyes.

"Portus?"

The old man's eyes sprang open. His hand shook. "Ellis?"

"I'm here."

Swiftly Portus turned his head, then winced with pain. But his eyes were clear of the confusion that they'd held the last time Hagan had seen him. Portus's hand, though it trembled, gripped Hagan's with weak vigor.

Hagan was vaguely conscious that Nilander had pulled a chair to the side of the bed, then indicated he would wait outside. Sinking into the chair, Hagan searched Portus's face for the anger he'd been so certain the old man felt for him. He found none.

He searched for words. "How do you feel today?"

"Tired." A twist of dark humor entered the old man's voice. "Thirsty."

Glancing around, Hagan saw a tall covered beaker and drinking tube on the low chest next to the bed. He offered it and the old doctor eagerly accepted. When he'd slaked his thirst, Portus lay back, sighing. "I'd forgotten how good plain water could taste."

Hagan nodded sympathetically. "The hard stuff goes down easy, but packs an awful aftershock."

Portus held up a trembling hand and studied it. "A sickness. A sickness of the soul. On Mars they'd put me in the Caverns for retraining. Here—" Portus's voice broke, and then went on. "Here I could be sent out to that monstrosity of a hospital they're calling The Farm." The trembling increased in Portus's hands and Hagan reached out and held them in his own. Portus's hands were cold.

"No, they won't do that."

"You mean they wouldn't be doing it if Elias were still alive." Portus's raspy voice was bitter. "The General killed him, you know. Got his hands on an old Firewing weapon and used it on Elias."

"Can you prove it, Portus?"

"No."

"Then don't say it out loud."

"No. No, of course not."

"Not even to me."

"No. But I wanted you to know. It wasn't the Firewing." Portus's voice trailed off weakly and his eyes closed. But not to sleep. His hands moved restlessly within the confines of Hagan's. Hagan thought again of the wild accusations Velia was throwing around the Colony about his birth, thought of the questions he had to ask, and wondered how to go about it.

Watching the lines of pain and fear deepen around the old man's eyes, Hagan felt a surge of sympathy for the old doctor who was so out of his depth. "Portus, Merrick bade me find you. He was worried when he couldn't get in touch."

"The General—clamped a lock on all outgoing communications. I couldn't even get word as far as Diana. Meeriam was willing to go again, but I couldn't let her take that chance."

A protective anger surged through Hagan at the thought of the girl even thinking of doing so. "It would have been very dangerous."

"Yes—" Portus lay quietly, whatever he'd started to say lost in another perambulation of his mind. Hagan was swamped by early memories of this gentle old man who'd always had time for an attention-starved boy. He bowed his head against the weight of the memories, and was almost startled when Portus spoke again. "I—I seem to've lost a, a few weeks. Have you presented your claim to the Council?"

"I've tried. Velia's fighting with all of her considerable claws."

"Whose side is Graeber on?"

Hagan glanced down at the uniform he wore and a slight smile twisted his lips. "Mine, I think. Or perhaps he's waiting to see which of us will be more easy to manipulate."

Alarm wrinkled Portus's brow. "If he thinks you're not, he'll get rid of you the way he did Elias. What's Velia's case? Surely the laws of inheritance are clear."

Hagan hesitated, distrusting the fate that would so easily let him ask the question that above all others he had come to ask. "She says I'm illegitimate and therefore can't inherit."

"Nonsense." Portus said it, but Hagan felt the tremor that ran through Portus's weak body as if it ran through his own. He tightened his grip on Portus's hands, willing the truth from Portus's suddenly dry lips.

When it seemed that Portus would not, could not speak, Hagan urged him on. "Of course it's nonsense. Elias's first marriage papers are there in the records and you signed my birth record yourself. No one knows better than you—"

"No—" Portus jerked his hands from Hagan's and covered his face.

Driven by a hot anger that started somewhere at his most inner core, Hagan insisted. "Portus, tell me the truth. I have a right to know."

After a moment of silence so intense it seemed that Hagan could hear the blood pounding in his veins, Portus spoke, his broken words whispered with anguish. "Elias—Elias was so in love—I couldn't convince him—I told him such a relationship was unacceptable—that no good could come of it, but—" Tears welled in the old man's eyes. Ran down his cheeks unchecked. Hagan slowly came to his feet, staring without seeing as the essence of the words seeped into his soul.

Almost unnoticed the door behind Hagan hissed open and Meeriam's soft but angry voice preceded her into the room.

"What are you doing to him? Why have you upset him? You have no right." She set a steaming bowl on the low chest and turned, trying to push Hagan away from the bed.

Hagan took no notice of her. The core of anger in him had grown to a fury that he could control no more than he could control the Kama River in flood.

He stared down at the old man, but he saw instead the man who'd fathered him. Meeriam's words, even her physical act of pushing at him couldn't penetrate his anger.

So Elias, who'd always set himself up as so moral, so righteous, the standard by which other men must act and feel, had been no more nor less than other men, a whoring bastard— no—a smile bent beyond recognition covered his face. No, he was the bastard, wasn't he? Velia was right. Some poor woman without the benefit of law nor the protection of family had given him birth. And if Velia had any shred of proof beyond wild accusations, he'd be dead.

"Portus," he said, still ignoring the protestations of the girl at his side, "is she alive, this woman who gave me birth?"

"No," Portus said softly, as though the memory hurt. "No, she died when you were born."

"Where was I born, Portus? On one of the farms?"

"No. No, not there. Not there."

"Then where?" Hagan asked.

But Portus, as if sinking under the memories, shut his eyes, and his hands went limp upon the bed.

Hagan exited Kassine's tall gates and stood, fighting to control the anger that was trying to tear him apart. Anger so great that for a brief time he'd even forgotten his fear of the Firewing. Hands clenched, head bowed, he was filled with words he would never say, at least not to the person who should have been alive to hear them.

Damn the Commander! Damn that old soldier for taking his pleasure where he may, and using the excuse of love to mitigate his guilt. Damn him—

"Sir? Captain Hagan?"

Hagan spun to the voice. Loomis, eyes widening in a seeming instant of fear, made him aware once more of his surroundings. Aware of his need to keep this deep anger from ruining his chances of staying alive.

Hagan forced open his hands, and took in a gulp of cool air. What the Commander had done with his life in the distant past couldn't matter now except as it would endanger Hagan's real purpose in coming back. As he'd realized a week ago while he listened to Graeber in the map center, the trip across the mountains would have to be made soon. Now it was even more imperative that he move quickly. Given time to dig, no telling what the General might find. Or manufacture, if the hard evidence was truly lost.

He drew in another deep, controlling breath, and felt a calm center replace the anger that had burned so hotly, and a teasing of curiosity touched him. Who was she, that woman who'd given him birth? All these years he'd believed the Freefarmer genealogy supplied by the Commander. Was there any reason to doubt that what had been truth then was still truth now? Did he really want to know? His earliest memories were of Velia, from the time he was two or three. He remembered no other mother though the Commander had told him he had been kept by a farming family when he was an infant. How much was true? How much lies?

Catching sight of Loomis's curious expression, he shrugged a slight apology for ignoring the younger man. "Yes, Loomis, what is it?"

"You asked me to stay and find out what the new assignments will be."

Remembering how important that had seemed just hours ago, Hagan stifled an impatient sigh. "Yes. Were they posted?"

"Yes, sir." Loomis grinned. "We're on Kama Patrol starting tomorrow at 0:400."

Dismay that he was being sent away before anything was settled on his claim ebbed and flowed with his need to leave as soon as possible for the Ancient City. Or at least, to get beyond Graeber's reach while he searched for the best way to go. The maps in the map room had been helpful, such as they were. But he'd know much more once he reached the mountains.

An echo of his earlier anger burned for a moment. If only Portus—but no, there'd be no help from Portus. The poor old man couldn't even help himself, and the Firewing —Meeriam's perfect mouth, her deep blue eyes, took image in his mind, soothing him before he even realized it—in the name of God, why did she have to be a Firewing?

Hagan was unaware his groan was audible until Loomis said, "Sir?"

"What?"

Loomis shifted uncomfortably. "I thought you were saying something, sir."

"Nothing important." Hagan indicated the path. "Let's get back."

Entering Late Mess an hour later with Loomis at his heels, Hagan felt the ordinary sounds of men talking while they ate dampen the sense of danger he had experienced since his talk with Portus. Loomis stopped near the door to speak to one of his friends, and Hagan went on, choosing a seat that put his back against the far wall. A young cadet, no more than fifteen, Hagan guessed, made his way between tables, taking orders. Hagan waited for him to approach with patience, his mind busy. Tomorrow he and Loomis would be out in the Valley, on their way to the mountains. A residue of anger still mixed with his dread. What he'd learned from Portus made his leaving even more imperative. It had to be soon, before Graeber figured out just how useless he was in the grand scheme of things. How easy would it be to leave the rest of the unit behind? What would he need to make the trek over the mountains? Clothes for the higher altitudes. Food for the first part of the trip. Later, with some distance between himself and Graeber, he'd live off the land. Though he'd thought of these things before, he'd been caught off guard by the speed with which this opportunity arrived. Could he find what he needed tonight? Once he was in the mountains, would he run into the Firewing? Only if they wanted him to. He repressed a shiver.

Loomis, skirting a raucous group in the middle of the room, grinned cheerfully as he dropped into the chair on the opposite side of the table.

Hagan felt a moment's envy of the younger officer's cheer. "You look like you've had good news."

"Yes, sir. Hawkins said he got a look at our itinerary. We'll be out two whole weeks."

Two weeks! Hagan controlled his excitement. Perhaps a whole week before he'd be missed. Maybe. He frowned. "What can the General find for us to do out there for two weeks? You can traverse the whole Kama Valley in three or four days."

"We're supposed to take the new river road. We're to follow up on some Firewing sightings. Graeber told Galt he thought they'd try to tear the road up, so we're supposed to make sure they don't."

Hagan understood that. The roads were cerafoam, thrown by a foam-thrower almost as big as a HOGG, the military carrier built for the smooth roads of Mars. HOGGs needed the smooth cerafoam surfaces to function properly. They were useless on rough ground.

"What Firewing sightings have there been? I haven't heard of any."

Before Loomis could answer, a loud burst of laughter from the center of the room drew his attention. An elegantly dressed soldier with a thin, aristocratic face filled with anger—seemed to be the target. He'd jumped up and his chair crashed backward. "Screw you, Johnson." He spun and eyed the rest of the large room with wild anger. "I'm getting out of this damned place. No one's making me stay. It's a damned killer."

The noise level quieted. Loomis turned in his seat, eyed the man, then turned back. "Small loss," he muttered.

"Who is he?"

"Name's Bennet." A young cadet arrived that moment to take their order, and Loomis waited. When the cadet was gone, Loomis started again. "One of Graeber's new style soldiers."

Hagan tried to read the meaning behind Loomis's dry tone. There was much more to the young lieutenant who'd become his aide than he'd first realized. Loomis himself was a career man, having been a cadet from the age of twelve, and a graduate of Arcola's top military academy. A soldiering family, he'd mentioned in passing. Though young, he had good instincts. In the week they'd been associated, Hagan had come to appreciate him. Though Loomis wasn't usually given to gossip, he managed to hear a lot that Hagan didn't.

"What's his complaint?"

Loomis hesitated, then his mouth quirked in a reluctant smile. "Says the Firewing have put a curse on him."

"And have they?"

"Could be. Or it could be just a guilty conscience."

Hagan glanced across the room at the big double doors in time to see the blond soldier disappear. "Oh?"

"Or," Loomis went on, "it could be just his imagination."

Hagan drew reign on his impatience. "What is?"

"What happens to him every time he gets near the Thomas homestead."

"What is that?"

"He gets the shits."

"Every time?"

"Yes, sir. Serves him right, though. He used to brag that he'd lay Thomas's wife some day. Thought to try it when they had that big fire out there. Must have been about the time you arrived." Hagan remembered hearing about the fire. He nodded, which was all the encouragement Loomis needed. The younger man's grin broadened. "He was laying for her that day, but he got the shits instead, and every time he gets near the place now, he gets them again. Justice, I say."

"What does Graeber say about it?"

Loomis's grin faded and he looked down at his fist, curled tight on the table. "The General says his men can take whatever they can get."

"That's more than harassment."

"That's the idea, I think."

Hagan felt a tight knot of revulsion in his chest. "Not on any patrol I lead."

Their meal arrived, and Hagan, tuning out the other voices, tried to concentrate on what was placed before him, but the thought of the type of harassment condoned by Graeber made him lose his appetite. He remembered Liam Thomas, and vaguely, Thomas's wife, Belle. Good people, hard working. They had young children. A large, neatly kept farm. They didn't deserve that kind of treatment, any more than the Firewing deserved what the General was trying to do to them. If he destroyed the City that was Graeber's goal, where would

Graeber aim his revenge? Would he turn on the defenseless freefarmers?

The large mess room crowded in on him, and the need to be out in the night air was overwhelming. The sense of danger that hadn't completely vanished since his talking to Portus that morning became stronger.

Before he could act on his need, however, the outer door burst open again, and Graeber stalked in, Galt at his side. A fat, poisonous toad, flanked by a lean hungry vulture.

Graeber swept the room with an angry, searching gaze, ignoring the voice that shouted "Attention!"

Every soldier in the place came swiftly to his feet. *He's looking for me.* The certain knowledge raised the hair on Hagan's neck. Though he didn't glance again at the door he felt Graeber approach. Strange, like the day he'd found the young Firewing in Kassine's abandoned garden—he could sense the danger moving closer. He darted a look at Loomis. Though stiffly at attention, Loomis was watching him with a puzzled frown.

Then Graeber was upon them.

"Captain Hagan."

From habit ingrained in him since he was first a cadet, though his urge was to flee Hagan stood frozen in place. What had he done wrong?"Yes, sir?"

A tense and fearful silence deepened across the room.

The General's hand rested on the instrument, the psychoprobe, strapped to his thigh. His voice was gravelly soft yet carried to every corner of the breathless room. "Do you think because you are the Commander of Kama's son you can with impunity ignore my orders?" Momentarily it seemed the General had forgotten the elder Hagan was dead. He continued, without waiting for an answer. "Do you think that any man on Earth ignores me when I give an order?" With each word the General seemed to reach new heights of fury. This time he waited for an answer.

"No, sir." Hagan held himself rigid. No matter that it was safer to act the cowed, weakling son of the Commander of Kama, his pride would not allow it.

His quiet answer seemed to enrage Graeber further. Using his words like a club, Graeber battered at the impassivity that

Hagan pulled around him like Jolando's cloak. But beneath his impassive face Hagan's mind raced. What message was Graeber talking about? He'd checked his message board before leaving his room less than twenty minutes ago. There'd been no messages waiting for him, other than the one about tonight's briefing for tomorrow's patrol.

Could there have been another? He flicked a glance at Galt and surprised a gleam of satisfaction in the other captain's cold blue eyes.

Graeber reached the end of his tirade more from lack of breath, Hagan thought, than from a paucity of words.

Hagan, aware that he'd never been so close to someone else's madness, none the less spoke softly, pinning Galt with his gaze as he did so. "Perhaps it was a message not delivered."

The swift rise of color on Galt's face said that Hagan's guess was accurate. Graeber's mouth opened, then shut again. The mad light in his eyes faded. Hagan could almost feel the very moment reason took over from emotion. The very moment Graeber realized he might have made a tactical error in front of the largest part of his officer staff.

Graeber's hand clenched dangerously around the butt of the psychoprobe and his voice grew soft. "We'll see about this." He whirled on his heel and lumbered toward the door.

Hagan stood at attention until Graeber had exited the room. At the door, before he followed Graeber through, Galt paused and looked back. "Good try, Hagan, but it won't work. He'll never believe you."

Hagan trembled with the need to control his temper. "Bad try, Galt. You'd better guard your back."

As the words sank in, Galt paled. A moment later he was gone. But still Hagan stood, his gaze taking in the other officers who'd been reluctant witnesses to the scene. One by one they looked away, none willing to meet his eyes. Now knowing the extent of the enmity between Graeber, Galt and himself, not one would give him the support he needed. Not one of them could be counted on to help stop Graeber. He could feel it. He knew it. Slowly he sank into his chair. Loomis let out a long, slow breath and, doing the same, reached again for his plate.

Hagan was reminded of Josh's theater; the scene played

out, the curtain dropped, the audience departed. Shuddering, he stared at his food, knowing there was no way he could force it down. If only this was one of Josh's plays. One that he could leave behind when the night was over. But it wasn't, and tomorrow was soon to come.

Chapter 14

Norcanna Bay

In the foggy air outside the carriage sheds at 0:400, Hagan watched the shadowy figures of the men he'd been assigned. An odd mixture of six young recruits from God knew what walk of life, and two noncoms, older soldiers, the kind he'd run into before who had the drill down pat and screw the brass. He didn't like the type.

The two older soldiers inspired no trust. Hagan found himself automatically rechecking the equipment and supplies, rechecking the charge of the HOGG's fuel cells. Doing all of those small ingrained acts that he'd been doing since the first time he'd gone on patrol. This morning, of necessity, they would also be towing an RMV, the tank-like c'foam road-thrower, to repair any road they might find torn up. The HOGGs were inefficient medium-speed vehicles, suited only to the smooth roadways of the Domes of Mars. There were rumors that soon they'd get wheeled equipment, but if he remembered correctly, that rumor had been around for years. The promise that was never kept. He'd heard the Commander say once that it was one of the ways the High Council on Mars made sure the Colony would stay small. Hagan wouldn't have been surprised to find that Graeber had set up a manufacturing plant to create wheeled vehicles to help him in his push to the Ancient City. But if he did, what would it entail? Finding the iron to make the steel, smelting, machinery to turn the parts—technology that would have to be rediscovered. Was that what Graeber was hoping to find still buried on the high desert? The technology to conquer Earth? Kali thought the General's goal was Mars. But if he were doing it, Hagan thought, his goal would be Earth itself.

Moving along the far side of the HOGG, Hagan bent and tested the coupling on the RMV, and found it secure. Two of the young crew members, he'd been informed in the briefing last night, had spent three weeks on a road construction crew and would handle the road thrower should the need arise. Should it arise. It most probably would.

They were also armed, recruit, noncom and officer alike, with s'darms, the small energy-charged hand weapons that were so deadly at close range, and so useless otherwise. Did being armed make them feel safer? Maybe so, but it didn't do much for his own peace of mind.

Hagan stepped forward from the shadows just as Loomis appeared in the doorway, and Loomis's face lit. "There you are, sir. Just got a small change in itinerary. The General wants us to spend the first night out at Old Man Crossing."

"Do you have it in writing?"

Hagan wasn't joking, but Loomis laughed anyway. "Yes, sir." He patted his uniform pocket. "Right here."

"All right, then, let's load up and get out of here. We want to be half way to the river before sunup." Casually Hagan moved toward the pack he'd leaned against a back wall, hefted it and carried it back to the cab of the HOGG where he and Loomis would ride with the driver. In the dark of the fog shrouded night he'd thrown together those items that he thought would help him get through the mountains. But two things he'd wanted most he'd been unable to find on such short notice. The soft yet tough Firewing boots, and a curly-skin vest that was both light and very warm. They were items not easy to find in these dark days, though he was sure that at one time he'd owned both. He threw the pack behind the seat and glanced toward the rear of the HOGG. "Come on, Loomis, what's holding it up?"

With only a smattering of grumbles, seven men climbed into the rear of the HOGG and settled down.

Two hours later, while Loomis and the young soldier who had pulled driving duty talked, Hagan watched the sun come up. They were on the downward slope of the coastal hills, traveling eastward into the sunrise.

First gray-pink and purple lines streaked the sky, light catching lines of clouds and making a strange roadmap of unreadable paths for cloud soldiers to follow, then the deepening reds and oranges, and then the ball itself, too bright a gold to let the eye perceive. Directly ahead of the ribbon of gray-white roadway lay the meandering river, still wreathed in tendrils of mist, green and gray against the browns and golden yellows of the dry valley floor. The first of the farms, the Thomas Homestead, lay to the Southeast, an hour away. Because they still had the advantage of being above the actual floor of Kama Valley, they could see in the far distance the gray-green line that denoted the beginning of the Hojoi plantation in that direction. They could also see the brighter green line of the river in the other. They were bypassing the homestead on the way out, Hagan's choice, not the official itinerary.

Reaching the river a short while later, they followed the straight course set by the white c'foam roadway until they reached a turnout by the river which already showed signs of having been used for a rest stop. Hagan, already tired of the enforced inactivity, and sure the others were too, called a halt.

A few moments later, standing at the HOGG's side, he let the familiar sights and sounds wash over him, enjoying the dawn as he had never done on Mars. In truth, for years he'd never seen a dawn. This morning the weather was perfect, and in spite of a lingering chill, promised heat later in the day. Closer to the river tendrils of fog still wound among the willows and other trees, evidence of water in an otherwise parched land. If he turned just so, he could even see the sun bathed peak of Mt. Kama in the distance, in bright relief against the deep blue of a perfect sky.

"Shall we set up the syn for a brew, Captain?" one of the youngsters grinned.

Hagan curbed a wash of impatience. He'd wanted a brief respite from the thunder of the HOGG, not a prolonged stop for a meal. But, looking beyond the young soldier's hopeful face he met Loomis's amused eyes. "Is there time?"

Loomis nodded.

"All right, then, twenty minutes."

Drawn by the sound of the river which he couldn't yet see, Hagan stepped off the cerafoam roadway and walked slowly down toward the bank. As he moved closer to the water, the sounds made by the unit faded, leaving only the bark of someone's irrepressible laughter on the air.

Climbing a grass and gravel dune, he studied the area. Back toward the roadway, the young boy who'd asked the question

163

had hefted the small ball stove over one shoulder and tossed another pack to an even younger boy. Boys, not men, he thought. And not soldiers. Probably had never seen the inside of the Academy, nor had more than a week's training. Not like the two older men who were coming down off the HOGG content to let the younger men do the work. Unobtrusively Hagan watched the two weathered VMP follow the younger ones down the trail toward the low grassy bank above the water's edge. One of them, at least, was Graeber's type of man. A tall Arcolan, probably older than Hagan, with a face weathered as much by hard living as the elements. The few words Hagan had heard him say were derisive, cutting. When one of the younger men bumped into him, his response had been harsh and quick. The younger soldiers gave him wide berth.

Hagan's eyes narrowed. All of the men, even Loomis who drew up the rear, walked carelessly, either sure of their safety or ignorant of the possible dangers. A feather of apprehension moved up his spine. Loomis glanced up, smiled and moved to the bottom of his little rise. "Shall we post a guard, sir?"

"Yes," Hagan snapped. "That one there. What's his name?" He pointed out the tall Arcolan.

Loomis's smile disappeared. "Sergeant Warren, sir."

"Get him up there on that point above the bend."

"Yes sir." Quietly Loomis moved down to the group gathered around the ball stove and gave his order. Shooting a black look in Hagan's direction Warren moved slowly up to the point opposite Hagan and took up his post. Hagan was vaguely surprised that he'd done as he was ordered. Neither of the two older soldiers had yet challenged him, but he expected they would before too long. Strange that he should feel a growing danger from them almost as strong as the danger he suddenly felt from this empty land. But, he guessed, the challenge would come later, when the heat had made tempers shorter.

"A cup of coffee, Captain?" Loomis called.

"No thanks." Hagan cut down from the path across the gravel and reached the edge of the riverbed. The river was low, but the level of the earlier spring run-off was indicated in the high water mark less than a foot below the bank. On the far side of the river a deep channel flowed next to a much higher bank, and grass- exposed roots stood in early morning shadow. The clean smell of the river was almost intoxicating, and Hagan would have enjoyed it more had he not begun to feel an anxiety for which he had no name.

Carefully skirting the damper sand, he walked slowly up the river's edge. Above and to his right he could still see Sergeant Warren, and knew that Warren was watching him.

A dozen Firewing could pass before the soldier's eyes, and he probably wouldn't see them, Hagan thought with disgust.

His strange anxiety growing, Hagan stopped at the water's edge and studied the quiet river. And then the banks on either side. And then the rise of trees and brush beyond the opposite bank. The feeling swept him, as it had in Kassine's abandoned garden, of being observed. The hair rose on the back of his neck.

Definitely not the same feeling he had knowing that Warren had watched him.

Without seeming to, he studied more closely the copse across the river. That was the place, he decided. That was where the Firewing was hiding. Turning, he slowly retraced his steps back toward the grassy bank where the younger men had sprawled, talking among themselves of the hot day ahead, of the families they'd left behind on Mars, and in the case of the young driver of the HOGG, of the farm he'd hoped to obtain from the lottery held by Kassine each year. A trace of bitterness laced the driver's voice. Quietly, not sure how far the sound of voices carried in the still air, Hagan broke in. "Back to the carrier, men."

"Aw, but—"

Loomis, catching a tight nuance in Hagan's voice, rose smoothly to his feet. "You heard the Captain. Get moving there. We didn't come to spend the morning, we only stopped for a cup." His good humor seemed to soothe their ire. "Sergeant Warren—"

The sergeant moved, and at that moment the crack of an old-style projection rifle rang across the river basin. The sergeant dove for cover. The younger men stood, mouths gaped open.

"Get down, you fools," Hagan yelled and dove for the protection of a sandbank. The others followed his example. Hagan watched the sergeant reach a clump of low bushes, apparently unhurt, then motioned Loomis closer. "Get the others back to the HOGG, before someone does something stupid."

"Sir, the sergeant—"

"I'll take care of him."

"But—"

"Move, Lieutenant."

"Yes sir." Clearly Loomis was reluctant to leave Hagan but saw the sense of getting the young recruits out of the way.

As Loomis herded the others back toward the roadway Hagan studied the point of land where Warren crouched behind a protective clump of deadwood. Any way Warren moved he'd be exposed, and he seemed to have figured that out for himself. But he'd been totally exposed out on the point. If the person shooting the old-style weapon had wanted to kill him, wouldn't he have succeeded?

Hagan studied the opposite bank. Firewing. But how many? As he had in Kassine's garden, he sensed now only one, and didn't question his knowledge.

"Warren, can you hear me?"

"Bloody well—" growled the angry soldier.

'Then listen. I'll move upriver and draw his fire. He's out of range of our s'darms and we'd need a blaster to reach him from this distance. We won't even try. As soon as he fires again, you get the hell off the point. Do you understand?"

"Yes."

"And as soon as you get back to the carrier, tell Loomis to get out of here." He visualized the maps he'd studied in Graeber's map room. "There's a place upriver where you can pick me up. About ten minutes by roadway. Wait for me there. It'll take me about thirty minutes. Have you got that?"

"Sure thing, Captain."

Hagan hoped the sergeant did. He didn't relish having to walk back to Norcanna through the heat of the day.

"Now!" Hagan shouted and, bending low, spun into the open. Even as he ran, he felt a frustration bombarding him from across the river, and with the next several cracks of the rifle realized the rifleman was a damned poor shot. Thankful for even that small advantage, Hagan gave the Firewing little target to aim at and kept running. As each further crack of the rifle rent the silence of the morning, sand flew up behind him. Finally winded, Hagan fell into a shallow depression and lay gulping great breaths of air. From the distant road he heard the whine of the HOGG's air thrusters start up, and hoped once more that Warren had passed on his orders in full. Silently he gathered air into his lungs for another charge.

Disgusted with his limited ability with the weapon, Condor rubbed his sore shoulder and glared at the metal and wood instrument in his hands. He should throw it into the river. He who read the ancient tongue, who had discovered the cache of weapons and had had the nerve to take some for his own—obviously there was more to learn than the mere aiming and firing of this weapon. But, remembering the way even his wildest shots had caused the men on the opposite side of the river to go to ground, he smiled tightly. Next time he'd will himself to aim better. As for this time—he'd known as soon as he heard the whine of the soldier's carrier that this time they'd escaped, though where the one who'd been running had gone to ground he still didn't know. Though he'd pushed out his thought and searched, he'd found no one. Glancing at the rising sun, he grabbed up the bag of ammunition and balancing the rifle on his shoulder, trotted up the river trail. He had only six hours before he was to meet the cousins from Delinore, and he was already anticipating what they would say when he told them about this morning's work.

Hagan, picked up by the others at the place he'd designated, said little about what'd happened at the rest stop, letting the incident itself be the lesson. He knew, too, that if he himself had been more alert, perhaps he might've prevented the Firewing from using them as target practice. It was a sobering thought, and a lesson for himself he didn't mean to repeat.

For the rest of the day they traversed the river road, sometimes close, sometimes cutting across tilled land to reach another meander in the river, stopping three times to repair some minor road damage, always, though, bearing south east under the blazing sun. They were still two hours from Old Man's Crossing but Hagan, choosing to camp before dark, by mid-afternoon found a site along the river that had the added advantage of being fairly open beneath tall trees. It wasn't the camp Graeber had wanted them to make, but Hagan thought he'd feel safer here than at a place they'd have to set up after dark.

Finally, with the others setting up their camp, Loomis found him alone on a small rise of land overlooking the river, and asked the question that had obviously been uppermost on his mind all day.

"Sir—about what happened this morning—" Loomis began, then seemed embarrassed to go on.

"What about it?"

"What was that all about? Was someone waiting for us? If he was, how did he know that's where we were going to stop?"

Loomis deserved answers that made sense, though Hagan wondered if they would make sense to anyone but himself. How could he explain what he knew, when he couldn't even explain it to himself? Searching for a coherent answer, he watched several of the young men awkwardly working on their small tents under the derisive eyes of the two older soldiers, and shook his head at their ineptitude.

"Or maybe," Loomis went on, "it wasn't a Firewing. I mean—"

"I know what you mean, Lieutenant, but you're wrong. It was a Firewing. Someone as inept as our young friends over there."

"Well, it seems damned convenient that he should be there."

"Look at it this way, Loomis. It was the first decent cover we came to along the river. We stopped because it was a perfect place, a nice, grassy slope, easy access to the river, and close to the road. Why couldn't the Firewing have also chosen it for all of those reasons?"

Loomis nodded. "Or chosen it, I suppose, because he knew we would."

"Not us, particularly. Any soldiers traveling the road today."

"I guess so." Loomis was biting back a grin. "He wasn't a very good shot, was he?"

"Meaning he didn't hit Warren?" Small loss had he done so, thought Hagan.

"Assuming that he was really trying," Loomis added.

Hagan stared at the young soldier, remembering the frustration he'd felt emanating from the man across the river. "Oh, he was trying all right. Next time we run into him, you can bet he'll be more accurate."

"You think there'll be a next time?"

"If one man can rout a unit of soldiers so easily," said Hagan dryly,

"don't you think he'll try again?"

"I—I see your point." Loomis glanced around the open campsite they'd chosen.He didn't seem unduly upset by the thought, but Hagan could see that he studied the area with new, more critical eyes. "I guess we'd better set out the ears."

"Not a bad idea, Lieutenant."

Loomis had the grace to blush at Hagan's sarcasm, but as he started to leave he turned again. "You know, I didn't believe the General when he said the Firewing were arming against us. Where do you suppose they get the weapons?"

"I don't know. Perhaps the clans still have a few stashed around. Some of them do hunt." He'd run into small-game snares also, when he was younger, but he had to admit he'd never heard the crack of a rifle until today. The deadly sound had shocked him, it seemed so out of place. Maybe—the idea crept into his mind—maybe the weapons were coming from the Ancient City. Even as he thought of it, the logic seemed inescapable. If there were interplanetary ships waiting in their silos, why not smaller arms too? His skin prickled at the thought. And what else did the ancient City hold? Wheeled vehicles, surely. Small air-ships. In Graeber's hands they would all become weapons that he could use against the people of Earth, as well as the people of Mars. A vision of Earth flashed into his mind, Earth as it must have been, with its teeming billions, the planet beating with the heart of humanity, all destroyed, destroyed suddenly within the space of weeks by leaders like Graeber who couldn't be satisfied with control of a part, but had wanted the whole.

And then the vision was gone, and all he could see was the softly flowing river, the green banks and the sheltering trees. But he was shaken. Could it have been like that? Could it happen again? Of course it could. Graeber was proof of that. Kali was right. Graeber had to be stopped! Hagan's sense of urgency deepened, and he thought of the pack he'd stashed behind the seats of the cab. Waiting for him to retrieve it and strike off on his own through the mountains. His resolve strengthened.

Slowly Hagan became aware that Loomis had been speaking. With a self-deprecating smile he apologized for his inattention.

"I only said, sir, what do you think of this place to camp?"

Hagan turned his own critical eye on the area. Shaded by tall leafy trees, the grove was green and cool compared to the road they'd traveled on all day. Unlike the rest stop this morning, there were no high sand banks, but the main channel of the river flowed once again against the opposite bank where the river pooled deep and quiet. A good place to swim, he thought suddenly and wondered if these young soldiers, direct from Mars, had yet had the experience of swimming in the river or bay. Probably not. He said as much to Loomis and the younger man grinned. "I was thinking that, sir. After we're set up, would it be all right to let them do it?"

"I don't see why not. Sergeant Warren and I'll place the 'ears', and you make sure one man is on the scan-board at all times."

A few minutes later Hagan lead the cadaverous older soldier away from the activity at the campsite.

Warren stalked at Hagan's side giving the impression that he'd rather be anywhere else. All day the dark looks from his angry eyes had told Hagan that the man had something he wanted to say, and Hagan thought it best to let him say it without an audience.

A few minutes later Hagan pointed out the final two placements of the listening posts. "There and there." The others were in a wide circle around the camp and once activated, would sense any movement larger than a rabbit over a wide area throughout the night.

With a grunt Warren hammered the last narrow post into the ground.

"Damned well won't creep up on us this time."

"No, he won't."

Dropping the hammer, Warren straightened and rested his fists on his hips. "It was just one bloody Firewing this morning."

Hagan silently indicated his agreement, waiting for the rest of whatever was on Warren's mind.

It didn't take long. "We should have gone after him."

"With what?"

"The bloody blaster."

"He would have been long gone by the time we got it across the river."

"Maybe. Maybe not."

"We'll never know, will we?" Scooping up the hammer and empty post pack, Hagan started to turn back to the camp. Hopefully the discussion was over.

But Warren, gaunt face ugly with anger, wasn't finished. "You're just like the old Commander," he spit out. "Bloody Firewing lover."

Hagan spun and faced the angry soldier, fighting to keep the commingled emotions of pride and disgust from his face. If Warren only knew how little like the Commander he really was. "You're out of line, Sergeant."

"So what?" Hate filled the sergeant's face. "We got our orders."

Unable to hide his own anger, Hagan's voice softened . "Who gives you orders, sergeant?"

Warren's eyes narrowed as he paused to assess the threat Hagan posed. As Hagan took a step closer, Warren took an involuntary step back.

"Who, sergeant?" demanded Hagan softly, and took another step.

"Galt said—"

"Ah, yes, Galt." Hagan nodded slowly as if he now understood, as indeed he did. He pinned the sergeant with icy eyes. "Galt," he barked abruptly, "is a dead man." He lowered his voice to an almost whisper. "You'd do well not to take orders from a dead man."

The quiet warning, in stark contrast to Hagan's deadly tone, drained the life out of the sergeant's face. Waiting a long moment for any other response the sergeant cared to make, Hagan was satisfied with the effect of his words. On this patrol, at least, Warren would obey him.

Afternoon slid into early evening. After their prearranged

contact with GHQ wherein Hagan had Loomis report only that they'd had one Firewing contact and hadn't made it as far as the first stop chosen by Graeber, Hagan had the two older men give the younger ones lessons on handling the soundboard, on sidearm safety, and, when he found that none of the younger men had even been given a map to read, elementary lessons on the mapboard. Evening meal was synthesized stew that was no better nor worse than any other Hagan had ever eaten. Who knew what would happen if any of these men were ever forced to live off the land. All of them would starve, no doubt.

Taking his plate away from the direct light of the ball lamp that someone had set in a floating pattern just above their heads, Hagan found a low flat rock nudged into a low grassy bank and stiffly settled himself, half listening, half remembering all the other times, in his father's command that he'd done the same. Six years ago. A long six years. And he was already feeling the effects of the morning's strenuous activity. Activity, hell, he thought with disgust. He'd been running for his life! Though it seemed strange to do so, he almost smiled at the thought. He'd been so certain he'd never come back to Earth, almost as certain as he'd once been that he'd never leave. If it hadn't been for meeting that Firewing—

A throbbing started in his head, and his thoughts shied like a startled fawn from the painful memories. Memories that seemed to crowd closer the nearer he came to the mountains. Perhaps tomorrow he'd face them, when his body didn't ache and he wasn't so tired. Tomorrow, when they crossed the river into what the Commander had always designated Firewing territory.

Reaching that decision he was relieved when Loomis appeared and dropped down at his side. Loomis's groan was half amused, half real. "Captain, you know, I'm not very old—"

Hagan grinned. "You mean, compared to me?"

"Well, yes, sir, I guess, compared to you. But I feel old, for God's sake.

These—these kids—"

Hagan laughed. "I sympathize."

Loomis flashed his irrepressible grin. "Yeah, I thought you might." And then his frown returned. "Isn't there something we can do when we get back to Norcanna? I can't believe that none of them had ever been swimming before. Not even in the bay. And the training—" Loomis shut his eyes in despair. "The closest they've come is to walk by the Academy on their way to the agricultural school."

Knowing that he had no intention of returning with Loomis and the unit, Hagan lost his desire to laugh. What did it matter to him, after all, what kind of training these young soldiers had. Leave that to Loomis, and the other career men. It wasn't his problem any longer, no matter what sense of guilt might assail him. "Are they conscripted right off the ships?"

"Usually. Thing is, they aren't military people. Anyone can see that. They make me sorry for them, but hell, what can we do?"

"Try to keep them alive until they learn some sense," said Hagan. "That's the main thing."

Keep them alive. The phrase seemed to run through his thoughts throughout the evening, and then on into his dreams throughout the night. Coming awake with a strange restlessness several times during the early hours, Hagan was thankful that at least he wasn't dreaming the eagle dream.

Awakened finally from a light sleep by the sound of a borobird he crawled from his bed-sack. Damned bird. The coo of the borobird came again, accompanied by the flap of giant wings as it rose from its nesting place high in the top of a tree across the river.

Hagan felt a chill of danger that drove all images from his mind except the hard, cool reality of the camp around him.

Silently , the dampness of ground mist in his nostrils, the disquiet of an unseen presence growing in his thoughts, he pulled on his clothes and boots.

The unseen presence. He could feel it now. As if someone were roaming without restraint past the sleeping bodies wrapped in their bed-sacks, around the dark ball stoves, then the equipment piled close at hand.

On the opposite side of the camp one of the young soldiers sat guard at the soundboard, watching the flicker of lights and obviously unaware that an intrusion was taking place.

Stilling his mind, subduing a very basic panic, Hagan made

his way between the row of sleepers and approached the young soldier. He placed a hand on the younger man's shoulder to keep him from rising. "Sh—"

The young guard jerked with surprise, then relaxed when he realized who was with him.

Hagan gave him a reassuring smile then turned his attention to the broad, glass-enclosed board. The soft flicker of lights indicated no intrusions, but still he felt the presence.

The Firewing, he thought, and his heart beat faster. The Firewing was back. The same one? In spite of himself something in Hagan opened, like a door being cracked slightly, so that he might peer out into the unknown, and the moment it did a feeling of recognition swept him. The Firewing in the garden— the Firewing across the river yesterday morning. For a moment he thought he could even put a name to the man, but promptly his logical mind denied that it was possible and the inner door slammed shut.

Shaken, Hagan stood staring at the board until the young soldier stretched, and grinned up at him. "Everything's quiet, sir. Has been for hours."

"Good." Hagan drew a slightly shuddering breath, and nodded at the ball stove. "Make us some coffee, why don't you."

"Yes, sir. Shall I wake the others?"

"It's early yet. Let them sleep."

Whistling softly to himself, obviously glad to be allowed to use his cramped muscles, the young soldier moved off quietly to do as he was told.

Hagan sank into the seat vacated by the young soldier and promptly forgot him. How powerful was the Firewing across the river? In the years of his absence from Earth Hagan had tried to come to terms with the fact of a Firewing's power. Patlos, the Firewing he'd killed—his hand trembled and he clenched it tightly in his lap. His own intimate experience with that power would haunt him forever.

But this Firewing across the river—again he almost put a name to the man—had a different power, weaker perhaps. A much younger power. An angry power. Even as he died, Patlos had not been angry. Here, Hagan had a sense of the anger. And this one was dangerous, too, in his unpredictability. But the power of his mind seemed weak compared to what Hagan knew was possible. Yes, even Meeriam was stronger. Strange that the knowledge wasn't as terrifying as it'd been two days ago. Maybe he was just getting used to the idea.

Or maybe, somewhere along the way, he'd realized that these people, these Firewing, were merely human too. Not gods, not supernatural demons or ghosts, but people who merely had extraordinary power. However this sensible idea didn't stop the hair from rising on his neck at the thought of dealing with them.

Was that the secret his father had known that let him get along with them so well?

Because the thought of the Commander was still painful, Hagan deliberately turned his attention back to the Firewing across the river, and knew the presence was still with him. Without volition a name slipped into his consciousness. Condor. The name that had been trying to reach him was Condor. He shivered with the sureness of his knowledge.

The smell of coffee preceded the young soldier's return. Hagan vacated the chair and motioned the young man to reseat himself. Taking the offered cup he glanced around the still sleeping camp. "Shut down Quadrant Four. I'm going down that way."

The young soldier nodded.

Cup in hand, Hagan moved from the soft circle of light cast by the board. Pausing at the edge of the clearing to let his eyes adjust to the predawn twilight, Hagan waited until the trees became distinct shapes, discernible from the bushes, discernible from the path. He then walked quietly, the way his father had taught him, until he came to the bank of the river. You are over there, he thought. You, Condor, with your anger. I don't blame you for your anger. You should be angry at what's happening to your people. I admire your anger. He raised his cup in a half-salute, then sipped the hot liquid. The sense of Condor's presence left him. He waited, but the feeling didn't return, and finally he started back to the camp. Today they'd cross the river into Firewing territory. In three more days he would leave the unit and start on his long journey to the Firewing's city of Phinx.

Chapter 15

Kama Mountain

At first light the People convening around their sacred hearths held counsel with each other. Anahata, eldest of the Clan Lissone, drew the Mind of the tribes to her fire. The Fire bed, laid to an ancient ritual, burst into flame and drew those who worked fields in the sun far to the east back to their sacred fires, drew those who were just rising far to the North to sit at their sacred fires, drew those who had just bedded under a sickle moon back to their sacred fires.

Mind called, and Mind answered.

High on Grandfather Mountain hidden from the rising sun in a deep cleft whose entrance path was a tribal secret, shadows flickered against sentinel rocks and trees, and etched valleys in the faces of her companion elders who occupied the nearest row.

Taking time, she let the fire settle.

And by his fire in the valley below Condor had his own waking dream.

Then, minds meeting Mind, Anahata spoke to the assembled tribe, and to all those of the Mind who had chosen to come to her fire.

Through my heart you have seen the events of the recent past. What might have been joy has turned to sorrow. I seek your counsel again.

The flame flickered higher as though fed by the energy of Mind. The thought came instantaneously across the vast expanse of the planet.

Our heart is sad for our loss. We feel the pain.

Our sorrow is great, Anahata agreed. *We have only defiance or retreat left open to us. It is time to make a decision. We have considered retreat.*

If that is your choice, our Fires would welcome you.

A flicker of humor tinged Anahata's thought, then vanished. *As we would welcome you at ours. But we now find ourselves divided in ways we have never been before.* An image formed in her mind and was shared across the vast reaches of Earth. *We must remember our sacred trust. As keepers of the City we must protect it. We cannot retreat.*

The ancient city was that which lay sleeping beneath a shallow non-reflective dome. One, Elias Hagan had once told her, that would have been recognized instantly by any engineer on Mars as a forerunner of something called the Davies Domes, which protected the burgeoning anthills of Mars.

The image shifted to a small encampment where bodies of four men lay where they had fallen and a group of black and red clad soldiers stood by with weapons drawn, standing for eternity linked to an act that took only a blink of time. Then the images vanished.

The thought came instantaneously from mind. *Remember — the dead do not protect, only the living. What say your own elders?*

Without opening her eyes, Anahata glanced into the minds of those around the fire. All of the arguments were there, all of the indecisions. Not since those first dark days after the Earth burst into flame had the People been so divided. *Our counsel is divided, she said. We seek the collective wisdom of the Mind of the People, and we will abide by the council of Mind.*

Having laid the problem into the lap of Mind, and knowing that all would abide by what Mind decided, if indeed, Mind decided anything, Anahata withdrew. Around the fire the others waited.

Then, from the far side of the fire the shadows broke, spun and solidified into the form of Condor. Staring around, he appeared shocked by the sight that greeted him. Then his face darkened with fury.

Anahata, knowing that a smile would infuriate him further, merely nodded. Watching him a deep sadness swept over her. Condor, her grandson's son, looking like a painting from the past. Paintings she'd seen in the Ancient City when she was a child.

Fierce and warrior-like, he'd not be guided by the elders. He would deny Mind. He had, in fact, already done so, and thereby diminished himself.

She grew heavy with her weighty thoughts. It had been so

much easier before the Return. He would have had the land—the weather—these would have been his foes. He would have fought them, and in the end would have been a better man for it. Now he had to fight the Wanderers, and himself.

"Well," he said into the silence, "what does Mind say? Will we flee like children before a lion-cub?"

Though she could have been angered by his insolence, Anahata chose not to be. "Do you equate the Arcolans with cubs, Condor?" She recreated for him the picture she had shared with Mind. Because his own abilities were weakened by his intense presence in the present she helped him look closely at the faces of the dead.

Abruptly he shook his head, driving out the images. "They slaughter the defenseless. We don't have to be defenseless any longer. I will not let it happen again."

Anahata hesitated, for the first time uncertain of her control over Condor. Mildly, though, she agreed. "No, it will not. We will abide by the Counsel of Mind. Perhaps it is time we gave this land to the Wanderers. Earth is vast and there are areas untouched in a thousand years where we could go."

"No! We will not give up what is ours! If we run from them now, there's no place on Earth that will be safe from them. You must see that." His tone became desperately pleading. "Listen to me, Grandmother. No one is safe from them. They will destroy us."

"If we do what we know is wrong, we will destroy ourselves. We will abide by the counsel of Mind."

Her curt words seemed to inflame Condor further. "No, Grandmother. Mind will not contain me." In his anger he seemed to grow in size until he stood massive against the shadows. A young and vengeful God of Retribution. He would be a leader to be feared, should he gather many followers, but his retribution would be merciless, indiscriminate, and with no understanding of who the real enemy was.

Mind, as he said, would not contain him. That was true. She knew it. She bowed her head. So be it, then. Neither would he contain Mind, nor would those who chose to follow him.

Anahata drew closer to the fire. Felt the pull of the Mind of Earth and closed her eyes. The others did the same. They became as the rocks and the trees, minds joining with Mind. Communion.

Sister and Mother of us all—spoke Mind.

We are Earth, she replied.

Your people are our people. Any who wish to come will be welcomed at any fire they choose. It would be abhorrent to Mind to perpetrate pain and destruction. Given time those not of the Mind will destroy themselves.

Sadly she agreed. *Yes, that is my greatest fear. They are a part of us, and yet apart.* She felt urged to defend the Wanderers, even though some had done nothing to deserve her defense. *They need help.*

Your efforts and your compassion fill Mind with hope. Perhaps, however, the clash is inevitable, and it would be better to meet it now rather than at some future date when the others fill the Earth once again with their separate ambitions. Knowledge died for is dearly bought.

True. Would that it was otherwise, she agreed.

There was a pause as if Mind were searching for words of comfort. *There are infinite possibilities. But the choice, as always , belongs to each individual heart. There is one who has returned. You know him.*

I know him. A chill that was part excitement and part apprehension touched her. *He is of my blood. I have called him.*

But he does not know himself. He must know himself before he can know Mind.

The way to self-knowledge is painful, she replied.

The fire will forge a strong steel.

I understand. We are Earth. Anahata bowed her head, feeling the withdrawal of Mind.

Again she felt the heat of the open fire on her face. A silence fell broken only by the crackling of the flames.

"Well?" Condor's insistence broke her concentration. "What was the decision?"

She stared at him across the fire pit. The elders watched. One leaned forward and threw another small log into the low flame and sparks snapped upward and disappeared in the rocks high overhead.

"You make your own decisions," she said finally.

Confusion flickered across Condor's face. "Mind—"

"Mind will neither help nor hinder you."

"But how—" Condor looked from one to the other of the elders as if he'd by force take the answers from them. Ferrian returned his stare, Hallat peered into the depths of the Fire. Maltoc watched Anahata, a small frown on his ancient brow.

"Each of us makes his own choice," Anahata said gently. "Mind will not be used, not by you or by anyone else. What is to be forged on this land in the coming days will be used here for eternity. Evil does not come from good, nor good emerge from evil, but the choice is and always has been yours. And mine. And each one of us individually and together. The main difference between the People of Earth and the Wanderers is that we of Earth understand this concept and they do not."

"And what if there is no clear choice?" Condor sounded agonized.

"There is always choice. You either build the universe or you diminish it."

Condor raised a fist to the distant sky. "I will not let the Others destroy us piece by piece."

"As I said, your choice." Tired now, Anahata felt every one of her years pressing her down. Condor still did not understand. He thought he could remake the world to fit his image of it. So be it, let him try.

Drawing silence around her, she disappeared from Condor's view.

And one by one, the others did the same, until Condor was left alone, staring at his own fire, knowing almost in a panic that for the first time in his life he was truly alone.

Before noon Hagan's VMP unit came to Old Man Crossing, where the road laid down earlier in the Spring bridged the river into Firewing Territory.

Unable to keep his uneasiness at bay, Hagan sat in the cab and stared at the slim bridge that gaped in the middle, torn apart by an energy he could barely comprehend.

He rubbed at the knot of tension building at the back of his neck.

On the downstream side of the bridge giant blocks of gray-white cerafoam had been tumbled like blocks on a nursery room floor.

"Jeez, will you look at that?" Awe filled one young voice.

Another didn't seem to comprehend what he was seeing. 'Wonder why they call it Old Man Crossing?"

Loomis chuckled. "Because, by the time we get this bridge rebuilt, we'll be old men."

Laughter rippled from the younger men, and with it came a lessening of tension.

Hagan continued to study the gap. At least twenty meters, he judged. Washed out by the river at flood? Not likely. The road crews hadn't built this road until after the short wet winter had passed and the spring runoff wouldn't have brought the river up enough to wash out this bridge.

Ignoring the chatter of the men as they exited the HOGG, Hagan swung down and walked the roadway to the gaping edge of the hole. Deliberately he shut out the sound of rushing water, the cheerful bird calls, the subdued whine of the waiting HOGG. Carefully he tested the resiliency of the construction beneath his feet. To this point, at least, it held under his weight with no vibration. How long ago—

"Hey, Cap, will we turn back? Damned old HOGG can't walk on water," someone called. Again irrepressible laughter ran through the younger men.

Hagan heard, and for a moment was tempted. They could go back and reach the old Valley Roadway and then go as far as Kama Garrison without once crossing the river. Postponing the inevitable. But there was no excuse. They had the road-thrower. Graeber would be expecting their report tonight.

He frowned as a niggling thought tried to make itself known. Old Man Crossing. This was where Graeber had wanted them to spend last night.

But the only place to camp, obviously, would have been across the river in that stand of trees. Surely then as of the beginning of this week at least, Graeber hadn't known the bridge was torn apart. Which meant recent damage. The Firewing? He studied the far trees, but sensed nothing of the feeling he'd had before, the feeling of presence from the Firewing.

If they had been here, they were gone now, and he had a bridge to repair. And the sooner the bridge was finished, the sooner he reached the mountains, and the sooner he'd be on his own.

The by-now-familiar sense of urgency hit him, making his voice sharp. "Loomis!"

"Sir?" Loomis was right behind him.

"There's only a twenty meter gap. Tell the men to pile everything they can lift into the hole. Get those blocks of cerafoam down there, they'll help. And any river rock you can move.When it's high enough, we'll cement it together with c'foam and throw a road over it."

"Will it hold that way?"

"Long enough to get a HOGG across." Turning, Hagan met Loomis's doubtful eyes. "Also get someone on the comboard and tell Staff what we're up against and what we're doing."

The work progressed at a steady pace throughout the late morning. By early afternoon the gap in the slim arc of bridge had been filled with rock, cemented with c'foam, more rock and river-smoothed driftwood and two small trees cut from the far bank. Hagan let the men stop for a late noon break, then set a team to throwing another layer of new c'foam into the fill. When the first layer was finished they paused, waiting to see how much the foam would settle before it set.

"Damned hot work, Captain," Loomis said. He, like the others and Hagan himself, had stripped off the heavy uniform blouse and the hard leather boots that weren't water tight, and now glistened with sweat and water.

"Yes, it is. But we're almost finished. Come on, keep them moving."

Hagan had no inclination to slow down. He wanted it finished before dark. "We've been working pretty fast, sir. Think it'll hold up?"

Hagan caught the worry in Loomis's voice and paused in the act of shoving another rock into the upriver side of the makeshift buttress. He straightened. Loomis's eyes were shadowed with concern.

"It'll hold." At least long enough to get the HOGG across. "I've seen whole buildings thrown up in less time than it's taken to repair this bridge. Don't worry.'

Loomis's irrepressible optimism returned. He grinned. "Yes

183

sir, if you say so, sir."

Hagan flashed him a grin and wedged in another rock.

"Hey, Cap," called one of the young soldiers. "Can we have another early camp tonight?" The others faced Hagan hopefully. Sergeant Warren sneered a word under his breath. Hagan ignored him. Glancing up at the sun he guessed another two hours of daylight at least. Time enough to be well away from the river assuming they ran into no more roadblocks.

Then he glanced across the river to the thick stand of shaded wood that grew down to the river's edge. By the good Lord, yes, it was hot, and the woods opposite promised a cool relief. And tomorrow they could rise extra early and be half way to Kama before dawn. Stilling a small internal warning that he was making a mistake, he smiled wryly."All right. As soon as the carrier's across we'll stop for the night."

After that the pace picked up again. The top layer of c'foam was laid without incident. Waiting for the c'foam to dry, Hagan sent Warren with two of the young soldiers to scout out a site for a camp down the road through the trees. When all that remained was to drive the HOGG across, Hagan sent the others on ahead. Loomis lingered behind.

Sitting near the water's edge, Hagan pulled his damp boots on. Beside him Loomis shrugged into his uniform blouse. When Hagan stood, once more dressed, Loomis did also. But as Hagan moved to the driver's side of the HOGG, Loomis spoke.

'Sir, I can drive the HOGG over, if you want me to.'

Wryly Hagan studied the younger man. "Don't you think I'm capable, Lieutenant?"

Loomis turned red under Hagan's scrutiny. "I didn't mean that, sir."

"Then I wonder what you did mean." Loomis's concern touched him but it was, he thought, like the chick mothering the hen. "Walk over. I'll be right behind you in the HOGG."

The other men had already disappeared into the trees on the opposite bank. Hagan, mounting the cab of the carrier, checked the fuel cells, and kicked in the thrusters. The whine of the air turbines roared into the poorly insulated cab. Under any circumstances the HOGG was an awkward vehicle to drive, especially compared with the small personal carriers found on

Mars, and to a lessor extent, in Norcanna. But the necessary skills hadn't deserted him. Once on its air cushion the troop carrier responded to the secondary thrusters like a well-trained warhorse. Slowly he followed the ribbon of cerafoam onto the arching bridge. Half a meter of clearance on either side allowed for little sway. Loomis, walking slowly, his eyes on the smooth c'foam roadbed, squinted in the bright glare of sunshine reflecting back from the fresh white foam. Cutting his speed until he was merely creeping, Hagan followed. Thank God for a still day, the thought came and went with the half-way point of the bridge. A bad crosswind would have been disastrous. The downward side was shorter than the upward side because the bank was higher, and Hagan felt a relaxing of the tension in his shoulders as he reached the end of the bridge. Loomis, ahead of him, turned, and grinning again, gave him a thumbs-up.Stepping off the roadway, the younger man waited until the HOGG came abreast of him. Hagan had slid open the cab door and started to say come aboard when a splintering of glass came simultaneously with a sharp, loud report. Shards stung him from every angle. He shielded his face and automatically kicked the off lever of the thrusters. The HOGG settled with a jar. Another report slammed loudly into the sudden silence and the HOGG shook sharply beneath the impact. He heard a harsh cry, and Loomis's hand reached out to him and then disappeared as Loomis fell.

Throwing himself out of the cab, Hagan hit the ground with a heavy thud. Against the carrier Loomis lay, a bright red stain running to the roadbed beneath him.

Shaking off a numbing horror, Hagan crawled to Loomis's side. The carrier had settled to solid contact with the roadbed. Its bulk seemed to be the only point of safety that Hagan could think of. Another loud report accompanied a sharp thud right above their heads, and without comprehension Hagan looked up at the hole that had suddenly appeared in the carrier door.

Get out of here, the thought screamed, and a moment later he'd pulled Loomis around the end of the HOGG and had fallen off the roadway on the other side, leaving a trail of bright red blood on the new white c'foam to show where they'd been.

In the protection of the ditch, working quickly, not knowing if their unseen attacker would shift position and try again, Hagan stripped off Loomis's uniform blouse and tore it into pieces, making pads for both the front exit wound and back entrance wound high on Loomis's torso. Hagan strapped the pads in place with his belt, speaking assurances in quiet tones, even though certain Loomis didn't hear.

A silence fell, a brooding, waiting silence that was broken only by Loomis's gasping breath and his own heart beating loud and fast in his ears. Movement in the trees to his right caught his eye. One of the sergeants, Warren, he thought, moved low and fast in their direction. Close behind him came three of the younger men. Hagan found himself trying to sense the Firewing presence in the trees, but found nothing. No alien presence, no disturbance. The feeling grew that the attacker had fled. He looked down and saw blood on the back of his hands, the small crisscrosses of cuts caused by flying glass that were minor but numerous. He reached up and brushed grains of glass from his face, thankful that none seemed to have found his eyes.

Loomis gasped and his eyes blinked open. The fear in them faded as his gaze settled on Hagan's face.

His lips quirked in a small grimace. "You look like hell."

"You don't look too good yourself," Hagan replied.

"I don't feel too good either." Loomis's eyes fluttered shut again.

In that moment Hagan knew that all his plans had changed. There was no more question of going into the mountains now. Loomis must be returned to Norcanna. And as soon as possible.

His responsibility for what had happened ate at him. If he'd let Loomis drive the HOGG —if he'd turned back before they crossed the river—if he'd stopped a second sooner—The ifs threatened to drown him.

The numbness he'd been fighting crept up on him. He watched Warren scan the opposite side of the roadway. No one there, he thought, then pushed himself to his feet. He drew no more fire. Still using the scanner, Warren rose to his feet and moved closer. He was pale. "The damned Firewing's gone. Are you all right, Captain?"

Looking down at Loomis's blood mingled with his own, Hagan wanted to deny that he'd ever be all right again. "Yes.

Round up the men, Sargent. We're going back to Norcanna right now." If they were lucky they'd get there before Loomis died.

Throughout the rest of the afternoon and on through the long dusk as the orange heat of day faded to purple night, Hagan sat in the cab of the HOGG trying not to think of Loomis stretched out on an airbed pallet in the back, slowly bleeding his life away. The young men kept silent vigil at his side. As the night grew darker, a sliver of new moon appeared riding low over Kama's peak. Mars, unblinking and red against the velvet of space, rode a few degrees higher. Red, the color of blood. Shifting in his seat Hagan wondered how far they'd come, but decided not to ask. More than likely the young driver didn't even know. Ahead of them the white ribbon of c'foam roadway seemed to disappear at some point just this side of infinity.

"What do you think that is?" The young driver pointed off to the right where a distant pale glow lit the sky. It might have been a small distant city or a nearby farm.

"A Hojoi farm," said Hagan absently. Ball lamps would be floating in their endless hypnotic patterns here on Earth just like they had done for centuries under the Domes of Mars, mindlessly repeating patterns made obsolete by the transfer to Earth. Immense Earth, where violence lurked behind trees, and young men like Loomis who hurt no one could be hurt themselves for no apparent reason.

Odd that he hadn't sensed the Firewing's presence this time. He certainly had that morning in Kassine's garden. And just yesterday in camp before the others had risen. The day before, at their rest-stop—

A Firewing. He'd not believed it was possible. What a marvelous piece of propaganda Graeber would make of it for the nightscreens of Mars. With all the blood and gore intact. It might be the very thing Graeber had been looking for.

Of course, if he himself had been the victim, Graeber might have claimed a double victory.

"Sir, look. A shooting star."

Hagan looked where the young man pointed. It did appeared to be a star, traveling low over the horizon. "Not a star, soldier. A landhopper—" A landhopper. A damned landhopper could get Loomis back more quickly. All they had to do was find where the branch road took off. Not too hard, they'd passed it some time yesterday.

An hour later Hagan ordered the young driver to turn off the road onto the secondary branch that went to the Thomas Homestead.

Warren's face appeared in the doorway between the cab and the rear. "You're crazy," he sputtered. "Those freefarmers won't give you the nod, let alone give Loomis space on a 'hopper. Hell, they'd just as soon see him dead. Be one less soldier to worry about."

"Nonetheless," Hagan said firmly, "we're going. Now."

The branch road took them east and then north. On either side of the ribbon of c'foam he sensed rather than saw the rows of Hojoi stretching to some unseen boundary many stadts away.

In some places the smell of damp Earth indicated unseen irrigation ditches, in others a deep earth smell drew mind pictures of rich plowed land and a feeling of kinship with the earth rose in him.

The memory of his father rose too, hard, unforgiving, implacably angry . You do not deserve Earth. That's what Elias had said. True. Everything Elias had said was true. He'd fled that beautiful glen while the morning mist still shrouded the trees, had gone straight to the Kama Garrison to tell Elias what had happened. By the next morning, before the others had climbed from their bunks, Elias had stripped him of his rank, of his youth, and if Elias had been able, he'd have been stripped of even his name. Only when he'd lost everything had he been able to value it.

Three days later Portus had put him on the Diana Shuttle. Weeks later, still numb from shock, he'd arrived on Mars with no idea what he'd do with the rest of his life. Only an odd fate had thrown him in with Josh and the troupe. He'd never seen professional acting before, but Josh had taken a look at him, liked what he'd seen and put him into classes with the other apprentices. Hagan glanced down at the sleeves of his uniform blouse. In the dark he was unable to see the blood stains, but he knew they were there.He thought of Loomis who clung to life by invisible threads of determination and hope. Would Loomis be lying there now if he hadn't come back? He shuddered.

"Sir, we're almost there."

"Good." Hagan shrugged his bitter thoughts aside. "Pull into the area by the stacking sheds."

"Sir—"

"What?" he snapped.

"A new rule came out just this last week. We're not allowed to take military vehicles past the gates."

Impatiently Hagan shrugged. "Then stop outside. I'll walk in."

"Sir," the young soldier glanced doubtfully at him. "Shouldn't you take a s'darm?"

The rumors of the Freefarmers arming was more widespread that he'd thought. He weighed the risk against the protection a s'darm might give him. "No." He swung down from the cab. A small sign hung on a standard to the right of the open gateway, the legend visible in the glow of the running lights of the HOGG. Thomas Homestead. Would it be a help or a hindrance if Thomas remembered him?

Sergeant Warren stepped off the back of the HOGG, followed by the other more silent sergeant. "You'd better take some men in with you."

A show of force? "I want cooperation, not coercion, Warren." Though why Liam Thomas should give him any he didn't know. But the Freefarmer had the landhopper. And damn it, he couldn't be so angry as to let a young man die. Seeing the anger flare in Warren's eyes, Hagan forestalled an argument "Wait for me."

Five minutes later he approached the stationary circle of ball lamps surrounding the hopper pad. A crew of four men were busy unloading the cargo hold of the awkward looking air-vehicle. A fifth stood to one side, watching. Liam Thomas, the Freefarmer himself. At the edge of the shadows by his side a large stack of brown crates stood in orderly rows.

There was a quietness to the whole scene that struck Hagan forcibly. The moment he stepped into the light Thomas whirled facing him. A s'darm, larger than any military weapon Hagan had ever seen, appeared in the Freefarmer's hand as though it were accustomed to being there.

The other four men froze, and the eerie silence was broken only by the soft rumble of the landhopper's air turbine.

"What the hell?" breathed one of the men.

"VMP" Another straightened slowly, his face uncommonly pale in the unnatural glow of the stationary lamps.

Hagan took another step into the pool of light, his hands lifted outward showing that he carried no weapons. "Thomas?"

With a quick, silent gesture Liam Thomas sent the four men scurrying into the shadows. Hagan heard them moving around behind him, and the hair rose on the back of his neck.

"How did you get here?" Liam Thomas grated out.

"A HOGG, out on the roadway."

"At this time of night?" Thomas's mouth tightened. He used his other hand to steady the large weapon pointed at Hagan's chest. "Troops?"

"Only a unit. Still out on the road." The sounds behind him abruptly ceased. Though the night had cooled somewhat, Hagan felt a trickle of sweat crawl down his back.

"Why? How did you know?"

Hagan glanced at the crates that had been unloaded. Were they weapons? Machinery? Contraband goods? "I don't know anything, Van Thomas. I've come for help."

The weapon in Liam Thomas's hand rose menacingly, its lens muzzle glinting in the bright light. "You've come to the wrong place."

"Thomas—" Hagan spoke quickly, trying to keep the desperation from his voice, "I've got a badly injured man. He has to get to Norcanna as quickly as possible. I'm asking you to take him in the landhopper—"

"No."

"Yes. Please. If you turn us away the unit out there'll want to know why. They'll be suspicious. Even if you kill me the word will still get back to Graeber. He'll wonder what you were hiding—"

"You're Ellis Hagan, the Commander's son, aren't you?" Thomas's tone was accusing. "It's said you've thrown your lot with Graeber. The Commander'd give me a medal for removing some of Graeber's scum."

Bone deep fatigue moved through Hagan. A sadness, a

certainty that Thomas was right. He was almost too tired to argue, but Loomis—no.No, he wouldn't let Loomis die. He met Thomas's angry eyes, and let his own certainty show. "The Commander would've approved of the young soldier out there who's so badly injured, Thomas. He's everything the Commander thought a soldier should be. He'll die if you don't take him back to Norcanna."

"Who is he?"

"Lieutenant Loomis. He was in Captain Moss's unit before being assigned to me."

"Loomis?" The name seemed to mean something to the Freefarmer. Or perhaps it was the mention of Moss. Slowly the lethal looking weapon lowered. Hagan had no doubt thoughts were moving with the speed of light behind Thomas's impassive face. Finally, with a practiced movement, the Freefarmer holstered the s'darm. "All right. I'll take him as far as the Processing plant. You'll have to have someone else take him on out to the hospital. We don't go near that place."

Thinking of all he'd heard about the hospital euphemistically referred to as the "Farm" Hagan's stomach knotted. "No, I don't want Loomis out there. Dr. Portus can help him." Better yet, Meeriam, the Firewing. If one Firewing could shoot Loomis, perhaps another could heal him.

Once Thomas had made up his mind, he moved swiftly. One argument arose when Hagan insisted he'd go to Norcanna with Loomis. Thomas said no, but Hagan remained adamant, and Thomas conceded the point.

Thomas stood behind in the shadows when Hagan returned to the HOGG. Warren stepped away from the cab and Hagan saw that he'd once more armed himself. "At ease, Sergeant. They've agreed to take him."

"That's a blasted miracle. I'll call Staff and let them know he's coming."

"No need. I'm going too. I'll call them from Kassine's."

Warren shrugged as if it made no difference, but Hagan felt a surge of resentment from the older man that was almost physical. As if he could read Warren's mind, Hagan knew that the moment they were out of sight, he would contact Graeber anyway. There was a way, one way, he knew, to keep the Sergeant from doing that.

Using the moments of confusion while the men unloaded Loomis, Hagan found the Comboard, brought it down over his knee with a loud crack. Cursing angrily, he muttered about trying to work in the dark and got an answering chuckle from one of the younger men. Let Warren later make of it what he would.

Thomas waited until the HOGG had disappeared from view before he ordered his men to pick up the pallet and bear Loomis to the landhopper. Thomas and Hagan followed the shadowy figures back toward the waiting circle of light. One of the men, Hagan noticed, had been left behind to make sure the soldiers didn't return.

"How long before you're ready to go?" Though Hagan was trying to control his impatience, the sound of it was in his voice. He felt Thomas's silent regard.

"Not long." The Freefarmer's voice brooked no further conversation.

Having no choice, Hagan impatiently endured the wait. Finally the hiss of a closing hatch told him Thomas had finished the job. He stood as Thomas appeared in the cab doorway. "Strap in," the Freefarmer ordered.

Hagan regained his seat and did as he was told.

After dropping a trip-card into the control box, Thomas slid into one of the recliners, snapped the locks on his retainer straps and swung his chair to face Hagan. He ignored the rising pitch of turbines, and the lumbering movement of the landhopper as it lifted off the pad. His eyes were hard. "How long before you tell Graeber what you've seen tonight?"

"What have I seen? Men working at night to beat the heat of day? Cargo being off-loaded?" Hagan glanced at Loomis who was deathly white and struggling for breath. "You might save his life, tonight, Van Thomas. I won't thank you by carrying tales to Graeber."

A subtle tension seemed to flow from Thomas's stiff body. "You're more your father's son than people think." For the first time fatigue lines crept around his eyes and mouth. He studied Loomis. "What happened?"

Hagan told the tale. Then suddenly, in the middle of one

thought, he had another and a wave of fear washed over him. The pack of clothes and supplies he'd left in the cab of the HOGG, hidden behind the seats.

Good God! How long before they were found?

Chapter 16

Kama Valley

The pack, even if Warren and the unit drove straight through the night, and reached Norcanna by late tomorrow afternoon, might not be found until someone cleaned out the HOGG tomorrow. On the other hand, the broken comboard would give Graeber a clue, but how in the hell could he have done otherwise? Still, it would only give him hours at the most. He had only hours before Graeber learned what was going on.

Drained of everything except mounting anxiety, Hagan glanced at the freefarmer, who'd leaned back in his recliner and closed his eyes. He looked asleep. Hagan tried to emulate Thomas, but sleep was elusive.

Why hadn't he sensed the Firewing who attacked them? And how in the hell had the Firewing improved his aim so much from one day to the next?

Elias had been killed with an old-style weapon, though of course not the same kind, but —his stomach knotted—but the Firewing hadn't killed him.

Then, if not the Firewing, who? And why? Why Loomis? Why not he himself? Or should he also have been lying there in his own blood, the way Loomis was? His tired mind circled the questions without finding answers. Finally he drifted into a space where memories and images chased each other in restless disorder across the nightscreen of his mind.

When the memory of Patlos came, as it had tried to come more and more often lately, he pushed it away, but it left a residue of cold sweat on his face and arms, and he shivered slightly in spite of the warmth in the small cabin. He was almost grateful when Loomis stirred and groaned, and drew him from his thoughts.

Quickly, Hagan released himself from his recliner and moved to Loomis's side. Raising a hand to his chest, Loomis was exploring his injury. Hagan placed a hand over his, stopping him. "Careful. You don't want to knock the bandage off."

"Captain?" Loomis's eyes were glazed with pain and held little comprehension. "Where —"

"Liam Thomas is giving us a ride to Norcanna." Hagan glanced at the Freefarmer, ostensibly relaxed in sleep. Desperation deepened in Loomis's pain-filled eyes. "I—I don't want to go out to the Farm."

"No, of course not." Hagan chilled at the strength of his own conviction. From what he'd heard of Graeber's hospital, some said it had been made into a major retraining facility, no human should be allowed into that monstrosity.

A shadow of his former smile crossed Loomis's face, and he relaxed into the pallet. "Thanks."

Regaining his own seat, Hagan also tried to relax, but the anxious knot that had tightened his stomach seemed to grow larger. By the minute it became more imperative that he reach the Ancient City before Graeber did. As soon as Loomis was settled at the clinic he had to leave again.

That decision reached, he should've been able to rest, but the moment he tried to clear his mind the memory of Loomis lying bloody in his arms returned, and when he tried to blank it out, the body became that of Patlos, and he finally gave in to the memory.

Patlos.

Even as he thought the name, a feeling of helplessness swept him. The same feeling that he'd had staring down at the Firewing's body. And he was cold. As cold as he'd been on that day by the river, on winter patrol.

They'd been on patrol from Kama Garrison, he and his unit, following the south fork of the Kama River into the lower reaches of the mountain range. A report had come in to Kama that Freefarmers were homesteading a little clearing on the far side of the river, in an area that had previously been a Firewing settlement. Intent on protecting the Firewing, the Commander had ordered Hagan to find the farmers and move them back on their own side of the river barrier.

Hagan had been angry at the assignment which he guessed was nothing more than punishment for having incurred Vana

Kassine's displeasure over his attention to her daughter. "Stupid young pup," had been his father's first angry summation of the matter. Two weeks on patrol in the middle of winter was guaranteed to cool him off.

But it hadn't.

If anything, the patrol to the far reaches of the Kama River had increased his resentment. He hated winter patrol. He hated the cold damp days, the miserable wet nights. He dreamt of holding Luan, sweet, soft Luan, in his arms all night, and he burned with jealousy wondering who she was with. He had no doubt she was with someone. She was a sickness in his soul. He knew he was going mad, slowly and surely mad, and that the only cure was to return to Norcanna as soon as he could.

Even Hugh Moss had laughed, he remembered. "You, Ellis, a Matriarch's consort? God, you wouldn't tolerate the position a year."

None of them, not his father, not Moss, not Vana Kassine herself realized that he'd be anything Luan wanted him to be. He loved her, by the good Lord above, he loved her.

The previous evening, though they'd only been out five days, he'd decided he'd take the unit back to Kama Garrison. They'd moved as far upriver as was humanly possible without starting to climb the mountain itself, and had found no sign of life beyond the river's edge. Not even a herd of deer, or a pack of coyotes. And so he'd tell Elias when they returned. And then he'd leave. He'd go back to Norcanna, whether he had permission or not.

He was awake early that morning. While the other members of his unit stirred themselves out of their warm bed-sacks, he pulled his long hooded weather cloak tighter and left the camp clearing, following a faint river trail, the scout's scanner looped around his shoulder, his s'darm strapped to his thigh.

He meant to give it one more try. The Commander wouldn't be able to say he'd shirked his duties, though he had no idea what man in his right mind, whether he be Freefarmer or Firewing, would choose of his own volition to be out in this weather.

But as he walked, a memory of Luan laughing as she pulled him with her into the heated waters of Norcanna's largest spa flushed him with corresponding warmth. The memory filled him to the point where he almost forgot where he was, what he was doing.

The river itself reminded him.

The river was rising with voracious appetite, eating at the banks and the brush on either side. The trail ahead crumbled in front of his eyes into the raging tide. The roar of the river wiped out every other sound.

The rage of the old man river matched the emotions raging inside of him, and momentarily he felt at one with the river, flowing angry and deep in this tight canyon, barely contained by conditions over which he had no control.

Then his purpose for being on the trail reasserted itself. He'd not have the Commander saying he'd ignored his reason for being there.

Raising the scanner to his eyes he studied the opposite bank. In the gray light of dawn, with a mist that was fast becoming icy rain, he found a small clearing, but there was no sign of human occupancy. Only a small herd of miniature deer which seemed to sense a hidden observer and floated with their peculiar gait up into the heavy stand of trees on the opposite hillside.

Turning the scanner to the river itself, Hagan saw floating logs, whole bushes uprooted and swept away, the water itself mud-colored and dull in the early morning light. Angry. Wild.

The closer bank, his side of the river, was more crowded with undergrowth, the path ahead lost to the river, the water-soaked bank still crumbling under the force of the current.

Lowering the scanner, he stared at the disappearing path, fascinated by the power of the water, by the sense of immense danger it evoked.

Then, as if someone gripped him from behind, he was pulled back from the edge, the tugging on his arm insistent, not to be ignored. He shrugged off the touch, then became aware of what he'd done.

He whirled, expecting to find one of his men at his back.

No one was there.

Fear flashed through him, but also curiosity. Someone was here or had been here just a moment before. The path he'd come down was empty. A smaller path almost hidden by encroaching

bushes disappeared up an incline to his left. That way, he
thought, someone must've gone that way. Someone was playing
games. His resentment burst forth again. Why the hell would
anyone want to do that?

He plunged up the faint path into the undergrowth, beating
the bushes in a futile attempt to flush someone out. When the
long weather cloak caught and tangled in thorn-covered vines, he
shrugged it off and went on.

Then, between one breath and the next the trail was
swallowed by a tangle of undergrowth, willow, fern and fennel,
and wild thorn-covered vines. He spun around, searching for
the path, his heart pounding. Careful, he cautioned himself.
Keep a clear head. It's all right. There's a way out. Behind
him, somewhere not too distant, he still heard the angry voice
of the river, though its roar was now muted. Ahead through the
driving rain he made out a steep hill whose summit was lost in
the low cloud ceiling. Useless to try there.

He could go back toward the sound of the river, but as he
studied that way, the underbrush seemed impenetrable.

Quieting his growing, unnamed fear, he moved forward,
taking the only way that seemed possible, the way of least
resistance, until he came to the base of a huge tree whose top
vanished like the hill into swirling clouds. One hand on the cold
wet trunk, he stepped carefully around roots and muck, sliding a
little and catching himself on one low limb.

A moment later he stepped into a small sheltered clearing,
stepped into it before he even realized it was there.

An open fire, smaller than a ball lamp, flickered in the middle
of the cleared space, drawing his wary gaze. The fire seemed
untouched by the rain, and the dampness of the air. To one side,
seeming to wait with uncommon patience for Hagan to notice
him, a man stood. A man dressed in brown. Brown soft-boots,
brown leggings, a brown shirt and vest, brown padded jacket
exquisitely decorated in brown thread designs shot through with
pale blue.

Raising his gaze to the man's face, Hagan experienced a flash
of recognition, but it passed as quickly as it came.

A Firewing. Fear swept Hagan. An unreasoning fear that
had been with him since childhood, and for which he had no

explanation.

His hand flew to his s'darm. He'd grown up hearing the tales of the dangerous Firewing, had thought he didn't believe all he'd heard–of course Firewing couldn't fly–of course they didn't glow with their power—but he believed enough to make him panic. Firewing could make you see what wasn't there. They could invade your mind—

In all his twenty-six years he'd never come face to face with a Firewing. He wanted to run, but felt rooted to the spot like the huge old tree he'd skirted to get here.

"You're a long way from your Garrison, young man." The Firewing spoke the Norcannan dialect with inflections of Arcolan crispness.

Hagan tried to contain his surprise and failed. His throat was tight. He was amazed that it even worked at all. "You're a long way from your mountain, Firewing."

"My mountain," the Firewing gestured at the surroundings with a smile, "my river, my fire, all of which you may share if you wish."

Hagan glanced at the unconfined fire and a deeply instilled horror of the unconfined flame flickered through him. He shook his head, but couldn't speak the denial that was on his tongue.

"The fire will warm you if you let it," the Firewing continued. He seemed both amused and sad.

Hagan frowned. "Open fire's dangerous." His panic growing stronger, Hagan glanced around the tiny clearing. The Firewing seemed unencumbered with either tent or pack. Or weapon. Some, he knew, carried the ancient projectile weapons, either cartridge or shot, when they hunted , but this one seemed not even to do that. Hagan turned his fearful gaze back to the Firewing. "Why are you here?"

"I'm waiting."

Waiting for what, thought Hagan.

Waiting for you, came the thought in reply.

The panic rose in Hagan's throat, threatened to choke him. His hand trembled around the butt of his s'darm.

Again the thought intruded. *I am Patlos. You're—*

Words burst uncontrollably from Hagans icy lips. "No! Stop that! Stay out of my mind!"

200

"It's nothing to fear. It's—"

"It's wrong." Dark swirls of fear clouded Hagan's vision, and panic, painful in its intensity, gripped him. He backed toward the shelter of the huge old tree until he came up against the hard wet trunk.

The Firewing stepped toward Hagan, hand held out. "Please, don't be afraid of —"

Hagan fired the s'darm at point blank range straight into the Firewing's chest. The brilliant flash of the charge drowned out the light of the small flame, bounced light against the sparkling drops of rain water dripping off the leaves overhead, then vanished, leaving the small glen darker than it was before. With a cry that cut through Hagan's very soul the Firewing clutched at his chest, then crumpled to the soggy earth. In horror Hagan stared at the fallen body. Trembling with dread, he nonetheless dropped to the Firewing's side and hesitantly reached out and turned him over. The smell of burnt flesh filled his nostrils.

I did this, he thought numbly. I did this—in anguish too great to name he threw the s'darm down and gathered the fallen man into his arms. I did this—

The Firewing opened eyes already clouded with approaching death. "I'm sorry—" His words were soft but spoken with determined effort. His hand clutched Hagan's arm with uncommon strength. "I made you fear me. It is not your fault."

Uttering a quiet sound meant to soothe the dying man, Hagan stood, lifting Patlos with him, barely conscious of the man's full weight. "I'll get you back to camp. I'll take you to the Garrison. We have a doctor—"

"No." The voice was both in his hearing and in his head, but now Hagan's anguish was too great for the knowledge to frighten him. "No. Tell—your father—tell Elias—I absolve you of blame." With a sigh the Firewing named Patlos died.

Hagan stood, the Firewing's body in his arms, barely aware of the rain pelting down upon his head, or of the small fire which flickered and died as if it had only been kept alive by the Firewing's breath.

A painful despair greater than any he'd ever known welled up in him. He had done this act. He'd committed this crime.

Everything that followed, his father's rage, the stripping of his rank, his banishment to Mars and a strange new life, all these he'd deserved. Because he had killed Patlos.

And the pain of the memory was as undiminished this night as on the day it had happened.

In a strong echo of that earlier despair, Hagan wondered if he would ever finish paying for Patlos' death.

With Hagan still shivering in his memories the trip ended. Liam Thomas had called ahead, and they were met by Meeriam and two young plant workers. In the early hours of the morning, they reached the small new medical facility. Loomis was their first patient.

Tucked into a curve of the heavily wooded hill, the small clinic's entrance faced a stone pathway that followed the curve of the incline to the major path through Old Town. Its back wall nestled in comfortable proximity to the tree-covered hill.

The smell inside was newness rather than antiseptic. Nilander's men shifted Loomis from his pallet to the white sheeted bed and silently removed themselves. Meeriam worked over Loomis, removing his shirt as gently as she could, approving the makeshift bandage, but not removing it.

"Will Portus come?" Hagan asked, unable to keep his anxiety at bay. He'd not brought Loomis this far only to have the doctor mess up now. He'd drag the old man out of his bed if he had to.

"Yes. Help me remove the remainder of his clothes."

Hagan was grateful for something to do. As long as he was busy he could forget how tired he was. Silently they worked until Loomis was stripped and covered with a soft white blanket sheet. His eyelids flickered once or twice, but it was only after Meeriam strapped the small reader to his upper arm that Loomis opened his eyes, looked at her and tried to grin. "I've died," he whispered, "and gone to heaven."

"Don't you wish," Meeriam said, and smiled. She brushed a hand across Loomis's face, then raised the other and simply held his head until his eyelids fluttered closed again, and he breathed deeply, the pain lines gone.

Hagan watched, almost holding his breath until she drew her hands away from Loomis's head.

"What did you do?" Hagan demanded in a whisper.

Meeriam eyed him gravely. She hesitated, then almost

imperceptibly sighed. "I merely removed his pain. Dr. Portus will be here soon with Gerald to look at his shoulder. There's no metal lodged in the wound?"

"It went clear through."

"Good. There are other things I must do. If you'd wait outside, I think Gerald wants to talk to you before you leave."

"I need to talk to him, too. How soon will they be here?"

"In a few minutes." Gently she pushed him toward the door. "There's a chair in the hall. You can wait there."

Urgency stabbed at him like a familiar pain.He stood firm."I don't have time to wait."

A quick, worried frown shadowed her eyes. "Why? Is it because you're still angry with Portus? He doesn't blame you for the way you feel, you know."

Hagan hadn't even considered what he'd say to Portus, considering how angry he'd been the last time they'd talked. In truth, his suspect parentage had no meaning except that it gave Graeber a better excuse to do away with him. He'd grown up knowing Velia was not his real mother, so why should it matter any more who was? And Portus was not the brunt of his anger. No, that rested solely on the Commander of Kama, who had lived a lie. "Nor do I blame him for keeping a secret."

God, he had to reach Phoenix before the general did. But now it was a matter of transportation. He had to have transportation. He had to.

"Captain," Meeriam eyes shadowed, "is Graeber looking for you?"

"Most likely. I've made a huge mistake. I left a pack in the cab of the HOGG we were driving." Somehow it didn't seem strange to be confessing about the pack to Meeriam.

"Oh," her voice was distressed, "but why did you—" she looked embarrassed. "I'm sorry. I have no right to ask."

He looked down into her concerned face, at her hands clenching in restless unconscious action. And it struck him that this was totally the wrong time to realize he wanted nothing more than to give her the right to ask all the questions. He also wanted to give himself the right to touch her with the touch that lovers use. Where had his fear gone? Had it vanished with the memory of Patlos? Or even before? For the first time he thought of Patlos, remembering only the pain, and not the fear. An upwelling of need rose in him, and he wished that he could sense an answering need in Meeriam, but he couldn't. There were only half- formed thoughts in her eyes, and more questions than he could answer right now.

He reached out and stilled her hands. "You have a right to ask. It has to do with the ancient city. I wish I could tell you more, but I can't."

"You're going there?"

Her intuitive question shook him. "If I can."

"And you need Vana Kassine's help?"

"Hers or someone's."

A great sorrow appeared in Meeriam's eyes.

Sorrow for the Firewing? Sorrow for the City? Did she know anything of Phoenix that might help?"What do you know about the Ancient City?"

"I've been there," she whispered. "Most of the People have. It is strange, and beautiful in its way, but Elias said it was also a bomb, waiting to go off. He was afraid of what he saw there."

Hagan wasn't surprised that the Firewing had actually taken the Commander to their most sacred places. That the Commander had never passed this information along to the University, or to the High Counsel didn't surprise him either, but it made him angry to think of Merrick's frustrations, of Kali's fears that could have been eased had the Commander chosen to share his knowledge. All of Merrick's searching through computerized maps and geographic land shifts, all of the worry and frustration, and agonizing by the group around Kali meant less to the Commander that keeping the Firewing safe. And all for naught. "He was right to be afraid. If Graeber reaches the City first, all that technology will be aimed at Mars, and then turned on Earth."

"We would not allow it."

"You couldn't stop it."

"I don't know. Maybe not, but what would you do? Destroy the City? Will that stop the General?"

Hagan's voice hardened. "It will keep him contained on Earth."

"Nothing will keep him on Earth but to die here."

"Maybe. If I reach the City before Graeber, I'll make sure he won't use the technology he finds. I can—" Hagan hesitated, not wanting to put into words the enormity of what he'd said he would do.

But Meeriam was quick to understand. "You can destroy it, is that what you're saying?"

"Someone has to. We can't afford to let a megalomaniac have it."

Meeriam shook her head. "So much will vanish that's good. It hardly seems right." Loomis groaned and she broke off. As she moved to the side of the bed and touched the young soldier's arm, she glanced across at where Hagan still stood by the door. "But I understand. I really do. Please," she added softly, "wait for Gerald. You need to rest, and you might as well do it here." A warmth stole through him, and a smile crept into his mind. She was a place of warmth and rest, if she but knew it, a center of peace and contentment. Not a young girl, as he'd first thought, but a woman to love without reservation.

Dismay at the path his thoughts had taken drew him up short. He made a mental retreat. "I'll wait a few minutes more."

Swift approval filled her eyes, and she smiled.

Dazed by the warmth of her expression, Hagan was reaching for the door when, with a slight burst of sound it flew inward.

Moss, in the doorway, froze. Hagan reached for his s'darm before he remembered he'd handed it over to Warren out at Thomas's Homestead. Instantly Meeriam was at his side, gripping his arm.

"No. Please. It's all right."

Hagan laughed tightly. All right, was it? He stood where he was, blocking Moss's entrance into the room. Moss would play holy hell trying to take Loomis out of here and to the Farm. He wouldn't allow it. "Captain," he acknowledged Moss with a grim nod. "What brings you here?"

"Warren called in. Said you were bringing Loomis in on Thomas's landhopper. How is he?"

Hagan tried not to show his surprise. Had Warren met up with another Unit? Had he a second Comboard stashed somewhere on the HOGG? His mind filled with questions, he failed to answer Moss's, and the Captain turned impatiently to

Meeriam. "How is he?"

Meeriam's smile was reassuring. "He'll be all right. Gerald's on his way with Dr. Portus."

Moss's eyes closed briefly in relief, and his head bowed. "Thank God."

There was more here than Hagan's tired mind could comprehend. Slowly he stood aside, and gave Moss access to the room. Hesitantly Moss walked to the bedside. Looked down into the still white face of the younger man. Reached out and touched him with tenderness so lightly that Loomis only sighed and slightly stirred without opening his eyes. Moss drew back.

His voice softened, but his usually passive expression was twisted with anger. "Who did it?"

"Graeber will say differently," Hagan said, "but it wasn't Firewing. We had one dogging our camps the first two days out, and I'm also sure it was the Firewing who destroyed the bridge at Old Man Crossing, but—"

Meeriam's eyes grew dark. "Condor?"

Surprised at her accurate guess, Hagan nodded. "Do you know him?"

Moss answered before Meeriam could. "He's a young leader who's gathering a group of dissidents around. They harass the soldiers, break up the roads. They don't bother the Farmers, and they've never come too close to Norcanna."

Hagan thought again of his meeting with Condor in Kassine's garden and could have told Moss differently. "They're also practicing with an old-style weapon," he said dryly. "though I can't say much for their abilities."

"Condor has no such weapon," Meeriam said. "No clan would give him one. The few weapons that are held by the clans are used only for hunting."

Hagan smiled without amusement. "He was taking aim at us the other morning."

"Not Condor," she insisted.

"Yes, your Condor." Hagan remembered the strange sensation he'd had of knowing, truly knowing the name of the presence roaming the camp. The face that he put with it was the face of the young Firewing in Kassine's garden. "Is he a friend of yours?"

"He's a cousin, but not of Lissone."

A faint blush colored her cheeks, and Hagan wondered if Condor was more to her than cousin. Then he had to laugh at himself. What right did he have to wonder? He drew in a tired breath. "It does't matter. He didn't shoot Loomis." Quickly he described the facts surrounding the incident at the bridge, and the conclusions he'd come to earlier. "If I had to choose one of those men with us, I'd say Warren."

Grimly Moss nodded. "He'll pay for it."

"Oh, please, Hugh, no," Meeriam said softly. "It won't help."

"Graeber's gone too far."

Watching Meeriam and Moss, Hagan realized they knew each other much better than he knew either of them. And Meeriam's concern for Moss, and yes, even Moss's knowledge of Meeriam, left him feeling shut out. It was an empty, hollow feeling that brought with it a strange flash of memory, a group of men and women around an open fire. An image that came, and then vanished, leaving him sad and aching for something that he couldn't name. He shook away the feeling. He was just tired. He'd feel better when he got some sleep. Wearily he looked around the sterile room, at the sleeping figure of Loomis, at the faces of Meeriam and Moss and it was as though he could see their lips moving, the gestures they made, but the words soft and insistent on one side, deep and determined on the other, meant nothing.

It was past time to leave. He couldn't wait for Gerald. He still wished he could see Kassine, but perhaps it was hoping for too much to think she could help him now. He'd find a place to rest, and by the time the sun set again, he'd be able to make his way out of Norcanna. On his way again to the mountains, and the Ancient City beyond.

Exiting the door, he slipped into the darkened hallway, then stopped to get his bearings. Behind him the soft argument broke off and a moment later Moss paused beside him. "Ellis, you can't go back to the barracks. When you don't show up at the Farm, Graeber will have everyone looking for you again. It'll be just the excuse he needs to come down hard on you."

"He won't find me." And if Loomis was lucky they wouldn't find him, either.

"I hope not. Do you have any plans?"

"Only to get some rest." Hagan was reluctant to share the rest of his intentions with Moss.

"You need something to eat, too. Let me help. I know a place—"

Hagan eyed the other captain. Why was Moss involving himself? In the shadows of the hall only the broad outlines of Moss's face could be seen and only the alertness of his posture as he waited for Hagan's decision. "Why, Moss? Why get involved? Why endanger yourself?"

"You really don't know?" When Moss started speaking, it was as if a cork had been drawn and the bottle tipped letting loose a flow of words. "By bringing Loomis back here," Moss said softly, "you've drawn more trouble on yourself than you needed in a lifetime. You could have let Warren do it. In front of the others he'd have had no choice. But by coming back, by insisting that it wasn't the Firewing, you'll throw a real knot in Graeber's rope. He'll have to remove you now, Ellis. He won't brook opposition." Moss took a deep breath. "But I'll be forever grateful for what you've done. That boy in there, he's my brother, Ellis. He's the only family I have left. He came to Earth just like I did, right out of the academy, two years ago, shortly after Graeber came. It was obvious even then what was going to happen. Your father suggested that we keep our relationship a secret. Graeber uses anything, everything, to get his claws in, and once he has you, he never lets go. I couldn't keep Will from coming to Earth, God knows I tried, but I've done my damnedest since then to keep him from catching Graeber's eye."

"Then why did you assign him to me?" How much more visible to Graeber could a young soldier be?

"Because we knew he could be trusted. Because you needed him."

A soft anguish was wrung from Hagan. "And to what purpose?" To say that he was sorry couldn't even begin to cover what he felt. To say that he was angry was only half of it. "Hugh, do you know why I came back?"

"Yes. The Ancient City."

"Do you agree with what I have to do there?"

"God , yes. You'll get any help I can give you. But Ellis, you can't do anything right now. Think, man. It's less than an hour to dawn. If you show yourself anywhere in Norcanna Graeber will have you picked up. This is all the excuse he'll need."

All the excuse, God yes. Hagan felt a strengthening of his resolve. Moss was right. The time had come to go to ground, at least until he got some sleep. After that, maybe the problems wouldn't appear so insurmountable. It seemed he might get the help he needed, and Loomis was in good hands, though how long it would take Graeber to think of looking here, only God knew. He nodded at the now closed door. "What about Will?"

"He'll be all right. We'll move him as soon as Portus sees him. Do you still want to wait for Nilander?"

Did he? In truth he was too tired to make sense of anything Gerald might say. "No. Not now."

Moss clasped his shoulder. "Then come with me."

Chapter 17

Diana Moon Colony

The Nix Olympica had been offloading to Diana Colony for one full day. Ken Kali, from his vantage in the observation rim of the Nix Olympica's control area, an area usually off-limits to all but the ship's elite crew, watched the last of the supplies and equipment disappear into the yawning maw of the supply tube that probed deep into the mining caverns beneath the Moon's surface crust and knew it'd soon be his turn to disembark.

"By this time tomorrow, Captain, you'll be there." The ship's security officer, Laurence Colbert, dark faced and dark skinned, bred at Trithonius Lacus but not of Xanthe's cast, gestured at the beautiful blue planet that hung partially hidden by the silvery rim of the moon's horizon. "I hope you know what you're doing."

Hoping he did, too, Kali hid a shiver of anticipation. Earth! The dream that was soon to become the reality. "What's it really like down there, Colbert?" He hadn't needed to tell the security man that he'd never been there before. It'd been in his voice, in his interest, in the excitement he could barely contain each time he'd come to the view station. "Big," Colbert answered promptly. "Bigger than you can think. More gravity, you'll feel that immediately. The variety of vegetation alone will astound you. And water, so much of it. So much water, they play in it." Colbert's face grew darker still. "For the amount of room, there are few people. It's downright eerie to stand alone on the surface of the planet, with no one around you. Blue sky." His knuckles whitened around the rail that enclosed the viewport.

There'd been other indications during the past weeks that Colbert had adverse feelings about the blue planet, and Kali had often wanted to ask why. He didn't, though, because he'd also sensed Colbert's reluctance to speak truly what was on his mind and had respected the security officer's reluctance.

Now, evidently, Colbert wanted to say his piece. "It's not

that I don't like it. I never said I didn't like it."

"What then?"

"It—it gives me the feeling of, well, like being outside this ship with no support systems. I'm always afraid to take a deep breath, for fear there'll be no air."

"Blue sky fever?" Kali asked.

"Maybe. Something like that. Maybe you'll be the same."

"Maybe." But Kali doubted it. For years, in his imagination, he'd lived without domes. He could hardly wait to make the dream real.

"You know, my friend," there was now even more reluctance in Colbert's voice, "our General Graeber is not going to appreciate your unannounced arrival."

Kali's smile faded. As Colbert's opinion was also his, he merely raised his chin with arrogant disdain. "So?"

"Don't take the danger lightly, Kali."The slightly accented sound of the 'thonius native's speech became more pronounced with agitation. "As emissary of Demar herself landing at his doorstep with no warning, he'll not only see you as a threat, but one to be removed with all possible dispatch. Splat! Like a bug he'll squash you before you even have a chance to spread your wings."

"No, not that soon," Kali disagreed with a hard smile. "He'll be curious first." He was counting on Graeber"s curiosity.

"And angry," Colbert went on as though Kali hadn't spoken. "Never underestimate the man's anger, or his strength of purpose."

The words were so familiar Kali's jaw tightened. Hadn't he said almost the very same thing to Hagan months ago? Kali turned his gaze to the beautiful globe that was Earth. Hagan was down there somewhere. If he was still alive. Surely they'd have heard by now if he wasn't. Graeber wouldn't keep news like that to himself. He'd find some way to use it.

Or Hagan could be lost somewhere in the vastness of the planet. No, there was no way he could get too far, and yes, by now, Graeber might have squashed Hagan, to use Colbert's own word for it. Kali grew cold. If he hadn't talked Hagan into coming back the player'd still be safe on Mars. Or at least, if not exactly safe, he'd have had the protection of Xanthe. Kali's sense of guilt brought with it an increasing anger. There'd been no other way. Hagan had been their only line of defense. Now Kali himself had to try, had to succeed, where the player had failed.

Hagan awoke from a strange dream, not knowing the time but alert to the sounds coming from the next room. He'd been surprised to recognize his safe place was Vana Darrow's round transient tower, but when he was ushered through the kitchen into the small, concealed room behind, with its own tiny utility closet attached, brought a hot stew that he could've sworn had never seen the inside of a synthesizer, and left alone, his surprise had already turned to shock. How many other people had used this room, and for what purpose? How many other rooms were there like this in Norcanna?

Nonetheless, stripping, he'd used the facilities, then stood under a luxuriously hot stream of water until he'd felt his bones ready to melt. Truth was, he'd almost gone to sleep standing there, and had barely dried himself before falling into the bed and into a deep sleep.

Now he lay on his back, staring up at a faintly luminescent ceiling trying to pinpoint what had awaken him.

The dream he'd had of Kali on Diana? Though it'd seemed very immediate a moment ago, already the images were fading.

The soft sounds coming from the kitchen? No. He realized he'd heard those sounds off and on throughout the day, until they'd become familiar and safe.

Time? He sat up quickly, his heart beating drum-like in his ears, drowning out all other sounds. What time was it?

Adrenaline high, he stood, abruptly alert to every nuance of the room.

The clothes he'd stripped off and dropped on the chair by the utility room door were no longer there. In their place instead was a pile of soft brown clothes and a pair of soft-leather boots. A light-woven white long-sleeved combination shirt and undershirt such as the Firewing wore was draped over the low back of the chair, obviously for his use.

And a good fit, he thought moments later. And, came the additional wry thought, someone had given him no choice in what to wear, had they? Finally stepping into the soft boots, he stood, momentarily disconcerted by how comfortable, how right these clothes felt. How familiar.

As if they'd been made for him. Or he for the clothes. But he'd once thought that about the uniform too, hadn't he?

No. Another role, that was all it was. Another costume, and another part to play. How many parts did a man play in his lifetime? How many more would he play before he reached the end of the script? He shivered slightly. How did it end?

Maybe he should demand a rewrite.

Before he had time to carry that thought out to its farcical end, a soft knock sounded at the door.

He grew still. "Yes?"

A lad who looked almost old enough to enter the Academy stuck his head in the door. One of Vana Darrow's sons, he thought, recalling that he'd met the boy once while he'd stayed in one of the rooms up above. "Good Evening, Captain Hagan." The lad wasn't a bit surprised to see him, even in these different clothes, and Hagan was struck again with the question of exactly what all went on in this place that Graeber didn't know about. The boy went on, "Van Nilander is in the small-room waiting for you. He said you were dressed."

Gerald Nilander would know, Hagan thought grimly, but kept a tight rein on his sense of outraged privacy.

The room the lad guided him into was a slightly wedge-shaped area running from the kitchen core to the outer wall. Windows, floor to ceiling grey-glass, looked out onto a small, enclosed and overgrown garden. The extreme slant of the sun indicated a time close to sundown. He'd slept the biggest part of the day. Establishing the fact to his satisfaction, Hagan turned his attention to Gerald Nilander, who sat at a small rectangular table set for four. With a slight nod and smile, Kassine's manager indicated the chair opposite him.

"Come to table and break your fast, Captain. The food is good, though not quite what you're used to."

At the very thought of putting food into his mouth, Hagan's stomach growled hungrily. He did as Gerald suggested but glanced at the empty places. "Are we expecting company?"

"Shortly. Hugh Moss and Meeriam are coming, but I wanted to talk to you before they arrived. Have you recovered from your sleepless night?"

"Of course." Not bothered by the thought of eating off the land, indeed the Commander had insisted on it at certain times, Hagan watched Gerald serve up a clear broth from a tureen in the middle of the table. The smell was rich with a spice he couldn't name, and his mouth watered. And somehow, he knew what it would taste like before he drew the first spoonful to his mouth. He wasn't disappointed.

Gerald watched him, an odd warmth in his eyes. His next question was a non sequitur. "What are your earliest memories, Captain Hagan?"

Hagan paused, the spoon half-way to his mouth. The question made him strangely uneasy . He frowned. Still, he felt a gentle compulsion to answer."Velia yelling at me, I suppose." He smiled slightly. "She yelled at me a lot, but then I gave her a lot of excuses." The Commander, after having established his estate among the others in Norcanna, and having installed his wife and son, seldom lived there. Hagan had always assumed it was because of Velia's viperous tongue. The Commander's wife was a shrew, and it was no wonder the Commander preferred life with his men. Hagan had never blamed him. He had, in fact, made his own escape to the Academy at a young age, leaving Velia in sole possession of the large house and larger walled garden. A garden like Kassine's. Hagan frowned down at his bowl, feeling something had gone awry with the taste. Nevertheless, he had questions of his own for Gerald Nilander.

"Does Kassine know what you are?"

"What I am?" Gerald's expression didn't alter as he echoed Hagan's question.

"Does she know you are a Firewing?"

Gerald's quick, faint smile held a touch of self-mockery. "The possibility has occurred to her once or twice, but when the thought comes she rejects it out of hand. The possibility doesn't fit her ordered world. Do you remember at all your very early years?"

"No. Does anyone?" Impatiently Hagan pushed his bowl away. "How long have you worked for Kassine?"

"Since she came to Earth with her first ship load of Freefarmers. She needed an assistant who'd been here before

215

her, someone to coordinate her efforts. I volunteered. She soon found me indispensable." Gerald glanced at Hagan's half-empty bowl and shook his head disapprovingly. "Vana Darrow will be disappointed if you don't finish each course. She worked in her kitchen most of the afternoon to produce this meal."

"She could've put a meal card into the synthesizer."

"True, but she believes fresh food is better for you."

"Where does it come from, what she cooks? The Firewing?"

"No. Some of the farmers are growing food to eat along with their Hojoi." At Hagan's obvious incredulousness, Gerald smiled. "Surprising, isn't it, Captain?"

"Yes." Somehow he'd thought it would never happen in his lifetime. "It sounds like the Freefarmers are more adventurous than I gave them credit for."

"Only some of them. And then only for certain products. Most farmers still prefer their meat from the synthesizer. The venison you'll eat later was shot by one of the People. Will that distress you?"

"No." Hagan toyed with his spoon, remembering. "The Commander often brought meat to the mess at Kama. He had a cook who would lie and say it came from the synthesizer, and most of the men believed it."

"But you never did?"

"No, of course not. It doesn't taste the same."

"And yet before you went to your father's command, you'd never tasted fresh meat?"

Hagan lifted one shoulder in a small shrug, wondering what Gerald was getting at. "Probably not." He thought it his turn to pose another question. "Did the Commander know what you are?"

"Yes." Gerald looked down at his soup, stirring it gently as though he were stirring up pictures of the past. "The Commander and I had no secrets from each other. I took him to his first council fire. I took him to Lissone, the first time he went."

"Did he go often?"

"Yes."

Hagan felt an odd tension. Was Gerald waiting for him to ask another question? His mind shied from the possibilities like a startled deer. Instead he focused on the empty places to either side and changed the subject. "When are Meeriam and Moss coming?"

Gerald hesitated, then sighed, accepting the change. "Soon. They'll be here soon." He stood and removed the soup bowls and tureen. From a chill-cupboard against the core wall he produced a bowl of greens and, filling two plates, offered one to Hagan. Curtly Hagan refused. His remembrance of the previous night's events was returning full force, and with the memory his sense of urgency. He wondered about Loomis, but before he could form the question Gerald said, "Loomis is all right, if that's what worries you. Portus cleaned the wound and sewed him up, and then we moved him to a safer place. Meeriam stayed with him."

"That's dangerous. You shouldn't let her be involved."

"What makes you think I could stop her? She knows her own mind, and she has learned to be careful of herself."

Remembering the way the soldiers of all ranks talked of the women of the town and the farms, Hagan wondered if even a Firewing's skills were enough protection. He shuddered to think what Galt, for instance, could do to someone like Meeriam. A protective anger surged through him before he could control it. Deliberately he shook the feeling away. She wasn't his problem. She wasn't his concern.

Like hell she wasn't.

The thought came from a deeper level of his mind and shocked him with its intensity. He leaned on the table for a moment, his face in his hands, trying to get his emotions under control. When he looked up Gerald was watching him with sympathy and understanding. "Are you in my mind?" he asked.

"No. Of course not. That would be an unforgivable invasion of your privacy. But that doesn't stop me feeling something of what you feel, or understanding something of your concerns. You're thinking of Meeriam and what you're thinking is in your face. You have an expressive face. I'm sure as a player you've been told that before. I understand you're very good. Did you enjoy the art?"

Momentarily diverted, Hagan frowned. "Yes, of course I did, or I wouldn't have continued for so long."

Gerald smiled. "To be a good player you need both talent and skill."

"Yes, and motivation." Hagan had the impression that they weren't, now, just speaking of his own career.

"And motivation," Gerald agreed. "Meeriam has all three. She believes in what she's doing. She knows that one day our peoples will come together and she feels it's her duty to help bring that about. Not even you will change her mind."

"Especially not me." Hagan wished that he'd taken some of the greens, if only to have something to concentrate on besides the man sitting opposite. Or the image of the woman in his mind. And then his attention swung to the door, and a moment later it opened silently and the object of his thought stood there. He felt like a magician who'd accidentally conjured a genie.

"Are we late?" Meeriam asked, her smile including both of them.

As Gerald answered in the negative, Moss entered on Meeriam's heels.

"We went by and saw Will," said Moss. "He was sitting up in bed wanting to know where the solid food was."

Gerald chuckled, and Meeriam, laughing, took her place at the table to Hagan's right. She wore a dark green dress with wide stand-up collar that framed her exotic face. The bodice of the dress fit her curves like a soft glove and the skirt flared around her calves and then settled lovingly around her ankles. It was the first time Hagan had seen her in anything but the farmer's green uniform-like tunic she usually wore. Meeting his mesmerized eyes, a faint flush rose in her cheeks. Quickly he turned his gaze to Moss and tried to catch what the VMP Captain was saying.

"—thrown the General into a state. He's still looking for you, Ellis, and he's damned well furious. He's posted guards around the processing plant but he's been discreet about it. He doesn't want Kassine to know. He thinks you might have gone to ground there. I wouldn't put it past him to try to get a unit inside this evening, Gerald, when your night shift comes on."

"I'll make sure he doesn't. What about the landhopper? Is it being watched too?"

"Yes. It'll have to be one of the carriers, El. There's none scheduled for Kama tonight, but perhaps by morning there'll be one." He accepted a plate of meat, vegetables and yellow squash that Gerald filled and passed it on to Meeriam, accepted a second for Hagan and then his own. The impression they gave was one of old friends meeting often. Comfortable, and almost ordinary. If one could forget that two of the three were Firewing. Or was Moss? No. As surely as he'd known Condor for a Firewing, he knew Moss was not. The fact that he knew chilled him. He made himself concentrate on the problem at hand. "I'd rather stow away on a HOGG. They're big enough to hide in, and the further I go before he finds out where I'm heading, the better off I'll be."

"The further we can go, you mean." Meeriam corrected softly. "I'm going too."

Hagan stared at her until the blush rose once more in her cheeks. But her gaze remained steady. "You need a guide through the mountains. I can be that guide. You need someone to be your contact with the Clans. I can be that contact."

"No." He wanted to sound stern, but he was afraid he only succeeded in sounding stubborn. He didn't care. He wouldn't take her. It was too dangerous. For God's sake, what would happen if Graeber caught up with them?

Meeriam's eyes darkened with frustration. "You need me."

"No." he said again. Perhaps he needed someone, undoubtedly he did, but not Meeriam.

He became conscious of both Gerald and Moss watching them. "I won't take her."

Moss shrugged and picked up a small knife and put his attention to the venison on his plate. Gerald considered Hagan a moment longer before he did the same. Though neither said a word, Hagan felt rebuked, but for the moment victorious.

His sense of victory was short lived.

After a brief silence in which he ate but tasted nothing, Meeriam said, "If you run into Condor before you reach Lissone, he'll kill you."

"Why should I run into Condor?"

"What makes you think you won't? He dogged your steps all the time you were on patrol, didn't he?"

"That's not to say he's still out there, or that he'd do it again even if he is." Though he was getting angrier, Hagan tried to conceal it, then wondered why he bothered.

"Of course he's still there. And he'll find you. You named him. Do you think, with his greater abilities, he can't name you? He knew exactly who he was dealing with. He's waiting for you to come back."

"He's on foot, isn't he? The HOGG will get me by him before he even knows I'm in the area."

"But once you're also on foot, once you reach the mountains, he'll catch up with you. He knows the trails better than anyone." Small even teeth caught at her lower lip. Her eyes darkened with thought. She darted a questioning look at Gerald.

Gerald hesitated. "It might work," he said slowly. "It might. We can try to enlist Condor's aid. Let Meeriam take you as far as Lissone. Undoubtedly Condor will be still somewhere in the vicinity. Perhaps Meeriam can convince him to take you over the mountains to the City. He can do that. He's been there many times. There's no question but that he knows the way."

"Would he do that for me?"

"Not for you," Meeriam met his eyes squarely. "But maybe for me."

Dropping his utensils into his plate, Hagan gave up all pretense of eating. He didn't want the young Firewing's help. Restlessly he stood and paced to the window. Outside the shadows were deepening. Soon it'd be time to leave. But by the Lord above, he didn't want to take Meeriam into greater danger.

Even if he was beginning to believe she could help.

As he sat within his office urgently conscious of the passage of time Graeber considered where else they might look for Hagan and Loomis. The town itself was covered. Both his staff captains were out searching the surrounding area and neither had yet called in to report. Was there anywhere else Hagan could have gone? Had he gone back to the homestead? The longer Graeber waited for Hagan to show up, the more his tension built. Where was the bastard? Of course, he thought, it wasn't the first time Hagan had dropped out of sight. The man was as elusive as a Firewing. He went to ground as easily as a rabbit went to hole. He couldn't be doing it alone. He must have help, but who would dare? Surely there was no one now he could turn to. Portus? Bah! The old doctor couldn't scratch his own balls. And the Matriarch wouldn't give Hagan help. Not after he'd screwed her daughter.

His eyes narrowed as he considered the pack sitting in the corner by the door. Something about that pack bothered him. Galt had brought it in earlier. Sergeant Warren had found it stashed behind the seats in the cab. Cribbs, the young driver, had denied any knowledge of it. That left either Loomis or Hagan as the possessor, and out of hand he rejected the younger man. No, it had been put there with purpose, but what purpose?

Graeber eyed the pack, a coldness growing in him. Rough mountain clothes, a thin but lightweight insulating blanket, a regulation-issue emergency pack of concentrated foods, thin but strong rope and several wraps of thin wire, a compass. Items a man might take if he were going into the mountains.The thought burst into his mind. Items Hagan might take if he were going to the Firewing.

Or beyond.

Hands suddenly shaking Graeber continued to stare at the pack, seeing all of his plans of the last three years cracking, splitting, coming apart. The conclusion took no great leap of the imagination. Hagan knew. Hagan knew what waited out there. Perhaps the old Commander had told him. And if he knew, no doubt others did too. The Professor at Xanthe. The High Council of Five on Mars. Ham-like fists clenched together on the desk in front of him, Graeber felt his rage build. No—no, they didn't know on Mars. They couldn't, or by now they would've tried to stop him. Again he said it to himself. They couldn't know. Only Hagan. That was why he'd come back. He wanted the fruits of the ancient city all for himself. For himself! Well, by God Hagan couldn't have it. It was his. Only he, Gordon Graeber, knew how to use the knowledge and might of the ancient city. It was his. His.

Graeber's inward quaking calmed under his rabid certainty and his thoughts grew clearer.

Loomis. Where was Loomis? Why hadn't they taken him out to the Farm? Badly injured, Warren had said. Should have been Hagan. God damn, why hadn't it been Hagan? Warren's excuses had been just that. Excuses. Grimly Graeber smiled, his hand clenching around the psychoprobe at his thigh. Warren would give no more excuses. For a moment his gaze rested on the spot where Warren had fallen, and a thrill of power surged through him. Next time it would be Hagan.

Unable to sit still any longer, Graeber pushed his bulk out of the chair and lumbered to the door. He had just opened his mouth to demand information from the cadet manning the communication board when that young man looked up with excited interest.

"Oh, sir, here's a bit of news just coming in from Diana. President Demar has sent a Captain Kali to us to pave the way for her vis—" His eyes on Graeber's face the young man broke off.

Kali? From Xanthe? Merrick's tame bear? Graeber felt dizzy with rage. His fist swung out, slamming into the door with a loud crash. "Absolutely not. Keep him on Diana. He can't come here. Tell him there's a state of emergency."

"We can't, sir. The shuttle's already on it's way. They left Diana over two hours ago."

Graeber's mind raced with possibilities. Another four hours before the shuttle arrived. Enough time to send a message to Mars and get one in reply. Enough time to find out why he wasn't warned of Kali's visit. God damn it, enough time to ship those technicians training out at the Farm on to Kama. They'd be safe from discovery out there. Surely they could keep the Arcolan away from Kama. Send Galt—no, no, he'd go himself to meet the Arcolan captain. But take Galt, too. Galt was better at intimidation than Moss. Moss was too damned reasonable. "Tell Galt I'll meet him at the Terminal at 2100 hours. And you— you'll get drivers and HOGGs, all six of them, out to the Hospital."His hands clenched into giant fists and a cold core of urgency settled in his chest. We'll see about this, he thought. He wouldn't have that man running loose in his colony, poking his nose God knew where. Not now. There was too much at stake.

Kali knew the shuttle arrivals were timed to arrive on Earth after dark, nonetheless he'd have preferred his first closeup view of the blue planet to have been in the full light of day. Watching the descent on the screen at the front of the cabin with two dozen other new arrivals Kali felt, on this very last leg of the trip, that they were falling into darkness. Very appropriate.

Though he'd been warned, the difference in gravity struck him first. Even the Nix Olympian's gravity grid that was meant to help prepare the passengers for their meeting with Earth, wasn't enough. And the artificial gravity grids of Mars, originally meant to approximate the normal gravity of Earth had, over the millennia, become something less. His first few steps across the high-domed terminal toward the barred gates with the other incoming passengers made him feel as if he'd taken on a double load of baggage. His glance at his fellow passengers showed some who looked bemused as he felt, and others who didn't seem to notice.

And then all thought of the differences he was experiencing vanished. Up ahead, beyond one of the barred gates, a delegation of soldiers had appeared. His stomach tightened. In the middle stood the short General, bulky, heavy brows lowered, exuding fury and power.

Kali didn't hesitate, but his inner smile felt a trifle grim. Arrogance, my friend, he said softly to himself, arrogance is the key.

He corrected his path to meet the General head on.

Chapter 18

Kama Valley

Through that first long night out of Norcanna, Hagan, with Meeriam, had clung to his precarious perch atop the HOGG with a tenacity bred of desperation. They had been prepared to wait out the night in Norcanna hoping for a ride, but Moss had reappeared and told them of the sudden movement of the carriers first out to the Farm to pick up technicians, and then on to Kama Garrison. If they hurried, they might find a way to use the movement of the carriers to their own advantage.

"Why now? What's going on?" Hagan had asked.

"A big-wig, coming in from Mars. The General really has the wind up. I've never seen him move this fast."

Big-wig from Mars. Hagan had wondered which one. But the opportunity to leave Norcanna on top of a carrier was too good to pass up. It would have taken them a week to walk that far on foot.

Slipping away from the HOGG in the early dawn hours several stadts before Kama, Meeriam and Hagan had made a cold camp along the river and slept most of the morning. By mid-afternoon they were on their way again, making a wide circle around Kama Garrison before starting into the mountains. Meeriam was very quiet, and Hagan was grateful. Though he had questions to ask about where they were going, and how, there were few questions he wanted to answer. For a while he'd be content that she led the way.

By the afternoon of the second day Kama Garrison was far behind. Hagan, calling a halt in late afternoon beneath a stand of ancient trees, watched Meeriam shift the pack from her shoulders and move her arms to relieve the strain. He wanted to ease the soreness from her neck and back but resolutely turned away. It was hard not reach out to her. Harder yet to keep his thoughts from dwelling on her to the exclusion of all else. He couldn't afford that kind of obsession.

Shrugging off his pack, he stretched, feeling his own muscles protest. Sweat trickled down his cheeks and ribs, and down the middle of his back. He hadn't expected the heat this early in the year. Dropping down beside his pack, he leaned against the broad base of one of the ubiquitous red barked trees, breathing in the scent of its oil, mixed with dust and the smell of his own sweat. He wiped his wet face on his sleeve. He was already tired, and they still had a long trek before night. Meeriam, he noted, seemed tireless.

Closing his eyes for a moment's rest, he returned to something else that had been bothering him. Why had Graeber so quickly moved all those men and that equipment? What was going on there that he didn't want the Arcolans to know?

He frowned. In the several months he'd been back, he'd learned of nothing going on out at Graeber's hospital except the retraining, though that alone was bad enough. Now he had to wonder what else Graeber had been hiding. He thought about asking Meeriam, but surely if she or Gerald knew, they would have mentioned it.

"It must be a grim thought." Meeriam's voice held a curious lightness. She dropped her pack beside his. Scrupulously, though they'd walked side by side for hours, she'd kept herself out of his mind, and for that he was grateful.

"Grim enough," he agreed. "I was thinking of Graeber and the hospital."

Her eyes filled with pain. "So was I. Those men on the carriers —"

"The soldiers?"

"Most of them were not soldiers —" Again she stopped. "Why would he want to do that to anyone?"

Hagan felt his skin chill. "Do what?" True, from the shadows on top of the carriers they'd seen the men loading into the back, along with cartons and crates of equipment, but the loading had been swift, and for the most part silent. He'd noticed nothing more extraordinary than the swiftness and silence.

"Some of those men, no, not really men, shells—where were their minds? What happened to their thoughts, their memories?" Her voice broke. "What has he done to them?"

Slowly the horror of her meaning swept over him. Men without minds? Nothing he'd heard on Mars led him to believe it was possible. Could a man live without a mind? And for what purpose? What use would a man without a mind be?

"He is horrible. I'd not thought he could be worse than we suspected, but he is."

"All the more reason to stop him."

"Yes." Her shoulders straighten. Shading her eyes from the glare of the sun, Meeriam studied their back trail. In the heat of the afternoon nothing moved. The smell of dry grass and bush, and the pungent odor of the tree permeated the air. Even the small birds that usually chattered in the distance had sought refuge from the penetrating sun.

Still searching their surroundings, Meeriam turned and studied the steep hill they'd been skirting for the past hour. Who did she think to find, Hagan wondered with quick irritation. Condor? His frown deepened. Where was Condor? Why hadn't the Firewing found them by now? Or was he stalking them—Hagan shook the thought away. Meeriam would say if Condor was in the vicinity.

Finished with her study of the land, Meeriam turned back, a determined smile in her eyes. "Above us in that rocky outcropping there's a small spring." She touched the half-empty water sack at her belt. "Would you like some fresh water?" Since leaving the river early this morning they'd had only the water they carried.

"If you're going that way." Handing over his almost empty water sack, Hagan wondered where she got the energy for such side trips. He himself had tired rapidly with the steady climb and the steadier heat, but she seemed to have been revitalized by the mountains. Her step was as sure as when they'd started, and her mood had changed. A sheen of sweat touched her brow, but she didn't really look hot. She looked—perfect.

Hagan shut his eyes against the thought.

"I'll be back in fifteen minutes."

Hagan nodded.

Meeriam watched Hagan shut his eyes, hooding his expression from her, and smiled slightly. She could smile, she knew, as long as she didn't think about Graeber and what he'd done to those men. It was easier and more interesting to think about Ellis Hagan, who was tired, but not complaining. He'd been a silent companion most of the day, but one who needed no direction on how to hike a trail. He seemed to have a sense of the mountains, and a tread almost as light as one of the People. She'd found herself thinking several times how natural he looked in her mountains, how attuned he was to the sounds, and to the signs. She'd caught him more than once studying the tracks left in the soft dirt, identifying to his own satisfaction what had gone before. Someone had taught him well, and she wondered if it was Elias himself who had done so.

Strange how the pain of Elias's passing had softened over the months. Possibly it was knowing that he'd never loved her the way she'd thought she loved him. As Meeriam climbed the steep trail up the side of the mountain she found herself wondering instead what had happened between father and son that drove Ellis Hagan away. Portus knew, she was sure. But Portus also knew something else, something that made him fear not only for his own life, but for Ellis Hagan's too. But whatever that secret was, the old man guarded it, hugging it to him with fear-laced determination. Her heart went out to him, poor old man.

Reaching a particularly steep part of the path, Meeriam put her full attention to the climb. At the top massive granite outcrops jutted upward, stark buttresses against the deep blue of the sky. The faint path wended its way between. The rocks, she knew, hid a small pool and a cool little depression where willows grew. Perhaps she should have invited Hagan to climb with her to the water, but habits died hard. The water places were sacred, and soldiers had been known to foul a spring simply to keep the People from using it. Not that she thought he'd do that. No, of course not. But still—uneasily she pushed the thought aside. Concentrated instead on keeping her balance across a narrow ledge, then pulled herself up over a gateway rock.

The smell of water reached her first, and then a strong command.

STAY AWAY. STAY AWAY.

Startled, she sank into the protection of one of the boulders. Immobile, she studied the scene below. The trail she crouched on

228

curved away and disappeared around the edge of the small pool. The water level was up, but that was natural this time of year, and she took in this information automatically, filing it for future use. The pool itself seemed undisturbed, the clear fresh water beckoning her with its promise of refreshment.

Who is it? Who has spoken? She sent the thought out and waited, but the mind that had spoken to her was silent.

Then a small movement at the far side of the pool, deep in the stand of willows, caught her eye.

Again she cast out the thought. *Who's there?*

Go away, came the thought in return.

She ignored the command. *Who are you?* she asked.

Reluctantly the answer came. *I am Glyn. Go away. I do not want you here.* The mind voice was defensive and growing weak. Injured, she surmised.

The proper identification would have been Glyn of— somewhere. But where? She couldn't identify him as anyone she knew. She kept her mind voice gentle. *I mean you no harm. I've come for water.* In her mind's eye she sought him out. He lay beneath a thick stand of bush, following its shade. He was injured. His leg lay out in front of him at an odd angle. *You are hurt,* she said into his mind. *Let me help you.*

The protest he offered was so weak she knew he couldn't mean it. At that moment a sound behind her made her spin. Hagan stood, watching her, a puzzled look on his face.

Her heart beat loudly in her ears. How had he gotten there without her hearing him? Where had he come from? Her confusion of thoughts must have been in her eyes because he frowned.

"What's wrong?" His glance swept the small pool below, and the surrounding glen, probed the trees on the opposite slope, then swept past the clump of willows. And then abruptly returned to the willows again. "Someone's over there." His whole perusal had taken only seconds.

"Yes," Meeriam said softly. She'd leave the question of what he was doing here for later. "Please don't move. He's young, frightened, and injured."

"One of your people?"

"Yes, though no one I know. Let me go around and talk to

him. Perhaps I can ease his pain."

"Maybe you can. Is he one of Condor's men? If so I'd like to talk to him."

Meeriam hesitated. "All right, but let me help him first."

Hagan accepted her stricture, but reluctantly, she noted. Frightened men were often dangerous, she could almost hear him think. Not giving him time to change his mind, she gave him her place in the shadows of the rocks and moved quietly down to the water's edge and then around the clear pool. Behind her she could feel Hagan's uneasy acceptance of his waiting role. Ahead of her was a young man's fear.

Hagan, taking another grip on the two packs he'd brought with him from down below, followed Meeriam's progress around the pool toward the shadow side. Her movements were slow and unhurried. He shook his head again at what had taken him up the path after her, still not willing to credit that for a brief moment he'd been aware that someone was waiting at the pool. Someone unseen and perhaps dangerous. It'd happened almost the moment she'd disappeared up the steep trail. By God how did the Firewing handle that knowledge? Feeling a growing tension, Hagan settled on his heels, ready to wait until she called.

Meeriam, knowing Hagan's thoughts were following her if not exactly with her, hoped he'd do as he'd said, and stay where he was. And then, as she came into the small nest of grass the boy had made for himself, all extraneous thoughts vanished. The boy's palpable fear and pain had brought sweat to his face and a fine trembling to his body. His shirt was torn and dirty, but she recognized it as Deran thread. So he was Glyn of Dera. He looked at her with eyes that silently hated her even as they pleaded for her help.

"I am Meeriam, of Lissone," she said quietly. Kneeling at his side she placed a hand on his injured leg and he flinched. "I'll help you. Please, don't be frightened."

The boy's gaze slid from her own to seek out the place where Hagan squatted, though Hagan himself couldn't be seen from where they were. "Who is he? He's not of the People."

"He's a friend. The Commander's son."

"What's he doing here?"

"We're looking for Condor. Why have you been left in this state? Why haven't you had a healing?"

"There's no one—no one to do it."

Meeriam touched him again. The heat from his injury burnt through his clothes, clothes that she realized now had blood on them. "No one? But surely Condor himself—"

Glyn of Dera laughed shortly. "They're afraid of him and they've taken away his power."

"Who has?"

"The Elders. They've denied him the power—" Hit by another wave of pain, the young man's voice broke.

Meeriam bit her lip to keep from telling Glyn that he spoke pure nonsense. Only Condor himself could give up his power. But obviously the young man was in no condition for argument, nor even for a few basic truths. "Is Condor coming back?"

"Yes. Of course. He wouldn't leave me here."

Meeriam didn't point out that Condor had already left him here. She merely nodded. "I see. I'll help you, as I said, but I'll have to have also the help of the Commander's son."

"He is a soldier." The boy spit the word soldier out with a feeling of both fear and loathing.

"He was," soothed Meeriam, "but he isn't now."

"He's one of them."

"Yes, but now we need his help."

"No—" as he moved in protest the young man's resistance submerged under another wave of pain. Meeriam knew they had to do something now, before infection set in. Before Glyn of Dera lost his leg completely.

Across the pool, Hagan, as soon as he saw Meeriam beckon, started down into the shallow depression where the water glittered like a jewel beneath the late spring sun. Quickly he came to the pool's edge and skirted the damp earth and finally reached her side.

Meeriam's hand stayed on the boy's shoulder. "This is Glyn of Dera. He's broken his leg and we'll have to set it before we can help him. Do you have any experience with broken bones?'

"None at all." In spite of his admission, Hagan's voice was deep and quiet, and somehow reassuring.

"Too bad. I only know what Dr. Portus has shown me, and I must say, I've never actually set a bone, and it must be set before it can be healed."

"We'll manage."

Yes, Meeriam thought, he gave her the feeling they would.

Hagan watched Meeriam drop to the boy's side. "Glyn, this is Ellis Hagan, the Commander's son." The young man's pain filled eyes opened briefly, but with a wealth of feeling, anger, fear, and something that Hagan could only read as a plea for help. Meeriam reached out, and placed her gentle hands upon the boy's head, much as she'd done to Loomis not so long ago.

Her eyes closed, and Hagan wished suddenly that he could hear what she was saying to Glyn, what words she was using, if indeed she was using words at all. Slowly, he saw the tension flow from the young Firewing's body as if it were air released from a balloon.

A short time later, using a strength and skill he hadn't known he possessed, Hagan, with Meeriam;s help, straightened and set back into place the boy's bone. Then they found small, straight branches that they used for splints and bound them to the leg with strips torn from their shirts. Afterward, Meeriam settled by Glyn's side and indicated Hagan should sit on the other. "We don't have time for a proper healing, but this will help. Besides, he said Condor was coming back for him."

Hagan didn't bother hiding his disapproval of Condor's conduct. "How did it happen?"

"He didn't say, but I—I saw it in his memory. There was a fight with a unit of soldiers. There's blood on his shirt. Someone was killed—" she reached out almost without conscious volition and touched the bloodstain. "A soldier's blood. Oh, Condor—"

Hagan stared at her, mesmerized. "You can tell all that just by touching him?"

"It's in his memory, and he feels very bad about it. It's easy to read."

Hagan turned his gaze to the sleeping boy, trying to judge his age and placing him at possibly sixteen or seventeen. "Will he wake soon?"

"He needs to sleep."

It was an answer that was no answer, and Hagan knew

it. Impatiently his mouth tightened. "Is Condor really coming back?"

"Glyn believes so. But I think rather that Condor will send someone for him. Most probably he'll let the people at Dera know where Glyn is, and they'll come for him."

"How long will that take them?"

"Too long."

Anger at Condor's cruelty flashed through Hagan. Abruptly, needing the movement, he grabbed the water sack Meeriam had set aside and strode through the bushes to kneel by the water. Meeriam followed and knelt at his side.

"Why are you so angry? Have I done something —"

"No, of course not." He turned, facing her, so close that he could have reached out and touched her, but so angry he didn't want to. "Condor is a fool. He's left this boy behind, a perfect target for the soldiers if they should come this way."

"But why should they? They don't know where this pool is. And Dera's not far. Someone will come before too long."

"I wouldn't count on it. If Condor and his friends have actually killed a soldier, you can bet that the other soldiers are on their trail." A mental picture flashed on the screen of Hagan's mind, of soldiers dogging a trail, and even as it disappeared a sense of urgency filled him.

"But Glyn—" Meeriam started.

"Glyn is expendable."

"He's not."

"Tell that to Condor." Scooping up his water sack, Hagan brought the cool water to his lips.

"What a horrible thing to say. I'm sure —"

Hagan lost whatever she might have said. A different sound cracked into his mind, hard boots against rock. Whipping around he searched for its source, staring first at the rocks through which they'd come, then at the skyline, part of it hidden by trees, part of it stark rock towering high above the higher ridge.

"What —" Meeriam started.

He silenced her with a gesture. "Someone's coming." He moved away from the pool. The air felt oppressive with heat and silence. What had he heard? He turned back to Meeriam. She was totally still, eyes closed while she searched with her mind's eye. He knew that was what she was doing. "Did you hear it too?"

Silently, eyes still closed, she denied that she heard anything.

"I did hear something," he insisted angrily.

This time she opened her eyes. "Yes, but —"

"Hard boots —soldier's boots on the rocks."

"Yes." Her eyes widened in horror. "It's a unit of soldiers. They have a man with them trained to track—and they're following the old trail. The one Condor took when he brought Glyn here.

The hair on Hagan's neck rose. "How far away?'

"A stadt, perhaps. No more."

"Impossible! They must be closer than that. I couldn't have heard them otherwise."

"No, really—"

Impatient with her protest, he spun and studied the shallow little depression that sheltered the spring. It was shaped like the cone of a small volcanic cauldron, with the water taking up only a small portion of the center. Around the edges grass, tall and thick, grew down to the water's edge. At the end where they stood the ground was soft underfoot, and he guessed that it would be much dryer later in the year. There was no place to hide unless one counted the thick growth of bush and brush where Glyn had secreted himself, and even that was poor shelter if someone was looking. A fine trembling chilled him. The soldiers had to be closer than Meeriam thought or he wouldn't have heard them.

But this beautiful little glen was a damned poor place to be caught by a unit of soldiers. No cover. "Where is this old trail?"

"Up there." Meeriam indicated the high rocky ridge opposite the side from which they'd entered.

The decision was made by the sense of urgency hounding him. Grabbing Meeriam's arm, he pulled her with him into Glyn's little nest. "We have to take Glyn and get out. Now."

Meeriam didn't argue. He felt the touch of her mind reading his certainty, and after helping him pull the young Firewing up and onto his back she retrieved the packs.

Though the afternoon heat had not abated, nor the sun's glare diminished, the map room below Norcanna's General Headquarters was cool and dim except for the bright projection on the screen wall. But as Graeber's voice grated softly from the darkened half of the room, the staff captains ignored the projected map of the Kama region of the Colony.

"He's slipped away." Graeber's lethal voice contained a wealth of sarcasm. "He was here and because I am surrounded by imbeciles, he has escaped." Graeber paced the length of the room. Time. Time moved too quickly. He wasn't ready yet. So damned much to do, and now Hagan was gone again. But Graeber knew—Hagan could no longer hide what he was. A spy. A damned spy. The fool! To think he could—white hot rage curled within Graeber but found no release. Plans. He had to make plans. "Galt, get out to to Kama Garrison and make sure Hagan does not make contact with the Firewing. Commander Barrows is useless. He's chasing his tail if he thinks to capture any of the Firewing who slaughtered that Road Unit." Among other infuriating news that very morning, Graeber had heard that because of an attack on one of his road units, Commander Barrows, the man appointed to take the old Commander's place, had not been at Kama Garrison to receive the shipment of weapons and men he'd removed from the Farm. Removed right from under the nose of that inquisitive Arcolan prig sent by Demar. By God, if he dared he'd squash that arrogant bastard—but not yet. Not while Hagan was still at large. Carefully Graeber clamped an iron control on his rage. "I want Hagan alive, Galt. If you find him, I want him taken to the Farm immediately. Under no circumstance is that Arcolan to be allowed to see him."

"I'll take care of the dammed AMP—" Galt began.

"You'll stay away from the Arcolan, Galt. He'll be very useful to us."

"Arrogant son of a—"

Graeber's grip on his temper broke. "Galt, you fool. Get out of here. Get out to Kama. If Hagan slips through, you'll be the one to go to the farm. Do you understand?"

Graeber clenched the butt end of the psychoprobe, the threat implicit in the action. Galt's eyes shifted nervously from the probe back to Graeber's face. "Yes, sir."

Satisfied that Galt had gotten the message, Graeber turned to his other staff captain.

"Moss, find that young soldier that Hagan brought back. He must know something or Hagan wouldn't have taken such pains to hide him. When he's found, take him out to the Farm too."

"And the AMP?"

"Keep a man on him at all times. Do it yourself, if you have to. Under no circumstances is he to see either Hagan or that young lieutenant."

"What if he tries to see Vana Kassine?"

"Let him. After all, what can the old woman say?"

"And Dr. Portus?"

"I am tired of Dr. Portus. We will dispense with the good doctor's services. See to it."

Moss nodded impassively.

Dismissing Portus's fate with no more than a blink of an eye, Graeber returned his thoughts to the Arcolan captain. Though Captain Ken Kali had arrived only the night before, Graeber had already, in the small hours of the morning, revised his master plan to meet this new contingency.

Genius, he thought, was always flexible.

Yes, the new plan was ideal. He couldn't have planned it better if he'd tried and, after all, as soon as the Commander's son was in his hands and the ancient city under his control—and when Madam President of the Grand Council arrived, ah, yes. Yes. Nothing would stop him, then. Nothing would stop him from taking his rightful place as Master of Civilization, perhaps, he thought with a feral smile, he would crown himself Emperor. Emperor of Mars. He liked the sound of it. And Emperor of Earth as well. He smiled.

We are Earth.

Anahata bent down and gave the small boy's shoulders a warm hug, but even as she did so she felt a pull of thoughts away from the camp, away from the busy, bustling life going on around her. A thought request that was coming from afar. Sending the child on his way, she straightened slowly and moved into the soft-sided tent and sank down upon the cushions that flanked the small table. The pull grew stronger.

Slowly she closed her eyes, and the sounds of the camp of Lissone faded and disappeared.

We are Earth.

We are Earth, she replied in her heart.

We of the Clan Dera are saddened. There has been blood emptied into the Earth this day. One of our people has died, another is injured.

The pain of loss struck Anahata sharply. *Can we help?*

One of yours is already helping. But the young one, the young warrior Condor, leads his followers in a destructive course. He has spilled the blood of the Others, and is even now leading them further into the mountains. Closer to your door.

You speak of Condor of Quill. He has chosen not to heed our advise and no longer speaks to Mind.

Nonetheless he brings destruction in his wake and you who guard the Way must protect yourselves.

Anahata bowed her head under the weight of her pain. She had seen already that it would come to this, but she had hoped that it might not come so soon. After thanking Clan Dera for the warning, and assuring them that because Lissone was closer, their injured clansman would be taken care of from here, and feeling the withdrawal of the Deran Mind, she sat bowed with the weight of her sadness.

But finally sadness and pain brought with them resolution. Casting her thought out, she moved swiftly in ever widening circles, searching, searching until she found what she sought. In her mind's eye she found the small band of men, Condor at their head. She frowned, knowing them all, knowing their parents, and their family lines. Two from Lissone, three from Dera, two plus Condor from the Valley of Quill. There had been ten, she knew. One had died in the river ambush, but where was the other? Had he been left behind? These wasted no time on the trail, their pace a steady ground-eating trot though one lagged behind, his pain obvious in his face each time he bore down on his left foot. His energy was going to block the pain, not block his mind from her entrance. That one she chose.

His memories were also painful. She ached for his anguish at seeing his comrade fall, and she saw the fierce battle in which they had engaged.

The powers of Mind had not been well-used against the weaponry of the soldiers. The discipline and training of the soldiers allowed them to fight in spite of their fear, and Condor had led his men too close. They had succeeded in destroying the HOGG by flipping it over on its side, trapping inside three men; two others had panicked and tried to run and Condor had stopped them. But the others had stood their ground, and used their weapons and in the end Condor had led his men away, all but one.

Sadly she was certain Condor had learned nothing from the battle, either about the soldiers, or about himself. And worst of all, in her eyes, he'd lost one man and left another of his own behind, injured and vulnerable. It was a decision that sat uneasily upon the mind of this young man whose thoughts she read as easily as she read the sky or sea.

As well it should.

Gently she led the young man's thoughts back to where Glyn of Dera had been left and immediately retained a sense of someone having been there and recently gone, taking the injured one with them. Filled with worry, she quit the young man's thoughts and renewed her mind's quest, and only when she'd located Hagan and Meeriam, and recognized Hagan's burden did she sigh with relief. Silently she touched Meeriam's thoughts, not even pausing for the ritual greeting.

Where are you bound for, my daughter.

Meeriam didn't falter in her step. *The mountain, Grandmother. And beyond.*

You bear a heavy burden.

Glyn of Dera, came Meeriam's reply. She glanced over her shoulder. Hagan carried the heavy weight of the injured young man without complaint, but she could see that he was using the last of his reserve of energy. Again her anger at Condor almost overpowered her. How dare he go off and leave one of the People behind, injured and unable to defend himself.

Remembering just in time that her Grandmother was with her, she checked her anger. *Grandmother, I bring Hagan to you. He needs our help to go on to the Ancient City.*

Why does he wish to go there?

Meeriam, her heart sore, shared all with her Grandmother.

238

Having seen firsthand, as it were, the unwavering determination of the General, she had no trouble expressing her fears, which were the fears of all thoughtful people. Truly the General must be stopped.

Anahata bowed before the conviction within Meeriam's mind. So it had finally come, the way her friend Elias had once said it would. The way she had told Mind it might. And Elias's and Adriana's son would make himself the vehicle of that destruction and ask for her help to wreck it? No, no, not with her help. The Clans of Earth had too long kept the city safe. There were secrets there to be shared with all mankind. Not secrets to be lost forever in some senseless destruction. She had wanted Ellis to come back to Lissone, to discover what he was. She did not want him to come to destroy his heritage. Hardening her heart to the plea in Meeriam's inner voice she made her decision. *I cannot help him do that which is repugnant to me she replied into Meeriam's mind.*

What he has to do is not wrong. What is wrong is to let the City of Phinx fall into the hands of the Arcolan General. Grandmother, please—at least hear what he has to say.

I will listen, child, but understand, I will not alter my decision.

Meeriam closed her eyes briefly, knowing that for now it was all she could hope for. Later, perhaps, when Grandmother and the elders heard everything Ellis Hagan had to say, they might change their minds.

Chapter 19

Kama River

With muscles strained to the breaking point Hagan eased to his knees and slid Glyn off his shoulder and on to the soft humus of the forest floor. Night was coming and with it the easing of the intense afternoon heat.

Though he knew he should move and let Meeriam attend to Glyn, Hagan wondered if he'd ever again make his body obey his command.

How far had they come? Fifteen or twenty stadts? Most of it steadily climbing into ever more rugged country. He'd walked until he was numb and then had continued walking. Even Meeriam, growing tired, had fallen silent, speaking only to offer water, or offer directions. Now she knelt at Hagan's side and touched him softly.

"I've camped here before. We can build a small fire. It won't be seen."

Chilled by the exhaustion that swept him, Hagan wanted nothing more than to lie down beside Glyn and sleep. Deliberately he drew himself to his feet. "His leg needs tending to."

"It will wait. Come sit over here."

Meeriam had dropped their packs by an outcropping of rocks on the other side of the clearing and now removed a lightweight overshirt and slipped it on. She then pulled one out for Hagan and slipped it over his head. He stood, letting her tend to him as if he were a child, too tired to protest. She then led him to the large rock outcropping and he sank down and leaned against the smooth boulders. They still retained the heat of the day, and he closed his eyes and let Earth's stored energy warm him.

With no wasted movements, Meeriam worked quietly until a flicker of light played against Hagan's eyelids. His eyes flew open. He stared at the small flame, and Meeriam's fearless movements around it. Once ballstoves with their minute nuclear cells had been invented the people of Mars had not had to deal with open flames. On Mars the flame itself would consume too much oxygen, and the threat of fire was always present. Returning to Earth, the Arcolans had retained their fear of the open flame. He wished he'd insisted on bringing a ballstove.

Fixing his attention on this one small detail seemed to ease his fatigue, until he had to laugh at himself for his mind trick. If flame was all they had, then he'd learn to live with it. Meeriam, who seemed to have been waiting for him to resolve his problem with the fire, came to his side, a spoon and small bowl she'd retrieved from her pack in her hands. An aroma rising from the bowl made him almost dizzy with hunger. She passed it to him with a smile, then went back for her own.

He knew they would have to talk soon, about Glyn, about what had happened, and where they would be heading tomorrow, but for the moment he found it hard to concentrate on anything but the delicious food in his bowl. With relish he consumed the stew and wondered if it was polite to ask for more.

"There's more on the fire," she said. Finishing her own, she dipped another full bowl from the pot and carried it to Glyn's side.

After Hagan had dished himself a second helping, he settled once more against the smooth warm rock and watched over the rim of his bowl as she moved in and out of the light making Glyn comfortable for the night.

When she finished she returned to the fire and drew herself the final serving of stew, then settled near him to finish it.

"Have you done this often? This traveling between Norcanna and Lissone?"

She nodded, the small movement almost lost in the play of flickering light. "More when your father was alive than now. He traveled quite freely wherever he chose, but it was always better to have one of us with him. He was known to Lissone, but a stranger to many others."

"So you acted as the—the go-between?"

"Yes." Her voice softened as she stared into the fire. When she glanced at him again, her expression seemed to ask for understanding, and something more. Belief, perhaps. "I would have been much more to him if he had been willing."

A knife of unreasoning jealousy tore through Hagan, and left him bleeding. He mended only a little when she continued. "I had mistaken my admiration for love, you see. I think he was much wiser. He never treated me other than as a favored daughter." A smile played around her softly curved mouth. "He taught me many things. He was well-versed in literature and history, as you know. And he was so patient with my attempts at the language. He was a very patient man."

Another kind of jealousy filled Hagan. Had he ever known the Commander's patience? In fact, did he even know the man she described? Not he. His father had been a cold hard man. Harsh and disciplined, and curt to the point of rudeness and proud to the point of arrogance as were most of the soldier breed. Where was the man she described? He'd learned no lessons from Elias Hagan except how to be alone. In all the years Hagan had known him, there'd been no softening of his attitude, nor his actions.

No, he and Meeriam weren't remembering the same man. His lessons in history had come from Portus, his lessons in family from the viperous tongue of his step-mother Velia. His awe-filled regard for the man who had fathered him had made him try to walk in the Commander's boots, but it had only been after he fled to Mars that he'd realized he was not of the same bone and flesh of which the Commander was made. He blinked rapidly, trying to dispel the images carried in his memory. How could he hate a dead man? When would his memories release him?

Meeriam, from near at hand, watched the emotions flow across Hagan's face and she ached to soothe away his pain. But some hurts had to be lived with until growth brought an end. It was the only way. He wasn't yet ready to let go. But someday, she thought, someday he would.

Using his pack for a pillow and his Firewing jacket for cover, Hagan finally slept, and dreamt. Of an eagle, of Luan as she had been when they were young, of Loomis and Moss —

It was after midnight that he came awake fully, cold and shivering—hearing voices that were almost dream-like in their softness, yet very real. An argument.

Without moving Hagan studied the shadowy clearing. The

fire had died, leaving only the glow of hot coals behind, and it cast no shadows. The star-studded sky sparkled between the canopy of trees high overhead. Meeriam was not on her bed.

Hagan, starting to rise, froze when the voices rose and the words became clearer. They came from the vicinity of Glyn's bed, but the voice was not the younger man's.

"You should have left him. He'd have been all right." The words were foreign, and yet Hagan had no trouble understanding them. As if they were still part of the dream and of course all was possible in dreams.

"No, Condor. The soldiers were coming. He would have been found. They would have killed him."

"So now you see into the future too?' the other voice sneered.

"No, of course not, but—"

"So you admit you didn't know for sure. The soldiers could have missed him. And now they have a trail they can't possibly miss, all because of a stupid—"

"Condor, stop it. What we did was necessary. If you hadn't been such a fool in the first place—"

"I wondered when you'd get around to that. I suppose Glyn told you what happened—God, if he hadn't gotten clumsy none of it would've happened."

"It wasn't his fault. You led him there, and then left him when he was hurt."

"Shut up, Meeriam. Shut up. He's safe now, and that's all that matters."

"Is it?'"

Hagan rose slowly to his feet. Meeriam and Condor stood near the place he'd laid Glyn. Both Meeriam and Condor were dark shadows against a lighter background of starshine seeping through the trees. Condor seemed massive measured against Meeriam's smaller shape.

He'd not realized his movement was noticed until Condor broke off in mid sentence, and he felt the Firewing's full regard. The hair prickled on his arms. He held himself immobile, waiting for Condor to move first.

A brittle silence stretched between the three of them until Condor laughed. "He's only one of them. Why do you travel with him when you wouldn't travel with me?"

"I'll travel with you now, if you'll come with us."

"With him?" The sneer of contempt was back in the Firewing's voice.

"She says," Hagan spoke softly in the Norcannan dialect, not wanting Condor to know that he'd understood the Firewing's speech, "that you know the way to the Ancient City and will show me."

"She's wrong."

"I thought she was." Hagan made his voice as contemptuous as Condor's had been. "They wouldn't trust you with that kind of information, would they?"

"You don't know anything about it. They trust me. I'm accepted at the sacred fire—"

Hagan wondered at the slight tremor he detected in Condor's voice, but ignored it as he strove to force home his point. "But you do not know where the Ancient City is."

"By The Mountain, I do."

"Then show me the way."

"The Elders won't like it." As if aware of sounding too hesitant, Condor rushed on. "Why do you want to go to Phinx? You won't see anything. Most of it is underground, and dark. The way in is hidden."

So he did know the way. Had he even been inside? Hagan asked.

When Condor hesitated again, Meeriam answered for both. "We have both been inside, during Ritual."

Hagan thought Condor had been inside more often than that, but perhaps he wouldn't want Meeriam to know. As the Firewing had said, the elders wouldn't approve.

"Yes," Condor agreed. "During Ritual. That doesn't mean I'll take you."

"Show me the way across the mountains and I'll take myself in."

"Take yourself across the mountains. I haven't the time."

"Condor, please—" Meeriam lapsed into the rapid, fluid speech of the Firewing. "Hagan has come to help us. I know you don't like him, but you like the General and his troops even less. Hagan can help us."

"By doing what? Will he kill soldiers? Can he tear down

245

those Garrison walls? How good is he at breaking up roadway? You are a child, Meeriam, if you think he can help me."

"Then you help him. Help him stop Graeber. Please, Condor, you're the only one who can take him through with speed. He needs the speed."

"What do I get out of it? Will the soldiers go back where they came from? Will they restore our dead? Will they leave us alone then?"

His answer was spoken so that Hagan would understand and his tone was full of the contempt Hagan had come to expect of him. Hagan stepped closer. "With Graeber gone, the killing would stop."

"So what will you do at the ancient city that'll get rid of Graeber?"

"Lay a trap for him. He wants the technology buried there. He'll stop at nothing to get it. And if he does get it, no one will be safe."

"The killing won't stop. Even if you rid us of Graeber, there'll be someone to take his place. Killing is ingrained in you people."

Was he right? Hagan shivered. Had they become a race of killers? No, please God, not if he could help it. "It wasn't me who tried to kill you in Kassine's garden."

"So that was you. I thought so. I should have slit your throat when I had the chance."

Try it, thought Hagan.

"No." Meeriam stepped in between them. In a spate of Firewing dialect Condor berated Meeriam for her foolishness, for her lack of Clan feeling, for her attraction to the stranger making her forget who and what she was.

Meeriam waited for him to finish. When Hagan would have interrupted, she held up her hand. As Condor ran out of words, she shook her head. "You are so self important you make me sick. It's no more than I should have expected from a man who would leave a friend behind to die."

Hagan expected an angry denial from Condor. He expected a violent reaction of some sort. He didn't expect the stunned silence that was louder than words, nor the feeling of anguish that suddenly hung in the air.

Then, still in silence, the shadow that was Condor was gone. Meeriam stood trembling, silent tears on her cheeks.

Quickly Hagan drew her into the protection of his arms. Anger and hurt flowed from her quivering body, and he held her close, comforting her with his heat, with his strength.

"I'm sorry." Her voice was muffled against his shirt when she finally recovered enough to speak. "I ruined it for you."

Hagan rested his cheek against the smooth cap of her hair. "No, you didn't. You couldn't have changed his mind."

"He's different. He wasn't like that before—"

"I'm sure he wasn't."

"I—I meant what I said. I'll take you to the Ancient City. It won't be as quick a trip as you were hoping to make—"

There was no question now that he would accept her help. "As long as we get there before Graeber, that's all that matters."

Meeriam nodded and little by little he felt the tension flow out of her, replaced by a new awareness of how closely she was held. She turned her face up to his, her eyes questing, her lips soft, and responsive when he bent to taste them. Hagan felt himself grow hard with need. But the need was coupled with a fierce protectiveness. A need to hold her gently, to proceed with caution. To treat her vulnerability with care. Torn by the conflicting emotions he held her more tightly and groaned his frustration. This was neither the time, nor the place.

"Come back to the fire," he said, knowing he had to let go or give in to his raging need. "There's nothing we can do until morning."

Nodding, Meeriam let herself be led back to where their packs lay.

By mutual consent, they settled down in the space where Hagan had slept. Given the tension that still filled his body, it wasn't the most comfortable bed Hagan had known, but he found a rightness with her that he wouldn't have traded for all the beds of Mars.

Exhausted by her encounter with Condor, Meeriam fell asleep quickly within the circle of his arms. Hagan, with the hellish pleasure of having her so close, was awake far into the night.

In the gray light of dawn, when they rose from their bed,

Glyn was gone.

Hours later, shrugging into his padded jacket Hagan admitted to himself that he loved this rugged mountain country. He would've loved it even more had he not felt such a sense of urgency. He'd never been this far into the mountains, not in all the time he'd been stationed at Kama Garrison. Even so it seemed familiar to him. Brief flashes of something close to memory seemed to tell him when a trail would take a turn, which fork they'd take. The thinner air had taken on a snow-laden chill. And why not? In spite of the heat at the lower elevations up here it was still late spring. And the country was spectacular. Hagan found himself fascinated by the creek they had been following. It was icy, sparkling in the flashes of sun that penetrated the trees, it's sound sometime muted, but always present. Like the calling birds whose voices echoed in the church-like silence.

And always present in the background was the sound of the wind high overhead. Glyn had been taken from the camp during the night with less noise than the wind made now. The knowledge left Hagan with an uneasiness that grew greater with the passing hours.

Following the swift, swinging pace set by Meeriam, Hagan thought about the strange events of the last few days. Seeming to use a special sense that let her see beyond herself, Meeriam said that Glyn's vanishing was all right, that men from Lissone had come for him. They were taking him back to Lissone for a healing. "It's where he needs to be."

Hagan accepted Glyn's disappearance because he had no choice, just as he accepted that Meeriam must lead him where he had to go.

The trail, by late afternoon, brought them to the base pool of a long, wide cascade of water. Here the giant trees crowded close by the mossy bank and the air was cooled by the mist.

As they drew closer to the cascade, all other sound was drowned out in the hellish roar.

Meeriam leaned close and shouted in his ear. "The trail starts over there—" she pointed to a break in the rocks to the left of the falls, "but," she frowned, "I don't understand. There's been a recent rock fall. It looks like the path might be blocked." Her words faded under the voice of the tumbling water.

She gestured him to stay where he was and cautiously started toward the base of the rocks.

He couldn't let her go alone. Catching up, he caught her hand and made her look at him. Leaning close, he yelled in her ear. "What's wrong?"

"Nothing. I just.." she frowned as she studied the mountainside. "I want to find a way around the rockfall."

Impatience vied with Hagan's growing sense of dis-ease. He watched her make her way through the strewn boulders, some as large as small personal carriers, some no bigger than their packs, and the conviction grew he'd seen something like this before. The bridge at the Kama crossing, where the blocks of cerafoam had been tossed about like children's toys. By a Firewing's temper tantrum?

Just like this. Had Condor done it?

With sharpened senses he studied the way Meeriam had taken. "Meeriam, come back—" he tried to raise his vice above the cascade's roar, but the human sound was lost against the water's louder voice. He waited, and finally, above and between the rocks, a moving patch of brown against the gray granite showed him she'd found a way almost to the top. Much higher, in fact, than he would've thought possible in so short a time.

Carefully he started upward. Felt the rocks shift beneath his feet. Thrown off balance he fell forward, scrabbling for a handhold. When he regained his balance, he pushed himself to his feet. With a strange booming sound the giant boulders settled further.

His heart caught. Meeriam had disappeared. Had she fallen? Angry strength surged through him. Using both hands and feet he scrambled over loose shale and small rocks, up and over huge boulders, trying to reach the place where he'd last seen her. Damn that idiot Condor.Was the Firewing willing to endanger her just to stop him?

"Meeriam!" He jumped and grabbed a handhold on a huge boulder and pulled himself up.

Go back—Her voice was in his head, the warning loud and clear.

Topping the boulder he came to his feet. Above him Meeriam was standing in full view. Safe. His first reaction was relief.

She spoke again into his mind and the words were accompanied by a sense of her fear for him. *Go back—*

"Come down," he called, but even though his voice seemed loud, he knew she couldn't hear over the roar of the water.

No, I can't — Her voice spoke into his mind.

A figure appeared by her side. Condor, looking as large by daylight as he'd looked in the shadows of the night.

*Go back, soldier—*Condor's voice filled with intensity. *The mountains are not safe for you. And go alone. Meeriam is coming with me.*

No, Condor, I'm not! Meeriam's voice was strong in Hagan's mind, a voice that didn't depend upon the clarity of sound for understanding. He leapt up to the next boulder, searching for the way.

Condor snaked out an arm and caught Meeriam. *Tell him to go back. You have no need of him here in our mountains.*

Hagan heard the Firewing's words as if they'd been shouted in a quiet room. "Leave her alone—" Hagan's words seemed to reverberate angrily in his head like a drum. Leave leave leave— He topped another boulder, closer now.

Condor's hand dropped away from Meeriam's shoulder as if he'd been burned and Meeriam pulled herself quickly out of his reach.

Condor stared down at Hagan, a stunned expression on his face. *Who are you?*

Hagan, still furious that the Firewing would dare use his strength against Meeriam, let the question pass him by. "Are you all right?" he shouted to her, anxious to be heard above the roar of the water.

Yes. Please, don't come up any farther. The rocks aren't stable. Condor sent them down.

"Why?"

"Because the soldiers are coming. He has led them here to catch you. They're very close. You must hide until they're gone.

"All right. But come down with me."

"Yes." Meeriam crouched down, reaching for the boulder where he stood.

No! Condor yelled. *Let the soldiers have him. They won't hurt*

him but they will you, Meeriam! Don't put yourself in their hands!
He turned to Hagan, a plea entering his voice. *Don't let her do that!*

Hagan paused, feeling the sudden anguish in Condor's words. Feeling the honesty. Truly now Condor was worried for Meeriam's safety.

Wait, he shouted, trying to stop her descent. The curious reverberation was still in his head, making him dizzy. *I'll come up.*

Watch out! Meeriam's cry rang in his ears, but it was too late. The boulder on which he stood turned beneath his feet. He jumped for the next boulder but it too was now rolling. They were all, everything around him, turning beneath his grasping hand. He heard a scream.

A moment later he slipped into space and hurtled downward accompanied by a fall of rock.

Pain exploded in his head. The strength fled from his arms and legs, and he was only vaguely aware of falling through space. A curiously light feeling, diving as an eagle dove.

Darkness closed around him, and he felt like he was falling through time.

Chapter 20

Norcanna

Time seemed to have a different meaning here in the Colony than it did on Mars. While Kali bided his time seeking an opportunity to contact Kassine or Dr. Portus, he suffered Graeber's attempts to keep him occupied. It was a measure of the threat he posed to Graeber, he supposed, that he was assigned one of Graeber's top Staff Captains as escort. Moss was a treasure of reticence, but at least he didn't throw his weight around, not like that other one, Galt. He was thankful for small favors.

From his place at the table in the small eatery where Moss had suggested they have their noon repast, Kali eyed the two men and a woman who had just entered, and hid his growing impatience behind an uncaring mask. His keeper Moss was no where in sight.

A feeling of unease feathered up his spine. Though he tried not to, he found himself covertly staring at the newcomers. Each of them was taller than the average Arcolan and weathered, he supposed, from the sun. Each of them also wore the common farmer-green tunics that one never saw on Mars except within the Agridomes of Pavonis.

But it wasn't the mere fact of their being farmers that had brought on his sense of unease. It was more, perhaps the way each of them had glanced at him when they first entered, but now seemed oblivious to his presence. Everywhere he went he received more notice than that simply because of the uniform he wore, and he hadn't decided which was worse; to be studied like he was some cavern freak or to be ignored like he was less than the lowliest tower servant.

He cared for neither extreme. Where the hell was Moss? And why, after having Moss stick to him like oily hojoi paste, had the VMP Captain suddenly just moments before asked to be excused and disappeared?

Well, not completely disappeared. There he was, beyond the square windows out on the walk. He was talking to someone, another Freefarmer by the look of him.

Kali glanced down with distaste at the remains of the meal he and Moss had been eating. He found himself no longer hungry. The meal itself had been disappointing. It was nothing more than he could've had on Mars, synthesized down to the last drop of coffee in the cup. He'd hoped for more than that when he came to Earth.

Kali switched his dissatisfied gaze back to the group by the door. Three farmers. What were they waiting for? The two men, though they looked alike, were too close in age to be father and son, and were muscled in a way that only came from hard work or hard exercise. The woman—

The woman was both young and beautiful, he decided. Or she would be if she hadn't affected quite so severe a hairstyle, and had worn something more flattering than the shapeless tunic and trousers. Even belted, the costume gave the impression of being too big on her lithe frame. He started to smile.

He was surprised when she turned, offering him the same scrutiny he'd just given her. Then smiled back.

His smile broadened, but at that moment the younger of the two men with her said something sharp, and she turned away.

Disappointed, Kali swung his chair toward the windows again, cursing the heat he knew was in his cheeks. Just one friendly person, that's all he'd ask. Just one. He hadn't realized Earth could be so lonesome. Damn him for a spurious priest if he knew exactly how to act here in Earth's Norcanna Colony. Before his arrival five days ago he'd have assumed that one acted the same no matter where he was. If a girl that beautiful had smiled at him under the domes of Mars, he'd have thought she was as interested in him as he was in her. Here he dared assume nothing.

Abruptly Kali became aware that while he'd been thinking of the girl at the door, Moss had reappeared. Would the freefarmers let him through? What were they waiting for? A confrontation?

Graeber's warnings of trouble between the soldiers and freefarmers rang in his ears, and though he'd taken them lightly at the time, he tensed.

And then, strangely, Moss spoke to the Freefarmers, and with a quiet word, indicated the way to his table.

Slowly Kali stood, wondering what to expect.

Approaching, Moss placed a hand on the older Freefarmer's arm. "Captain, this is Freefarmer Liam Thomas. He has the largest homestead in the valley. And this —" he indicated the younger man, "is his brother Garth, and this his sister, Lira. Lira and Garth are farming down at Pioneer Cove." Kali was aware of Pioneer Cove. It was an area below Norcanna on the coast which had within the last year opened to homesteading. Kali had recently been involved in a search for homesteaders for the area or he possibly wouldn't have known it even existed. It wasn't a place that received extensive coverage on the Mars nightscreens. He acknowledged each of the younger people, then turned his attention to the older.

Moss went on. "Liam, this is Captain Kenneth Kali, recently of Mars."

The freefarmer held out a strong, dark, calloused hand. "Welcome, Captain. You are the Liaison officer at Xanthe, are you not?"

"I was, yes sir." Liaison from President Demar was Kali's official title now. "At the present time I'm here acting in another capacity."

His answer caused a slight smile to appear in Thomas's eyes. "You've done a good job."

Kali shrugged off the compliment, more embarrassed than pleased. "But not a perfect one. Some do slip through who have no business here." From the corner of his eyes Kali saw the young man's scowl deepen in agreement and the girl's expression grow troubled.

"No system is foolproof," answered the Freefarmer. "But that's not the purpose of our coming here." Thomas hesitated, seeming unsure of how to continue. He glanced at Moss, who nodded encouragement. Then at Kali again.

"Captain, do you want to help Ellis Hagan?"

Hours after meeting the Freefarmers at the small cafe, the inky dark closed in around Kali as he reminded himself of their mission. Never in his years of service had he done anything like this. He'd been a babe in arms during the Southern Domes uprising. He'd deliberately avoided Cavern duty. He'd spent his required year in the Presidential Guard, and then had gone on to duty with the Expansion Council. God! Where was the training for what he was doing now?

As they'd waited by this lonesome roadside the new moon had vanished and the night shadows had grown deeper, leaving him with a feeling of isolation and danger that was painfully intense.

Moss, another dim shadow, crouched nearby behind a jutting granite outcropping. Waiting. Below, on the roadway, were three large HOGGs that had appeared only minutes before.

Kali's famed arrogance had deserted him. Moving closer to the shadow that was Moss he crouched on one knee. "What are they waiting for?"

"The HOGG from the farm."

"Is Hagan with them?" So far nothing indicated Hagan was.

"If Thomas's information was right, he is."

Kali clenched his fist in silent frustration. He was crazy to be here. If Graeber found out, the careful cover he'd constructed would shatter in a thousand pieces. But what choice did he have? Hagan was down there in one of those three HOGGs. Injured, according to Freefarmer Thomas. And it was his fault Hagan was there.

Moss was, at best, uncommunicative. He'd asked Kali a scant six hours ago if he wanted to help Hagan. Until then Moss had been a silent, remote guide assigned by Graeber to make sure that Kali saw only what Graeber wanted him to see, heard only what Graeber wanted him to hear.

Hagan had been mentioned only once before this afternoon, when Kali asked if he was still in the Colony, a question he thought was only natural when one considered the splash he'd made after his father died. Yes, Kali had let himself exhibit that small curiosity, but nothing more. Not by a word or a blink had he given himself away. He was positive. If Moss's grunted affirmative had raised more questions about Hagan, Kali had been too wise to voice them.

Why then, when Moss had sprung his question, had Kali met

the taller man's searching gaze with his own, and made a split-second decision that he hoped he didn't live to regret?

Leaning forward, Kali peered around the black bulk of rock. Below, on the cerafoam roadway that gleamed silver in the starlight, the three HOGGs waited, their air turbines humming softly in the quiet night, their running lights dim. Ahead of the carriers, the cerafoam road forked into smaller ribbons, one leading to Norcanna, the other disappearing into the hills. Ending, Kali knew now, at the place called the Farm. Graeber's retraining facility.

Retraining. Kali shivered. No one should have that kind of power over men's minds. No one. Least of all a madman like Graeber.

Beside him he felt the VMP Captain tense. Then Kali, too, heard the sound of another HOGG. After a moment that seemed to stretch forever another carrier appeared, coming from the direction of the Farm.

The new arrival stopped a short distance down the ribbon of roadway, and the driver quickly emerged. A shadow broke from the side of the middle waiting vehicle and moved forward, stopping not quite within the circle of dim light.

"Hagan?" Kali queried softly.

"Not yet. The one that came from the Farm, that's Galt." Moss spoke softly but with a wealth of contempt.

"Graeber's man." Kali remembered him well.

"To the core."

The two men who'd met and talked briefly now moved past the circle of dim light toward the middle of the three HOGGs. Moss touched Kali lightly and motioned down the hill to the left. From their position above, Kali could see three distinct bushes that looked hardly big enough to afford any kind of cover, but would let them get closer, perhaps even close enough to hear any conversation taking place. He nodded, and bending low, made his careful, quiet way down the hillside.

He hardly dared breathe as he moved close enough to see the guard standing at the rear of the middle HOGG who saluted as the two black red clad soldiers approached.

"There's one guard," Kali whispered in Moss's ear as the quiet captain settled gently at his side.

"Yes. Maybe more than one." A sharp, low-voiced command came from beyond their line of sight, and a moment later three more men emerged from the HOGG's rear gate, a heavy burden between them.

A lifeless burden—Kali's despair came unexpectedly. Hagan dead, and all because he had insisted that Hagan return—

"At least he's alive," whispered Moss.

"How do you know?" Kali couldn't keep the bitter sound of defeat form his voice. A savagery he'd not known he possessed surged through him, and only Moss's sudden hard grip on his arm kept him in place. For a brief second he fought the VMP Captain's hand, but Moss leaned closer.

"He must be, otherwise why bother to bring him back to the Farm? See, they're transferring him to the other carrier."

Kali's thoughts cleared. Of course. Moss was right. But a new tension filled him. Was Hagan badly injured? Unconscious? Or drugged, perhaps? He thought of the brief recounting of events delivered earlier by Moss. All they knew was that Hagan had been hurt in a fall. No one yet knew how it had happened or how badly he was hurt. The message had come from the Firewing, passed to Freefarmer Thomas, and from Thomas to Moss. It had happened two days ago.

Suddenly Moss tensed. "Galt's leaving. Come on."

Without waiting to see if Kali followed, Moss crouched low and ran through the shadows bordering the road. The HOGG ponderously revolved on it's air cushion, preparing to return the way it'd come. Kali pressed a prayer to God that the drivers of the other HOGGs would be blinded by their own dim lights and wouldn't see the two of them.

Then, as Moss gathered himself to jump for the rear gate of the barely moving HOGG, the lights of the other carriers came up to full power. Moss, already moving, would have burst into the full glare of the first advancing carrier had not Kali, in another split-second decision, thrown his weight on the taller man, taking them both down into the safety of the roadside shadows.

Only after the three large carriers lumbered by, their air turbines throwing a whirlwind of dust through the black night, and only after that same dust had settled and the silence returned, only then did either man move.

Kali drew a shuddering breath, coughed and sneezed. Rolling off Moss, he helped the other man sit up. "You all right?"

Moss's voice was husky. "Yes. Thanks." Then strong with bitterness. "By God, though, we've missed the best chance we'll get." Slowly Moss stood. Brushing himself off, he looked in the direction the first carrier had taken and shook his head. "We won't catch up with him. Not tonight. And tomorrow might be too late."

Returning in the small personal carrier that earlier had brought them from Norcanna, Kali sat silent, lost in a well of frustration. Questions he had, plenty of them. But Moss seemed content to handle the manual controls, lost in his own silence.

Finally Kali could stand it no longer. "Are you going to tell me the rest of the story?"

Moss glanced at him and smiled slightly. "I wondered if you were curious."

"Very. How did you suspect I'd go with you?"

"Portus. He assured us you weren't the arrogant bastard you seemed."

Kali's jaw went slack and then his sense of humor asserted itself. He laughed. "Nice of him. How is the good doctor?" Portus had been, like Hagan, conspicuous by his absence.

"He's been ill. But he's better now. He wanted to see you, but we thought it'd be dangerous. For both of you. Graeber's still looking for him."

Kali frowned into the darkness. Moss's answer merely raised more questions. He wanted to ask about Hagan, about what would happen next. He chose instead another question he considered of paramount importance.

"How do you manage to convince Graeber you're loyal to his cause?"

Even in the shadows of the small cab Kali caught the Captain's searching glance.

And then Moss's gaze turned back to the roadway. Just when Kali began to think he'd get no answer, Moss sighed. "I never argue with him. I'm a good soldier."

"And of course you always do as you're told."

"Whenever possible," Moss agreed.

"And when it isn't?"

"Graeber doesn't find out."

"You play a dangerous game." Kali considered, then softly amended his statement. "A very dangerous game."

A rare grin flashed across Moss's face. "You're playing the same game yourself."

In silence Kali conceded he was. A game he meant to win.

Into the long moment of silence that followed, Moss said, "Is Demar really coming or was that story just an excuse for your own arrival?"

Before he could help himself, Kali laughed. "She is coming. We couldn't stop her."

"She's foolish."

"She's old. And Graeber is family-connected. She refuses to see a threat."

"Then she's also blind. She must know that the old ways are coming to an end. If she's not careful Graeber will teach her that lesson before she dies."

"She'll have to learn it for herself. She won't listen to anyone else. She pushed through the new outliner over the objections of most of the rest of the High Council. God knows we needed something faster than the Mendoza, but still, it was a tremendous expense. It was all anyone could do to keep her from making the first flight. Yet she has a certain style, and the people of Mars seem to regard her highly. It's that regard that has kept her in power for so long."

"Too long."

"Yes." The problems of Mars were deep and involved but, Kali thought, the problems here were worse. "Tell me, Captain. How do we get Hagan out of Graeber's retraining facility?"

Hagan came awake slowly, the falling sensation still with him. Falling toward a pinpoint of light that was becoming bigger with each passing fiery breath. The light burst on him and involuntarily he groaned, because with the return of light came pain.

"He's coming around," said an almost familiar voice. "Call the General."

"I'll call him when I'm damned good and ready," growled another, easier to identify. Galt. With a note of triumph in his voice.

Hagan slitted his eyes, trying to make out form or substance, but though there was movement, it was only the movement of blurred shapes, patches of light and dark. He blinked, trying to clear his vision, trying to get the overwhelming pain to localize. In his shoulder, yes, and his legs. How long had he been here? He tried to lift his hand and came up against a cold metal strap.

"Hagan—Hagan, do you hear me? Do you know where you are?" A cruel hand dug into his jaw and forced his head to turn. Hagan choked on the animal cry of pain that welled in his throat. "Do you know?" A gloating sound entered Galt's voice. Hagan escaped again into darkness.

Kali paced. The broad gathering room of Kassine's tower residence four stories above ground was catching the first dawn light, and a young girl was waving the floating ball lamps into darkness. Another was filling a sideboard with food. On a long padded divan a young man introduced by Moss as Lieutenant Will Loomis, though he wore a green tunic rather than the black and red uniform of the VMP, sat with white-faced care. Kali had seen a too quick movement causing flashes of pain. Moss, his uniform jacket open and his military collar undone, stood at a window staring outward toward the bay. The farmer's sister, Lira Thomas, talked quietly in a corner with her brother Garth.

Kassine herself had arrived only moments before, not bothering to hide her surprise at the number of people gathered here. After his quiet introduction Moss turned back and leaned tiredly against the window and Vana Kassine moved to a large conforming chair. Now she watched them all with an angry anxiety.

Kali had a thousand questions of his own, but he, like Kassine, for the moment kept them to himself. Freefarmer Thomas had been gone when he and Moss had returned to Norcanna some time in the early hours of the new morning, but according to his sister he was due to return with Gerald Nilander, Kassine's manager, at any moment. It was for this they all waited.

And so Kali paced.

"Young man," Kassine said suddenly, "Earth would not cease

to spin if you sat down. If you have not exhausted yourself yet, at least you have managed to exhaust me."

Kali drew himself up short and bowed a very formal bow to the old woman. "Your pardon, Vana Kassine. I didn't think to annoy you." Termagant was the word that came most quickly to mind.

"But you have. Does the general know you're here? Gerald said your every move was watched. Where does Graeber think you are right now?"

"In my bed I hope, Vana Kassine."

Before he could say more, Moss turned from the window. "They've come."

Moments later the door hissed open and Freefarmer Thomas entered, followed by a dark-haired girl, and Nilander. Warily Kali eyed them. Nilander of course he knew by reputation. The power behind Kassine, someone had said, but he noted the genuine regard which which Nilander first went to the old woman and made his small bow. Kassine accepted this as her due, but none the less looked relieved to see him.

Kali had no more than registered that the girl with them was dressed differently, even to her soft brown boots, when Nilander turned to him.

"Captain Kali?" Kali nodded. "I'm Gerald Nilander. I understand Hagan has been taken to the General's hospital."

Before Kali could answer, Moss pushed himself away from the window. "They brought him in during the night. We came close, but not close enough." Moss hesitated, then asked what Kali considered an odd question. "How badly is he hurt?"

The girl who'd come in with Nilander answered. "He was unconscious for several hours, Hugh. He must have hit his head when he fell. His shoulder's broken. And his legs are badly bruised."

"But can he walk?"

"Probably."

Kali studied the girl, his impatience building. Moss had told him nothing of what Hagan was doing before he was caught. Was he going to the Firewing for help? Was he trying to make his way to the Ancient City? And how did she know what Hagan's injures were? Was she there? Was she the cause? Because his anger now had a focus, it spilled out harshly and without conscious volition. "How do you know? Were you there?"

A flash of pain swept across her face. Her shoulders slumped, and he sensed a deep and searing fatigue, as though she'd traveled hard and not slept for several days. "Yes," she said, "I was there."

Kali was immediately contrite. But Moss, spinning toward him, seemed ready to defend her. Quickly she caught the soldier's arm. "Please, no. It's all right. He's only worried."

Nilander agreed. "We all are. We must devise a plan —"

But before he could continue the young house-girl reentered, saying with a hesitant voice, "Vana Kassine, Van Nilander—there are soldiers banging at the gate. They want in."

"Soldiers? Nonsense —" Kassine rose stiffly to her feet. "They know better than to come here."

"But—but they have," the girl protested.

Liam Thomas broke the tense silence with a quiet expletive. "He's feeling very sure of himself."

Kassine leaned heavily on her cane and stalked toward the door. "He will not force his way in here! I will not have that man in my home."

"No, Glena." Gerald intercepted the old woman before she could reach the door. His eyes were hard, his voice was not. "Perhaps admitting him is just what we must do. What better way to disarm him?"

That Gerald used her familiar name seemed to go unnoticed by Kassine. Briefly Kali wondered how many other Matriarchs would have allowed such familiarity by one who worked for them. Was Nilander so much more than he seemed? Hadn't Merrick intimated as much? It was to Nilander he spoke. "We can't be found here, Van Nilander."

"No, of course not." The manager bent toward the old woman. "Glena?" Nilander awaited the old woman's decision.

The old woman's sharp gaze traveled from one to the other of her uninvited guests. "Very well. Meeriam, you take these three —" she swept her cane in the direction of Moss, Loomis and Kali, "through the tunnel to the plant. Tell Butcher they must be kept until the all-clear from here. Van Thomas, would you and your family care to break fast with us this morning?"

Accepting Kassine's invitation the Freefarmers moved toward the table, and Meeriam beckoned the three soldiers. "Come, it'll be quickest if we take the central lift to the basement."

Within minutes they had entered the smooth tiled tunnel that began in the basement beneath Kassine's double-towered residence. Kali paused, catching his breath. Sounds echoed down here, their harsh breathing, the click of their hard-heeled boots, the short soft instructions from Meeriam. The slight downward slope was lit at long intervals by high-powered ball lamps that cast harsh light directly below but left large patches of shadow in between. Loomis was also trying to keep pace, but running out of breath he leaned against the wall beneath a ball lamp. "I'm not as strong as I thought." He flashed Kali a painful grin. Kali offered him an arm, and they moved on. "How long ago were you injured?"

"A week or so—before Captain Hagan and Meeriam left for the mountains." He clenched his fist in angry frustration. "I wanted to go too."

Assessing the younger man's condition, Kali smiled. "I doubt you were in any shape to do so."

"No." Loomis's face grew hard, making him look like a younger version of Moss. "But at least I'm alive, thanks to Hagan. I'll do anything I can to help him now. Will he be—" Loomis stumbled over the words, "what will the General do to him?"

Kali's face tightened. "Depends on what the General wants of him, I suppose. The Share, perhaps." And who knew what Graeber would do when he found out Hagan couldn't give him the Share. Had already assigned it to Xanthe and considered it no loss. Kali shivered. Not anything he wanted to think about. Deliberately he hurried Loomis forward, effectively cutting off further questions.

As the tunnel continued, an acrid smell grew stronger. Ahead Meeriam and Moss had reached a gate that seemed almost as solid as the walls themselves. Meeriam had already pressed her palm against the lock, and even as Kali and Loomis arrived the gate slid upward with a deep, rumbling sound. The acrid smell of processed Hojoi immediately became stronger.

Before the gate slid shut, they heard the tramp of heavy footsteps echoing in the distance, and then the closed gate shut off the sound.

Meeriam led them into a side room that was obviously used for storage. "Come. There's no time to waste. You must be hidden before they come around to the main doors."

"What about you?" Kali asked.

"I work here sometimes. No one will think my presence strange."

The next room she led them to was also a storage room, but here open bins along the walls held green bundles of clothes, and a clothes recycler hummed in one corner, spitting out a bundle every two minutes. Grabbing a bundle from a bin marked Male-large, she thrust it at Moss, then pulled two from the one marked Male-med. "No time to strip. Wear these over your clothes and make sure the cuffs are tight. If you don't the smell will penetrate and you'll never be rid of it. Everything you need is there. Pull the boot coverings up to above the knee and tie them, and pull the hood down to your eyebrows. The face protector fits over the edge of the head cover, making a seal. No —" she reached up and adjusted Kali's head cover. "That's it." She did the same for Loomis and then for Moss.

Kali uneasily eyed the last piece of protective clothing, a cone-shaped breathing mask. The mere thought of putting it on made him want to gag. Meeriam watched him with concern. "You'll need the cone. The smell of raw Batch—"

Kali understood. He'd never been in a processing plant before, but the smell was reputed to turn even strong stomachs bilious. He took a deep breath and slipped the mask over his face. As long as he believed the alternative was worse, he could tolerate it.

As a hiding place, the vast noisy floor of the processing plant was ideal. Leaving Meeriam behind, the three soldiers had passed through a sterile room, and then on to a high platform above the processing floor. There they were met by Kassine's morning shift supervisor, an extremely large man who wore the name Butcher on a shoulder patch. He was dressed just as they were. Even the face cone could not muffle the sharpness of his tone. He'd obviously been told of their coming and had been waiting for them. "This way."

Moving quickly, he led them down onto the floor and along one moving belt. Taking a long-handled rake from a surprised worker's hands, he put it into Kali's. "Stand here and rake," he said. "Watch the others and do as they do. It's not hard. Even a soldier can learn."

Kali knew he wasn't imagining the bite in the large man's voice. He might help them, but obviously he wasn't liking it. Loomis and Moss were given places on the belt at his back.

Within minutes Kali felt the heat of the steam belts rising around him, causing sweat to stand on his face under the mask, and to trickle down his ribs. Because of the heat he guessed the other workers wore little but the basics under their green-wear. Also within minutes he was feeling the unaccustomed weight of the long-handled rake in his shoulders and forearms. How did they stand it? And how god-awful primitive, compared to the automated plants of Mars!

But when the double doors at the far end of the building rolled smoothly back, all discomfort was forgotten.

Kali paused, as did every other worker on the processing floor. At the end of the vast room, behind the glass sterile-screen, Graeber stood, his face covered by a conical faceplate but his clothes, his head and his hands unprotected from the acrid fumes of the processed hojoi. He pointed at the sterile door, and it was obvious though they couldn't hear the words, he was demanding it be opened.

Suddenly Butcher stood beside them again, speaking with no fear that Graeber would hear over the constant noise of the ancient machinery. "Go back to work, friends. Nothing to be alarmed about. By God, look at the ugly toad. He'll never get the smell from his clothes. Pick up your rakes. He won't last in here more than a minute or two. Ignore him like the toad he is. That's it, friends, back to work."

Slowly the workers took up their spreading, pushing and dividing until not one looked up again at the General.

From the corner of his eye Kali saw the General step through the sterile screen and gesture down the aisles, sending his conically masked soldiers onto the vast floor. When the soldiers on his aisle passed behind his back Kali studiously eyed the oily black goo on the dryer belt and prayed to God that the soldier was too conscious of the smell to notice a difference between their more bulky clothing and that worn by the workers on either side. He was hardly aware of holding his breath until the soldier passed by. Then Kali breathed again. Graeber, fury in every step, left the way he'd come. The big double doors banged shut and sealed, and Kali, with a sigh, lifted his rake off the moving belt.

A prodding finger hit him in the middle of the back. "Not yet, soldier, not yet." He met the giant's harsh eyes. "He's posted a guard to watch over us. How greatly he cares for our welfare, see? Keep working. The shift changes in two hours. You're not safe until then." The giant went on down the row of workers, talking to them, calming them. Kali glanced across the wide belt to the worker across the way. A woman, he realized. Watching the ease with which she handled the rake he groaned softly. Two hours? His mouth tightened and deliberately he turned his mind to what would happen when they left the safety of the processing plant. To the need to get Hagan out of the General's hands. To anything that would let him endure the damned torture of the next two hours.

It was a matter of endurance, Hagan thought. When all else failed, you endured.

And when all sound in the small room ceased except the beating of his own heart, except the sound of his own breath moving in and out, Hagan opened his eyes.The small room was featureless, white and glaring in the bright light that floated overhead. He'd been awake, aware for some time. Aware of the voiceless attendants who'd injected him with another dose of strong body-numbing drug that left him floating but his mind alert. The same ones who'd then strapped his shoulder. The same ones who'd lifted his head and forced a tasteless gruel down his throat. He'd swallowed to keep from choking.

Either he was no longer strapped down, or he couldn't feel the straps that held him. Nor did he feel pain though he remembered that his shoulder had felt broken, and his legs might have been, too. The attendants had only worked over his shoulder. And yes, he did remember at one point being on his feet. Yes. It'd hurt, but he had stood. A wave of relief washed him, than vanished. His thoughts grew soft around the edges, like fog creeping into the corners of his mind obscuring the clear bright pictures. Damn the drug. He shook his head, trying to clear it. Si ought to know about this miracle drug. Ah, the uses he could put it to.Danielle would like it too. What time was it? How long had he been here? Where was Graeber now? Was he on his way—on his way—an ingrained need to keep the thought secret didn't let him articulate the name of the place he needed to reach. The place he and Meeriam—Meeriam. Meeriam, come back. Why had she gone with Condor? Would they reach the place—that place—and would Graeber—what time was it? What time—he had to get up—get out—

Then of course he was on the stage, and it seemed right and proper that he be there. On the stage in Jolando's tight black uniform and long flowing cape, giving him identity and power. Jolando who had said words written by a master playwright some two hundred years before. The words Josh had reformed to fit the present day. Words that were used like weapons. As his father used words. He shook his head, trying to drive the accusing vision of Elias back into the shadows of his mind, and it seemed to work until he became the eagle screaming through the sky. Down—down. Falling into merciful dark.

Shaking with rage, Graeber stood in front of the monitor at the central guard's station and stared at Hagan's image projected on the screen. "How long has he been like that?" In his rage he shouted and heads turned as far away as the reception room doorway down the hall.

"A little while." Miles, the General's personal aide, edged a little further to one side, his attention torn between the General's words, and the General's hand. "Galt woke him up when they first brought him in. He's been real restless since. We tied him down and strapped his shoulder."

"He's irrational." Graeber's fist slammed on the side of the large screen. The picture wavered, then sharpened again.

Miles sidled further away. "Yes. Could be the drug, though we don't usually get that effect."

Blind with his rage, Graeber ignored Miles. After this morning's abortive attempt to catch Kassine with Firewing spies under her roof, and being made to look like an idiot at the processing plant—even after a bath and clean clothes he could still smell the stench of raw Batch—Graeber wanted to smash something. Anything. Hagan—he would break this Hagan the way he had broken the elder. Consumed by fury he stared at the screen. In this state Hagan was useless to him.

He shifted his icy gaze to Miles. "Two hours. I want Hagan on his feet in two hours."

Miles' bland face grew tight. "It'll take longer than that for the drug to wear off."

Graeber's fingers flexed on the probe and a surge of power flowed through him. He licked his lips. This evening, then. By God, this evening.

Waiting on the steps a short while later for his carrier to come around, Graeber considered what to do next. He had Hagan right where he'd always wanted him, he'd have had the old lady this morning—he glanced down at his crisp clean uniform and his satisfaction disappeared. By God what a stinking place. How did they stand it? If there'd been anyone at Kassine's they'd disappeared into the processing plant. He knew it, though he couldn't prove it. Let her laugh this time. It wouldn't be much longer—

Graeber's mouth tightened. He was still waiting to hear from those idiots out at Kama. The old roads were there. They had to be. The Firewing couldn't block them all. He'd find a way. He damned well would.

Glancing at the sun, he gauged the time. Shortly after thirteen hundred hours. Wind caught at his jacket though he hardly noticed. Nor did he take much notice of the storm clouds on the horizon. A smile grew on his broad face. He had a whole unit of retrained farmers who would kill anything they were pointed at, that he could send into the Kama Valley on an instant's notice. Yes, hit the biggest farm and the others would fall right into his hands. But not yet. Not yet. When Demar came—

His smile disappeared. Where were Moss and that arrogant bastard from Mars? Not that he particularly cared about Kali, but he needed Moss. Never knew what the man was thinking, but he could always be depended upon to keep a cool head.

A chill ran through him. Nothing was wrong. Wasn't everything falling into place just the way he wanted? No hitches, no snags. Everything on line, and yet—

Impatiently he turned, searching the curved white driveway in front of the low right wing of the hospital. Where was the damned carrier? A flash of movement in the distance between a stand of trees beyond the gates caught his eyes. As it came closer he made out a carrier, a small one such as civilians used. Going full tilt and coming this way. In the harsh early afternoon sun it seemed shadowless and vaguely disquieting.

And then it appeared again at the end of the drive, entering the gates as if there were no gate lock to be manipulated.

Stupid driver—get himself killed. What did he think he was doing?

He didn't believe this! Graeber backed into the recessed doorway, almost stumbling in his hurry. The dry taste of fear was in his throat.

Then, as the small carrier sped by the door flew open and a man came tumbling out. Stunned Graeber watched. Sweat stood out on his face. He stared at the black and red-clad figure which rolled twice and then came to rest face down on the cerafoam roadway.

With a feeling of horror, Graeber stared down at the body at his feet.

The figure was bloody and beaten, but recognizable.

It was Moss.

Chapter 21

Norcanna

Long after Moss had departed in the small carrier Kassine had lent them, Kali stood on the drive of Kassine's abandoned estate, staring down the empty roadway. His bruised hand curled into a fist. They had small hope of fooling Graeber for any length of time. In fact, if the General swallowed any of it, Kali would be surprised. But one of them had to get into the Farm, and Moss was right, of course. Of the three he was the most likely to succeed.

"Sir," Loomis said quietly, "it's time we left." The young soldier had once more donned his uniform, and though the morning's excitement seemed to have done him no harm, the pallor of his skin indicated his continued weakness.

Kali agreed. Worried, he glanced up at the blue sky. The temperature was dropping, and the wind had risen. "I've never read of storms this late in the spring." He shivered with a sense of foreboding. Rain was another event outside his experience. He wasn't sure he was looking forward to it.

"Happens sometimes, sir. If we get a low-pressure trough in off the ocean. Won't last long.' Loomis moved toward the gate of the abandoned garden, behind which another personal carrier waited. "If we hurry we can reach Van Thomas's homestead before Graeber starts a search for the carrier Hugh took. And we don't want to be caught on the road in the rain. Water on the roadways plays hell with these little carriers."

Loomis passed through the gate, and Kali followed. A gust of wind swept dead leaves into a swirl that seemed to take human shape before it dissipated into another dead pile of leaves. He shook his head at the fancy. He'd be ready for the caverns himself, if he wasn't careful. Loomis climbed into the little carrier's control seat and activated the thrusters. Their power added strength to another gust of wind and the small carrier wavered on its column of air.

"Go ahead," Kali shouted. "I'll get the gate."

Loomis nodded and the small carrier moved out unsteadily into a sunlight that seemed curiously muted. Using muscles made sore by the morning's work, Kali slammed the gate and forced the corroded lock home. Glancing behind him as he jumped into the control cab with Loomis, Kali noted that the strange wind was already wiping away any evidence they'd been there.

Night came early. Meeriam lay in the dark and listened to the wind. She had already tried sleep but the moment she closed her eyes the image of Hagan sprang to life, more vivid than any image she had ever visualized. But each time she tried to touch the image with her thought it dimmed. It was as if he was deliberately pushing her away, though how he could was beyond her understanding. Frustrated, she lay staring at the ceiling.

Meeriam—the thought came to her as if on the wind itself. A strange, electric tension filled her. She waited for it to come again, making herself empty, receptive, aware.

Meeriam—the thought was a cry that became a scream, full of pain and anger. She tried to follow it to its source, but a void threatened her, a dark horrible place where she dared not go. As if the residence tower were one with the wind, she felt it shake with the wind's force. Trembling she rose to her knees and caught a floating ball lamp and waved its light into existence. The light seemed to help. It was Hagan. She knew it was. He needed her. She knelt in the middle of her bed and closed her eyes, again, concentrating on the image. When it came she enveloped it within her mind, experiencing an emotion she had hardly yet given a name. Love. It filled her and flowed out of her into that strange void. When the next scream came, filled with such pain and anguish she thought she'd die of it, she wrapped the image within her giving it strength, giving it life, until finally she was swallowed by darkness, the same darkness where, somewhere, Hagan dwelt.

High on the flank of Grandfather Mountain the sacred fire burned low, flaring only when an errant finger of wind pushed its way through the winding secret way between the boulders. Anahata, eldest of elders, bowed her head, at one with the fire, with the rocks, with the shadows of night. She felt the approaching storm encroach on her communing mind like a shadow cast behind a setting sun. A powerful storm, she knew, and dangerous, because it was not controlled.

She did not ask who caused the storm. She knew. And though it was surprising to many, she was not surprised. She had always known he was powerful, even though he was without that elusive strength called Power. She bowed her head into her hands and called upon Mind to help her now. She felt the scream like a jagged bolt of lightning, shattering the night of a soul into mere shards of life, burning, destroying. Damaging beyond repair—

No. she would not believe that. He would survive. He had to survive. He will survive, Mind spoke to her, comforting her. He will survive.

"He will," she whispered, confirming what she already knew. But shame filled her that he should have to go through this experience. Shame that she had not wanted to involve the People in goal. Shame that she had thought she could keep them safe at what cost—at what cost?

Lightning cracked close by, and the smell of ozone filled the air. A powerful smell that raised prickles on her skin. Thunder followed quickly after the brilliant light, rattling the very rocks on which the sacred fire burned. Yes, his anger was well-deserved, and well placed. But such unconscious control would vanish— would vanish— God help them all should he wake to his power without control.

Kali stood on the covered porch of the homestead's main building, watching the electric storm race across the broad expanse of sky. The wind had grown stronger, and even the Freefarmers who had gathered silently to watch said they remembered nothing to match this storm's electric ferocity.

"There'll be fires in the mountains, you mark my words," Garth Thomas strove to keep his nervousness from showing, but failed. Liam's younger brother had a habit of chewing on his thumbnail that Kali hadn't noticed before. Lira frowned. "We should have gone back to the Cove tonight. The children are there. If the soldiers come before we get back—"

"They won't go out in weather like this," said Garth. "They wouldn't want to get mud on their leggings."

Lira's glance at Garth was full of sisterly derision. If the mood had been lighter Kali might have laughed.

Then another farmer said, "Lucky if we don't get another fire in the fields."His worry was well-founded. Kali had been told earlier that half the homestead was at dry-point, waiting for harvest.

The next flash of lightning illuminated more worried faces as other workers joined them on the porch. Soon a small crowd had gathered. Waiting. Watching. Hoping against hope that the heavy moisture in the clouds overhead would pass the valley by.

Kali found himself counting the seconds between the flashes of light and the thunder, willing the seconds to lengthen. He was still counting when Belle Thomas, Liam's rotundly pregnant wife, appeared in the doorway. Another mystery, said a part of his mind. A woman pregnant and happy about it. Earth was full of mysteries.

Then the thought fled. Vana Thomas's face in the flickering light was white with worry. "Liam, Van Nilander is on the 'screen. He says it's important."

With a soft curse the Freefarmer strode through the doorway and disappeared inside. Kali intercepted the uneasy looks among the other farmers, and interpreted them to mean there was now a greater worry than the strange unseasonable storm. He was right.

When Thomas reappeared a few moments later, his face was a hard mask of anger. "The soldiers have been sent out from Kama Garrison. Van Nilander says we have at best several hours. I've put out a call to the other homesteads."He paused, looking at Kali. "This isn't your fight, Captain. You don't have to stay."

"What good can you do against the soldiers? They'll be heavily armed."

Liam Thomas's faintly savage smile gave Kali more hope than the farmer's words. "We ourselves are not without arms."

Kali hadn't expected to make his stand against Graeber so soon, nor had he expected to do it with Freefarmers, but looking at the determined faces around him, he knew there wouldn't be a better time or place.

He nodded. "I'll stay."

General Gordon Graeber faced Hagan across the small retraining room, his eyes glinting with a steely madness, his hand wrapped tightly around the butt of the psychoprobe at his waist.

Tethered to the metal pole in the center of the bare room by a metal strap attached to his free wrist the soldier-turned-player was of necessity on his feet, and though his face was pale with pain, his eyes were contemptuously steady.

Hagan's injured arm was bound to his body by cloth strips. His bronzed body was otherwise bare, and gleamed with a fine sheen of moisture, but he stood still, waiting.

There was no hint of fear in his eyes. Like father like son, came the uneasy thought. Graeber shook it away. "I'm glad you're feeling better."

"I'm sure you are." Hagan's voice matched his eyes, steady, waiting, merely hinting of well-controlled anger.

Graeber's frown deepened. Where was the fear? He needed the fear. Fear made men malleable. A deeper thought intruded. The old Commander hadn't shown any fear either. Not even when faced with the weapon that had ended his life. The thought made Graeber irrationally furious, and he grabbed the probe from its holster and his grip was painfully tight. Within the white, windowless room no sign of the strange storm that raged outside intruded, yet Graeber seemed to feel it all around him, an electric current as powerful as the sun going nova, as dangerous as an unchecked tide.

Dangerous? Nonsense. He banished the thought with a harsh laugh. "Tonight, player, you'll give me what I want, and we'll dispense with this stupid game."

"What do you want, General?" Hagan's voice had grown soft.

"Your cooperation, Player. A signature on a conveyance. Your presence with the forces this night that I send to destroy Kassine."

A smile briefly touched Hagan's lips but went no further. "The one I can't give you, the other I won't."

Can't? Won't? "Proud words, Hagan. But meaningless. As your father found out before he died."

"He gave you nothing before he died."

"Wrong. He gave me everything. He had no choice, and neither will you." Abruptly and without further warning, the bulbous eye of the probe came to life and with a short bark of triumph Graeber swung out and connected with Hagan's genitals.

Moss fought his way to consciousness. His face felt stiff, and sore. Blinking owlishly, he stared around the small hospital room. Empty, thank God. Yet it was late! Too late? Was he too late to help Hagan? Maybe not. Hagan was strong. But no man could hold out forever against the probe. Not the way Graeber would use it. He tried to roll off the bed and groaned aloud. Couldn't do it. Not yet. Damned if he didn't wish there'd been another way of getting in here without raising the staff's doubts. Hadn't he known the split second before he hit the roadway that he was going down too hard? Pushing himself into a sitting position he surveyed his surroundings. There was an electric tension in the air. Like an electrical storm in the making.

In one corner a recycler hummed away, and he wondered if his uniform had already been discarded. Probably. It had been a bloody mess. He, Kali and Will had made sure of that. He edged to the side of the high bed. It was easier now. He slipped off and felt his strength returning.

The room was large. His was one of four beds on this side, but none of the others were occupied. Grabbing a pillow from the next bed he added it to the one on which he'd been resting to make a passable lump under the light cover. In the dim light it would do. With a wince for the stiffness of his abused muscles, Moss moved silently to the bank of lockers at the end of the room. A swift search found his boots and leathers, the belt, the s'darm and its holster. His personals, including his ID were also there. With the card in hand he moved quickly to the recycler and ordered up another uniform. While he waited—and four minutes had never seemed so long—he used the utility room at the other end of the empty ward. The hot water was a relief to the bruise that had darkened and swelled one eye.

When he heard the small ding of the bell signal that said his clothes bundle was available he started back toward the recycler.

He was halfway into the room when the click of hard heels on the tile hallway outside the door threw him back into the utility room. His heart pounded. Had he left the locker door open? Would someone notice a clothes bundle resting in plain sight on the recycler?

He cracked the door slightly and watched a white-clothed attendant move past him toward the bed he'd occupied. Bright light from the hallway lighted the attendant's path but left the rest of the room in shadow. The attendant seemed to notice nothing out of line, but he was approaching the bed. Another moment and he'd reach out and touch the lump of pillows.

Though Moss had hoped to avoid announcing his intentions so soon, he had no choice . As soon as the attendant bent over the bed, Moss slipped behind him and brought the rigid edge of his hand down on the unsuspecting man's neck. With a soft grunt the attendant dropped where he stood.

Moss dressed quickly. Minutes later, after having used restraining straps pulled from the side of the bed to bound and gag the attendant and hide him in one of the lockers, Moss moved into the hallway and paused to orient himself.

At the end of the long hall to his right was a reception area. That and this wing were the oldest parts of the building, originally used as medical facilities for the whole colony. Only after Graeber came was the purpose subverted. How could they all have let one man control their lives so completely? The thought grated on his nerves. And yet, didn't he know? All the horror stories he'd ever heard about retraining, about the punishments meted out here, about men sent here and never seen again, stories he'd thought exaggerated or perhaps even false, came back now. No, not false. The hair rising on the back of his neck said they were not false. The urge to march himself to safety was strong.

Hardening his resolve, he turned his back on the way out and started in the opposite direction, hoping that anyone he met would think he belonged. He felt he was moving into the depths of a slimy monster's lair.

The feeling increased as he turned first one corner, then

another. Here the doors were closer together, indicating smaller rooms. Most were open and the first one he passed and glanced into raised the hairs on his neck. A bare room, except for the post in the middle. A wave of revulsion turned his stomach. He needed no pictures to tell him what happened in one of these rooms. Trying to shut out the thought he hurried on.

He traveled the length of that corridor and turned into the next, realizing that shortly he'd be back where he started. Here again each empty doorway looked exactly the same as the one before. He was almost ready to concede defeat when he heard a strange, keening cry. Abruptly he froze, his skin prickling with a response so basic he had no name for it.

The sound came again and without warning the lights went out.

Bracing himself with his back against the wall, Moss sought to still his fear of the total darkness. Down the corridor two voices raised in a frantic babble of questions and accusations. Someone else was blaming the power outage on the storm. Still another voice called for a portable ball lamp. Near at hand, too close for him to do more than hold his breath, a door scraped open slowly under pressure, and the burning eye of a psychoprobe thrust through, and then a thick hand and arm. Someone with harsh labored breathing emerged into the hallway. Moss was already sliding away from the sound when, in the meager light, he recognized the shape of the man.

Graeber!

The burning eye of the psychoprobe cast about in a semi-circle, seeming brighter in the otherwise total darkness, but all it revealed was the beefy hand and arm that held it.

Moss backed away until he came to another open doorway and slipped in. Slowly the eye of the probe came closer, than passed by, blocked out by the bulk of the man who held it. All that remained was the sound of Graeber's panting, panicked breath.

Moss waited only seconds, then, a sense of urgency pushing him on, slipped out the door and down the hall into the next room. The one from which Graeber had come. Cursing the darkness that hampered his search, he was fearful of what he'd find.

Moss was two steps into the room when he was caught by a strange, eerie light which was almost electric blue. The light filled the room bright enough to bring certain features into focus. Within it a twisted figure hung by one cuffed wrist from the post in the middle, his knees not quite touching the floor.

"Hagan?"

Moss spoke softly, and the eerie light dimmed.

Crossing quickly to the post, Moss reached out. Hagan flinched from the touch of Moss's hand on his arm. The strained muscles of his back bunched and shivered. The blue light faded to total darkness. Gently Moss pulled Hagan to his feet and supported him with one arm while he worked by feel in the now total darkness for the tether that bound Hagan to the post. Discovering it was metal, Moss drew his s'darm and laid its crystal nose on the post's center ring. Even through closed eyes the brilliant flash of the silent weapon penetrated. Hagan's arm dropped free and he sagged forward. Bending, Moss took Hagan's weight on his shoulder.

With a soft cry of pain that echoed the earlier desperate keening, Hagan went limp.

Hagan came to in the dark, lying on a bed that was totally unfamiliar. Hard. Still in the hospital? A violent shudder shook him. A movement at his side brought him to full alert, and he filled with unreasoning fear. Then Moss's soft voice spoke in his ear. "Here, El, lean forward and put this on." Relief filled him. With Moss's support he sat forward, every muscle in his body protesting the action. A soft material slid over his head and onto his shoulders. Hagan bit back a groan of pain that came with the slightest movement. The memory of Graeber with his evil, gloating eyes, and his evil instrument of torture made him shudder again. "Better?" Moss continued softly. "I've got a pair of pants for you, too. Found them in the locker. God—there's something strange going on here."

"Strange?" Hagan's voice croaked on the word. Even the act of speaking brought pain.

"Yeah." Moss laughed silently, as though doubting the evidence of his own senses. "There's a—a light. It's following you."

Hagan stared into the impenetrable darkness and saw nothing. "Nothing—nothing there." He tried to swing his legs over the bed, and another wave of horrific feeling rose up, swamping his senses and loosening his grip on consciousness.

Moss's voice came as if from a great distance. "See? There it is. God, it's—"

Caught by the sound of awe in Moss's voice, Hagan pulled himself back from the brink of darkness. Moss wasn't easily awed. But when he opened his eyes once more he saw nothing. Nothing! Panic swelled in him. And a feeling of urgency. And also a certainty. Fear raced through him. "Hugh, hide. A guard's coming."

With only a brief hesitation, Moss slipped from his side and disappeared into the inky darkness. Ignoring the knife-like fire that threatened to take his breath away, Hagan slipped his legs over the edge of the bed and groped in the dark for the pants Moss had spoken of. Yes, there they were. Working through waves of pain, with one hand, awkwardly he drew them on. Built for a larger man, they fit him loosely, and he was grateful. He'd barely placed the last fastener when the door to the hall opened and a pale light flooded in.

A guard, holding a weak ball lamp high overhead peered through the doorway into the shadowy room. After the inky darkness even that amount of light felt like a glaring beam to Hagan. He put a hand up to block the beam from his sensitive eyes. The guard saw the movement and leaned further in the doorway. "You there, what are you doing?"

Hagan froze. Sensed Moss somewhere in the shadows to his right. Waiting. Come in, he thought to the guard. Yes, come in a little closer—

Acting as if he'd heard the thought, the guard stepped forward, still holding the ball of light high. With a flash of movement, Moss stepped from behind a screen to the guard's left and brought him down with a short, sharp chop. The guard dropped, his forward movement sending the floating lamp spinning into the room toward Hagan.

"Hagan, the light —"

Hagan's intent was to stop the lamp before it hit the wall and shattered over his head, but before he could force his tortured muscles into action the lamp halted, still spinning, right above his head.

As he registered what happened, Moss stared at the lamp, then at Hagan. A question was in his eyes.

Chills brushed Hagan, but he could find no explanation for the questions either of them had. His stomach knotted and his sense of urgency returned full force. "Come on, Moss, let's get out of here. Do you know the way?"

His words jolted Moss into action. "Yes. We're in the old wing. The reception area isn't far. If the lights stay off, I think we can get out without being seen. Can you walk?"

Hagan wondered, but buoyed by an anger too deep to banish, he had no choice but to try. He was almost thankful for the pain, sharp and jolting in his shoulder and keeping him focused. He slid off the bed.

"Here," Moss reached out. "Lean on me."

The pain of movement left Hagan once more gasping. Angrily he brushed Moss's hand aside. He'd do it himself. He had to. He remembered Graeber wielding the instrument of torture, and his anger became focused and somehow it became easier to ignore the throbbing fire in his groin, the piercing stab of fire in his shoulders. The ache of his almost-dislocated arm.

Moss watched him a moment, then nodded. "I'll check the hall." Moving in short jerks on bare feet, Hagan reached the hall a few steps behind Moss. In the room at his back the light of the ball lamp faded, but even so the darkness was not absolute. At the very end of the long hallway a faint light glowed.

Moss uttered a curse. "That's the central reception area. There's a crowd down there. It'll be damned hard to get by them now."

Hagan knew what Moss meant. He also knew with certainty that Graeber had discovered him missing and was even now sending out the soldiers into the surrounding hallways. "Can't help it," he gritted out. "It's the only way to go."

At that moment Graeber's voice bellowed an order. A scream of pain followed, and it was as if Hagan himself had been hit again.

Something snapped inside, an unconscious and unknown restraint. Anger flowed out of him in strong, brilliant red waves that he saw. His stomach churned. With a tremendous roar the building trembled around them, shifting on its foundations, rolling and heaving with the motion of the earth beneath. Losing contact with Moss Hagan fell to his knees. An eerie glow of blue light filled the hall that even he could see. Moss grabbed him by the waist and hauled him up.

Moss's voice whispered urgently in his ear. "Earthquake, El. For God's sake, come on. Let's get out of here." Bearing the greater part of Hagan's weight, Moss continued down the hall toward the reception area.

As they approached, Hagan eyed the glassed-in guard's station, and watched it shatter, sending slivers of glass and cerafoam flying through the air. Ball lamps floated with random craziness.

The nightmare scene took on a hellish quality. Wind-driven dust, toppled desks, counters and shelves, and men pulled themselves from the rubble cast by toppling walls and sagging ceiling.

Pulling Hagan with him, Moss shouted to a man standing in a doorway, frozen with fear. "Out. Get out before the roof caves in."

A guard, crawling from the rubble of the guard's station, stared at them and began shaking. Again Moss yelled his order, and the wild-eyed guard sprinted for the wide front doors.

Two white-coated attendants, fleeing the building ahead of Hagan and Moss, had no eyes for anyone but themselves. An almost palpable gray cloud enveloped them. Their fear, Hagan thought. That's what their fear looks like. The white-coated men ran through the gaping doors behind the guard and disappeared into the night. Moss urged Hagan after them, and a moment later they too burst through the doorway and into the welcoming darkness.

A starless, electric night, within a wild, destructive wind. For the third time the ground on which they stood, shifted, throwing both of them to their knees.

Hagan's heart hammered wildly with fear, his pain and anger for the moment forgotten.

Calm. Safe. The thoughts sounded like his own but were intrusive. Wildly he searched the darkness for sign of something familiar, something real. Denied he heard anything but the crack of lightning overhead.

Calm. Peace. Safe. You are safe.

The words repeated again and again, but he denied them room. He thought of Graeber and trembled uncontrollably. Where was he? Would the bastard escape the collapsing building? He shouldn't. He should die there as he had caused others to die.

The anger drowned the quiet words in his head. A flash of lightning arced across the sky, illuminating the broad green lawn, the curving drive, the towering gates at the far end. Illuminated Moss, who had come to his feet and stood watching him.

"Where is the General?" Hagan ground out. "Where did he go?"

"I don't know. He might have gone out the back."

The ground heaved beneath their feet, and screams came from inside the destroyed building.

Meeriam had started to dream, and her dream was filled with Hagan. And then the dream had awakened her but the scene in her mind, the continuation of the dream, was all too real. The earth shifted and rolled beneath Kassine's resident tower and she grabbed the side of the bed.Still seeing Hagan in her mind's eye, she repeated over and over again the calming litany, but the words did no good. He wasn't listening.He was injured, and he was angry, so very angry.

Drawing back from the mind pictures she frantically searched outward for Gerald. It took her a moment to realize he was gone. Slipping into her green tunic, she hurried to the stairs knowing that something was terribly wrong right here in Kassine's tower.

She checked first the room that Portus usually occupied but he wasn't there. She felt his earlier occupancy, but knew that he'd been gone some time. Was he out in this mind storm? Meeriam shivered, and hurried on.

Up one floor and then another until she reached the Matriarch's living quarters. "Vana Kassine?" She paused in the doorway to the gathering room but the old woman was no where in view. She hurried on toward the office, seeing as she did so the faint light seeping around the door. She raised her voice. "Vana Kassine?" She pushed the door open then halted. The old woman sat at her desk, her back straight, her hands clenched together on top of a pile of thin picture sheets, her eyes closed. She was unnaturally pale.

"Vana Kassine—are you all right?" Quickly Meeriam approached the old woman and knelt at her side. "Please, are you —"

"Hush child. I'm—I'm all right."

"Then what is it? How can I help?"

"Help? Oh, child, you can't help." Kassine opened her eyes and stared at the picture sheets spread out before her on the desk. Meeriam glanced at them, and her stomach churned.

Each thin screen-print held a picture of the Matriarch's daughter, each indicating a level of depravity or abandonment that was beyond Meeriam's understanding. In each, Luan looked into the screen's eye with defiance as she allowed unspeakable acts upon her body. Sick with revulsion Meeriam looked away. Why? Why would she have done this?

"It was the General, he did this to her." Trembling, Kassine answered Meeriam's unasked question. "There is—there is a final picture." Her hand clenched around the last sheet, crumpling the thin film. "It was at the bottom of the stack as they were delivered." Kassine swayed in her chair. "I think I am going to be sick."

Meeriam didn't want to look at any more of the pictures spread across the old woman's desk, but as she tried to pull the one from the old woman's grasp so that she could help her away from the desk, she saw the last and most shocking of all. A woman silently screaming in death agony as her blood flowed down her naked body. Pain laced through her. Luan. Oh, poor, poor Luan. "No, it's not real. He has contrived them some way," she choked, not believing what she said, but wanting to say anything to comfort the old woman. "They are all lies. The General has made these up." Feeling Kassine's pain as if it were her own, Meeriam's tears ran down her cheeks and she took Kassine into her arms and rocked her back and forth as if she were a mother with an infant.

Slowly the unnatural stiffness went out of Kassine's body.

"My daughter is dead," she whispered. "My beautiful, willful baby. Why couldn't she have been happy to be just what she was? She had everything. She had family, position. Whatever I could give her, she had." Kassine groaned softly and tears started down her wrinkled cheeks. "But it was never enough. Oh, child," she whispered brokenly, "it is so hard."

"I know," Meeriam said. "I know." Leading Kassine away from the desk and the hateful pictures, Meeriam experienced an anger almost as great as Hagan's, but with a lifetime of control behind her she produced no catastrophic effects. She helped Kassine into a soft chair.

"The General has had his vengeance, hasn't he?" Kassine dabbed her eyes, and already Meeriam could feel the old woman exerting her tremendous will, and gathering her strength. "But will he be satisfied with that?"

The answer came more swiftly than Meeriam expected. From somewhere below a man shouted, and a door blasted open. Startled, Meeriam cast out and discovered soldiers flowing in the several entrances on the ground floor. Many heavy footsteps shook the tiled halls. Meeriam—Gerald's voice pressed quickly into her mind. *Listen. You and Vana Glena are in danger. I can't help. I am following Graeber's army of soldiers toward the farms. Hagan and Moss have escaped the hospital, but they won't be able to help either.*

Thinking of the pictures on Kassine's desk, Meeriam felt the blood leave her head. Had Hagan—had he also—*Is Hagan all right, Gerald?*

He'll make it.

A small part of Meeriam's heart sang with sudden joy. Hagan had escaped. He was safe. Gerald said so.

But she had another worry. *Gerald, I can't find Portus. Do you know where he is?*

I sent him to Pioneer Cove with a convoy this morning. He's safe enough for now. The General's spread too thin to chase him down just yet. But Vana Glena would not leave with him and now I see a great danger for you both. I know it's much to ask, Meeriam, but please. Stay with her. She needs you. Graeber is coming for her.

Yes, of course I'll stay. And you're right about the soldiers. They're already here.

Hugging her arms around the old woman, she shivered. *I hear them below.*

BOOK THREE

FIREWING

Chapter 22

Kama Valley

Shivering in the predawn air, Hagan pulled one of the blankets Moss had liberated from the hospital rubble tighter and drank in the quiet sight of the world coming awake. An unnatural silence lay over the land and with it the heavy scent of rain-soaked earth. Somewhere a borobird called and from the opposite hill another answered. Moss turned in his sleep and with skin that felt new and extremely sensitive, Hagan felt as well as heard the soft sound.

He thought about how Moss had gone back into the rubble time after time, first searching for Graeber, then continuing until he was sure no one else was trapped inside.

Hagan, swamped by a bodily anguish too great to allow movement, had lain on the grass in front of the ruined building and waited for Moss to return. His aversion to the place was so great he didn't think he could've gone back in even if he'd been in any shape to do so. For a short while he'd even hated Moss for trying to save the lives of those trapped, until he realized that Moss was still looking for Graeber.

The search, however, had been futile. Graeber had escaped, probably with the first wave of people fleeing from the building. The damned coward wouldn't help anyone if his life depended on it, Moss had said. Now, as surely as if he'd seen it happen, Hagan knew Graeber had already gathered his forces around him and was on the move toward the ancient city, and the Firewing wouldn't stop him.

Groaning with frustration Hagan threw off the blanket and stood. His freedom of movement was hampered by the bandages wrapped around his shoulder and binding his arm to his side. Twisting out of his shirt he unwound the white strips. If Graeber was on the way to Phoenix, then he was wasting time standing here. Graeber would take a hand-picked unit with him. He'd have a HOGG, maybe even several. For a short while he'd be limited to what roadways there were. No doubt he'd abandon the awkward vehicles once he reached the mountains.

Hagan visualized the map on the map-room wall. If he cut across country he had a chance of getting through the mountains almost as quickly as Graeber did. Would Meeriam be willing to go with him again? His heart stirred with a strange protectiveness. No. As much as he wanted to be with her, he wouldn't ask. It was too dangerous.

"Hagan?" Moss's voice behind him was filled with disbelief. "What the hell are you doing?"

"Taking the—" Hagan looked down at his left shoulder. The last of the strapping fell away, and there was only a residue of aching muscles where yesterday there'd been broken bones.

The cuts and bruises that had covered his body were only shadows in his memory. A dozen explanations, all of them ridiculous, took frantic flight in his mind and were discarded. He was left with one either/or. Either his injuries had not been as bad as he'd thought, or he had somehow healed overnight. And somewhere in his memory was the residue of pain that the injuries had brought. He had not dreamed his injuries.

"Good God," Moss said. "You look a hell of a lot better than I do."

Hagan switched his gaze to Moss's battered face. How could he have missed that last night? "What happened to you? Did Graeber—"

"No." Moss didn't elucidate. Ever pragmatic, he came to his feet, snatched Hagan's shirt off the ground and tossed it to him. "Better put this back on or you'll damned well freeze to death."

Stunned by the magnitude of what had happened, Hagan did as he was told and didn't dwell on Moss's reaction.

An hour and a half later at the fork of the road, a small personal carrier confiscated from one of the back sheds was waiting for Hagan's entry. He swung a makeshift pack of supplies scavenged from the hospital onto the floor beside the driver's seat and mounted the cab. Held out his hand to Moss.

Moss took it reluctantly. "Are you sure you want to go alone, El? Give me the word and I'll go with you."

"I know you would. But no. Go back to town, Hugh." They had both detected the haze of smoke from the direction of Norcanna. Who knew what Graeber might have done before he left. "Someone needs to take charge. Better you than anyone Graeber leaves behind."

"But are you sure he's headed for Phoenix?"

They both knew there was nowhere else for Graeber to go. "I'm sure."

"I still think the Firewing at Lissone will stop him."

They'd been through this discussion before. Hagan merely shook his head. By now Moss knew as well as he did that the Firewing wouldn't lift a hand, not even in their own defense. Except for Condor—

A rising wave of anger at the young Firewing choked Hagan. If he hadn't interfered—if he hadn't let his own jealousy get in the way—

Resolutely Hagan pushed the thought from his mind. He had a long way to go before nightfall, and an even longer way to go to reach the ancient City of Phoenix out on the high desert beyond Mt. Kama. If he could do it in a week, he'd be surprised. He didn't have time to spend in futile anger at one lone Firewing.

With a last brief goodbye, he started down the empty roadway.

But certain knowledge was firm in his mind. If Condor was still out there, he'd damned well better not get in the way.

Through the warm night, as he had for two nights running, Condor paced the dark shadow below, stopping when it stopped, resting when it rested, sleeping in small snatches when it slept. Though the man below paused seldom, and faltered never, Condor still felt the searching, probing thought that emanated from him.

At first Condor had thought this was one of the People, not of his clan, of course, but still one of them. He'd have challenged the stranger, but then something familiar, something dangerous, stopped him.

He knew this man, this shadow who moved like one of them. It was Hagan, the soldier, traveling more swiftly, more surely than a soldier should travel. Once Condor had tried to probe the mind of the man below but had come up against a barrier of mind that defeated him. So he had watched, and waited and followed.

At noon the following day Hagan rested in a grove of tall trees beneath the craggy Bluff of Sinjon. A small trickle of water formed a fountain that he drank from. Condor frowned, watching. He even drank like one of them.

Would he rest now? Condor found himself hoping so. Then, abruptly he saw Hagan stiffen. A wash of fear touched Condor before he could control it. What had Hagan seen or sensed? What had he himself missed?

Shutting his eyes he quickly cast out, sensing, seeing with his mind the path ahead, the path behind. Nothing. No one. Small animals, a mountain cat lazing in the sun up the ridge. No threat. Nothing.

The thought came into his head with the force of a blow. *Who are you? What do you want?*

Hagan? Speaking into his mind like one of the People?

I know you, the thought went on. *Yes, of course. Condor.*

Yes, I am Condor.

How long have you been following me?

Three days. How did you know? When no answer came to that thought Condor rushed on. *Where are you going? To Lissone? You have taken the wrong path.*

Why would I go to Lissone? What good would it do me? Would those Firewing help me defeat Graeber? I think not. The answer was short, sharp, stabbing with intensity. Condor wondered at that wealth of feeling revealed by Hagan's thought. His bitterness was Condor's own, but a belated sense of loyalty to the People welled up in Condor.

They would help if they understood.

I doubt that. Not any more than you would.

Condor's anger at the passivity of the elders of Lissone surged to the fore, and he had to agree. Neither did he want to help this soldier, but perhaps it was better than either of them going alone.

Curious but wary he probed. *How would you stop Graeber?*

I will destroy his goal. I would destroy the city so that he will not use it.

You can't!

Watch me.

But that—Condor was stunned by the magnitude of Hagan's proposal. The ancient city was the beacon that was meant to bring the wanderers home. All of their old stories said so. Destroy the beacon—destroy the hope of the ancients?

With unseeing eyes he stared into the far distance. *No. No, you can't.*

Abruptly he lost the mind contact with Hagan. Spinning, he searched the ground below his vantage point. Gone. Hagan was gone. Fear-laced anger brought him a fine trembling and he tightened his fingers around his staff.

"Hagan," he shouted out loud. "Hagan you won't do it. I won't let you."

"You can't stop me."

Condor whirled to the sound of the voice so near at hand. Breath caught in his throat and his pack slipped from his shoulder and his staff came automatically up to defense level, but it was too late. Hagan dove under it, hit him midsection, and they tumbled backward over the edge of the ridge and rolled down the rocky slope.

A moment later Hagan's hands were around his throat, choking the breath, the life out of him. No. No, he wanted to shout. It won't end like this. But the world faded around him.

Hagan stared down at the limp, unconscious form beneath him, fully aware of what his anger had almost made him do. Carefully he checked the younger man's breathing, saw the marks that would be bruises by dark. He was aware that he was sweating profusely, aware that the birds had grown quiet. God, he'd almost taken a life. Condor's life. He shivered in spite of the noonday heat. He was no better than Graeber.

Rising swiftly he lifted the younger man, staggering slightly under Condor's weight. Carefully he carried the younger man to the small stream and its trickling waterfall. Placing Condor on the bed of feathery fern that alway grew around these pools,

Hagan then located and retrieved the Firewing's pack and staff.

Not knowing how long the young Firewing would remain unconscious, Hagan delved into his pack, looking for any clue to the reason Condor had been following him. Trail food, a solid dark and salty substance, wrapped in a broad leaf. Hagan laid it aside. A soft leather vest that'd give additional warmth come night. Moss had found him one similar. Another small pack of food, nutlike in flavor. And something hard, something carefully wrapped and deposited at the very bottom of the pack. Unwrapping the package, Hagan stared at the knife revealed. A fighting knife, very old. He'd seen the like in a museum on Mars. Where would Condor have come by such a weapon? Were they carried by the Firewing? No. No not a Firewing weapon. An old Earth fighting knife. Carefully Hagan rewrapped it and put it back. He replaced the other items and put the pack to one side. He himself had food enough for tonight's camp. Tomorrow he'd have find more, but he wouldn't take Condor's.

Ten minutes later the young man stirred. Drew a rasping breath. From his own pack Hagan had taken a light wooden cup and he used it now to offer Condor water. Watching the younger man swallow, Hagan's own throat ached in sympathy. Almost without thought he reached out, felt the heat in his own hands increase with the need to touch Condor. Slipping his hands onto the Firewing's neck, his only wish was to undo the damage he'd done.

Fear in his eyes, Condor jerked away.

"Lie still, you idiot. Let me help." Though the words were strong, Hagan's voice held a hypnotic quality that calmed Condor. Hagan felt a strange energy flowing, flowing through his own body, an energy which he seemed to control though he did not know how. A heat that seemed so natural, so right he didn't question it.

A moment later, of its own accord, the heat ceased to flow. Drained, Hagan sat back on his heels and closed his eyes.

He shivered. What was he doing? What had he done? This wasn't taking him where he had to go. How long before Graeber reached the Ancient City? A sense of urgency filled him. He had to go on.

Only after he'd picked up his own pack and settled it on

his back did he turn and look at Condor. The Firewing was watching him with a guarded question in his dark eyes.

"Who are you?" Condor asked.

"You know who I am." Hagan's voice was hard. "I'm Hagan, son of the Commander of Kama."

"No. You are one of us. Why are you pretending otherwise?"

"A Firewing? You think I'm a Firewing?" Hagan laughed. He was no Firewing. He wasn't even a soldier any more. In truth he didn't know what he was, or what he would be if left to his own devices. "I've left you your food. Don't follow me."

"You won't make it through the mountains. Not without help."

"Whose help? Yours?"

"No—why should I help you?" Condor touched his neck and his eyes narrowed. "You don't even know what you did."

"Oh, I know all right." Hagan repressed a shudder. What he'd done was something he'd only heard about. Rationally there was no explanation. Neither did he want one so irrational he couldn't believe it and thinking about it had begun to give him a headache.

Quickly he turned away.

"Soldier—wait. I—I will show you the way."

"Why would you? You don't believe in what I have to do. Not any more than the elders at Lissone."

"But you say it will stop the General. You must do it. I must, too."

Hagan eyed Condor, wondering at the speed of his change of mind, wondering if he could trust it. "How fast can you get through these mountains? Do you really know the way?"

"I've been there before. Many times. I have been there with the People, and I've been there on my own. I know how to get inside the Ancient City."

"And you'll show me the way?"

One final time Condor hesitated, but his decision had been made. "Yes, I will."

"Can you travel now? We don't have any time to lose. Graeber's already on his way."

"I know. We'll arrive before he does. I promise you."

"You promise me." *And what do your promises mean? Not a damned thing,* thought Hagan, but he held the sharp words at bay. Warily he watched the younger man scramble to his feet, touch his throat and neck with remembered awe before he shook his head and reached for his pack and staff. He looked at Hagan uncertainly. "I'll lead the way."

Hagan let him.

Well into the afternoon and evening they hiked, and that first night they camped by another small stream, beneath a tower of craggy granite. Though Hagan had sensed water somewhere ahead, the stream came as a surprise.

"It's protected here. We can make a fire."

Hagan remembered it was the same thing Meeriam had said about the fire on their last night together. He still didn't like open fires, but he wasn't as adverse to the idea as he might have been once. He watched the Firewing gathered dry grass, twigs and a few larger pieces of wood. The flame, when it came, both fascinated and repelled him.

Condor noticed, as he seemed to notice all things about Hagan, but he said nothing. Instead, he pulled the dark foodstuff from his pack and shaved off a section. Hagan shook out the last of the nuts and dry fruit Moss had given him and ate slowly.

For long minutes the small flame's occasional crackle and hiss was the only sound that broke the night silence.

When Condor spoke, it was into his mind, not into the still night air.

Why did you chose this path instead of the old roadway. You must have known the other way would be easier traveling.

But longer. And more obvious. And keep the hell out of my mind.

When you didn't want me there before, you put up a barrier. Why don't you do that now?

If I knew how, I would.

But of course you know how. You did it before.

"I told you," Hagan burst out angrily, "stay out of my mind."

Condor switched his curious stare from Hagan to the flickering flame, put another small dry branch into the center of the fire pit, then glanced back at Hagan. "It scares you, doesn't it?" A smile of superiority flickered on the younger man's bronzed face.

294

"Yes," Hagan admitted after a long moment of consideration. "Yes, it does." Everything about these new sensations scared him. He distrusted the messages that came intuitively. Like the feeling he'd had of water being ahead. He'd known it, yet not believed it. God, yes, it scared him.

Condor changed tack with a suddenness that left Hagan confused. "The going from here on gets harder. Will you be able to keep up?"

"Why shouldn't I?"

"You soldiers, you're soft." The contempt was back in the younger man's tone.

"I'll follow anywhere you lead, as long as you remember that the goal is to get there, not to test my strength."

Hagan didn't mean for Condor to mistake the steel in his voice for anything but what it was. A warning, a promise. Condor's gaze met his. He nodded.

Before dawn they were on the move again. Time after time they climbed hand over foot, seeming to go straight up, then straight down again. For a short while they followed the banks of a fairly good-sized stream, Lee-Zone. The name came to Hagan's mind before he had a chance to doubt it. The stream descended from the high valley where the Firewing lived. He also knew that without asking. If he thought about it the knowledge bothered him. He tried not to think about it. Instead he watched the land, smelled the air, so different from the salty seacoast where Norcanna lay, or the always slightly acrid air under the Domes of Mars. The sun grew warm on his back and neck and he removed the warm vest and without stopping stowed it in his pack. He envied Condor's staff which seemed to be almost as handy as a third hand.

We'll cross the ancient roadbed soon, Condor said without words. *Watch for guards. If your general has passed here before us, he might have posted them.*

He's not my general, Hagan grumbled, but he was too interested in what lay ahead to be truly angry this time at Condor's thought penetration. He was, in fact, getting used to it.

Then they were on the downside of a steep ridge, and Hagan caught his first sight of the ancient roadway that crawled and curled its way through the mountain passes. He thrilled to the sight before he even knew for sure what he was seeing. The road to Phoenix! Merrick, who had guessed it was there, Graeber who had insisted it must exist, even Kali who was afraid it did, all of them right, yet all this time Hagan had thought it was just the figment of someone's imagination.

The realization grew in him. Here the ancients had driven in their high-powered vehicles, cruising at speeds unimaginable to the Arcolan's air-turbine technology. Here more people had passed in the course of time than lived under all the Domes of Mars.

Reaching the flat broken surface Hagan smiled at his own fanciful imagination. In reality the place where a many laned road had once been was nothing more, now, than a man-made valley, narrow in places, dotted with low bushes and tall grass. Without the perspective of their earlier height he wouldn't have known what he walked on.

Hey, soldier, Condor's words jabbed into his mind. *Hurry up.*

Exhibiting a Firewing's reluctance to expose himself, Condor had taken off at a quick jog across the open area. Hagan choosing a slower pace, studied the surrounding hills as he ran. If he had not been doing so he might have missed the glint of light off a reflective surface to the west.

Condor- his warning thought traveled out before he could stop it. *Someone's watching.*

Condor had reached the far side of the man-made depression. He crouched among man-high bushes and waited for Hagan to catch up.

Keep going, damn it, Hagan shouted into his mind. They might not have seen you yet.

Condor disappeared into the rocks, vanishing right before Hagan's eyes, so thoroughly he might never have been.

Hagan neither slowed nor sped up, but his feeling of being watched, of being studied through a high-powered scanner grew rather than faded. His mind flashed an image of soldiers, a compact unit. Road throwing equipment. His mouth twisted. Graeber had come well equipped. And there, another vehicle. A face. Meeriam. He faltered and almost tripped. What was Meeriam doing there? Another face superimposed itself on the grasses in front of him. Graeber.

Momentarily he choked on an upwelling of hate and fear, and his mind pictures dimmed.

Hagan—

Condor's voice in his head seemed to come from a long distance. *Hagan, don't stop. Don't.*

Hagan clamped an iron control on his rising emotions. Not the time, not the time. Later he'd think about it. Not now.

Minutes later he reached the protection of the rocks on the other side of the ancient roadway and dropped to the small patch of shelter Condor had found. He was sweating profusely.

Graeber has a whole troop coming this way. Condor's thought was eager.

Wearily Hagan shook his head. He couldn't convince Condor to stay out of his mind, and for some reason he didn't seem able to erect the barrier that would keep the Firewing out, but at the moment he couldn't even care. Leaning his head on his braced knees he drew deep, gulping breaths until gradually he began to feel himself calm. Meeriam—God, what was she doing there?

Then the import of Condor's words sank in.

Coming after us?

Condor grinned. *You're good for bait, if nothing else. We can set up an ambush.*

No. No, we'll leave them be. Carefully Hagan let his mind return to Graeber's position and the pictures took on a super clarity. Meeriam. Hagan's stomach knotted. Neither bound nor gagged, but deep within a drugged state. And—the Matriarch Kassine. Graeber had both of them. "Graeber's insurance," he said aloud, the words bitter on his tongue.

We have them, Condor laughed. *We have them. Don't you understand, soldier? They are fools, and we—*

Hagan flowed to his feet, speaking fiercely in his mind and hardly realizing it. *Don't you understand? You attack those soldiers, Condor, and Graeber will see that Meeriam and Kassine die.*

You just don't want to face them. You don't want to fight.

In the face of Condor's angry charge, Hagan's own anger melted away. "We'll leave them alone and go on. Even with your power, there's too many. We have to push on to Phoenix. At this rate, with those vehicles, they'll beat us there."

In disgust Condor threw up his hands. "Coward's way. If Meeriam's with him, it's because she wants to be. She always thought more of the soldiers than she did of her own—"

Hagan exploded. For the second time in two days he found himself at Condor's throat. As they went down, he on top, Condor's surprise still in his eyes, Hagan regained a small measure of control. As quickly as he'd taken Condor down, he rolled off the Firewing and stood trembling. Condor lay stunned, staring up at him, anger fading to an almost reluctant respect. He sat up slowly, rubbing his elbows. *I wish to hell you'd stop doing that.*

"Get up," Hagan ordered, ignoring Condor's half-humorous thought-spoken complaint. This time he was not the least sorry for what he'd done. He pointed at the path. "Get going."

That night the dream which had not bothered Hagan for many weeks returned. Bolting to a sitting position he trembled with the vividness of it. The feel of flight. The eagle's view. The scream. Condor, instantly alert, pushed up on one elbow. *What is it? What's wrong? Sleep demons, soldier?*

"No. A dream. Just a dream." Hagan sank back on his pack and cushioned his head with his arms. Why now? Why, after all this time, had the dream returned? It must be the mountains. He'd been in the mountains at Kama the last time he'd seen Elias. All he could remember of that time now was the furious mask of the Commander's expression the last time they'd parted at Kama Garrison. It was a memory he'd never wanted to confront again. Elias, furious and condemning. White with—with what emotion? Hagan frowned into the darkness. Grief? Would grief explain Elias's actions that final day? But why? Why would he grieve more for the dead Firewing than for his remorseful son? There had been no understanding in him, nor forgiveness. No compassion for the fear that had made his son commit the unforgivable act of taking another's life.

God, he'd been so scared that day. And so sick. And shocked by the violence of what he'd done. Elias couldn't possibly have hated him any more than he'd hated himself. Perhaps that was why he'd not protested more. Why he'd suffered being banished.

Deliberately Hagan stilled the trembling that memory brought. Felt again the pain of his father's rejection.

You have killed my brother. You are no son of mine.

Perhaps the pain was in knowing that Elias had thought more of the Firewing than he had of his own son. What other reason could there have been in the Commander's mind for such strong emotion?

Perhaps he'd never know. Perhaps he had simply to accept that it was there, and go on. Perhaps it was time to let it go.

Maybe, even, it was time to forgive the Commander, and time to take the further step and forgive himself for that blind, panicked act of destruction that had changed his life. For the first time in years a sense of peace stole over Hagan. A sense of rightness. Patlos, after all, had not blamed him. Patlos.

The memory of that kind, strong face rose in his mind, the face of the Firewing as he'd seen it in the misty glen that day. And suddenly a much younger face was superimposed on the first. Patlos still, but a much younger Patlos, someone no older than Condor. And the memory of arms around him, supporting him, giving him strength. Confused, Hagan tried to hold the memory, but it slipped away.

Unable to will the memory back, Hagan let it go, and began to slip into the shadowy world of sleep.

Another mind picture jarred him awake again.

Meeriam.

Or was he awake? He looked around, half frightened yet determined, too. Meeriam lay on a flat pallet, her eyes closed, her breathing deep but her mind shadowy, unfocused. Outside-outside what? The smooth walls had holding racks that he'd seen before. Of course. The interior of one of the large carriers. Before he had time to wonder how he'd gotten there, a harsh voice on the other side of the door overrode his fear. Galt?

"Hell yes, the girl's still here. Got so much lotus tea in her she won't wake up for a week." The heavy door in the tailgate of the HOGG slid back with a bang and a handheld light flickered inside, illuminating first a pallet on the opposite side. Kassine, limply asleep. And then the light illuminated Meeriam's dark head, the pale vulnerability of her undefended cheek.

The small beam of light moved down her soft, unprotected form. Hagan's anger swelled, and suddenly the beam of light paled, flickered and went out.

Galt's hard, frustrated curses cut the air. And then he gasped painfully.Hagan, without actually seeing what happened, knew Galt held up a hand burned by a malfunctioning light. Hagan smiled, and the scene vanished. Hagan once more felt the bare comfort of his insulating cover and the hard ground beneath him. This time when he slipped into sleep it was to the dark, dreamless world of rest.

Chapter 23

Kama Mountain

By noon the following day Hagan had come to grips with what had happened last night. In his mind he had grown an understanding of what happened, but not how, or why. When he and Condor had settled beneath a sentinel pine at a place they could watch their back trail, he wondered how best to ask his plaguing questions.

But Condor gave him no chance. As they shared berries and nuts they'd gathered along the way, Condor said into his mind, *Who are you really, soldier?*

Who was he? It was a question he couldn't answer. Rather than try, he countered with another. *Who do you think I am?*

Considering Hagan, Condor's face shuttered. Hagan had the eerie feeling that he could have followed the Firewing's train of thought if he'd wanted to. He didn't want to.

You are of the People. One with Mind, should you so choose, said Condor finally.

How can it be? Hagan thought the words, rather than spoke them out loud, just the way Condor had spoken into his mind. Each day it was getting easier, and each day it felt more right. He went on. *Everyone knows the Commander of Kama was my father. I look too much like him to deny it.*

I don't know. It is a mystery. Are there more people like you on Mars?

God, I hope not. Yet, how did he know there weren't others?

For all of our sakes, I too hope not. Grabbing up his pack, Condor stood and gestured at Hagan's things. *Come on. We can't sit here all day.*

Later that afternoon, after a particularly long and difficult climb, Hagan stood, hair prickling down his arms, looking upon the ancient desert that everyone had speculated about yet no one but Firewing had seen for a thousand years. And there was the ancient roadway, winding through the mountains in sweeping curves like an ancient riverbed that finally disappeared in the fold of lower hills. From this height he could see the grand concept in a way he'd not been able to do when they'd jogged across it earlier in the day.

Condor's expletive jerked him around. Condor pointed into the distance.

From this high vantage point the winding course of the old roadbed below was obvious for some distance in either direction. As were the HOGGs, the troops and the small personal carrier in which no doubt the General rode that were inching their way along. Thirty men, he judged, if all the carriers but the one which held Meeriam and Kassine were full, along with Graeber and Galt. At the point of the column was a road crew which had moved out ahead of the others, the RVM silent from this distance as it smoothed the roadbed with c'foam.

Why had they brought the women with them? Insurance? Hostages? For a moment he considered touching Graeber's mind to find out, but the very thought made him sick. Graeber's was a dark, sick soul. A mind he feared.

Condor touched him mentally, drew his attention away from the sight below. *In another hour*, he said, *they'll reach the place where the road disappears. It'll slow them down. They might abandon the carriers. We could take them there.*

No. We still have a chance to beat them to Phinx, but we must move on!

Though it was obvious Condor still disagreed, he shrugged and picked up the pace.

The thought of leaving Meeriam behind scared Hagan. Still drugged, still unable to protect herself, she needed their protection. His protection. A fierce tenderness grew in him. He shouldn't leave her behind.

Before his next thought was fully formed, Condor interrupted. *No.* The sound was a mind shout. *No. You were right. We must go on. You'll never reach the city if you go for her now.*

You can't be certain of that.

I touched the soldier's mind. She's been given Lotus Tea. Even if she wakes, she'll be sick for days.

A growing dread made Hagan cold. *What do you mean if?*

302

The tea is a poison. It affects the mind as well as the body. She's of the People and very powerful. If she wakes before the drug is completely gone from her system, it'll be very painful for her. At least let her wake naturally.

Hagan remembered his one bout with Lotus Tea, the euphoria, the sexual awareness, the ecstasy, and the powerfully sick hangover he suffered for three days afterward. The heightened physical awareness hadn't been worth the pain.

Hagan nodded his understanding but went back to his original question. *What do you mean if she wakes?* His mind-voice was deadly.

Condor took an involuntary step back. *It's possible she'll never wake from her sleep.*

Anguished denial filled Hagan's soul. Meeriam couldn't die. He would not let her. A glance at his expression turned Condor pale, and he turned away and started down the path, leaving Hagan to follow or not, as he chose. With a last look at the carriers crawling along the narrow roadbed, Hagan took a grip on his dread and followed the Firewing.

The days and nights that followed fell into a pattern that once set, never varied. They had left the ancient roadway. Condor followed a trail that was evident only to his eyes, though once in a while Hagan thought he felt another presence or the residue of someone who'd passed that way not long before. They were once more climbing. The way became steeper, the vegetation more sparse the higher they climbed. Soon it seemed to Hagan they were walking up the spine of Grandfather Mountain itself. The peak that had been on the horizon of his youth and at the edge of his memory all of his adult life now towered above them, shrouded in mist and mystery.

As one day flowed into the next, Hagan wondered if their trek would ever end. It seemed the more he hardened to the trail the harder Condor pushed. The days weren't easy.

The nights were worse. And always the same.

First the dream. The eagle screaming in its downward dive. The waking, trembling, to Condor's puzzled eyes.

And then finally the drift again into sleep, the waking to another place. Twice Galt had entered the carrier where Kassine and Meeriam slept on, and twice he'd turned back, once because

303

his knees had suddenly suffered a great pain, once because his vision had blurred to the point of near blindness. These weren't symptoms Galt wanted to share with anyone. His frustration was great and Hagan wondered with trepidation how long Galt's temper would hold. Hagan's only consolation was the fact that Meeriam's sleep did not seem as deep, her inner images weren't as vague. In spite of Condor's harsh assessment he chose to think it was a positive sign.

Hagan considered whether they should destroy the vehicles and leave Graeber and his men on foot, but would Meeriam and the old woman survive if soldiers had to carry them? Wouldn't Graeber be more likely to kill them on the spot? Hagan knew he couldn't take the chance.

On the fifth day a flurry of bad weather held them immobile on the crest of Mt. Kama. The cave Condor found for them was little more than a covered crevasse where the wind howled with slightly less ferociousness, and the cold was a little less piercing.

He helped Condor gather dry wood that someone had scattered in the sheltered depths even though he had no intention of coming too close to the resulting fire. Clammy and cold, shivering and miserable, he finally settled against a smooth rock.

Condor had trouble understanding Hagan's aversion to fire. *It won't hurt you, unless you touch it.* Hagan was so used to the Firewing speaking into his mind by now he no longer offered even a token protest. *Sit closer, man, so that your clothes can dry or you'll end up sick.*

Because he knew Condor was right, Hagan finally did as the Firewing suggested, and after a while his shivering stopped.

The small fire was curiously lulling, brighter and warmer than its size would suggest, the depth of the red-gold flame drawing at Hagan, pulling him into curious mind pictures that might have been memories. His eyes drifted shut and he was almost asleep with the first true sleep he'd known in days when Condor's muffled expletive jerked him alert.

Condor had come to his feet, a strange, almost wary look on his face, his gaze fastened on the wide open mouth of their cave.

Hagan's attention whipped to the direction of Condor's gaze.

An old woman stood blocking out the gray light of late afternoon. She wore a heavy robe-like cloak that fell to just below her knees. Leggings wrapped with rawhide lacings covered her calves, and disappeared into the tops of soft brown-leather Firewing boots. As Hagan watched, awed by her appearance of age coupled with the an aura of youthful resiliency, she opened her cloak to the warmth of the fire. Her smile took each of them in equally.

What are you doing here, Grandmother? Condor's harsh mind-voice sounded rude.

The old woman's expression didn't alter. "I knew you would not come to me, so I came to you. Welcome me to your fire, Condor. Introduce me to the Commander's son." Her words were spoken aloud. Was it in deference to his presence, Hagan wondered? Her gaze touched him, then lingered. Seeking, but for what Hagan couldn't tell.

Slowly he stood, the memories closer now. He knew her. He knew her voice. He had heard it in his dreams, calling him. He had heard it even deeper—in his memory. And her eyes were velvety dark and alive with unnamed emotion.

"You look like your father looked when he first came to our mountains."

"So I've been told." His voice sounded stiff. He was startled by a surge of resentment that had no source that he could name. "Who are you?" That his rudeness almost matched Condor's both surprised and shocked him. But the resentment had swept away other, gentler emotions.

"I am Anahata, Clanswoman of Lissone. I am Condor's great grandmother."

"And Meeriam's?"

The old woman nodded, a shadow clouding her eyes.

"Then why the hell aren't you helping her?" Hagan had no idea where the words came from, but as soon as he'd said them he knew they'd been there all along, festering in his soul. If the Firewing were so God-awful powerful, why weren't they doing something for Meeriam?

"Meeriam will help herself when the time comes. She has chosen a way that is not ours to judge."

"In other words you are turning your back on her." *The way you did me when I was a child.*

The thought sprang form the depths of his mind with the

trueness of a well-shot arrow. He stared at the old woman, stunned by the mental images that accompanied it. Sunlight dappling the forest floor, his uncle, the young Patlos, holding him in strong young arms. His uncle Patlos—his father's brother—or his mother's brother. Angry, aching knowledge filled him. He had, it was true, killed his father's brother.

The old woman nodded.

But why hadn't Elias told him?

She answered thought in his mind. *His own grief and guilt were in the way.*

Condor growled with an animal impatience. "What does it matter now?"

Hagan stared at Condor. Was he seeing all these images or did Condor think they were still talking of Meeriam? He shook his head in confusion. Too many memories were crowding in, too much information arriving that he had no time to process.

His gaze returned to the old woman's kindly face. He spoke directly into her mind, aching with the question that had been in his soul for years. *Why, Grandmother, why did you send me away?*

The question hung between them like a flaming dagger, threatening to cleave him apart. The memories were there, now, and a pain too great for tears. He was being sent away—away from the only home he'd ever known, away from those who loved him, whom he loved. He felt the tears on his child face. She had sent him away. She had banished him from Lissone the way his father had later banished him from Earth.

Slowly the memories faded until he could see the old woman again by the light of the fire between them.

Her eyes were shadowed with regret. "I had to send you to your father. You evidenced no power. It would have been too cruel to keep you and raise you among those who were stronger than you. More powerful. You would have come to hate us and all that we are."

"So you sent me to my father."

"To Elias, yes. There was no other action I could take."

"And more cruel than if you had kept me with you."

"I did not know."

Condor laughed. "So I was right. He is of the People."

"No." Hagan's quick denial drew a frown from the old

306

woman, but he went on anyway. "I'm not one of you. I won't sit back and watch Graeber destroy life on this planet and do nothing to stop him." He pinned Anahata with his scornful gaze. "I don't see how you could let him go so far."

"You don't end killing with more killing."

It was a tenant Hagan agreed with. He had no rebuttal. What was there left to say? There were other ways. Graeber would reach his own end, but Hagan knew it was his job to make sure Graeber didn't reach the Ancient City.

Anahata, grandmother of the Clan of Lissone, drew herself up, and wrapped her calf-length cloak around her. Her mind voice filled with authority that brooked no opposition. *You will both come back to Lissone with me.*

"No." Hagan spoke with a quiet determination that matched the old woman's. "I must go on."

"Even if I admit that I was wrong those many years ago? Even if I say there is a place for you now beside our fires?"

"Even so." Hagan glanced at Condor. The younger man's puzzled frown deepened. "You don't have to continue with me, Condor. I'll find my own way from here."

Condor's angry shake of the head was all the denial needed. Relieved, Hagan went on. "It's too late for me to return to Lissone. I would fit in there as poorly now as I did when you sent me away."

"You do have power. We could teach you."

"Teach me what? To sit back and watch Graeber repeat the mistakes of history? He won't be content with controlling Mars. He'll come back again, and again until he has stripped the Earth bare of its humanity and resources. He will breed the very destruction you are most afraid of."

You must not destroy the Ancient City. It is not necessary. The words were spoken with quiet anguish into his mind. After a small pause, Anahata went on. There is much there that is good. Much that the wanderers can use.

Then help me.

No. The word contained more sadness than anger.

Then leave us alone to do our job.

The old woman drew her cloak tighter, and with no seeming motion retreated until she disappeared into the gathering dusk.

After a moment of silence Condor laughed again, but now there was an uncertainty to the sound. *She won't give in that easily.*

Hagan drew a shuddering breath. The memories were still too fresh, his resentment too deep for him to care how the old woman felt.

Yet it was all there, wasn't it? Sorrow, compassion. His grandmother. His logical mind might have debated the point, but his heart knew the truth. Yes, not only Condor's and Meeriam's, but his Grandmother, too.

Settling by the fire, Hagan considered which of the thousand questions he should start with. Which Condor might answer best, if at all. "Tell me, Condor. Tell me about the People."

Much later, resting by the glowing embers of the burned down fire, Hagan found himself still too tense to sleep. Condor, some time before, had grown impatient with his questions, and had rolled himself into the light sleep blanket and shut himself off from Hagan's probing mind. Still the questions came, but now he knew they were questions to which even Condor didn't have the answers.

Who had his mother been? What was her name? How had Elias met her? Had he really loved her, or merely taken her with a soldier's disregard for anyone but himself?

As much as Hagan would like to believe the worst of his father, he knew that wasn't true. The old woman would have had no respect for a man who'd taken her daughter in the throes of a soldier's lust. Neither, if he were to be honest, could he see his father in the role of despoiler.

Later Hagan slept, but the questions followed him into his dreams, and there, in that soft dreamworld, the old woman also beckoned.

Come to me, she seemed to say, and I will give you all the answers you seek. Come to me.

When morning dawned, a morning still gray with the dampness of heavy fog, neither Hagan nor Condor wanted to linger at their small fire. Hagan had dreamed neither the eagle dream, nor of Meeriam, and his sense of urgency grew, making it imperative that they push on.

Because of the bad weather they were three more days on the

down side trail, but on the third day, as the skies finally cleared, Hagan had his second, closer glimpse of the desert. It stretched as far as his eye could see, and nothing moved in the sky but an eagle.

The next morning he had in the tracks on the desert floor indisputable evidence that Graeber was there ahead of them.

Chapter 24

Phoenix

Heart pounding against his ribs, Hagan flattened himself against the hot rock wall of Phoenix. Across the narrow freestone path Condor did the same, his eyes slitted against the glare of the late afternoon sun. For once Hagan and Condor seemed in perfect accord. Quiet, waiting, wondering. Though he sensed with his Firewing senses the immediate vicinity, Hagan found no one waiting just inside.

Is your General that confident, or is he merely careless, Condor asked silently.

Or was it a trap?

No trap. Wordlessly Condor nodded his agreement. Whatever that screeching metal-on-metal sound had been that had brought them to a halt had vanished into the silence.

Hagan was tensed, ready to thrust him inside when another sound, this time distinguishable as a voice, reached them.

Meeriam!

Hagan's stomach lurched. He'd not believed the old woman. Though he'd hoped, he hadn't really believed Meeriam would survive the lotus tea.

The brief joy he felt vanished. Awake she was in even more danger than when she'd been drugged. The sound of voices came again, fainter.

Sound carriers through the tunnels, Condor said into his mind. *They could be quite deep by now. The city goes down many levels. and spreads out for miles.*

Hagan wiped the sweat running into his eyes. Eased the tension from his shoulders. They had to hurry. Each moment that passed put her in more danger.

He glanced across the tunnel opening toward Condor. *Are you ready, Firewing?*

Any time you are, soldier. Condor made a slight sardonic gesture. *After you.*

Accepting the challenge Hagan slid into the shadowy tunnel.

And was blinded by the contrast between light and dark. He stood sightless against one cool wall, aware of a temperature drop of at least twenty degrees. Then, as his eyes adjusted, he realized with a sense of awe that he was gazing upon an artifact of man that was at least a thousand years old yet looked as if it had been built yesterday. A shiver chased across his skin.

Condor touched his thoughts. *There's that sound again.*

Hagan listened.

Metal on metal. Giant metal doors came to mind, and moving stairways. Sounds that seemed to be coming from deeper still into the vast system of tunnels beneath the empty desert floor. But the enormity of what was before Hagan's eyes kept him rooted to the spot. Looking, absorbing. The tunnel stretched out into the shadowy distance, becoming mysterious and dark. The tile beneath his feet, once glossy white, he was sure, now a millennium after it had been laid, was dull in the dim light.

But there was light of sorts. Where did it come from?

Perusing the hallway, Hagan saw no fixture, but as his eyes became more adjusted to the dimness, he saw intervals where narrow hollow shafts entered the hallway from above. One was near at hand, and he leaned forward and peered up into a mirror-lined tube. Mirrored? A pinpoint shininess hit his eyes as he stared upward. Sunlight? He breathed a soft sigh of admiration for the engineering skill shown by the ancients. Clever of them to free themselves from the need to generate power to light this huge underground city. And at night? How did they store the sunlight for later use? And how long had these tunnels rested in darkness before the heavy clouds of the holocaust lifted and let in the sun? A strange anguish for all the questions that might never be answered rose in his throat. Deliberately he pushed the thoughts aside. Looked in Condor's direction to find that the Firewing was watching him with oddly sympathetic eyes.

It was once great, was it not? Condor lapsed into the old tongue, but Hagan had no trouble following him. Condor's sadness was as great as his own. *To think,* the Firewing went on, *that they had all this, and let it go.*

Inexplicably angry, Hagan pushed away from the wall.

You've been here before. Which way?

Depends on whether you want to go straight to the ancient ships, or to what they called the Command Center. The Command Center is four levels above the Hall of Ships.

Hagan considered briefly. Which way had Graeber gone? Would he split his men and try for both? Knowing how little Graeber trusted his own people, Hagan doubted he'd let them split up. Then, had Graeber headed for the ships?

Condor, can you tell where they are?

The Firewing, closing his eyes the better to turn inward, finally shook his head. *I—I can't. It's like looking into a place of—of desolation. Graeber has a dark barrier. I can't do it.*

Then try Galt or one of the others. Hagan curbed his upwelling of anxiety. *Try Meeriam.* Turning inward, he, too, opened the sight that had no center, opened that core of himself that he'd always, until this moment, protected. An immediate breathlessness gripped him, choking him and bearing him down. Emotions that had lingered in the ancient hallways for a thousand years swirled around him, anguish, pain, and a deep, black hopelessness. Images swirled around him, images that reminded him of the disastrous end of Graeber's retraining facility. Feeling he could drown in the images if he didn't do something quickly, Hagan forced the pictures and memories away. He was almost surprised to see Condor still standing at his side, seemingly unaffected by the destruction that lingered like an abysmal fog in the psychic atmosphere.

Condor frowned. *What did you see? Graeber? Meeriam?*

No, neither, Hagan said. If Condor hadn't seen it, then he, Hagan, couldn't explain.

Then, which way, Soldier?

Hagan could hesitate no longer. The Command Center.

Condor led them forward. Their soft Firewing boots made no sound on the floor.

The Command Center, when they reached it an hour later, was like nothing Hagan had ever seen. Large curved screens lined two walls, blank and gray. The third wall, where they stood, was banked by glass doors and the fourth side of the rectangular room was taken up by a large floor to ceiling window that looked out on a vast, shadowy vault whose bottom was lost in darkness and whose top reminded Hagan of one of Mars' smaller domes.

Without hesitation Condor pushed through the nearer of the doors. It was obvious to Hagan he knew where he was going. The floor on which they stood sloped to a row of glass-screened control panels. A low rumble, almost below the edge of sound, growled beneath their feet.

One lone man sat with his back to them, a large book of symbols open on a stand in front of him. The screen above that workstation was the only other sign of animation in the room.

As they stood taking it all in, the rumble beneath their feet grew perceptibly louder.

Condor spoke into Hagan's mind. *What's he doing?*

Hagan hazarded a guess. *Trying to activate a part of the complex?*

How can he? Those symbols must all be meaningless to him.

Maybe not. How long do you suppose Graeber's been planning this?

Months?

Or maybe years.

Condor seemed to grow older as the logic of Hagan's guess sank in. *What shall we do?*

If the Firewing had been halfhearted in his help before, Hagan now felt a growing resolution strengthen him. Indicating the lone soldier, Hagan said into the Firewing's mind, *You stop him. I'll find Graeber.*

Minutes later Hagan slid down the last few meters of a freight chute on his rear, then broke his fall into the vault of ancient ships by landing on his hands and feet. Picking himself up, he ran noiselessly past empty, ghostly silos, bottomless pits, he guessed, where once great ships had rested before beginning their long journey to the planet Mars. Perhaps once they'd even planned to go on to the stars. The thought made Hagan ache again for the mislaid plans of those long ago ancestors.

Ahead, in the distance, though, he could see the shining tubes—rockets, perhaps. Rockets had propelled those early ships into orbit. Or were they sister-ships of the Mendoza Class? Running through shadowy dimness that was an eerie approximation of twilight, Hagan came to the first silo that still held one of Earth's first planet to planet ships. In spite of his sense of urgency, he stared in awe upward into the vast dimness where the nose of the strange, sleek ship slept in deep shadow, waiting to be reawakened.

Compared to the Mendoza, though, which had strange protuberances, a multifaceted eye-like control area, and innumerable projections for fuel and cargo storage, this ship looked like nothing so much as a tube-train placed on end. And, as tall as it seemed, half of the ship, he realized with a jolt, was still buried in its birthing silo, still connected to its womb by the umbilical cords built into the surface on which he stood. For the first time he received a true impression of the immensity of this underground chamber. But even as he stood gazing upward at the giant monster ship the rumble which had become so familiar as to be almost unnoticeable, increased in power and intensity. A sudden shaft of light slanted from the high dome overhead and slashed a beam of bright illumination into the shadowy vault. The dome was opening.

He shot out an angry thought aimed at Condor: *What the hell are you doing? You're supposed to stop that—*

Condor's returning thought broke in, holding a trace of anguish. *I can't. He's started a sequence that works automatically. A built-in countdown,* he said. *Have you found Graeber?*

Not yet. How long do we have?

There was a stillness from Condor. Then, *Seventy-five minutes.*

A renewed sense of urgency filled Hagan. Where the hell were Graeber and his men? Meeriam?

The moment he thought of Meeriam, her image burst into his mind. *Meeriam? Where are you?*

Ellis? Are you here?

Feeling like the thought of her was a tangible line pulling him, he moved toward the next filled silo. *I'm here. Condor too. Where are you? Are you all right? Has he hurt you?* By God, he thought harshly, if they'd hurt her—a wash of almost uncontrollable anger flooded him, and a fearsome strength that wanted to break something.

Ellis, don't. I'm all right.

Hagan started to voice the questions that had pounded at him these last days, but knew this was the wrong time to ask. All he needed to know would come later. *What's your situation?*

Inside a ship. Inside a cell—the General says it was a sleep cabin but there's hardly room to turn around.

Are you alone?

No. Vana Kassine is here. She's—oh, Ellis, I'm worried about her. She's so fragile. I've tried to help her. Luan's dead and it's as if she has given up too.

Luan dead—for a moment Hagan remembered with sadness only the Luan she'd once been.

Ellis, Meeriam's voice was urgent, *be careful. I think the General knows you're coming.*

Hagan repressed a sigh, and relegated Luan once and for all to the past. The matter at hand was urgent. *Listen, Meeriam, you have to get out of there.*

Not without Vana Kassine. I can't leave her behind.

No, of course not. Check the men —

Abruptly he stopped, his senses giving him warning of what was about to happen. Then two guards in their black uniforms who paced the perimeters of the silo, s'darms drawn saw him. Before Hagan could dive for cover, one whipped his lens-nosed s'darm to eye level and fired.

In a bright flash of pain, Hagan fell. His last thought was a frustrated curse.

Disoriented, Hagan experienced a strange feeling of floating, not unlike a dream. No sense of the passage of time came to him. Only Meeriam's soft inner voice, urging him awake seemed an anchor holding him steady, though he did think her urging strange.All at once sensation seemed to come back into his limbs and he realized that the world he saw upside down was truly that way as he was carried quickly by one of the two guards toward the yawning port of the nearest ship.

Ellis—Ellis, please, wake up, Meeriam's worried voice spoke into his mind again.

I'm awake.

Are you hurt?

Though his hands were tied behind his back, with effort

Hagan kept his body relaxed while he explored his returning senses. Stunned, not hurt. The effects of the s'darm seemed to be wearing off quickly.

No, I'm not hurt. There are two guards. They're taking me into the ship. Through barely slitted eyes, Hagan watched the yawning entrance of the giant rocket open upward, then slide shut again almost noiselessly behind them. From somewhere overhead came a strange clanking sound, while underfoot the vibrations he'd felt earlier increased in intensity. Grunting under his weight, one guard let go his legs and dropped him to the floor of the passageway. He lolled his head to one side and through slitted eyes studied the spidery ladder that led up to another level.

Before the guard could even reach for a device hanging on the wall, Graeber''s voice came through a grill right below. "Bring him up here." Graeber's voice was ripe with satisfaction. "Bring him up, I say."

The control level of the ship was large and open. Hagan entered, pushed ahead by the guard who had been carrying him. Graeber, sitting in the command post, overflowed the upright flight recliner, once more reminded Hagan of a giant bloated toad. Graeber's eyes were small, self-satisfied slits. Galt, at the general's side, watched with that malicious smile on his face.

Graeber was the first to speak. "Ah, Captain Hagan, I've been expecting you."

Hagan faced the General, rage boiling just below the level of conscious control. A rage that could slip out and destroy anything in its path if he let it. As it had done before. He had a feeling that if he let the emotions go unchecked, he could bring the whole Ancient City down on their heads. Now, having seen only a small fraction of what the Firewing had guarded for a millennium, he found himself loathe to do it unless it was necessary.

He kept his voice calm, but wasn't sure he could keep either the hate or the fear from his eyes. "Have you, General?" Hagan looked around. There were only four men here, besides the General, and yet a whole field unit, at least thirty men, had been with Graeber earlier. Where were they now? Turning his attention back to Graeber, he smiled. "You'll be glad to know that I hurried as fast as I could."

"Were you afraid I'd leave without you? Never fear, Captain. I knew you would come. I already have another place for you in my plans."

Galt laughed, but Graeber quelled him with a glance. "And you'll be glad to know I have a friend of yours on board."

"Oh?" Sharp, tangible fear darted through Hagan. Did Graeber know about Meeriam? About what she was? Climbing up the long ladder from the entrance he'd known the moment he passed the level she was on, and he'd touched her mind with what reassurance he could offer. Her answering thought had been encouraging.

"Yes," Graeber was going on, "Vana Kassine has elected to travel with us, though alas, her daughter could not. I'm sure her family on Mars will pay magnificently for her return to the safety of the family arms. It's too bad you have no family left, Captain. Surely someone would have paid greatly for you."

Hagan's relief was so great that he almost missed the last of Graeber's comment. But then Hagan's reaction was tempered by a new worry. If Kassine was in as bad a shape as Meeriam thought, it would be even harder to get her out. He frowned at Graeber, trying to keep the train of conversation while he planned a way out. "I'm not worth much in the open market, General. Surely you've figured that out by now."

"You underrate yourself." The General's hands steepled in one of his favorite poses and he chuckled, the sound rippling through his gross body like waves upon a bay. "Ah yes, I can hardly wait to see the reaction of those bigots on Mars when they realize that I have them by the balls."

Hagan's gaze ran across the banks of dials and gauges, shapes and uses strange to his eyes, and undoubtedly stranger still to the General. "It won't work, you know. This ship will never make it to the Domes." Even as he protested, Hagan's mind seemed to push at its limits, his inner eye touching the face of one screen, and then another. At first it was just the feeling that his eyes had become sharper; then it was the actual experience of seeing both from his position in front of the general, and from a position beyond Galt. Another strange and frightening experience that dimmed the moment he noticed it. Fine sweat broke out on his face and hands. He choked back an inner scream. He couldn't let go now. He couldn't.

And then Meeriam's voice came calmly into his mind. *Don't be afraid, of it, Ellis. It's an ability, a talent. You can use it, make it work for you.* Meeriam's thought disappeared from Hagan's mind, leaving the sense of calm behind.

Obviously unaware of Hagan's inner turmoil, Graeber went on, waving a fat hand at the screens and control boards lining the console in front of him. "Oh, but this ship will work. It will work." His voice hardened. "I have not come this far to fail."

Hagan braced himself. He'd learn to handle this new facet of power just like he'd learned to handle the mind talk. He turned his full attention to what the General was saying. "And what will you do when you get to Mars? They'll be waiting for you, you know."

"Of course they will. I expect them to be waiting. Have you ever seen a human body burst in the vacuum of space, Ellis? Ah, you grow pale. I thought not. Neither have most of the people under the Domes. We're all so careful to don our suits if we need to go beyond a dome. However, I'm sure you'll make a good example. We'll put it on the nightscreen and let everyone watch. We'll have three other ships along with this one with the firepower to smash a hundred domes the size of—" A jar ran through the ship. Graeber leaned forward and peered into one of the screens. "Captain Stark, report immediately. What—" Cutting off Graeber's words, another jar and a distinct rumble vibrated through the latticed metal at Hagan's feet. Graeber jabbed a finger at Galt. "Go see what's happening."

Though he looked as if he'd rather not, Galt nodded and spun toward the ladder.

Once more solidly within his own perspective, Hagan stared upward at a big screen whose image was that of the surrounding vault outside the rocket. No wonder Graeber had expected him. The General had indeed seen him coming

Ellis—Meeriam spoke into his mind, *Condor is on his way down. He says Moss is nearby with your friend Kali and some soldiers. He says we have to get out of this vault of ships now!*

Moss and Kali here? Hagan worked to keep the shock from

his face. *Condor—Condor are you listening?*

Yes, soldier, I hear you.

Is the countdown sequence continuing?

Yes.

Jam it some way. Break a machine. Jam the dome so that it won't open. Anything. Isn't there a manual override?

If there is, this soldier doesn't know about it. Besides, we might slow the sequence down, but I don't think we'll stop it.

Then slow it down as much as you can.

The operator up here believes if you stop the sequence the fuel in the rocket will blow.

Get into his mind, Condor. Make sure. It's a chance we might have to take.

I've done that. He doesn't know much except that he was told to follow the sequencing in the book. The book says—

Blast the book. I'll see if I can slow it down from here. Are you coming down? If you do, be careful when you reach the vault. The ship's eye-spies are everywhere.

Hagan became aware that the General was watching him intently. What had he missed? A question? Another of Graeber's digging barbs?

"Yes." The General's eyes had grown hard. "You should have joined me when you had the chance, Ellis." He turned his chair so that the full force of his fury settled on the guard at Hagan's back. "Get him out of here."

Taken down two levels to one of the little sleeper rooms, the guard thrust Hagan inside. Before he had time to even regain his feet, Galt reappeared. With a gloating smile, the soldier dismissed Hagan's guard, and followed Hagan into the small room. Quickly he locked the door from the inside.

All the jealousy and rage that Galt held inside poured out in the fist he swung at Hagan. Hands still bound, Hagan hit the floor of the small sleeper with a hard thud then twisted sharply, trying without success to avoid Galt's heavy, swinging boot. Hagan's own anger flashed white hot, his memory of pain inflicted by Galt too recent to tolerate any more. Swinging his legs together he kicked up into Galt's groin, and the soldier, not expecting resistance, gasped and bent double. Hagan kicked out again, this time with his mind as well as his body, trying to hurt Galt any way he could. Galt paled and clutched at his head and crumpled. Breathing hard, Hagan watched him, waiting for his recovery, but the soldier lay still.

A pounding came on the door that Galt had locked and a muffled voice called out Galt's name. Still Graeber's captain didn't stir. Hagan gave a grunting command that was a passable imitation of Galt's voice, and the guard outside grew silent. Still furious Hagan tested the ropes that bound him. A synthetic rope, almost unbreakable. Galt had wasted no time in taking his revenge. Only minutes had passed since they'd left the General. Only minutes, and yet it felt like a lifetime. Slowly Hagan's breathing returned to normal.

Meeriam's voice entered his mind. *Ellis, you can untie the rope.*

Hagan's initial angry impulse went unspoken, even in thought. He substituted another. *How?*

Let yourself see it, Meeriam instructed calmly.

Can't you untie it for me?

No. You have to do it.

In other words you won't help. That she wouldn't help somehow hurt.

We don't have time for you to lie there feeling sorry for yourself, came her acerbic comment.

Feeling thoroughly rebuked, Hagan jerked at the rope again, and only succeeded in creating pain in his wrists and shoulders. Shutting out the pain, he concentrated on visualizing the way the rope would look wrapped around his wrists. The image was sharp and clear. The knot was hard, and he could see a thread of blood oozing above where the rope was wound.

His hands were growing numb, and yet it was as if he had another pair of hands whose dexterity remained unimpaired. He could actually feel the rope within his fingers, and he worked at the knots until they loosened, and then came free. The image vanished, and he brought his freed hands into view of his eyes. They were exactly as he'd envisioned them, even to the blood still oozing from the place the rope had gouged into his flesh. Had he really done that? He chilled. How long, he wondered, before things like this ceased to scare him?

Meeriam had told him not be be afraid, and yet how could the possessor of such abilities not be afraid? Did these abilities belong to all Firewing? Glancing down at Galt who still lay unconscious at his feet he wanted to deny that it had been the power of his mind that had disabled the soldier, but the evidence was there.

Meeriam's feather thought touched him again. *Ellis, please hurry. I need your help.*

I'm coming, Reaching the lock he sent the wheel turning. With a sigh the heavy door opened. The soldier on guard outside the door started to turn just as Hagan slammed down on his neck with a vicious, double-handed fist. The soldier fell without a word, but the act of violence left Hagan trembling. Quickly he stooped and grabbed the guard and pulled him into the sleeper and dropped him by Galt.

He hoped both the guard and Galt would be out long enough that he and Meeriam could remove Kassine from the ship before the others were alerted.

He opened the opposite sleeper lock. Meeriam, from her place kneeling on the floor beside a low bunk, looked up at him and smiled. It was a smile that held welcome and pride and something else he couldn't define. Something that he responded to in spite of himself. Reaching down, he pulled her up and into his arms. *Thank God you're safe.* He wanted to kiss her.

Please do, came her shaky thought.

He lowered his mouth to hers, and she met him half way. He was the first to exert his control and pull away. *You're were right. We have to hurry.*

Leaning over the bed he lifted Kassine. Her slight weight shocked him. Lead the way, he said. Meeriam led him toward the spidery ladder. They might be halfway free, but the next half seemed a long way to go.

They had descended two levels when Graeber discovered them on his spying screens.

The General's voice screamed over every intercom on the ship. "Stop them. Stop them. Galt. Stark. Guards, stop him!" The general's scream held madness. Though they were not touching, Hagan felt Meeriam shiver.

Moving more quickly now, Hagan pounded down the

spidery ladder to the entrance level, the old woman caught in a strong grip against him. Hagan hoped her ancient bones would hold up under this additional stress.

Meeriam, who'd gone ahead, was already at the entrance, and without touching it sprang the locks open. Condor's voice pounded in his head. *Get out. Hurry. I think it's going to blow up.*

Meeriam glanced over her shoulder and it was obvious she'd heard Condor too. As he reached the entrance level, Hagan heard the men below, visualized Stark and at least four others, and felt their frantic climb up from the lower regions of the massive ship.

He didn't take the time to stop them. Their own lives were more important. He wondered how much time was left in Condor's countdown.

Condor?

It's starting. Hurry.

Out on the floor of the vast vault he noticed the sun no longer pierced the dusky shadows. The dome covering the vault had closed again.

This way, Meeriam said, guiding them toward the further side, opposite the way he'd entered. In the direction she indicated stood a massive row of steel doors almost hidden in the shadows.

And then as he ran past empty silos, and past ghostly ships still in their wombs, he felt it again, that strange rumbling that seemed more mental than physical.

Far behind him now lay the ship that Graeber occupied, that he knew Graeber would not give up, no matter what happened.

Suddenly Kassine cried out, and the heart-rending sound stopped Hagan as nothing else could have. Shifting her in his arms, he looked down into her aged face and into alert eyes that looked back at him with anguish. And then the anguish was banked and the usual determination took it's place.

"Leave me," she said. "Leave me and save yourselves."

"I won't leave you."

"Young man," Kassine's abruptly imperious tone went strangely with her weakened condition, but a life-time of command would not be denied. "Put me down this instant."

"We have no time for argument, Vana Kassine." Hagan

started forward again, cushioning his steps as best he could to keep from jarring her any more than he had to. Behind him in the distance he heard Galt shout. The brilliant flash of a s'darm filled the shadows. The charge was too distant to touch them.

Ahead, beside one of the massive doors, Meeriam waited. He didn't need to hear her thought to know she urged him to hurry. Then Condor reached her side, and using his immense strength of mind and body helped her open the doors.

Another flash of the s'darm was accompanied by a deafening roar, and the vibrations underfoot raised in double decibels.

He heard Condor's thought over and above a tremendous roar. *That's engine ignition. It's going.*

Yes—Hagan looked upward, where the dome remained firmly shut. Then over his shoulder. Galt and the soldiers with him had come to a halt and had turned, and were staring at the ship.

Galt, you idiot, run!

Galt's shock at Hagan's voice in his mind was not as great as his fear of the explosion building beneath the ancient rocket. Shoving his s'darm into his belt, he shouted at his men and took off at a dead run toward the door opening under Condor's efforts.

Encumbered with the old woman, Hagan moved aside to avoid being trampled by the frightened soldiers.

Keep them running, Hagan shot the thought to both Meeriam and Condor. *Let them through but keep them running.*

Run yourself, Hagan, came back Condor's quick words. *Hurry.*

Giving a silent apology to Kassine for the pain he must be causing her, Hagan held her tighter and ran on.

The giant door shut behind him, bringing an eerie sense of peace. He leaned against a smooth tile wall and brought in great gulps of air. Condor and Meeriam were on the opposite side of this little chamber, doing the same. But it would soon be as hot as a furnace of ball-stoves.

He glanced down again into Kassine's face and found her watching him with a frown.

"I should have let you marry her," Kassine whispered. "It all would have turned out differently."

"I doubt it, Vana Kassine. Some things are meant to be."

Hagan shifted the old woman to a more comfortable position in his arms. "Let's get out of here."

When they entered the tunnel network a few minutes later, Galt and his soldiers had vanished. And, still in his arms, Kassine died

He took another deep breath and pushed on.

They were many levels away from the vault of ships when the tremendous explosion tore through the ancient underground vault and forever sealed the starships in their grave.

Chapter 25

Phoenix

Hagan, seeking solitude after all that had happened, finally made his way back to the empty Command Center. Moss, arriving with a victorious Kali and a unit of soldiers in time for the clean-up, had found the control room tapes, and from them it was obvious the General hadn't even tried to escape the doomed ship. Sitting in his captain's chair he'd proceeded with his own personal countdown as if in truth he'd already begun the flight to Mars. Preserved forever on the Command center's recorders his voice had contained the icy assurance of total madness.

Hagan wasn't sure what he'd hoped to see by coming back here, but after the dust and ash had settled in the enormous vault below, after Moss and Kali had flushed out Galt and his few remaining men, Hagan had sought the emptiness and now stood at the grayed blank windows that no longer overlooked the vault below.

The vault had been examined from the outside and declared sealed. No radioactivity incurred by the exploding ships had leaked out into the surrounding desert atmosphere. The Firewing had not allowed it. Miraculously, or perhaps miracles had nothing to do with it, considering the power of Earth's Mind, the dome overhead had sealed in the enormous heat and held against the force of the explosions.

Taking charge of the few prisoners, including Galt, Moss promised to deliver them to Norcanna within the week. Kali was expecting the Mars delegation sometime toward the end of the next month and was already requesting an interview with the Earth Clan leaders to set up a meeting with High Counsel Demar. Everyone expected the Clans to agree and that Anahata would be their chosen representative.

Hagan watched it all and should have been satisfied, but he wasn't. There was something unfinished. He thought at first it might be Portus that he still had to deal with. He wanted to talk to the old man, to know the Commander Portus had known. To know the story that Portus could tell. He thought he was ready to hear it now. But even after that matter had been resolved in his mind, the unrest in him grew, gnawed at him until he pushed away from the blank glass windows and paced the length of the great room and back.

The unusable vault of ships held no more interest for him, now that Graeber was dead. Those ships were a part of Earths previous life, a life that had ended in senseless horrific destruction once and if used again, would only lead to more of the same. He'd felt no regret to see them destroyed and the vault sealed. And there were other parts of the ancient city still untouched. Those would be interesting to explore. But not now. Not when this great restlessness, this incomprehensible incompleteness continued to build within him.

Meeriam appeared in the Command center doorway and stood, watching. He felt her presence like a warm fire, waiting and welcoming. And welcomed, he thought. He turned and stared across the breadth of the room. She seemed to glow with an inner golden light within the shadowy darkness of the consoles and control panels. He wanted her with an ache that wouldn't leave. But not yet. Not yet. He turned back and stared into the shadowy vault below. There was so much he needed to understand, and something he had to do.

She knew before he did when his decision to leave was made. When he turned, she came to his side. He held out his hand and she placed her smaller one in it. Her eyes were warm with compassion and something more that he wanted and needed, but had no right yet to claim.

And then Condor was there also, moving toward them with his quiet Firewing step, a leashed intensity in his gaze as he studied the two of them together.

His lips twisted in a wry smile, and as usual his words were spoken into Hagan's mind. *Will you walk away now, soldier? Are we no longer necessary to your ambitions?*

In the way that was beginning to feel most natural, Hagan replied in kind. *Do you think to get rid of me that easily? You can't, you know. I belong here as much as you do. I belong to Earth.* Even as Hagan said the words, he wondered if they were true. Did he indeed belong here yet?

Meeriam's hands tightened on his, and her thought was in quick answer. *Yes, yes you do! But we are only what we believe we are, and you have yet to discover what that is.*

Yes, of course. Hagan closed his eyes and the image of the Mountain flashed into his mind. The Mountain was calling him. *Yes, I must go.* Hagan held Meeriam in his arms, feeling her fragility as well as her strength. He could hurt her, he knew, but he wouldn't. *Wait for me?*

Yes, of course. I'll be in Lissone.

With Grandmother?

Yes.

She'll think it strange, won't she?

No, she'll know. She'll understand.

Hagan glanced up and met Condor's pained gaze. *Will you go with her to the Valley?*

If you wish. But I won't stay. Condor's eyes grew remote. Hagan had the impression the Firewing was already distancing himself from them. Condor went on. *There's much of our world I haven't seen. Many clans and settlements are spread across the Earth. I have a need to see them all.*

Nevertheless we'll meet again.

Perhaps.

There were other words Hagan wanted to say, but none of them would come. It didn't seem to matter. Hagan glanced down at Meeriam, who was still in his arms. He lowered his head, his mouth searching for hers in hunger barely repressed. Her answering fire filled him with warmth.

Lissone, he said.

In one week, she answered.

The moon rose as Hagan struck out across the desert floor toward the distant line of hills. Moon bright enough to read by, though not yet full. Tirelessly, like a Firewing, hour after hour he traveled. The time was approaching but he didn't know for what. He knew only that he had to go to the Mountain. The Mountain was calling.

Before dawn he reached the foothills, by night he was in the tall trees. He stopped and rested once by a small pool, drinking his fill, sleeping briefly until a new excited urgency woke him and pushed him on.

By sundown of the third day he reached the base of the secret path that climbed to the hidden place of the sacred fire. Just below the peak that was Grandfather Mountain. Kama.

The last rays of sun illuminated the ragged ridges and highlighted the path. As the sun sank in the west the moon, full and incredibly close, rose in the east.

No longer afraid of its power, grateful for its heat, Hagan built a fire in the lee of a tower of rocks. It was the place of sacred fires, a place he'd known instinctively. Ancient invocations rose in his mind and spoke themselves from his mouth. He heard the ancient words with his ears and understood.

I would join mind with Mind.

We are Earth, came the answer.

Hagan sank beside the fire and closed his eyes, the better to see the inward images. Immediately a sense of unnumbered faces also staring inward and outward at the same time filled him. A multitude of minds making up Mind. The Earth Soul.

And he knew he had been called to this tribunal meeting, called perhaps as long ago as the time of meeting Patlos in the little glen, but only now was he ready to heed the call.

Only now.

The knowledge humbled him.

Fueled by the thoughts of multiple earth, the fire flared higher. The heat brought out the sweat on Hagan's brow, glistened on his arms and legs. The power of Mind grew in him, but there was a barrier. He knew he wanted to merge his mind, his thoughts, his soul with the Soul of Earth. To be so close—a painful tension filled him.

He came to his feet, taut with need.

Then, abruptly, wings spreading wide, a great Golden Eagle appeared on the opposite side of the fire, the largest eagle he had ever seen. He wanted to call it Father.

Suddenly his sweat was the sweat of nausea. He knew what was happening, and he didn't want it to happen. He couldn't— wouldn't—

The dream is not the barrier, said Mind into his mind.

Uncertain of that truth, Hagan stood irresolute, the heat of the flaring fire no longer warming him.

You are also the eagle, Mind continued.

"No," Hagan said aloud. Not him. Closing his eyes once more he tried to close his inward sight to the image of the eagle but still he saw it before him, growing in size, terrifying and terrible. "No."

Inexorably the voice of Mind continued. *You have soared upon a stage, playing your part in a drama of your own making.*

I did not kill my father.

As though he'd not protested, the voice of Mind went on. *The only barrier is in your own heart. Open your heart, Ellis Hagan, and become one with Earth.*

A fine trembling feathered Hagan. The longing to leave himself, to leave the finite barriers of his body and to merge with something greater filled him. Then he stood outside himself and felt a calmness descend upon him. An eternal silence. "I cannot—"

It is your choice, came the voice of Mind, softly fading.

The eagle which had stood with giant wings extended shimmered as though losing substance. An anguished cry released itself from him. "No."

And as if in answer to his cry another shape formed next to the eagle. The old woman, long robe rippling as though in a light breeze, her eyes kind, too gentle to mean him harm—and yet he knew she was going to ask something of him. He knew it and braced himself the way one might brace against expected pain.

She held out her hand. Her words were spoken aloud and also into his mind so that he seemed to hear them with every cell in his body. "You are precious to me, Ellis Hagan. Not only for who you are, but for who your parents are."

The expected pain came. "They are dead. They are gone."

No, Anahata said gently. *They live. They live in many realms.*

Trying to deny the surge of hope that filled him, Hagan closed his eyes once more and bowed his head. No, the Commander was dead.

Live the dream again, Ellis.

Hagan's hope became fear. His head snapped up and his eyes sprang open. The shimmering eagle next to the old woman

331

seemed again to grow in size. The fire flared higher, sending flames into the star-studded sky.

You have written a drama that you now believe implicitly. You must learn that you may write a different ending. Or as many endings as you need.

Hagan felt the old woman's words enter into his mind and body even as he watched her lose substance. At the same time the eagle gained solidity. Though he still felt the rock of the sacred place under foot, Hagan's perspective seemed to be changing, flowing toward and then merging with the growing, shimmering form of the wide-winged bird of prey.

I am the eagle, he thought with wonder. He felt the giant wings outstretched within the muscle and bone of his own body. He felt the fire receding as the giant wings lifted him up into the star-filled night.

Above the horizon the rising moon had breached the sky and cast a silver glow over Earth. Living Earth.

Higher he went, and higher until his view extended far beyond the mountain to the desert on one side and the Kama Valley on the other. Until he could see the sparkling seas of Earth to the south and west. He soared higher until Earth's terminator indicating the demarkation between day and night became visible, moving like a majestic finger across the face of Mother Earth. Life-giving Earth. Before he had time to fully imbibe the intoxicating view, he was spiraling downward again. Down, down with breathtaking speed.

And he was within the dream.

The eagle's angled wings dipped, cutting into the updraft, starting the bird of prey on a slow spiral downward. Closer and closer to Mother Earth and to a strange drama being played out on the road below. The eagle catching movement, banked more steeply and, screaming, plummeted downward.

Two men, startled from their angry confrontation, looked up, their faces etched in time by the wild angry cry of the descending bird. A giant bird, monstrous in its proportions, its black wings blotting out the zenith sun.

The shorter man, bloated with avarice and hate, stood frozen in fear as the bird plunged, screaming. The older man, taller, iron gray hair close-cropped to his well-shaped head, looked upward. With understanding in his heart, he welcomed the Eagle with a fierceness of love overwhelming in its intensity.

The blast of the old-style weapon shattered the silent tableau and the man with love in his heart fell to earth. In anguish again the Eagle screamed.

The images shattered. Shifted.

Across the valley floor two eagles, equal in size and strength, floated toward the distant cliffs, searching for the hot updraft to take them aloft. Against the cliffs they found it, and at one with Earth, with Mind and with each other, sailed upward into the brilliant sun.

Dale Aycock is an award-winning poet, author of four published novels, the Starspinner series and Stardrifter. She lives in Los Gatos CA. She has been writing since she was a teenager, and has taught novel writing through the Community Interest Program of MetroEd, in San Jose, California, for which she wrote her own 115 page workbook, A Way With Words. Dale has been an insurance adjuster, and Bookstore owner, mother of five and spouse of one, as well as a writer and is a member of the California Writers Club, South Bay Branch, and the World Future Society.

www.ingramcontent.com/pod-product-compliance
Lightning Source LLC
Chambersburg PA
CBHW071202020726
47502CB00002B/513